LUV SHUV IN NEW YORK

N. M. PATEL

Cover Designer: Bhavi Mehta

Editor: Librum Artis Editorial Services

Proofreader: Judy's Proofreading

❀ Created with Vellum

To everyone who needs a little push to start chasing their dreams.

Do it. It's not as hard as it looks like.

AUTHOR'S NOTE

I started reading romance when I lived in India. Four years ago, I moved to New York City for my Master's degree. And it completely changed the way I read romance set in the U.S.

I started expecting to see more diverse group of people being written in romances set in big cities like New York, Chicago, Boston. I started looking for Indians and Chinese to make an appearance, even as side characters, in the books I read. Because I saw and experienced that diversity all around me. It was shocking to see such a huge presence of Asians in the U.S., yet so under-represented in books.

Every day I travelled in the subway, I saw so many interracial and intercultural couples having their little moments and living their normal life, and it warmed my heart. My need to read such romances increased tenfold. But I couldn't find enough of them.

So, I decided to write my own. A book where people from different backgrounds fell in love. I wanted to write a story that followed an immigrant student that adapted to a new country —its education system, its food, its culture, and its lifestyle. A story where an American fell in love with an immigrant who opened his eyes to a whole new world. A story that brings two cultures together and makes their love worth being celebrated, accepted and normalized. Yes, some of these experiences were my own, some were of my other Indian friends, and some were what I wish I had experienced myself.

I wrote my culture the way I've experienced it.

Everyone would have their own version of what makes them an Indian, what feels Indian to them, and I completely respect that.

When it comes to Indian parents, not all Indian parents are the same. There are many parents who would never accept a relationship between their Indian child and their American partner. There are parents who would never accept their child's partner if they're not of the same caste, let alone the same religion or country.

However, there are many who give power to love. There are so many parents who love their children so much that they sacrifice their happiness, comforts, take up debts, so that their children can achieve their dreams and all their heart's desires.

I wrote this book with a hope that it might give courage to anyone who is wondering if their love story is worth fighting for. To give them hope that maybe their parents would accept their partners. To tell them that it's okay to fall in love with a person, no matter their race, religion, caste, and sexual orientation.

We all deserve to choose the person we want to spend the rest of our lives with.

And if you find that person worth fighting your family for, you better give one hell of a fight.

Because you deserve a happily ever after.

PART I

CHAPTER 1

"This isn't going to be pretty. Rules will be broken. Friendships will be tested. And huge risks will be taken. But they're small prices to pay for true love and freedom, right?"
- Lisi Harrison

Akira

Ahmedabad, India

Chaos was inevitable when my entire family decided to come. *All fourteen of them.*

"Should we walk you to airport security?"

"That's not necessary, Mummy."

Everywhere around us, clusters of people were engrossed in their farewells and welcomes. The sharp tones of worried mothers and tense fathers, children screaming and running around, the sound of flights taking off and landing—and my own family talking over each other—had my heart pounding out of my chest.

"Are you sure you want to go to New York? You still have time to change your mind."

"Pappa, check-in is in five minutes. And yes, I'm sure I want to go to New York." And my answer to this question has remained unchanged for the last nine months, since I began my application for a master's degree in architecture.

"Where is that brother of yours? How can he be late to see his little sister off?" Mummy looked around the crowds as she dabbed at her face with a handkerchief, pretending to wipe the humidity off her cheeks. Every now and then, she swiped away a stray tear. She thought she hid it well, and it was evident how much she was trying to keep it together.

She was going to make me cry. I wrapped my arms around her shoulders and said, "Has Aakar ever been anywhere on time? Don't worry, Mummy. He should be arriving any minute now."

The late evening rain had cooled the harsh concrete pavement of the airport, and soft wind helped soothe the heavy emotions in the air. All of us stood near the entrance of the airport at midnight, preparing to say the final goodbyes.

Mummy's firm grip on the arm I'd wrapped around her shoulder almost brought me to my knees. She was trying so hard not to break down in front of me. I placed a kiss on her hand and brushed away a tear that had slipped down her cheek. I stayed silent. Words would be our undoing.

Was my dream of studying in New York worth leaving my family? Was it a better option than staying with my family, practicing architecture in India, and then marrying someone someday, hoping to God their family was open-minded enough to let me work? That scenario racked a shudder through my body.

As much as I loved my family, I was entirely dependent on them, against my will. I wanted to live on my own—make decisions without asking for permission from my family. Cook my own dinner. Pay for my own shit. Create a life of my own. And at the end of the day, I wanted to live a life I was proud of. And I wouldn't achieve it until I moved out. I needed to follow my passion.

So, when I got the letter of acceptance from Columbia University, I knew I had to go.

I needed to do this for myself.

When I'd announced my wish to my family, riddled with guilt and worry, Pappa had said, "It's okay to follow your dreams, Akira. We're here for you."

Since then, my departure had been a constant countdown, and the day was finally here.

Emotions from all my family members surrounded me.

My stomach churned. My heart sped up. I was drowning in the feelings around me and within me.

Nerves.

Excitement.

Guilt.

I was sorry for leaving, but not sorry for taking this step.

As I stood near Mummy, my eyes met my younger brother, Abhi. He noticed Mummy's strong hold on my hand and came bounding over from where he was hanging out with our cousins.

"You better make some hot American lady friends," he said, waggling his eyebrows.

"Abhi, watch your mouth," Pappa said as he came up behind Mummy and rested his hand on her other shoulder. He was the rock of our family.

I poked my tongue out at Abhi. "Even if I do, I'm never introducing them to you."

He poked his tongue back at me. "I think you're running late. You better go check in."

Pappa turned to me, his forehead etched with a worried frown. "*Beta*, I'm very proud of you for the courage you've shown. When you start living alone and get to experience that freedom, do not forget why you've decided to leave us. To study. To make something out of your life. Don't get blinded by everything. Don't get into a bad crowd. And do not fall into this *luv-shuv* with some American. We don't want anything to affect your studies."

Luv Shuv meaning *feelings like love.*

I quietly listened to his concerns, for probably the fiftieth time. He's said these exact words to me so many times, I could lip-sync with him at this point.

I nodded obediently. "I know, Pappa. Trust me. I won't let anything affect my future."

"Aakar's here," one of my uncles shouted.

Phew, saved by my older brother, like always.

"Aakar, how can you be late for something so important? Have we taught you nothing?" Mummy asked. Only my arm around her stopped her from going after my brother with her swinging handkerchief.

"Sorry, Mummy. I got held up at work," Aakar said and quickly dragged me with him to stand with Abhi and Ria.

"I'm so jealous you get to leave this madness behind, Akira," my cousin Ria said with a sigh as she watched the drama unfold. I nudged her with my shoulder and laughed. She was my roommate, my support system, and my best friend. God, who will I have midnight talks with?

I had just minutes before I had to check in. With so many family members here, it was time to start saying goodbye. Mummy was on the verge of crying, and my aunts stood ready to console her. The men, my father included, still believed my bags needed to be looked over and my grandparents peppered me with advice...mostly unhelpful. My brothers and Ria busied themselves with snapping as many selfies with me as they could.

I knew saying goodbye would be horrible, but I was

shocked at my grief. It took leaving the country for me to realize how close I held my family to my heart.

Mummy started crying, and I held her as she cried on my shoulder. Pappa gave me the tightest hug he'd ever given me, and by the time every aunt, uncle, cousin, and grandparent had hugged me, I was exhausted. Every loving word punched through my heart, and I hated myself a little for putting my family through this pain for the sake of my ambitions.

. When I hugged my baby brother, I whispered in his ear, "I'll miss you, Abhi."

"Don't you make me cry." He squeezed me tight before turning away and pretending to check over my luggage—just like my father had.

Aakar, who was patiently waiting for his turn, lifted me in his arms and gave me a twirl. "You better be safe, Akira. I won't be around to have your back."

"I'll miss you too, *bhai.*" *I'll miss you too, brother.*

No matter how crazy my family was, they were *my* crazies. And I was going to miss them so much.

I looked them over for a moment more, wanting the memory to be like a snapshot I could hold close to my heart. Tears blurred my vision, but only when I'd turned around and walked into the airport, did I let them fall. I didn't know if my decision to go to the United States was the right thing to do, but time would tell. I could only hope that whatever came my way was worth leaving this love and support behind.

∾

Sam

New York, USA

. . .

DRAFTING TABLE. *Check.*

Bed. *Check.*

Nightstand. *Check.*

Closet. *Check.*

Stationery. *Check.*

The loud vibration of my phone from my nightstand ruined my mental checklist. I huffed and plucked the phone off the charger.

Mom calling...

"Hey, Ma."

"Sam, are you all set, honey?" I could hear the chattering sounds of other teachers in the staff room of the school where my mother taught history.

"Yeah, I was going through my checklist."

"You and your checklist. How many times have you gone through it already?" I could feel her eyes roll through the phone.

"Three times," I said, proudly. *As if making sure everything was perfect was a bad thing.*

I loved my mom, but she was one of the most extroverted people in our small family. I was not. I'd rather spend my time sketching and taking a walk among the beautiful architecture of the city than go to a bar with people I barely knew.

I sat on the edge of my bed, my gaze fixed on a dirty spot on the floor while my mom continued. "Sammy, you need to go out more. Meet new people. Make new friends. You're only there for three years."

"I am perfectly happy with my current friends, Ma. I'm not going back to school to meet new people. I'm doing it to get my master's degree."

While my mom talked, I got the broom and scooped up the debris on the floor. I straightened the books on my study table in the corner of the room on my way to the bed. I'd kept as much open space in my bedroom as possible to fit my drafting table and to give me room to make my design models.

"Okay, Sammy. I understand." I heard her sigh and could almost imagine the shake of her head. My mother was stubborn, and I wondered when she'd stop worrying about me. "When do your classes start?"

"In three days. I need to go to the campus and see where my orientation is gonna take place. I also need to check out the library."

"Okay, Sam. Call me when you're back home. You know I worry."

"Of course. How's Dad now?"

"He's okay. Fever's gone. He's taking it easy for a few days."

"That's good. Only a few more years, Ma," I murmured.

"You take your time, Sammy. We aren't going anywhere."

"Say hi to him for me, will ya?"

My parents weren't exactly young. They had me in their forties, and I was twenty-seven now. Since Dad ran a construction firm with his partner, he couldn't retire like someone with a corporate job.

My parents have been waiting for me to take over the family business so my dad could transition to retirement. I wanted nothing more than to give them that, but I didn't want to just continue running his construction company. I wanted to expand. I wanted our firm to take up architecture services.

Luke, my father's partner's son, who was also my best friend, had been very supportive of that suggestion. In fact, he was the one who had encouraged me to apply for the graduate program in architecture at Columbia University. He's in his second year here and couldn't stop raving about the courses, the campus, the professors, and all the networking. So here I was, going back to school.

"Will do. Take care. And don't forget to have a little fun."
Ah, there it was—the teacher's voice. I pressed my lips tighter

to stop the laughter. She acted as if this was the first time I had left the nest. I did my undergrad at Boston Architectural College. Five years of that and five years of working in NYC had made me more comfortable alone. I don't think I could live with my parents for more than a week or two at a time now— I'd go crazy.

"I will. Bye, Ma."

After I hung up, I looked around my room. The gray bedsheets and comforter complemented my cherry bed frame. The dark gray curtains and carpet cooled my room in the sweltering heat of August. This was home now. At least for the next three years. I took a deep breath, taking in this new venture.

Drafting Table. *Check.*

Bed. *Check.*

Nightstand. *Check.*

Closet. *Check.*

Stationery. *Check.*

CHAPTER 2

"The future of architecture is culture."

- Philip Johnson

Akira

I was ready for orientation. I had enough time to make myself a cup of chai and have some breakfast. Megha, one of my roommates, bumped into me on my way to the kitchen. She was a computer science student, and their classes had already begun two weeks before the rest of us roommates, which put her in a pissy mood every morning. "What are you doing up so early? And why are you all dressed up?"

"Good morning to you too. And today's my orientation. You want some chai?" I asked.

Her eyes widened, and she moaned, "Oh God, you are the best. I'll have a cup."

While she ran to the bathroom to freshen up, I got the chai ready. It was my one true weakness and my ultimate strength. I needed Indian tea—aka chai—to get my motor running. And so did all three of my Indian roommates.

I'd made a conscious decision to find Indian roommates. It

was my first time moving out and living on my own. I didn't need to make it more challenging by living with people of a different culture. Living with other Indian women gave me a sense of belonging and comfort.

By the time I had everything prepared, Megha was ready for her classes. I handed her the cup, and I was about to sit down on the barstool at the kitchen counter when my phone rang.

Mummy video calling...

"Hey, Mummy."

"Akira, you ready for your first day?"

The loud chatter of the kids flittered in the background. It was almost dinnertime in India.

"Yeah."

I showed her my favorite orange blouse and white jeans that we'd bought together.

Mom squinted at the screen and said, "Oh, Akira, you look beautiful."

"Thanks, Mummy. So, how's everyone? Find any girls for Aakar?"

I loved riling up my mom. Especially when it was about my brothers. Aakar was twenty-eight, and Mom had been actively looking for a girl for him to marry for a few years now. She was obsessed with getting us married off—especially Aakar. The first thing she'd said when I'd announced my wish to get my master's was, "If you plan to study at twenty-six, when will you get married?"

I sipped my chai as Mom said, "You won't believe it. I have tried to show your brother two perfectly good women since you left, and he refused to meet both. Again. He doesn't even look at their photos, just outright rejects them. Do you know how many women I've tried to show him this past year?" I was pretty sure I'd be getting a call from Aakar within the next few hours. Thankfully, I would be in my classes then.

I took a few sips of my chai as my mom called some of the family members around her to wish me luck for my first day. We talked while I had my breakfast, and I told everyone I needed to leave after a few more minutes.

"Don't forget to have some curd and sugar, Akira. For good luck."

I've no idea what good that did, but Mom had been feeding me that combination for good luck for every new beginning. It hasn't failed me yet, so why risk it for my first day in grad school? Hopefully, the Indian good-luck gods are active in America.

I nodded. "Okay. I'll have it. Now bye, Mummy. I need to leave."

"Bye, *beta*. Let me know how your day goes later. God bless you."

After eating a spoonful of curd and sugar, which tastes like sweet yogurt, I ran out the door and down the three flights of stairs to the main entrance of my building.

The fresh, crisp air of New York greeted me as soon as I stepped outside. It'd been a week since I came to New York, and I was amazed by the hot weather. I don't know why, but I imagined New York to be cold all the time. I looked around the street as I walked to the campus. Why did people have their eyes stuck to their phones when there was so much to see?

Like all the symmetrical and ornamental facades of the buildings, and the diversity among the people. In India, virtually everyone looked just like me. Ahmedabad, my hometown, doesn't get as many tourists as some other popular cities. But ever since I'd stepped foot in New York, I'd been surrounded by people from all around the world.

American. Chinese. Japanese. African. Some I couldn't even figure out.

Since arriving in the US, I'd yet to have a conversation with anyone who wasn't Indian. I wanted to, but it made me nervous.

But no problem—I was going to orientation today with optimism and the assumption that everyone would be friendly and awesome. I was excited to make a few good friends here. Yes.

And like Pappa says, *Confidence is the key*. And a smile. That too.

I was huffing and puffing by the time I'd walked the stupid uphill and downhill streets of the city and reached the campus. By the time I'd reached my building, my calves were burning, and sweat had gathered under my arms, on my upper lips, and rolling down my forehead.

Please, God, don't let this be a disaster.

As I stood outside the closed doors of the classroom, I blew out a breath, said a silent prayer to Lord Ganesha, a god for new beginnings, and pushed the door open.

The first thought that came to my mind was it looked like a funeral. Almost everyone in the room was wearing black. Was there a dress code I didn't know about? I was about to turn around to go back home and change when one of the professors came up to me and introduced herself. "Hi, I'm Lily Bennett. I'll be teaching History of American Architecture."

"Hello, Professor Bennett. I'm Akira Mishra."

It was the first time a professor had walked up to me to introduce herself. In my undergrad in India, it had always been the other way around. She offered me a genuine smile and shook my hand and said, "We're still waiting on a few people. Please have a seat. There are coffee and donuts at the back. Feel free to grab something."

I turned to where she pointed and went for the donuts and coffee.

Once I'd grabbed a donut, I walked toward the front of the class and picked an empty seat on the second row. The moment I got seated, another professor, who introduced himself as Mr. Evan Smith, handed me a big folder that contained all the course documents, maps of the building, and other requirement lists. Once he was gone and I had arranged my folder, a book, and some pens on the table, I took a bite from my donut and looked around.

More faculty members sat at the long desk, facing us at the front. Nerves fluttered in my stomach at seeing the assortment of students, some sitting quietly and going over their documents, and some talking among themselves.

Would someone approach me to talk? Should I? What would I say? Would they understand my accent? Only one way to figure that out.

I turned to look at the guy sitting beside me—a handsome white guy in a black shirt, black jeans, and black-framed glasses. He was among the few people who were quietly reading the contents of the folder the professor had handed out. A frown marred his forehead as he read—he even took notes. Should I disturb him?

I might've been staring a little too long at him, because he turned his face to me, and raised his eyebrows. His eyes, hidden behind his black-rimmed glasses, were a vivid combination of blue and gray. I had a hard time looking away. *Keep your face neutral, Akira. Do not show your nerves. He's just a good-looking guy. With beautiful eyes. No big deal. Keep your cool. Offer a handshake to him, and just introduce yourself.*

"Hi, I'm Akira." I offered my hand.

The guy stared at my suspended hand for a little longer than I would've liked. Not awkward at all. I was about to pull back when he pushed up his glasses and took my hand.

"Sam White."

Thankfully, I didn't snort at his last name. "Pleased to meet you, Sam. Have you been to New York before?"

His brows scrunched up a little. Guess he wasn't expecting any further questions. Sam cleared his throat and put his pen in the small pocket of the folder as he said, "Umm...yeah. I've worked in the city for five years. And I grew up in upstate New York."

"That's so awesome." I couldn't imagine living near the city, and he had grown up around here. Sam's eyes were scrunched up in confusion, probably wondering why I found his living arrangements awesome.

I was about to ask for recommendations on places I should visit in the city when the professors announced that they were ready to begin. Both of us turned toward the stage, where five professors had lined up. Each took a few minutes to introduce themselves and explain a little about what they were going to teach us for the first semester.

The dean of our department announced that we were a cohort of forty students. Then it was time for the students to introduce themselves. We were asked to tell everyone our name and a little about ourselves—where we were from, our undergrad experience, why we chose to pursue a higher degree, etc.

Introductions began, and I couldn't wait to hear what everyone had to say. There were about fifteen people before me, and among them, eight were from different parts of the US, five from China, one from Sri Lanka, one from Kenya, and one from Brazil. Each of them gave passionate reasons for why they wanted to pursue a master's in architecture.

It was finally my turn.

I straightened my shoulders and said, "Hello, everyone. I'm Akira Mishra. I'm from Ahmedabad, a city in the western part of India. I did my bachelor's in architecture. I decided to pursue my master's because it's my dream to work as an architect in a place where our profession is valued. I want to live in a city filled with structures designed by master architects. It wouldn't hurt if the buildings I design in the future get to share a space with buildings like the Empire State Building, Grand Central, and One World Trade Center. I want to learn to design buildings in a manner that is more sensitive toward the environment, the people, the history, and the culture of the place. And finally, I want to be an architect in a city where I can make it on my own. The chances of that happening in India are slim. Architects aren't, you know, paid well in India. Or at all."

Why did I have to mention Indians not getting paid enough? They didn't want to know that. My cheeks were burning with embarrassment. The only relief was that a few people laughed at that.

Professor Lily said, "Thank you, Akira. We wish you all the success in making it in New York. We hope this course helps you along in your journey."

I felt a rush of relief as she moved on to the next student. I guess I had an answer to whether or not people could understand my accent—the question I wondered now was whether they would be interested to hear anything I had to say.

❧

Sam

Huh. She was funny. And honest. Blatantly so.

What did she say her name was?

Akira.

Before I could focus more on her or her blinding fashion choices, it was my turn to introduce myself. I righted my glasses and said, "Hello, everyone, I'm Sam White. I did my undergrad in architecture at Boston Architectural College. Since my family is involved in the construction industry, I have grown up around buildings. As a child, I used to go out on field visits with my dad, and ever since then, I've loved watching buildings take form out of nothing. Learning about buildings is my passion. I hope to expand my father's construction business into architecture, and I'm looking forward to learning as much as I can before I start this new venture."

N. M. PATEL

I could see the pleased smile on the professors' faces. "Great, Sam. I hope you use these three years to take advantage of as many opportunities as you can," said Professor Smith, then moved on to the next person.

I felt eyes on me. I took a glance around and caught Akira staring at me, her face lined with a genuine smile and anticipation.

I looked at her and raised my brows in question.

Since people were still introducing themselves, Akira leaned toward me and whispered, "Isn't it cool to see people from all around the world gathered in a single room? It's the first time I'll be working closely with Chinese people or Brazilian. I've never even talked to them before."

I was taken aback. I've never been asked something like this. I looked around the room. Yes, our class was filled with students from around the world. Having lived my whole life in big, American cities, I didn't even notice anything unusual about our class before Akira mentioned it.

I shrugged. "I guess I never noticed or thought about it that way. I've always lived in cities full of people from all over the world. India doesn't get many tourists?"

"It does, but not much in Ahmedabad."

I nodded, and we got back to listening to the introductions.

After a few minutes, Akira leaned in again. I almost rolled my eyes. She had a lot to talk, this girl.

I leaned in. "Yes?"

With an apologetic smile, she said, "You know, you're the first American person I've actually talked to. Except for the immigration worker at the airport, or at the billing counter in a supermarket and the professor. Like a friendly conversation, you know. It's exciting."

My shock at her statement made her giggle. She stifled it with a cough and got back to listening.

Wow. Never heard that before. I cleared my throat and said,

18

"Good to know...uh. Sorry to say, but I've talked to Indian people before."

She waved a hand in a friendly gesture with a smile and got back to the professors' concluding session.

I was surprised I was more focused on Akira than the professors. That never fucking happened.

Now that I'd shared a conversation with her without blinding myself with all that bright orange, I gave myself a moment to look at her.

She had a smooth, light golden complexion with gorgeous black hair tied into a high ponytail. Her black eyes, rimmed with heavy liner, had a depth to them like all she had to do was look at me to know my deepest secrets. And every time she smiled, her eyes got a playful glint in them. I wish she would turn and smile at me once more.

I waited, looking at her for a beat longer.

And she did. She turned around, looked at me, and gave me a small smile, acknowledging me, and I couldn't help but smile back at her.

Focusing on architecture might be a greater challenge than I had expected.

"Do you have some time to work on that new residential project?" asked Luke, who was now my roommate in our off-campus apartment. The university didn't provide on-campus housing for grad students. So, Luke and I decided to rent an apartment together close to the campus.

Luke and I became best friends when our fathers started their construction company, Wilson & White, almost twenty years ago. We were seven years old then, and twenty years later, our friendship had only gotten stronger. Both of us had already started taking up minor projects of our fathers' company and worked on it together every chance we got.

"Yeah, let's do it in the evening. Once I'm done with this design assignment," I said, as we walked to the university.

"I know I pushed you to do the master's, but I hope you're enjoying it." Luke had started in the program a year before me and had loved it so much that he had not stopped bugging me until I'd applied. I couldn't have been more grateful.

"Yeah, man. The faculty is great, and I love the courses. We can make some great contacts here for when we decide to expand Wilson and White Construction."

Luke laughed and shook his head. "You and your planning. Just focus on the now. Study. Learn. Get to know the people. Enjoy this time, man."

"Yeah, no. You'll thank me later when my planning keeps our business on top of shit."

We reached our building and, after a fist bump, headed in different directions to our classes.

It'd been two weeks since classes started. The first semester is all core classes. The professors thought that would help us get comfortable with our classmates and make new friends. What was it with people and their "make new friends" and "get to know people" thing? I had some friends. I didn't need more.

We had four courses: architecture design, architecture technology, history of architecture, and visual studies. I wasn't worried about any other classes except for the architecture design. That was the main design course that would take place in the studio.

I entered our studio, which was a massive, open room lined with tables along the walls and the center of the room. Each table had a computer and a shelf space underneath it.

I walked between the rows of tables to get to my assigned spot at the end of the room near the window. I placed my bag on the shelf under my desk and nudged out the chair with my foot. I guess I nudged a little too hard because it crashed into Akira's, who sat right behind me facing the opposite direction.

"Oh hey, sorry for that," I said, when she jumped and looked up at me from the computer.

A smile brightened her face, and she waved her hand. "Oh, hey, Sam. It's all right. Space is a bit cramped."

We were a lot of students, and it was not easy to remember each of their faces and names. Because our class was so diverse, and all of them with names I'd never heard before, it was a wonder that I distinctly remembered Akira's face and name.

Maybe it was because she was one of the loudest people in the class, not just in her voice but her personality as well. It had become impossible to ignore her presence. I switched on my computer and waited for it to boot up.

Behind me, Akira called out to her friend sitting beside her and said, "Hey, Mo, how is your design for the installation in a public square coming up? I'm hoping I can finish mine in the next two hours."

Mo, a Chinese woman, answered, "I'm a little stuck in a section. And I'm definitely not going to be able to finish the presentation."

Akira instantly stood up and shoved her chair back, which slammed into mine, shoving me into my desk and gouging my ribs. I glared at my screen and counted to ten to breathe through the pain.

"Oh God. I'm so sorry, Sam. I wasn't looking," Akira said, looking at me with worried eyes. What do you even say to that?

"It's fine," I gritted out through my teeth.

She smiled apologetically and turned around to discuss the design with Mo. Why wasn't I surprised? She'd done the same thing a few days ago with another friend. She always went around the class discussing her designs with others and encouraged others to talk about their design with her.

I hated it.

I didn't enjoy discussing my design process with others. I preferred the appearance of creating something out of nothing. I enjoyed giving that experience to people. Personally, it was no fun when an architect revealed his thought process, his approach, and his concept before finishing the design. It completely ruined the mystery of the final product. And that's why I always tried to steer clear of Akira's sphere.

Akira laughed at something Mo said. God, she was loud. Every time she entered a class, she greeted people around her, including me. However, the factor that contributed the most to Akira's loud presence was her clothes. Her bright, colorful, printed, blinding clothes. There was no theme in her outfits. Or maybe there was—the theme was "too much."

In the last two weeks, Akira had worn bright-colored tops with blue jeans, dresses with prints of big flowers, cats, lines, hearts, and even sushi. Every day was a surprise, and sometimes I was horrified by her outfits, and other days I couldn't stop staring at her.

For the past two weeks, my hours in the studio were spent working on my designs and trying to not concentrate on what Akira was doing. I hated it. But the more I thought about her, the more energy I put into my work. No wonder I was done with today's presentation three days early.

Hours passed, and the presentation for our two-week initial installation design exercise had already begun. The exercise was supposed to give us an introduction to the ideas and skills of our classmates. It would help us in deciding who we wanted to work with in future group projects. So far, I'd seen some exciting designs. It was apparent that everyone was extremely talented and would be fierce competition in the future.

Akira was already done with her presentation. Today, she wore a formal gray skirt and a tucked-in black shirt. She had tied her hair into a tight knot, and her look screamed professional. Usually, her dressing was colorful enough for me to immediately notice her in a crowd. But sometimes she threw a curveball and wore something so subdued that my eyes would instantly start looking for her.

We didn't talk a lot, but we made sure to acknowledge each other when we entered the studio or any class, be it a smile or a nod or a verbal greeting.

Akira's presentation and design were impressive. She had designed a public seating as an installation. Her concept for the design problem was openness and accessibility to the public. She proposed an interactive seating design where each sitting block was a different shape, with punctures of various shapes and sizes that could entertain children. The entire installation was intermingled with pockets of landscapes to provide privacy as well as a sense of otherworldliness from the chaos of the city.

It was something that could actually work for a public square in Manhattan. I think the only area that she needed to work on was her presentation skills. While her drawings conveyed her ideas clearly, a lot of other classmates had far more impressive presentation skills. The faculty felt the same and told her not to limit herself with basic architecture software, but to explore new skills.

I'd already practiced my presentation speech last night. Thrice. So, when it was my turn, I was prepared.

I went up to the podium and started my presentation, explaining my initial idea on exploring the context of the public squares, taking the inspiration from the verticality of the skyscrapers and creating a metal sculpture that would symbolize the history of the square, and its progress into the contemporary architecture. The base of the installation was at a high platform, whose steps served as a seating area for the public. I had even created a 3D rendering of the installation and how it would look at different times of the day. I concluded my presentation with a walk-through showing people milling about the installation, with some sitting on the steps and some taking selfies with the installation.

The comments started with Dr. Smith. "Sam, that was a great presentation. I love your concept of taking your inspiration from the verticality of the buildings around the square. The installation works well with its surroundings, as can be seen from the renderings. Well done."

"Thank you, Professor."

Like he did at the end of every student's presentation, Dr. Smith asked the class, "Any questions for Sam?"

Only one hand was raised.

Akira.

Of course, she'd need to say something.

"Yes, Akira." The professor nodded toward her.

Akira leaned forward in her seat. "Sam, great presentation. I just had one question in terms of accessibility. How would a person with a disability access your installation? And how do you ensure the safety of children from the top of the platform? Thank you."

Oh, fuck. Why didn't I think of that? God, this was a dumb mistake. I needed to make something up. Fast.

"Akira, thank you for that question," I said, stalling. "My presentation is focused more on exploring the general concept of the design and looking at the bigger picture. If I'm to take this design further, I will incorporate the accessibility issue and other safety regulations."

"Great," she replied and sat back with a polite smile. As much as I was embarrassed at Akira's question, I was almost glad that she was paying attention while I presented and cared enough about my design to ask intelligent questions.

I could say for sure that of all the people who presented before me, I didn't remember the designs of more than three people, including Akira. I definitely wanted to work more with her. Not only were her design philosophies opposite to mine, but also her approach to a problem was fascinating. She wasn't afraid of challenging me, and I wanted nothing more than meeting up to those challenges.

At the end of the lecture, the professors told us to settle down so that they could announce the next design exercise, which would start from the next week.

Prof. Smith began. "Great job, everyone. We wanted to introduce the next design exercise right now so that you have some time to work on the design problem and start your research before the next class. We will be working on this problem for the remaining semester. All of you will design a housing complex. We want each of you to pair up with a partner. Within the next two weeks, you will be choosing your site location, where you think a housing complex is needed. You will be working in pairs but just for the initial site visits and research of the site. After that, even though your site will be the same as your partner, you will work on your design of the housing independently. Any questions?"

We collectively shook our heads.

"All right then. For the entire week, you can go and explore the city with your studio partner and come up with your site options for the next week's studio. Let us know who you are working with during the next lecture."

The moment the faculty left, everyone jumped out of their seats, looking for a partner. God, why hadn't the professors made this decision for us? It would've been so much simpler. The noise of everyone making a move toward each other was deafening. Sweat ran down the back of my neck. This was the perfect moment to get Akira to work with me. I needed to hurry before her other friends asked her.

Just then, someone tapped at my back.

I turned around, and my eyes met Akira's.

She looked away as her cheeks turned red.

"Yes?" I asked. It was amusing to see her, dare I say, nervous. Usually, she couldn't stop talking.

"Umm...," she said as she rubbed her arm, "I hope you didn't mind that I questioned you in front of everyone."

How did I tell her that her questioning me was the very reason that had me hoping to work with her?

I smiled at her. "Oh no, not at all. I was glad to know that you were paying attention and interested enough in my design."

Her cheeks flushed.

She cleared her throat. "So... Do you want to work on this project together? With me, I mean."

Wow. No one said she wasn't bold. "Sure. I'd love to."

All tension left her body, and she almost sagged in relief. With a big, bright smile, she asked, "How do we do this? Do you have any general idea on where do we begin to start looking for the site? Or should we go to the library and start with research?"

Wow. Library and research. My heart swooned at those words. But this exercise demanded a different approach, at least according to me. "I think research is a good approach, but this is New York City. Being out and about might help us a lot more than research right now. Maybe after we've selected a few options, we can dig deeper into them. What do you think?"

She clapped her hands together and said, "Okay then. Let's hit the streets. This exercise seems to be the best excuse to explore the city. Where do we start?"

"Let's start with downtown around Wall Street, and we'll walk north. We'll get to see a lot of good buildings on the way."

"Oh, I'm so looking forward to it. I haven't had a chance to roam around the city since I arrived in the US." Her excitement poured out like a buzzing energy. She bounced on the spot, as if in the next moment she might dash out the door to begin her exploration.

I might've been staring at her too long, because she changed the subject and got back to the point. "So, when do we go?"

"Saturday at eleven a.m.?" I asked.

She looked through her phone, maybe checking her calendar. "Yes, that works. And where do we meet? At the university entrance?"

"Sure. That's perfect." I don't know why, but I wanted to keep talking to her. She turned around to leave, but suddenly turned back toward me as if she forgot to say something. "Thanks, Sam. I'm really excited to work with you."

She smiled her gorgeous smile, and my heart skipped a beat.

I couldn't decide whether I was excited to work with her or fucking terrified. Both. The answer was both.

CHAPTER 3

"The purpose of life is to live it, to taste it, to experience the utmost, to reach out eagerly and without fear for newer and richer experience."

- Eleanor Roosevelt

Akira

"Akira, where are you going so early on a Saturday morning?" Megha asked as she sipped her chai. My three roommates looked like they'd just rolled out of bed.

"I have this site visit with a classmate for our studio project. We need to roam around the city and find a prospective site for us to use for a design project for the rest of the semester." I knew Shruti, my other roommate, would relate to this.

Like me, she was in the construction industry and studied construction management, and had experience going for site visits. Poor Megha and Vidya were the tech people in our group and had to study all the computer programming jibber-jabber.

Shruti prodded, "So, who is this classmate? Is he Indian?"

"No, babe. Not an Indian. His name is Sam."

Immediately a chorus of *Oohs* and *Aahs* broke out, and I

wondered if I should proceed any further. That decision was taken out of my hands when Vidya said, "Tell us more. You and Shruti are our only hopes to meet hot and cute American boys. Megha and I don't even have any American classmates."

The considerable lack of Americans in their computer science classes was a huge disappointment for them.

On the other hand, Shruti and I had an abundance of American classmates. Maybe because most of the Americans had the freedom to study whatever they were passionate about, which gave them a hundred different career options.

Or maybe because Indian students were usually forced into two professions—engineering or medicine. The rest of us, who were interested in doing something other than that, were paid so little that we couldn't afford to continue our passion in India.

"Well, he has these gorgeous blue-gray eyes. You should see them. I can look at them for hours, not that I've had an opportunity. All we've exchanged so far are smiles, nods, and polite hellos. And, he is so smart. He doesn't talk a lot in the class, but he does have a hundred questions during the lectures. But I don't think he has a lot of friends here. He keeps to himself and doesn't talk to a lot of people. And you know, he seems like a very professional guy. Every day, he wears these boring clothes, like a sweater or a shirt or sweater over a shirt. And it's always either blue, black, or gray."

Vidya snorted and pointed at my dress, saying, "You want him to dress up in bright yellow clothes with insects printed on them?"

I snorted at the image of Sam in something as cool as that. What I didn't admit was how he made everything he wore look so sexy. Every sweater and jeans combo, or white shirt with the sleeves rolled up to his elbows, paired with the thick, black watch that he wore every single day, made him look lethal. Like just a glare from him would make you cower.

Every day, his hair was styled in a sleek look. Even by the

end of the day, not one hair would be out of place. I usually went from a ponytail to a braid to a bun in the span of a few hours.

I don't know why I kept noticing him. Maybe because he was my first friend, or more like my first acquaintance, in the class. Or maybe because he was so prim and proper, I wanted to ruffle his feathers a bit and make him less *him.*

"So, is he friendly with you? How are you going to work with him?" asked Megha.

"Oh yes, he is friendly with me, I guess. As I said, it's not like we've talked all that much. But he was the first person I talked to in our class. So, we kind of acknowledge each other with some sort of greeting every day. And some days, he sits beside me in lectures."

"So, when and where are you guys going today?" Vidya asked me.

"We're going to explore the Battery Park and Wall Street area and walk up north from there. See what we find."

I looked at my watch, and it was 10:25 a.m. already.

"We're meeting at eleven. I better hurry. He's very punctual. I'll see you all later."

I'd never been happier about having an apartment near the university campus. It was a ten-minute walk from the university entrance, so all I needed to do was pack my bag and leave.

In moments, I was out the door with my sketchbook, favorite pencils, a camera, and a water bottle. The crisp, fresh air hit my face, and I inhaled a big gulp of coolness. I'd never get used to it.

I didn't understand why some people thought New York City's air wasn't clean enough. Where I come from, the weather was so hot, and the air so polluted, that every time I stepped my foot out the door, I had to cover my face with a scarf, put on my sunglasses, hand gloves that covered my whole arms and a helmet to protect my head while driving my two-wheeler vehicle. The air in New York was heaven to me.

It was almost the end of September, and the weather had started to cool down a little after the brutal heat of August.

I opened the group chat my siblings and I shared as I walked toward the campus. And like every time, I was struck by the monumentality of the buildings around me. I sent them a selfie showing my morning time and the streets of New York.

I clicked a few pictures of the buildings along the "street," which ran east–west in Manhattan, and sent them in the group chat. They were mostly three- to four-storied pre-war structures, usually made of bricks, sometimes red and sometimes yellow, with stone quoins at the corners, and decorated with ornamental doors, windows, pediments, and cornices.

A few comments of *Wow* and *Amazing* popped up in the messages.

Once I walked along the "avenue," the road running in the north–south direction, I clicked a few pictures and sent them again. My attention kept getting divided between chatting with my cousins and looking at the delicious food people were having in the outdoor cafés. Despite being a vegetarian, everything looked and smelled delicious.

I was walking along Broadway Avenue, laughing at the photo Ria sent of Mom shouting at Abhi, when I spotted Sam heading toward the university entrance from the opposite direction.

He walked as if each of his steps had a purpose. Even when he entered the classroom, or went for a bathroom break, his stride didn't loosen. He walked with his shoulders straight and his gait smooth. His entire demeanor oozed confidence. I wished for half of his self-assuredness.

Today, he wore tan pants and a dark brown cardigan over a white shirt, which had been folded up to a little below his elbows. He always wore his thick black watch, which went perfectly with his square-ish, black-rimmed glasses. His dark brown leather bag was slung across his shoulders, his hand holding the belt of the bag.

Objectively, he was just a student walking toward the university. Personally speaking, why did he have to look so hot in something so basic? And how could a guy that hot be so aloof?

I waited for the signal to turn green when I noticed Sam waving at me from across the street. I waved back and gave him a smile, indicating with a raised finger that I'd be right there.

Today would be the first time that I would be out exploring the city, and I was so pumped. The only thing that could make it better was some good conversation with Sam and being able to find a site for our project.

∼

Sam

Akira walked down the street from the opposite direction as I reached the entrance of the university. She wore a bright yellow dress, which made it easier to spot her in the crowd of people. She walked as if she had all the time in the world—looking at buildings, peeking at people's food, and occasionally typing something on her phone.

She looked adorable.

Her dress reached a little above her knees, giving me a fantastic view of her smooth legs. They weren't the toned, even muscular legs that most women had here, the result of a life-time of walking on the streets of New York. Her calves had this curve that looked really soft to touch. She had slung her bag across her shoulders, and the strap of the bag was falling right across her chest, accentuating her curves.

She noticed me when she stopped at the traffic signal across me, and I forced my eyes to stop checking her out. The moment our eyes met, my hand instinctively shot up to wave. I looked at my hand in absolute shock and betrayal. A nod was more my style.

But she gave me a big smile and waved back. Just as she started crossing the road, a gust of wind blew her long, wavy black hair across her face, and her dress rode up an inch or so, giving me an even better view of her legs.

I tried my best not to react and turned my head toward the subway station. There was no need to creep her out on the very first day of the field visit. We were here to study and learn, not get into the complications of attraction.

The moment Akira arrived, she gave me a big smile that lit up her eyes. This girl. There was absolutely nothing subtle about her. Not her personality. Not her emotions. Not even her clothes—looking closer, her yellow dress was filled with prints of...bugs? *What the fuck?*

I smiled back at her and indicated the entrance of the subway station with my thumb. "You ready?"

She nodded and extended her arms, telling me to start walking.

We got in line behind other people and filed down the stairs, swiping our Metro cards and heading toward the platform that would take us downtown. Luckily, the subway seemed to have just arrived, so we ran down the stairs and into a car before the doors shut.

The train wasn't as crowded as it would've been if it were a weekday, so there were enough empty seats for us to sit together.

After a few minutes of sitting in silence, Akira asked, "So, how do you like Columbia? Is it everything you hoped for?"

Silence wasn't her strong suit.

I looked at her, and replied, "It's pretty good. What about you?"

"I love the campus. I have never studied at a campus this nice or a university this prestigious."

"My undergrad university in Boston actually had a better campus, but it's certainly not as prestigious."

"A better campus than Columbia?" Her mouth fell open in shock.

I chuckled. "It had more space, so lots of green, open space there. Columbia is in the middle of Manhattan. It's a lot more compact," I explained.

"It's the best I've seen," she muttered under her breath. Even her muttering was loud.

"So, what part in India are you from?" I asked, bringing her out of her musing.

"Would you even know the state and the city if I tell you?"

Huh. She got me there. "No. That's why I asked," I said, trying to minimize my ignorance.

She smiled at that. "My city is called Ahmedabad, and it's in the state of Gujarat."

"Do you miss it?"

She got a thoughtful frown on her face. "Sort of."

Sort of? I'd expect her to say yes. Now curious, I asked, "What do you mean?"

"I don't miss the weather. At all. And I'm not a big fan of Indian food, particularly Gujarati food. It's the vernacular cuisine of Gujarat. At least I wasn't when I was in India. But I miss my family. Even with roommates, my apartment seems quiet. I hate it. I miss having constant background noise. I miss having a lot of people around me. Why do you think I chose New York? I got into Cornell and Boston, too. But they seemed to be so isolated. I love seeing life around me. I'm sorry. Am I talking too much?"

Well, what do you say to that?

"Truth—yes." Her smile dropped before I'd even finished the sentence. Now she wasn't even looking at me. I touched her hand, and continued. "But I want to hear more. Tell me about your family, if you don't mind?"

What was up with me? Why couldn't I stop talking to her?

And she was back with her smile. Why did I feel so happy at the smile on her face? Akira turned toward me, our knees touching, and continued. "Oh my God...don't even get me started. Well, let's see."

I was still stuck on our knees that were touching right now.

She started counting her family members on her fingers. This was going to be epic. "It's me, Mom and Dad, my two brothers. I'm the middle child, by the way. Then, there are my two uncles. Two aunts. They both have two children each. And my grandfather and my grandmother."

I couldn't help but smile at that.

"I was asking you about your childhood home, like the people you grew up with."

"What do you mean by *childhood* home? And these are my family. We all live together."

Holy fuck. That was fifteen people. And I couldn't believe she lived with her family up until now.

"Like all the time?"

She stared at me as if I'd asked a ridiculous question. Yep. She was staring at me so hard that I tried not to squirm. I probably did.

Finally, she took pity on me and answered, "Yes, Sam. All the time. My father is fifty-five and is still terrified of my grandfather. He wouldn't dare ask to separate. I mean, I understand that's not what usually happens here in the West, but it's pretty common in India to live with your husband's family once a couple gets married. However, these days, people in big cities have started living separately from their parents."

"If you don't mind me asking, why did *you* leave your family?"

She was about to answer when a hoard of people climbed

in the subway at the Times Square stop, bringing in all sorts of food smells and screaming children. A few people stood holding the rail next to where Akira and I sat.

Akira chuckled at my obvious discomfort. The train had suddenly become a loud place.

I leaned into Akira, almost touching her ears, when an intoxicating fusion of vanilla and rose hit me. Akira. That was all her. All words left my mind. I wanted more of that smell... needed to take my fill and roll around in that aroma.

A leg hit my knees, and I realized what I was doing. I was leaned into Akira and not saying a word. *Way to not creep her out on the first day.*

I cleared my throat, straightened my glasses, and without meeting Akira's eyes, said, "You were saying something?"

I did not want to know what she thought of my leering. I needed to get my head straight.

Akira turned toward me, and her cheeks had a hint of red. Without meeting my eyes, she said, "Well, for privacy and freedom, first of all. You have no idea what it's like to live with fourteen people. Second, I had been completely dependent on my family, and I needed to be my own self. Know that I can make it on my own without relying on others."

She kinda looked sad.

"You don't look very happy."

She raised her eyebrows with a small, almost embarrassed smile. "I don't, huh?" She shrugged her shoulders and continued. "I'm glad that I left, but the decision made my family quite sad. And it's difficult to be alone when you've lived with so many people all your life. I miss their constant presence."

"I'm sorry. You're brave to move across the world," I said. And I believed it. It would've taken an enormous amount of courage to leave everything behind and start a life in a new country.

She snickered, shaking her head. "I'm no different than

hundreds of thousands of immigrants trying to make a life here."

She was right, but I'd never given as much thought to immigrants. I was so busy tackling my own problems, I had no time to focus on others.

Before I could say something, Akira said, "Now enough of my story, tell me something about yourself."

Her anticipation for my answer compelled me to share. I worked to dredge up an appropriate response.

"Well, it's my mom, dad, and me."

"C'mon, Sam. I word vomited my history. Give me a little more than that." She looked at me with her large, innocent, puppy-dog eyes, and I was so screwed. It'd been two weeks, and I was already starting to think about Akira more than I should.

Akira jerked to the side to look at the sign on the subway wall. "I think this is our stop! Isn't it?"

Oh, shit! I grabbed her hand and we ran for the door. I was almost glad for the interruption. I shouldn't be so involved in Akira and sharing all the personal stuff.

CHAPTER 4

"Throw your dreams into space like a kite, and you do not know what it will bring back, a new life, a new friend, a new love, a new country."

- Anais Nin

Akira

I didn't really notice when Sam grabbed my hand to get out of the subway. But I was very aware when he didn't drop my hand as soon as we were out.

His strong hold around my fingers sent a zap of electricity through my entire body. Must be static.

Had to be.

He was dragging me out of the station, always one step ahead of me, expertly weaving us among the hustling commuters of the city. While he seemed to have forgotten that he was holding my hand, I was highly aware of the feel of my small hand in his much warmer, stronger hand. I wasn't even gripping his hand, but rather passively resting it in his firm grasp.

The moment I closed my hand around his, he jolted in surprise and quickly let go.

The tip of his ears turned red, and he looked back at me, almost blushing, and ran his fingers through his hair. I'd never seen his hair anything but perfect. "I'm sorry for uh...holding your...um...I didn't realize I was holding it."

It stung that he regretted holding my hand, which was dumb because there was no reason for him to hold my hand or for me to feel any sort of hurt. *Shake it off, Akira.*

I shook my head and smiled at him. "It's fine. So, what's our game plan for today? What places are we hitting first?"

He relaxed at my attempt to casually let it go, and even got excited at the prospect of discussing our field visit.

He turned toward me as we climbed up the station staircase to exit and said, "Okay, so once we get out of the station, we'll come out at Broadway. I thought that if we started from the bottom, we could continue exploring and walking uptown for as far as we can walk and see where we get. We have a few exciting places that we can check out in the vicinity. We can walk up to Wall Street, hit up a few other streets in the Financial District, walk around Battery Park, and if you want, I can even take you to touch the Charging Bull's balls."

He winked at me while I stared in utter shock for two specific reasons—one, Sam's playfulness turned him into an insanely sexy version of himself, and I refused to blink and miss out on a single second of it. It was the most I'd ever heard him speak.

Second, *bull's balls? What the hell!* Why would I want to touch a bull's balls?

When Sam raised his eyebrows at my still shocked face, I sputtered, "What? Why would I touch a ball's bull? I mean a bull's balls?" I was pretty sure I had turned into a tomato by now.

He chuckled as we walked along Wall Street and said,

"Well, rumor has it that touching the balls on the statue *Charging Bull* brings you a financial fortune."

"Huh. Well then, let's go touch some balls." If touching balls of a bull statue was going to get me rich, who was I to say no?

We got out our supplies to note details for our potential sites as we walked.

Me, a sketchbook and a pencil.

Sam got out his sketchbook, a tape measure, a black pen, maps, prints of different buildings of Wall Street, a red marker, a grid-line book, and then clipped his student ID card to his sweater. Not only did he carry all of that in his bag, but he managed to hold it all in his hands while we walked along the busy sidewalks of Wall Street.

The moment we noticed each other's supplies, we stared at each other in shock for a blink and burst out in laughter.

In the two weeks since classes had begun, this was the first time that I saw Sam truly laugh. He had this weird laugh where his shoulders silently shook for a few seconds and then he made a loud, hiccupy sound, and then the whole thing repeated. Like a machine that suddenly started working, making sputtering noises, after being shut off for years. There was no smoothness to it. But surprisingly, that weird laugh worked for him. And I loved it.

Charging Bull ended up being our first destination. And it was surrounded by hordes of tourists. We stood across the street, and all I could see was the bull's hump. About a hundred people stood around the bull clicking pictures. A few people flocked in line near the bull's backside, while two guys groped the bull's balls. Holy. Shit. Sam wasn't wrong.

I turned to Sam's smirking, know-it-all smile and said, "You know, in India, we too have auspicious animals, like the cow, tortoise, elephant, mouse, each being a vehicle of different gods. We usually touch the animal's feet or hump or nose. Never their balls. Isn't that weird?"

Sam shrugged his shoulders, his eyes twinkling as the bright light streaked across his face and hair. He smiled and said, "A little weird, but it's as weird as praying to an animal, isn't it?"

I scoffed. "It's totally different."

"Says you."

"Of course. And I am always right."

Sam shook his head, trying to hide his beautiful smile. But I saw it. There definitely was a smile.

As we got a little closer to the gigantic bull, he explained, "An Italian sculptor, Arturo Di Modica, built this bronze sculpture of the bull in the late eighties, during a time of recession in the US. According to him, he made the bull, and I quote, 'as a way to celebrate the can-do spirit of America and especially New York, where people from all over the world could come regardless of their origin or circumstances, and through determination and hard work overcome every obstacle to become successful.' So, you see, this sculpture is a symbol of acceptance of people of different origins, and it gives hope to people who work hard to make a living in the US and strive to be successful."

I was awestruck by the end of his explanation. I hung on to every word he spoke; his passion flowed through his words and captured my undivided attention among the sea of tourists in the middle of the Wall Street.

He had no idea how much this story touched my heart. Or maybe he did. And that's why he brought me here. To make me feel like I belonged in this country. That I was wanted. I wasn't an intruder here. I had the right to study here, work here, and make something out of my life.

With a huge lump in my throat, I said, "Thanks for telling me this. It means a lot."

I smiled at Sam and showed him all my gratitude reflected in my eyes. He paused, and a bashful smile spread over his face.

He nodded and turned around to lead me to the line for clicking picture with the bull's balls.

Sam stared intently at my phone as he clicked pictures of me. "You'll be a billionaire if you massage and pet the balls with any more passion, Akira."

I scoffed and rolled my eyes. "Stop. You'll make me want to kiss these big balls."

He snickered and kept clicking.

After a few more shots, I asked him to join me between the bull's legs to click a picture of us together.

Once he sat beside me, after handing over my phone to a tourist, I said, "C'mon, Sam, hold these balls with me. They're big enough for both of us."

He snorted with a little smile, while I laughed at his expression of disbelief.

"Perfect picture," the tourist said.

Both of us looked at her in surprise. Guess we forgot why Sam was sitting beside me.

Embarrassed, both of us got up and I took the phone from the lovely tourist.

Once we were done, we walked across the city for the next three hours, and Sam continued his impassioned descriptions of different buildings: the New York Stock Exchange, Trinity Church, Federal Hall, the Woolworth Building, and many more, giving me little anecdotes of their history and building technology.

We jotted down notes and sketches, discussing the potential of different sites and clicking pictures of the site options. Amid the exhaustion of walking for three hours, I spotted a Starbucks. I didn't even realize that I had gasped, causing Sam to stop and catch my arm abruptly.

"Akira, what happened? You all right?"

Two frown lines appeared between his eyebrows.

I caught hold of his wrist in excitement and said, "Sam, it's Starbucks. We need to go there. Now."

Sam frowned at me as if I was talking in Gujarati. "What?"

Well, what didn't he understand? "What, what?" I asked.

Exasperated, Sam rolled his eyes and expanded, "Why do you want to go to Starbucks right now. If you want a coffee, we can have great coffee from any of the local shops in the hidden corners of Wall Street?"

While he did have a point, I didn't know how to begin my explanation. "But..."

Before I could get a word out, Sam continued, "And we would get far more authentic New York coffee in the local shops than a West Coast chain café that's on every corner."

Oh man, now he did it. What an asshole!

"It's not on every corner in my hometown. There is not even *one* Starbucks in my city. Hardly any cities in India have Starbucks, and Ahmedabad is not one of them. I've only had one Starbucks drink in my lifetime, and that was in Mumbai, when I got my visa to come to the US. So, sue me if I'm excited to get a Starbucks coffee."

Leaving the ridiculous, arrogant jerk-face behind, I stormed in the direction of the Starbucks across the street.

Sam

Nobody had ever made me feel like an entitled asshole. And for what? Not getting excited over Starbucks. How would I know they didn't have it in her city? *Well, you didn't, and now you made this gorgeous girl sad, you arrogant fucking asshole.*

I pushed my glasses up on my nose and ran after her. "Well, when you put it that way, it does make me sound like a jerk."

Akira seemed to soften a little at the acknowledgment of my

asshole behavior. I put my arm around her and started walking with her toward the green and white sign.

"C'mon, you should definitely check out their cold brew. It's awesome." I faked a big smile and tried to put all the enthusiasm that I could muster for the unnecessarily overpriced coffee chain.

A genuine smile lit up her entire face. "Thank you. Now let's hurry."

Kinda made me feel shitty for making her lose her sweet smile over a cup of coffee. She was already two steps ahead of me when she turned around and gave me a sexy little smirk. "You know, you might be a really good architect, but your acting sucks."

I burst out laughing. This girl was going to be so much trouble.

"You caught that, huh?"

She rolled her eyes at me. "Your fake smile had a little too many teeth. Never ever do that again." I gave her my own eye roll as we made our way to Starbucks.

As I opened the door to let her in, I realized Akira was standing a few feet from the door, scrolling frantically through her phone with a deep frown on her face. I rushed back to her and gently caught her arm to not spook her. "Akira, hey. Is everything alright?"

She chewed her lip, but then gave me a small smile and a nod. "Uh. Yeah. Everything's fine. It's just that I had made a list of 'secret' drinks that I wanted to try whenever I got the chance to go to Starbucks, but since I changed my phone, I've lost all those notes. What should I order now? I've seen people giving these crazy orders with different flavors and types of cream and milk."

Where was the damn wall when you needed to bang your head on it? I gave myself two deep breaths before I responded,

"Akira, they have a menu. And you can order something from that."

I gave her a you-walk-in-and-order-something-right-now-or-I-walk-out glare. As she walked inside, she turned, stuck her tongue out at me, and closed the entrance door in my face.

I walked in and stood behind her in the line. "How mature," I said into her ear.

As she turned her head to respond, she sneezed violently and banged her head into mine. I almost keeled over in the middle of the stupid Starbucks line.

"Fuck!"

"Oww."

I looked up to see Akira holding her palm over her forehead too. Our eyes, brimming with pain, met.

"Are you okay?" we asked at the same time.

My head throbbed, and by the look on Akira's face, hers too.

As I removed my hand from my forehead, so did Akira.

A lump had formed on her forehead. My finger lifted to tell her she had a lump.

But so did hers. Confused, I touched my forehead where she indicated.

Again, so did she.

We touched our lumps at the same time and cringed together, then burst out laughing in the middle of the crowded Starbucks.

Tears rolled down Akira's cheeks. I howled, bent in half, hands braced on my thighs. Akira's knees gave out, and she sat on the floor, laughing, her one hand clutching her head.

The moment her tear-streaked eyes met my tear-filled ones, the world stopped.

My heart stopped.

This moment.

Her.

I captured every single detail of this moment in my mind and carefully filed it with my favorite memories. This moment would be the one that I would go back to whenever I wanted to remember what pure joy felt like. When was the last time I laughed this hard? I gave her my hand to help her stand up. She took it as she put her weight on me, and I couldn't help but hold it for a few seconds longer than necessary. She didn't complain. I didn't mention it. She ordered a triple mocha Frappuccino. I ordered a regular black coffee.

Once we had our orders, we took a seat at the barstools near the front window. While she sucked the frosty, sugary liquid from her straw, I sipped my black coffee.

"I thought you were gonna get a coffee," I teased.

She shook her cup in my face and blurted, "Frappuccino has coffee in it."

I couldn't help but snort. "Frappuccino is not coffee."

She huffed, put her frap on the table and said, "Fine. I didn't want to risk it. I've never had a black coffee before. Doesn't it taste bitter?"

This girl could manage to shock me every fifteen minutes. "You've never had a black coffee before? What did you do during your late-night studio in India?"

She rolled her eyes at me, again, as if I was the weird one here. "We do have coffees. But they are instant coffee mix which we add in a little water and a lot of milk and sugar. Very few people invest in coffee machines, and typical restaurants and cafés in India don't have black coffee in their menu." She shrugged her shoulders as if that was completely normal.

"Do you want a sip?" I offered. Her eyes went round. So did mine. Shit. What did I just say? And why, *why* would I suggest for her to put her lips exactly where my lips had been a moment ago?

I didn't need to get into any complications with her.

As beautiful as Akira was, I was here to study architecture, not fall for the adorable Indian girl. *Fall? Not fall. Crush.* That's what it was. I didn't need to go crushing after Akira.

As if she could read my mind, she asked, "You don't mind?"

Did I mind? No.

Would it make *everything* impossibly harder? Most definitely.

"Not at all. Here." I handed her my cup as she gave me hers for a taste of the sugary shit. As if I needed anything sweeter in my life right now. She put her lips right where my lips were a second ago, took a sip and instantly sprayed it out all over me.

Before I could complain, she spewed, "How are you even drinking that thing?"

She grabbed her drink from me and started sucking on her frap while she handed me some tissues.

I glared at her as she raised her one hand in defense and said, "It's all on you. How could you hand me something that bitter and gross to drink?"

I tried not to laugh while I wiped my shirt with a napkin. "Let's go before you seriously injure me, you crazy person. We'll continue the rest of the work in the studio on Monday."

She laughed and punched me on my arm and said, "You're the crazy one to drink that awful, bitter concoction."

We didn't go anywhere for the next two hours.

We stayed in the coffee shop.

Sharing stories.

Exchanging smiles.

Laughing.

Feeling lighter than ever.

CHAPTER 5

"It is not our differences that divide us. It is our inability to recognize, accept and celebrate those differences."
   - Audre Lorde

Akira

I was in the studio discussing our field trip with my classmates on a Monday afternoon. I'd spent my Sunday putting together a presentation with Sam at the studio. And for the entire day, I'd struggled to concentrate on work.

Sam's small frown permanently etched on his face, his gentle but matter-of-fact voice describing different buildings and patiently telling me the stories associated with them, and his adorable, awkward laugh, were all doing something to my heart, my stomach, my cheeks, and even my sweat glands.

Every time he focused on me, my English started to trickle away, and broken, stumbling words came out. Thankfully, he probably misinterpreted my awkwardness as me stumbling speaking English, immigrant and all, and didn't comment on it.

I just had to spend a little more time with him and get used to his presence. English will smoothly fly out of my mouth in no time.

The professors hadn't arrived yet, which gave me time to catch up with my other friends and get a general sense of what everyone had done over the weekend. Dani, Aida, Mo, Tom, and I huddled around Mo's desk, going over her and Tom's field trip pictures.

Mo was my first Chinese friend.

Aida was from Kenya. Just like me, she was the only person from her country in our class.

Dani was a cool American chick who had initiated a conversation with me on the first day of the class.

And Tom was the first gay guy I'd talked to in real life. When I'd told him that, he'd laughed loudly and hugged me.

I never imagined that I would be lucky enough to have an opportunity to be a part of a group where people of so many different backgrounds came together to exchange ideas and learn from each other.

We all looked different, but our passions, dreams, hopes, and ideas brought us all together. And to think of all that we could achieve by contributing to each other's knowledge—it was incredibly humbling.

Not even three weeks had passed, and we all had started learning to say "Hi" in each other's native language, and freely asked each other about the things that had always fascinated us about each other's countries.

For instance, Mo asked me, "What is this caste system in India, and how many gods do you have?"

Everyone stared at me with wide-eyed curiosity, as if the two questions could be answered in two lines. "Well, as for the first question, I am not opening that can of worms. It's too complicated and extensive to explain quickly. Second, we have many gods. Every religion, sub-religion, caste, sub-caste, and communities have a god that they believe in. And some religions like Hindus have more than one god. We have a god for every aspect of our lives—agriculture, rain, wind, sun, money, vehicles, for a good husband, for being able to bear kids, for success, and on and on."

While I drank some water at the end of my answer, Mo, Tom, Dani, and Aida stared at me, slack jawed.

As Tom started asking Aida about some good Kenyan restaurants, I felt a tap on my shoulder. I turned around and my eyes met the brilliant blue-gray that had started haunting me in my sleep.

All the other conversations got tuned out, and Sam became the sole focus of my attention. He looked divine in his usual black, slim-fit pants that ended a little above his feet and gave a sexy view of his ankles. His black-rimmed glasses, perched on his nose, made him look even more serious than he truly was, now that I'd gotten to know him a little.

He politely greeted our classmates without contributing to any conversations as he dragged me off to discuss our presentation before the class began. I smiled at them, assuring to catch up with them later.

We reached our desks, which were right beside each other now that we were sort of friends and working together. I noticed a Frappuccino in a Starbucks cup beside my laptop. I was about to hold the cup and holler out to ask if someone had a missing frap when Sam informed me, "I got it for you."

Umm. I might have looked confused or shocked or a combination of both because Sam's stature went from indifferently informative to nervously twitching. It started with a frown, his hand started running through his hair, straightening his already perched glasses.

"What?" he asked, prompting me to speak.

"Why did you get me a frap?" Not that I wasn't grateful, but I had no idea why someone would just bring me a coffee. I certainly haven't brought a coffee for anyone in the class. I was genuinely confused about this gesture.

Sam was neither my boyfriend nor my best friend. I would call him a friend after the last two days, but none of my friends in India had ever bought me a coffee. I might have been lost in my thoughts, because Sam had started looking even more uncomfortable and was extending his hand to take back the frap.

Out of reflex, I brought the coffee closer to me and asked him, again, "Sam, why would you bring me a coffee?"

I took a huge sip and couldn't help but moan, "Oh my God, what kind of frap is that? And you didn't answer my question."

He mumbled something while looking at the cup in my hand.

"What?" I asked.

He resumed his fiddling with his hair and glasses and said, "Well, I felt bad for insulting you the other day. I didn't mean to come off as an asshole, but that's what I was. I didn't know your city didn't have a Starbucks. I shouldn't have been insensitive. That's why I wanted to bring you a Starbucks."

He shrugged as if it wasn't a big deal.

But it so freaking was.

I melted, just like that whipped cream in my cup.

I tried to say something. Anything. My throat closed up with all the emotions that were trying to escape, but I clamped down all those words. The stupid feelings might've escaped my eyes, because Sam was suddenly beside me and staring at me intently with a severe frown on his face.

"Are you going to cry? I can take back the frap."

"It's mine," I barked and pushed him off. Then promptly pulled him close, put my arms around him, and hugged him. My head landed near his shoulder, my nose near his collarbone.

I gave myself one moment to breathe.

One moment of that blissful warmth. Just one more second. And before he could hug me back, I let him go.

Feeling a little embarrassed, I smiled at him and said, "This is the first time someone got me a coffee. Thank you."

I took out my sketchbook and presentation notes from my bag, and gave him a nod. "Let's go. We have a presentation to give."

Because of Sam's fair complexion, it was pretty easy to see the blush on him. If I wasn't wrong, as Sam picked up his notes and book, his ears, cheeks, and neck were definitely red. I decided not to mention it, but as I joined the rest of the class for the presentation, I heard Tom ask Sam, "Hey, Sam, you've gone all red. You okay, man?"

"It's just a little hot in here," Sam muttered.

A laugh escaped me, and as I turned back to look at him, he glared at me, even redder now, consequently making me laugh harder.

IT'D BEEN THREE DAYS, and Sam had brought me a different Frappuccino every day. While it was by far the sweetest thing that anyone had ever done for me, it had to be expensive.

Personally, I wouldn't buy more than one Starbucks drink a month, and it was getting painful to watch Sam spend his money on me. In Indian rupees, one Starbuck coffee could buy me more than fifteen cups of coffee from an average restaurant in India.

That conversion itself made it even more painful to see Sam spending so much of his money on a coffee, just because he was sorry for something he did unconsciously. It was on the fourth day that I officially made him stop, telling him I was going to make him drink every cup that he bought for me from that moment on.

The next day, Sam showed up without a coffee in his hand, and I thanked the money goddess, Laxmi. While I gave him a thankful nod, he gave me a smirk and patted me on my head as he passed my desk to reach his desk beside me.

"Let's get to work," Sam declared.

After our presentation on our site visit a few days ago, the professors had given us the instructions to proceed with our individual design proposals.

Sam and I had chosen three four-story buildings on Wall Street as our site. Our plan was to build a modern housing skyscraper above the historic, smaller buildings.

Even though we'd started working on our individual projects, Sam and I had an unspoken agreement to continue to sit together in the studio. Over the days we'd worked together, I'd started to feel a strange sense of comfort around him. His silent and formidable presence, the way he tackled work with dedication, his willingness to teach me every time I stumbled, and his witty retorts all had me entranced.

The more time I spent with Sam, the more I got to know him.

Like how he did not like it when any of my stuff strayed over to his desk. This I learnt after I found him glaring at my purple highlighter for five minutes straight. Initially I thought he had a problem with the purple color. So, I left my black pen on his desk, and found Sam glaring at it again. Definitely wasn't the color.

He never called me on it, but my little experiment was enough for me to figure out he needed his own space. He seemed to have a system for his things. Every pen, pencil, highlighter was in a holder he'd gotten from his home. He did not use another pen until he had placed the pen he was first using back in the holder. There were no random doodles and scribbles in his sketchbook, which was so weird, because most of my design ideas came from my scribbles.

53

He also had a coaster. He would not keep his coffee anywhere else.

Every little thing he did, I noticed. I didn't want to though. Yet, I couldn't keep away. And I really wanted to.

It was getting tiring to constantly remind myself that I was here to learn architecture, be my own person, and be independent. Sam should be at the bottom of my priority list. In fact, he shouldn't be on the list at all. But then why did I keep putting him at the top of the stupid list?

∽

Sam

We had been working together in the studio for the past two weeks now. We sat next to each other—our desks were barely large enough to hold our laptops and sketchbooks—as we worked on our designs, our hands occasionally bumped, me being left-handed and Akira being right-handed.

Akira had her headphones on, her lips murmuring the song in her language. So, all I heard coming from her lips was gibberish. I'd gotten pretty used to the way she worked over the past few days.

A few minutes passed where we silently worked when she tapped her pencil on my arm. I pulled out my headphones and raised my eyebrow at her in question.

She bit her lip in a small grimace for disturbing me. I didn't know why she felt guilty anymore. She did this every hour.

"What's up?" I asked, just to prompt her to ask her question.

She looked relieved and turned her laptop to face me. "So, remember when you said the access and circulation looked a little chaotic? Well, I moved around the staircase and lobby, and tried to create a little more grid pattern for convenience. What do you think?"

For the next few minutes, we discussed her designs. I think the more she verbalized her ideas, the more ideas she got. It used to bother me but her discussions brought out some amazing ideas for me too.

Once we were done with the discussion, she turned back her laptop, and started looking for something in the clutter that she liked to call her desk. It was a mess that I tried to not look at directly. I was just happy that she was respectful of my tidy desk and limited the clutter on her side.

Two hours passed where we worked in companionable silence. To refresh our mind, we went to the little café in the basement floor of our building and returned with some coffee and muffins.

We immediately got back to work, and Akira doodled the shit out of her sketch pad, colors and markers dotting every surface of the paper.

I lost myself in my design, outlining the different options for my layout. My process of design—letting the space come alive in my mind, translating it to paper, getting the proportions right, researching the details of materials—was crucial in the initial stage. I needed to be immersed in it, follow it religiously for my satisfaction at the end.

So, when Akira kept shifting in her seat, I lost my focus. I tried to ignore her restless movements for a few minutes when she suddenly got up.

I turned to her and raised my brows in question.

She turned red and started packing a few things in her bag. "Umm... I'll be back in a bit."

Before I could respond, she had rushed out of the studio, leaving behind a sudden sense of emptiness around me. I looked around the studio to see if others felt the same way, but everyone was just busy working.

I turned back to my sketch and stared. And stared some more.

My hand hovered over the lines I had traced, but for the life of me, I couldn't get back on track.

My mind stopped imagining the apartments and the housing scheme that we had to design and kept turning into circles with questions.

Where did she go?

How long would she be gone?

To make it worse, this wasn't the first time she'd left the studio so abruptly like that.

This was, I think, the fifth time she'd run away like that in the last two weeks, but who was counting?

I took a sip of my coffee to get back to my work. Design. Housing. Sketch. I begged my mind to focus. Tried to imagine entering and moving through the housing scheme.

But all I did was drag my eyes to the empty seat beside me.

Did she go somewhere to meet a guy? Did she have a boyfriend? Because she always returned happy and relaxed, with a big smile on her face, and occasionally some Indian food.

Just the possibility of Akira meeting up with a guy made my stomach turn sour.

No matter how hard I tried to keep working, I simply couldn't.

And I hated it. And I hated that I hated it.

I didn't want this girl to disrupt my life. But no matter what I tried—listening to music, watching a lecture by my favorite architect, sketching—nothing fucking worked. For those minutes, I hated Akira.

Hated her for making me curious. Hated her for making me wonder. Hated her for making me care.

I stewed in my emotions for thirty agonizingly long minutes when the door of the studio opened, and she walked in. Happy and relaxed.

She walked toward me and gave me a huge smile. And for the life of me, I couldn't stay mad at her. We continued to work until 11 p.m. that evening, after which I walked her home, occasionally responding to her constant chatter. Sometimes when it was early, we took a longer route back and explored the streets of New York.

Still wondering about Akira's regular absence, I walked into my apartment and stumbled into Luke. He hovered over his city of building models which dominated our living room.

As soon as he noticed me, he called out, "Hey, man. What's up? And don't freak out. I'll clean up after I'm done."

"Hey. What's the model for? And I only freaked out that time because you hadn't cleaned up for three days," I said, grabbing a beer from the fridge.

"Preliminary studio review is the day after tomorrow. So, one more day."

"Cool. You want any help?"

"Sure. Could you start on the trees and streetlights? I'll join in once I'm done with this roof." Luke never declined any help. He believed that people wouldn't offer to help if they didn't want to, and if they offered to help just as a pretense, they'll learn not to do that again after he made them work for two hours.

I used to be the complete opposite. I never asked for help and declined any help offered. But lately, I'd been asking for help and giving more help, thanks to Akira.

"So, how come you don't work from home? You've had everything set up since you moved in," he asked, half of his attention still directed toward his roof cutout.

"Ah...I haven't had a chance. Staying busy. Making new friends," I rambled on as I picked up materials for a streetlight and started helping out.

"You don't make new friends. What're you hiding?" Luke

asked, assessing me in just a glance. Maybe a glance was all he needed.

"What? I make friends." I had nothing else to say.

"You have just one friend. Me. Now tell me what's up?"

I didn't know if I should be talking about Akira with him. It wasn't as if anything was happening there. *You want something to happen, don't you?* It had been three weeks since I met her. I didn't even know if she felt anything for me at all.

"Dude..." Luke nudged my arm.

"Sorry, I was thinking."

"About?"

Fuck it. "Akira," I admitted.

Luke got this big, stupid smile on his face. "Akira? Who's that? She hot?"

The moment he saw my glare, he shut up and asked me to proceed.

So, I told him.

Everything.

How she wore the loudest colors, the way she got excited about something like Starbucks, her huge family, her nonstop talking, us working together in the studio until late at night, and her regular disappearance from the studio that had been bothering me.

By the time I was done, Luke and I had finished off three beers each. He got this serious look on his face. "Sam, I haven't seen you go crazy over someone in a long time."

Like I didn't know that.

"Nah, man. We're just good friends," I claimed.

Luke snorted loudly. "Have you looked at yourself in the mirror, man? We've been friends for years, and I've never seen you like this over a girl. You fucking blushed when you started talking about this girl."

Even though everything Luke said got to me, I let it slide.

"C'mon, Luke, it's been just three weeks since we met. Akira's just interesting and funny. That's it."

"As you say. I know you heard me. And I'll be visiting your studio soon. I'd love to meet this girl." He then got back to work on his stupid roof while I silently made streetlights and trees for his model until I couldn't stay awake anymore.

CHAPTER 6

"We become not a melting pot but a beautiful mosaic. Different people, different beliefs, different yearnings, different hopes, different dreams."
  - Jimmy Carter

Akira

I made my way to our shared bathroom. In the kitchen, Megha was making *chai*. Being the only two dedicated chai drinkers of the house, Megha and I usually made two cups every time.

"Hey, Akira, good morning, babe," Megha said.

I grumbled a good morning as I went into the bathroom.

Disappointment stared back at me in the mirror above the sink. I looked down, unwilling to meet my eyes, as I freshened up.

I picked up my chai from the kitchen and sat across Megha at the dining table. Since it was too early for the lecture and I was in no state to make a good conversation, I started uploading pictures of all the places I'd visited to the family chatting group.

Megha surfed through her phone for the latest Bollywood gossip.

I could feel her eyes on me, but I was in no mood to acknowledge her stare down.

As I checked today's schedule while the photos were being uploaded, a notification of a message from Sam popped up.

S: Good morning. Studio today at 2?

As if I could feel any worse, the class genius had to message me. I did not want to look at his stupid face today. I didn't bother replying and went back to upload more photos.

After a few minutes of silence, Megha said, "That's it. Akira, what's wrong?"

Without meeting her eyes, I said, "Nothing."

"C'mon, Akira, you're worrying me. Whatever it is, I'll try to help."

After taking a big gulp of my chai, I looked at her. I tried to get the words out, but shame had my throat close up. Megha squeezed my hand, concern etched on her face. Her eyes were patient and calm.

I took a deep breath and let the words out. "I bombed one of my assignments. I had to write a research paper on the emergence of postmodern architecture in New York. And I failed."

Megha was up from her chair and had her arms around me before I could even blink. I tried to stop the tears from falling but failed. I broke down. I had come to the States to study. But I never knew that writing a research paper could be so difficult. I'd never had to write a research paper for my bachelor's in India, and now I had to write five in just one semester. I had worked hard for the past few weeks to get this paper right. But apparently, according to the professor, my paper didn't meet the requirements.

"What am I going to do, Megha?" I asked, biting my lips to stop the trembling.

She ran her hand over my hair. "You need to talk to your

professor and ask them what they're looking for in a paper. We clearly have a disadvantage when it comes to writing papers."

"You're right. Gosh, it's so freaking embarrassing. As if that's not enough, Sam wants to work together in the studio today."

Megha sat back on her chair and frowned. "How is that a bad thing?"

I couldn't stop the growl as I said, "Because he is the genius of the class. I bet he scored well in the paper. And what if he asks me my grade? I can't handle the judgment and any snide remarks. Not that he would do that. But what if he did?"

With a small, teasing smile on her face, Megha asked, "Why does it matter to you what he thinks?"

"I...uh... Because. He is a friend. And I want him to stay my friend. Yes. That's why it matters."

"Of course. And if he's your friend, wouldn't he help you with your paper if he finds out that you're having trouble?" she asked, clearly proud of her assessment.

"Ugh. Maybe. Fine. Yes, probably."

With a grumble, I texted Sam: See you at the studio.

THE MOMENT I entered the studio, without meeting Sam's eyes, I went to the desk where Tom, Mo, Aida, and Dani were gathered. I neared their desk to find that Mo and Aida were in distress. Tom and Dani were trying to console them about something but stopped the discussion when I reached their desk.

"Hey, you guys. Everything okay?" I asked.

Tom and Dani didn't say anything but looked at Mo and Aida in sympathy.

And I knew it.

I reached across the desk and placed my hands on Aida and Mo and said, "Did you guys get bad grades for the paper too?"

Mo gasped. "You too?"

I nodded, and Aida's arms came around me. "I wish the education system in my country included writing research papers."

"Me too," I grumbled.

Goose bumps lined behind my neck as I felt eyes on me. Sam. I wasn't going to look at him when I was so upset.

I talked to my friends for a while, and Mo, Aida, and I decided to meet the professor next week to ask for her help. With that decided, I turned and went to my seat beside Sam.

Without looking at Sam—who hadn't stopped staring at me —I got my sketchbook out, turned on my laptop and opened the drawing that I had been working on for a week now.

A few minutes passed in silence when he said, "Hi, Akira."

I turned toward him and said, "Hi." I did not meet his eyes. I just couldn't.

"Everything okay? You seemed upset when you were talking to your friends."

Of course, he saw all that.

I turned back to my screen, and muttered, "I'm fine."

"If there's anything I can do to help, let me know. You know you can tell me anything, right?"

Why did he have to sound so genuine? I met his eyes. And even though a frown marred his face, his eyes were sincere. It was those freaking eyes. They made me speak my mind to him.

"I didn't do well in the research paper," I said, looking him in the eyes. If he was going to look down upon me, I was going to look him in the eyes for that. I dared him to make fun of me.

But he didn't.

He simply frowned in confusion. "What went wrong?"

I shrugged my shoulders and said, "If I knew what was wrong, I wouldn't have made those mistakes. I'd never really written a research paper before. Apparently, it wasn't a properly structured research paper."

His eyes widened. "How have you never written a research paper before?"

I glared at him. "Because our education system doesn't value writing research papers. We study, we give exams, and we make drawings for the design studio. That's it. We had no courses focused on research."

Sam's cheeks reddened and he looked away. Not wanting to say more, I turned back to my laptop and started working. A warm hand covered my shoulder, and I turned to look at Sam.

He pushed up his glasses and said, "I'm sorry, Akira. I didn't mean to be rude. I'm just shocked. Research and writing are such a huge part of our educational system here. Would you like my help? I promise I won't act like an asshole."

I did need help. And right now, I'd accept all the help I could get. "Sure. I'm glad you want to help. What do you have in mind?"

He fidgeted in his seat, hesitating to say it. When I quirked my eyebrows at him, he shook his head and said, "Um...would you mind if I looked at your paper?"

I sure freaking would. I swallowed, sweat gathered at the back of my neck, and without meeting Sam's eyes, I asked, "Is that really necessary?"

"Well, I need to know where you're at, you know? I promise to be sensitive. C'mon. You show me your paper. We'll sit in the cafeteria, and I'll get you the special mocha."

I rolled my eyes and printed the paper. It was cute that he thought a mocha was somehow going to mitigate my embarrassment at him seeing my utter failure. But he was trying, and I appreciated his help.

"Fine. But if you make fun of me, I'll punch you."

He laughed. "I won't even stop you. Now, let's go."

I grumbled, mostly in embarrassment, while Sam led me out of the studio with his hand firmly planted on my neck. I absolutely did not focus on the strong weight of his hand, the warmth seeping into my heart, or the relief that it brought to my mind. Nope. I absolutely did not focus on any of it.

As we found an empty spot in the cafeteria, I took a seat and got my paper and notes out while Sam went to get the mocha. He scrolled through his phone as he stood in the line, and I couldn't stop myself from looking at him.

He was mesmerizing in his subtle mannerisms. His confidence, his self-assuredness, his unflinching belief in his work, were beyond sexy. He was my aspiration.

Yes, he turned into an asshole with his ignorance now and then, but he always corrected himself and apologized for hurting me.

I'd found him sexy the first day I'd seen him. Now, I knew he was smart but a little ignorant, brilliant in his work but a bit of an asshole, sweet and helpful but always frowning, and a good friend but not everyone's good friend.

I was pulled out of my musings when Sam put the mocha in front of me and took a seat beside me on the small round table.

He must've thought I was still fixating on my paper because he said, "Hey, don't worry, Akira. You'll be an expert in paper writing in no time."

"Really?" I asked, his words giving me hope.

"Really. I am a great teacher."

I scoffed and burst out laughing. And when I looked at him, he had this sweet smile on his face that made my stomach flutter, and my cheeks heat up.

"Let's get started, shall we?" he asked.

I nodded and handed my paper to Sam.

While he quickly read it and made notes in the margins, I sipped my mocha and tried not to stare at him. The moment he finished reading it, my nerves heightened again.

"So?" I asked.

He gave me a gentle smile and said, "Your writing is not bad. It's pretty decent, actually."

I nodded. "Yeah, I'm decent in English. My entire education was in the English language. All our books and exams were in English."

Sam frowned at that. "But you didn't converse in English outside of school?"

"No. It's not like we enjoyed talking in English. It's not our mother tongue. Even in school, we talked in English with the teachers and in Gujarati with our friends."

Sam shook his head, his mouth slightly agape in shock. "Wow. So you guys already knew two languages since you began school. That's really great."

I shrugged my shoulders. "It's pretty normal for all the students who attended English language school. And we also learn Hindi in school. And Bollywood is all Hindi. So, we all understand three languages."

Sam had a small smile. "If it makes you feel any better, you're already better than me in this aspect. I know only one language."

That did make me feel better.

Sam chuckled at my big smile of triumph and said, "Now that you're smiling, I have to say that you need to have a hypothesis in the beginning of your paper."

"What do you mean?"

And for the next hour and a half, he sat and explained to me how to begin my paper. Apparently, I had written an essay.

For a research paper, I needed to have an argument to put forward, or a question to pose regarding the topic, and through research, find an answer, or I needed to make a statement regarding the topic and support the validity of my statement through my research. Huh. That was a whole lot of thinking.

But I understood now. Sam wrote down a basic structure on how he wrote a paper. He compiled a few links of resources he referred to while researching and emailed me the document. He was patient as he explained.

Every time I worried over something, he rubbed my neck with his strong, warm hands. I tried to not let it show how much I liked his hands on me. His friendly touch was starting to feel like a lot more to me.

But I wasn't going to think about it. Not now. Not when I had so much to accomplish.

I was starting to realize that I needed to invest a lot more time in my writing than my fellow American classmates.

From that day forward, while Sam gave two days a week to work on his papers and the remaining to design, I gave four days a week to papers and four to design. I know. Some days I worked on both.

While Sam submitted his writing assignment after the first draft itself, I made three to four revisions after getting them checked by him and making revisions every damn time.

After six weeks of working hard, I was finally getting a good grasp of writing. Partially thanks to Sam and a lot of thanks to my hard work and Google, I was finally at a place where I understood the technique of writing a research paper. I still struggled with the language, and my writing style wasn't as fancy as Sam's, but I wasn't going to go crazy over that.

After three grueling hours of nonstop lectures, Mo, Tom, Aida, Dani, and I sat in the cafeteria for lunch. Sam seldom joined us, and only after a lot of insistence from me, so most days, it was the five of us.

"How late do you guys stay in the studio?" Dani asked.

"Are you sure you guys are just friends?" Tom added, waggling his eyebrows like a lunatic.

These questions had been popping up a lot in our conversations lately.

"We're just friends, you guys. And we stay till about eleven p.m.," I said after I finished the bite of my sandwich.

"How do you handle him for so long? He seems so stoic and uptight," Mo added.

I groaned. Poor Sam. He was also so much more. I didn't say it out loud though.

"So, have you guys kissed?" Dani asked.

I groaned and said, "Nope."

I got up. I tried to act as if I was late. "God, I need to go to the studio. I'm late. We'll catch up later."

Without waiting for anyone's answer, I ran away from the questions for which I had no answers to. I would've told them if I had any idea what was happening between Sam and me.

Since I'd already left early from the cafeteria, I went to the studio a little earlier than our design class began. At 2 p.m. sharp, Sam arrived, his stoic face in place, his glasses perched on his nose, and a coffee in hand.

His wet hair sent me into imagining various scenarios of him showering, him naked, him working out—no one would shower at 2 p.m. if they hadn't been working out before—him sweating, and the cycle continued. Every single time. In all the weeks that we'd been working together, I was still not used to his gorgeousness.

He smiled at me and took a seat beside me. "You been working for long?"

I turned in my chair to look at him properly and said, "Hello to you too. And I had lunch just a while ago."

He placed the coffee beside me and said, "I brought you this."

He winked at me and turned to switch on his laptop. I took a sip of the coffee, just to do something with my hands, because I suddenly wanted to hug him.

"Thanks for this. I needed it," I said and looked at my screen. I needed to stop looking at him before I did something I shouldn't.

"No problem. I wanted to show you the changes I made yesterday after our discussion. You got some time?"

Good. Yes. Let's talk about work.

When I nodded, he opened his file on the screen, and said, "Well, then get here."

Oh man. Not closer. Sam raised his eyebrows at me when I didn't move. Shit. I dragged my chair beside him and sat close enough that the arms of our chairs touched.

He started explaining his design, but all I could concentrate on was the fresh ocean smell of his body wash and something completely him. I took a deep inhale and held my breath for as long as I could to keep his smell inside. What was happening to me?

Every time he pointed to something in his laptop and came insanely close to my face, his deep, steady voice shut me up, making me wish he would keep talking the whole evening.

Every time he sketched something to show me his ideas, his long, elegant fingers hypnotized me, making me wonder about all the things that he could do with them.

Every time he laughed his weird, wonderful laugh, or smiled at me for no reason at all, my world brightened up a little more.

And every single time, in the late nights on the empty street of New York, when he came to drop me off at my apartment, he looked at my lips with so much heat and intensity that for just a second, I battled with my body to not grab his face and kiss him.

Every day, I waited for him to kiss me.

Every day, I prayed he wouldn't.

Every day, I struggled not to kiss him.

Every day, I hoped it would get easier.

It had to get easier. Being together was not an option. We were two very different people from different countries with very different cultural backgrounds.

But why didn't I feel those differences?

Why was Sam just "Sam" for me?

Every night, my mind wandered to thinking of what kissing Sam would feel like. What would his arms around me feel like?

A loud ringing voice from my phone dragged me out of my thoughts and hopes and wishes.

Dad calling...

And that was why I had to stop dreaming about Sam and enjoy the time I had with him. Because even if we did work out and fall in a fairy-tale love, my family would never approve of our relationship.

I squashed all my "Sam dreams," shook my head, put a smile on my face, and picked up the call.

Every day, one of my family members would call, with the rest of them hovering around the phone screen, and we would talk for 20–30 min, with them asking me questions about American culture and the way the people dress, the way they eat—I was actually shocked to see so many people having and loving salads as opposed to pizza and donuts—and the way they walk so much as opposed to the small two-wheeled vehicles that we use in India.

This. My family. I couldn't lose it.

I couldn't lose it over an American friend.

A friend I was wildly attracted to.

A friend I dreamed about.

A friend who had no idea the kind of thoughts I had in my head about him.

Fuck my life.

~

Sam

It was around 6:15 p.m. when Akira walked into the studio. I was working on my paper on skyscrapers in NYC for my History in Architecture course.

It was the end of October, and fall was here in full force. Trees had started to change colors, and the entire campus was covered in red, yellow, and orange, giving the university a warm and cozy vibe to it.

It was a little chilly today, but looking at Akira, you'd think there was a blizzard outside. She was zipped up in a thick jacket. As she stood near the coat hanger removing it, one more jacket appeared from underneath it. She already had a wool hat perched on her head—a hat with two cat ears sticking out— that instantly tightened my pants. I didn't understand how a hat could have that effect on me. Or maybe that was just Akira.

All she had to do was exist near me, and my body went into a state of arousal.

After removing all her extra layers, she finally took her seat beside me.

She switched on her laptop and turned to me. "So, what're you doing?"

I just had to ask her. "You know, I wouldn't be wearing that many sweaters and jackets even when it's snowing. What're you going to do when it snows?" I couldn't help but laugh when I wondered about that inevitable scenario.

She punched me lightly on my arm and pouted. "Hey, don't mock me. This weather is colder than the coldest day in Ahmedabad. It's an official winter season for my body."

I'd gotten used to hearing surprising things about her city and her country every day. If it wasn't the weather, it was food. If it wasn't food, it was Bollywood movies. So, it didn't surprise me when she proceeded to google the weather conditions in her city.

She continued talking as she googled. "You know, I feel so jealous of my family members. Ahmedabad still has warm weather. When Aakar called me this morning, he was complaining about the weather being so hot that he had to keep the air conditioner on for most of the day."

Then she proceeded to shout, "They still keep the air conditioner on, Sam!"

The anguish on her face over the weather made me burst out in laughter. My laughter made her eyes bulge out, and I could see her getting mad at me, which subsequently made me laugh harder.

"Keep fuming, baby. That should warm you up quickly." Even as she glared at me, her eyes were laughing, and her cheeks turned a little red. She looked away from me to the screen, and I could see the blush spreading down her neck and ears.

I thought back to what made her go all red, and I realized what I'd let slip through my mouth.

Baby.

I had called her *baby*.

God. Things were getting out of hand. The more I tried not to think about her, the more she popped up in my mind. All I wanted to do was touch her, kiss her, hold her, talk to her. More than three months had passed, and I still hadn't touched her other than a few not-so-accidental touches on her arm or shoulder.

Akira had me so fucking desperate and turned on for her, I've had to take matters in my own hands. Literally.

Her smile, her soulful black eyes, her long hair, her curves, were all I had thought about the first time I'd screamed out her name, pleasure coursing down my spine and into my hand. From that day forward, I knew I was fucked.

And I knew I wouldn't be able to think about her without my new, shiny, rose-colored glasses.

She was all I thought about. It had been months since we'd started working together.

I had my desk perfectly arranged at home. But Akira wasn't there, and so I went to the studio every day. Like clockwork. My priorities had started to shift. I didn't know when it happened, but Akira had started becoming an integral part of my daily life.

I looked forward to working with her every day, not that I got much work done, but I wanted to spend more time with her. I was unreasonably greedy for her attention. I even made her work on the weekends so that I could spend more time with her.

And Akira always showed up.

She showed up every evening and gave her whole heart to work. Even though she had fun while working, always chattering and singing, she was one of the hardest working people in the class. She accepted her academic limitations, and I was proud of her for working hard in overcoming them. And she had all my respect and admiration for it.

The smell of something delicious brought me back to the present. Akira had once again brought some dinner for us. By us, I meant everyone present in the studio. And not just Akira, her close friends were in on it too.

Every week, each of them brought some food of their culture for the rest of the class. This began two weeks ago.

Today was the third time, and everyone had started looking forward to Sundays. Akira and her friends decided on Sundays because there would be fewer people in the studio and more food for the rest of us. Once we set up all the food on a common table, Akira introduced her dish.

"So, today's dish is bottle gourd *halwa*. It's purely made of bottle gourd, milk, and sugar. I didn't add any dry fruits, because I didn't know if any of you were allergic to something." There were a few groans at the mention of bottle gourd. I had to admit, it was an ugly, green-colored goop.

Tom had brought some mini custard-filled eclairs. Dani had brought pecan pie. I was undoubtedly going to be filling up on that one. As delicious as Akira's curry was from last week's food fest, that green goop was not going anywhere near me.

Aida had brought some traditional Kenyan curry for every-one. Mo had gotten some Mapo Tofu, but vegetarian version. Akira had squealed in excitement and hugged her for the consideration.

We had started keeping paper plates, forks, and knives in the storage cabinet. Tom and I got them all out and set every-thing up.

These two hours that we all spent together were some of the best times of my week. No one talked about architecture or design or assignments. We all talked about our lifestyles, what we did in our free time, the good and bad things about our countries and cultures. Or just random shit.

Once we filled up on our plates—me not taking any halwa but trying not to let Akira see—Aida asked, "What's so great about America anyway?"

I decided to take that one. "Well, it's freedom to do whatever you want, to be who you are."

As my fellow Americans started nodding along, my dearest friend Akira responded, "Says the straight white American guy."

"Ooh, burn!" The entire group erupted in howls and laugh-ter, as I waited for the ground to swallow me up. I could feel the heat rising to my ears.

As if matters couldn't get any worse, Luke walked in during the mayhem. I introduced him to everyone and went back to hide my face in the wall.

Luke directed his eyes to Akira and said, "You must be Akira. I'm Luke. Sam's best friend."

She looked at me with a smile on her face and shook hands with Luke. "Hi, Luke. I'm Sam's...uh, friend."

Friend. What an awful word. I hated it. I didn't spend most of the day thinking about my *friend.* I didn't get lost in my *friend's* eyes. I didn't get hard when I looked at my *friend's* curves. I didn't laugh at my *friend's* bad jokes, and I certainly didn't jack off to my *friend's* name on my lips.

Luke noticed the apprehension and disgust on my face and fucking smiled the brilliant, mischievous smile that had always scared me. Luke went and put an arm around Akira, *my* friend, Akira, and said, "Akira, I'd guess you are far more special to him than I am. I'd guess I might be demoted to just *a friend*."

And then the fucker winked at me.

Akira didn't see the wink as she got over the initial shock. But after hearing Luke, she went red. She might've noticed my laser focus where Luke touched her, because she moved out of his arm, smiled at me, and handed some of her green goop to Luke.

It felt good to see the flash of terror on his face as he examined Akira's dish. I could see his struggle to say no to her but, to my delight, he couldn't do it.

She reassured him, "It's really good."

Just to show us she wasn't kidding, she took some in a spoon, took a big bite, and moaned.

Luke gave me another one of his devious smiles and started to pick up the same spoon that Akira had put back in his plate. I gave him the harshest glare I could muster. He realized how serious I was and quietly handed me the plate, with the spoon, grumbling.

He then slapped my back, hard, and said, "I'll talk to you at home."

I didn't doubt it at all.

I knew why I couldn't bear for Luke to eat from the spoon that Akira had used.

I just didn't know why I felt like such a possessive bastard when I had no claim over Akira. But for this moment, I needed to get that plate away from Luke. It was mine. I refused to understand the rationale behind my reasoning.

I just took the spoon that Akira had used, scooped up the

ugly mess, silently said a small prayer, and put the food in my mouth. The gooey sweetness melted in my mouth, and I got lost in the food. My eyes rolled back in bliss, and I might've moaned a little too.

I opened my eyes to Akira staring at me. Her eyes dilated, a flush on her cheeks and fists clenched tight. I met her eyes and held them longer. I dared her to ignore the heat brewing between us. A few seconds passed, and she turned away with a shake of her head.

It wasn't the first time I'd seen this reaction from her. Often, I'd see her checking me out, see her blush, notice the blatant arousal in her eyes.

But every time, she'd push everything down and go back to her cheerful chatter.

Her reaction was one of the most important reasons why I never went any further. I was terrified that once we crossed that line, things would change. I desperately wanted Akira to be in my life. It scared me to think that I would lose Akira as a friend if things didn't work out between us.

I knew there was something stopping her from crossing that line too. I could guess it was our cultural difference, but I knew Akira was open-minded, and she had no issues with people from different cultures.

Our food party was proof of that.

But there seemed to be an invisible line that forbid us from crossing it.

Once everyone was done eating, the rest of us who hadn't brought food took the responsibility of cleaning up the mess. After working for two more hours, it was almost midnight. It was especially difficult to work with a full belly.

The Luke episode had created a strange tension between me and Akira. She'd gone quiet on me, and I didn't know what to do. Akira's chatter and frequent questions had become my norm, and her silence was killing me. I couldn't handle it anymore.

"Akira, let me know when you're ready to head home. I'm done for the day. Too full to work anymore."

Without meeting my eyes, she nodded and said, "I'm done too. Let's go."

Akira shut down her computer, put all her winter clothes on, and we headed off. I took the shortest route to her house today. I couldn't bear her silence. Like always, we stopped at her apartment door.

She looked at me. Finally. Gave me a small smile.

I looked at her smile. Her lips. Her eyes.

She bit her lip. And my throat dried up.

I hungered for her.

I fucking craved to put my lips on her. Taste her.

She took a deep breath. I took a deep breath.

Our gazes never strayed.

I saw the heat in her eyes, the desperation, the desire.

But I also saw the hesitation.

So, I touched her hand. Just for a second. Just a graze. I allowed that to myself.

"Good night, Akira."

I clenched my fist so I wouldn't pull her into my arms and kiss her.

I looked at her for a second longer, turned around, and walked home.

CHAPTER 7

"Our diversity is our strength. What a dull and pointless life it would be if everyone was the same."
- Angelina Jolie

Akira

I stood there, breathless, until Sam's retreating back disappeared.

He was going to kiss me. One more second and I would've kissed him.

He was going to kiss me. I turned around, opened the door to my building and climbed up the stairs, battling disappointment and relief at the same time.

He was going to kiss me. He got jealous of his friend.

He was going to kiss me. He ate the halwa from the same spoon that I'd used.

He was going to kiss me. I wanted him to kiss me.

He was going to kiss me.

I entered my apartment in a daze.

Everyone was gathered in the living room. Megha sat on the sofa having a late dinner watching Vidya and Shruti, who were engaged in a heated discussion. I went and sat beside Megha and asked, "What's going on?"

With her mouth full, she said one word. "Navratri."

"What?" I couldn't help the shriek. I was off the sofa and into the discussion.

Vidya and Shruti went quiet for a second, stared at me, and then launched back to the planning and discussion. I was right along with them.

Navratri was my absolute favorite festival of all Indian festivals. I loved dressing up in the traditional clothes and doing the folk dance called *garba*. I had no idea that Jersey City in New Jersey organized the celebration of the festival for two consecutive weekends every year. I never thought I'd get to celebrate the festival here.

My heart warmed at the thought of bringing Sam along. And maybe my classmates too.

"Hey, Shruti," I said, "Can I bring my classmates?"

"Of course. The festival is going to be on the streets. It's open for all. The more, the merrier, right? I'll ask some of my classmates too."

"Awesome. I'll invite them all. Let's hope they come."

Before I could talk about the traditional dress with the girls, my phone rang.

Ria calling...

Ria and I were the only girls among all the siblings. She was two years older than me and was the daughter of my father's older brother. And she was my best friend.

But ever since I moved here, catching up had become difficult. We kept each other updated, but it'd been a while since we last talked. I had told her a little about Sam, though only the part about us working together and that he was a very good friend.

I excused myself from the living room and picked up her call.

"Hey, Ria," I said, as I shut my bedroom door behind me.

"Akira, what's up, babe?"

I always talked in Gujarati with my family, as it was my mother tongue, and in Hindi with my roommates since they came from a different state and didn't know Gujarati.

"Big problem, Ria," I mumbled.

"Don't tell me. Oh God, please don't tell me what I'm thinking."

I closed my eyes, hung my head and said, "I think Sam was going to kiss me today. I know he has wanted to kiss me for a while now."

Ria was an expert in handling a tense situation with absolute calm. "What do *you* want, Akira?"

As if that mattered. I took a deep breath and said, "You know it doesn't matter. I can't do whatever I want."

Ria made an exasperated noise and gave me her no-bullshit tone. "I asked you a simple question. What. Do. You. Want?"

For the first time, I admitted it out loud. "I wanted him to kiss me. Oh God, Ria. I so badly wanted him to kiss me. We were this close, you know. But then he didn't. I'm pretty sure the doubt and fear on my face made him walk away from me. I just don't know what to feel. I can't do this. Mom and Dad would kill me."

Ria made a shushing sound. "Akira, first, take a deep breath. Relax. Do you love him?"

I scoffed at that. "Ria, I've known him for three months. It's not like we've ever talked about deep shit, you know. He doesn't talk much, but I still love his company. Without even meaning to, I've started knowing him, you know. Like I know that he's left-handed. He starts running his hands in his hair or starts fiddling with his glasses whenever he is nervous.

"He drinks black coffee with one tiny pack of sugar. It's so gross. And he is so competitive. If I ever get ahead of him in any course, he'll stay in the studio working extra hours just to get ahead of me.

"He has no tolerance for spicy food. Last week, when I took curry to our class for everyone, he pretended to love it, but he sweated the whole time, went all red, and even went home early. And I hadn't even made it as spicy as I usually do.

"He doesn't talk to a lot of people, but he talks to me. He is funny, a little quiet, but sometimes he smiles at me with no reason at all, and it just makes my heart go all haywire. And anytime I need him, he is always there for me, Ria. Always. Even if it is dropping me home every night, taking different routes to explore the city, teaching me how to write a paper, giving me suggestions in design, he's there. And he cares, you know. And I've started caring about him too. I want to know what he does when he goes home. I want to know him outside of classes, but I'm terrified to take that step, Ria. I don't know if I even should."

I almost sobbed.

Ria stayed silent for a while. "You love him."

I rolled my eyes at that. "No, I don't. Not yet anyway. But he's kinda my best friend. Who I want to kiss. God, what do I do?"

Ria huffed and said, "Kiss him, you fool. It sounds like he feels the same for you. What's stopping you?"

How did she not understand the gravity of the situation?

"Ria, what about Mom and Dad? What about our entire family? What would they do when they find out I was dating an American guy?"

"Do you want him to be your boyfriend? Or is it just an attraction or a crush?"

I tried explaining to her in the best way I could. "Ria, if today I had to choose between Sam and our family, it would break my heart, but I would choose our family. Once I kiss him, cross that line, and let my heart free, I could fall for him. Given a choice then, I don't know who I'd choose when the time comes."

That got her serious. "Okay, babe. Let me tell you one thing. Don't be scared about what our family would think while making this decision. Listen to what your heart says. I know I sound like all clichéd Bollywood movies, but if your heart says 'Kiss him,' just freaking kiss him. If it has to happen between you two, it'll happen. We'll deal with the family. But don't do anything that you'll regret in the future. My only advice is don't tell the family about Sam unless you want to marry the guy. You don't want to fight this battle if your non-existent relationship is not going anywhere."

Hearing Ria, my mind finally calmed a little. "You're right. No one in the family needs to know anything. I'll tell them if and when I absolutely need to. Oh God, Ria. These past days have been hell. Thank you."

She laughed on the other side. "Of course, Akira, what are big sisters for? And don't you blab anything to your brothers. Aakar would always tell you to be sensible and Abhi might just blab it all."

"Of course. And you'll be by my side if things go south, right?" I needed to know my sister was behind me, even hypothetically.

"Always, Akira," Ria said.

Knowing that at least one family member would support my relationship with Sam gave me the strength to take that step forward. To finally accept that I wanted to give myself a chance to be with Sam. To not be afraid when he looked at my lips. It gave me the courage to give my heart a chance.

With that thought in mind, I sent a goodnight text to Sam and went to sleep with a smile on my face, thinking about new beginnings and new possibilities.

Me: Good night, Sam. :-*

Sam: Good night, Akira.

Sam

I WAS a little early in the studio today. Ever since I walked away from Akira, I'd been restless. I didn't want to ruin anything that we had, and last night, I almost crossed the line of our friendship.

But after I saw the hesitation in her eyes, I just couldn't kiss her.

I knew she was attracted to me and wanted to kiss me, but it would hurt me more if she regretted the kiss than us not kissing at all. So, I'd backed off. It had taken three cold showers throughout the night to get myself under control.

The studio was a lot more crowded than usual today.

Next week was our midterm design review, and everyone was tense. Some of them were sitting on their computer working on their design, some were making their design models, and some were making their final sheets and presentation.

I had finished my design two weeks ago. I'd been making my design model at home, which I completed last week, and my presentation was almost done. I planned to give myself three days to practice the speech for my presentation.

Akira wasn't far behind either. Since she had to devote extra time to write the research papers, she was still making her model.

It sucked that some of the international students were at such a disadvantage because of the difference in the education systems. To make it here, they had to put in a lot more time and effort than the locals, and I was in awe of them for making it in a whole new country with all its challenges.

It was at 2 p.m. sharp when Akira rushed in the studio. She stood at the coat rack, removing all her sweaters while she talked to Tom excitedly.

She wore a bright red top with big sunflowers printed all over it and black jeans.

She had a big smile on her face as she and Tom went to where Dani and Mo sat. All of them suddenly burst into excited squeals and laughter as soon as Akira said something. The studio that'd seemed like a funeral ten minutes ago transformed into joy and laughter within five minutes of Akira's arrival. She was a ray of sunshine.

I tried to focus on my work when Akira took her seat beside me and turned on her computer.

While her computer booted up, she turned toward me— like always—gave me her big, beautiful smile and said, "Hey, Sam, guess what?" So much excitement, she couldn't sit still in her seat.

That instantly brought a smile to my face. "What?"

"I'm going to Jersey City next weekend to celebrate Navratri. Oh my God! I'm so, so happy that people celebrate the festival here. I was so prepared to miss it now that I'm here, but my roommates informed me last night that Jersey City celebrates the festival every year, and all of us are planning to go."

I couldn't help but laugh at her excitement. She was like an excited little puppy. "That's awesome. And what's Navratri again?"

At that, she rotated her chair toward me and explained, "It's one of the most important Hindu festivals. Typically, the festival is celebrated for nine days. People celebrate it for different reasons in different parts of the country, each having its tale on a general theme of good defeating evil.

"It has nine days of fasting and nine nights of folk dance

called garba. It's a form of dance where you wear traditional clothes and dance together in a circle and perform the same dance routines for hours at a stretch. Oh, Sam, this is my absolute favorite festival. I don't do the fasting and everything. I'm all for traditional clothes and garba. You need to experience all of it to understand."

I'd seen Akira excited before. Almost every day. But today, she was something else. She was elated. Her eyes had gone wide, and an open-mouthed smile was stuck on her face. Her enthusiasm scared me sometimes, but this was downright terrifying. So, I said the only thing I could. "Wow. That's interesting."

She seemed to sober down a little, and with a nervous smile, she asked, "So, um, would you like to join me? Uh, it won't be just you. I've also invited some of my friends. Tom, Mo, Dani, Aida. You can invite Luke too. It would be fun. There would be dancing and celebration and music."

And then she proceeded to give me the puppy-eyes look and destroyed all my defenses. As if I was ever going to decline.

I wanted to see her outside of this studio, outside of academics. I wanted to know *her*. The things she enjoyed, the things she hated, things that got her excited, things she feared, and so much more.

Going to the festival would be a glimpse into her life, and I wasn't going to miss it for the world.

"I'd love to." I gave her a reassuring smile.

She squealed and jumped out of her seat to hug me. Since I was seated, her arms came around my neck, and my face rested by her shoulder, surrounded by her hair. I couldn't help but take a sniff.

She smelled divine, something fruity and fresh, plus something that was just her. I'd just put my arms around her when she squeezed me once more and let go of the hug. I hated when she let go of her hugs.

When I saw her face, she was back with her exhilarated face, and I promptly excused myself to get some coffee.

But before I could leave, Akira called me, "Thank you so much for agreeing to come with me. You'll see, Sam. You'll have a great time."

"I always have a great time with you, baby. But you better get done with all your work before next week, or you would be the one not having fun." Shit. I called her baby again. My mouth seemed to have completely detached from its filter.

Akira, however, blushed, and promptly started working on her model. See? Attracted but not ready.

A WEEK PASSED with all of us working rigorously, where days turned into nights and nights turned into days. Some of them stopped going home altogether.

The girls occasionally got together and watched videos of the dance steps in preparation of Navratri, and I'd occasionally find them practicing in the corner of the studio.

When Akira had asked me two days ago if I wanted to learn the steps with them so that I don't feel left out, my blank expression had told her enough. The next time she asked me the same thing, I'd asked her the status of her midterm presentation. She had stuck her tongue out at me and never asked me to practice garba again.

Today was our midterm review.

After six grueling hours of listening to all the presentations, I was officially done. I needed a break. I could hear Akira's never-ending chatter going on and on about the festival, the clothes, the timing, and whatnot.

I walked up to her and said, "Hey, I'm out. Let's take some break for a weekend. I don't think we have much work for now."

Akira agreed. "Yeah, I needed a little break too. I don't remember the last time I relaxed and just watched Netflix."

"So, when are we going for the festival?"

Her eyes lit up every single time she talked about the festival. "Friday evening. So, tomorrow. We'll meet around six at the university entrance."

"Do I need to wear anything special?" I asked. I didn't want to offend her religion or step on some boundaries.

She smiled at me. "I don't think you'd be comfortable wearing traditional clothes. Tom, Dani, Aida, and Mo are wearing traditional clothes, but you can wear a white or red or any colorful shirt and blue jeans or something. I'll get the dupatta for you and Luke. Okay?"

What did she say she was going to bring for Luke and me? Duptaa?

"Duptaa?" I asked.

She laughed and explained, "Doo-puh-atta. It's a long, scarf-like thing. Just google it."

"Got it. See you then, Akira. Take care."

I pulled her in for a hug. A friendly, casual hug. She fit perfectly in my arms, her cheeks at my chest and the top of her head right below my neck. I bent down, breathed her in, and squeezed her a little more. She put her arms around my waist and squeezed me back.

Tomorrow couldn't come soon enough.

After a last squeeze, I reluctantly let her go and walked back to my apartment.

It was very, very quiet.

CHAPTER 8

"We were together. I forget the rest."
 - Walt Whitman

Sam

I waited for everyone at the entrance of the university as I googled Navratri. The multiple images that popped up gave me some idea on what to expect.

After seeing all the pictures, I was excited to see Akira in the traditional attire called *chaniya choli*. The dresses were so colorful, with flowing skirts, cropped blouses, and a transparent scarf thingy called dupatta, as Akira had mentioned.

After about ten more minutes of waiting, I saw a small crowd in colorful clothes approaching me. They were about a block away, but the colorful clothes were evident from afar.

It was when they got closer that I saw her.

Akira.

And I stopped breathing.

She wore a traditional black blouse, just like the one in the pictures, and a long black and navy matching skirt with intricate designs in it. The blouse covered just her breasts, clearly showing off their roundness and that sexy fucking cleavage.

She had a long, yellow, translucent dupatta draped across her one shoulder, crossing her chest, and the other end tucked in her skirt at her waist. The entire outfit was so complex, and I didn't understand what and how she was wearing stuff. But every piece of clothing seemed to be designed for seduction.

This was the first time that I'd seen so much of Akira's skin, and it was fucking with my body and mind. I'd never seen her belly before, never even thought about it. But her short blouse, and her skirt starting right below her belly button, left a lot of smooth, brown skin exposed, and the transparent dupatta giving the occasional peek at it drove me crazy.

Every step she took had her dupatta swaying away from her body, giving me delicious views to her curves.

Her skirt, tight at her waist but freely flowing over her hips, had about a thousand tiny mirrors stuck on them, and every time she walked, her skirt gave a million reflections of light.

She had an ethereal glow surrounding her, or maybe it was just me who was blinded by her. It didn't matter. All I could see was Akira. And I'd gone hard as a fucking rock. Before she or others could notice me, I put my one hand in my pocket, and another at my side.

She neared me and she stole my breath away. Her long hair was pulled in a high ponytail. Her eyes were heavily lined with black stuff, making them appear like deep pools of black. She wore big, round earrings and a matching necklace. The end of the necklace rested on her chest, right above her cleavage.

And her lips. She'd applied red lipstick. They looked like sin and hot passion. As she stood in front of me, I could see the excitement pouring off her in waves. Her eyes traveled down my body, looking for God knows what.

Pleasure burned through my veins everywhere she looked.

She introduced me to her three roommates, all of them

dressed similarly to Akira. The differences were in the colors of their clothes and the jewelry they'd put on.

Akira then introduced me to a few Indian guy friends, who were their neighbors and her roommates' friends. Since we were already running late, we all started toward the subway station after the basic introductions.

But the moment Akira turned around to walk ahead of me to get down the steps, I saw it. Her. Entire. Fucking. Back. Was. Bare. The blouse. It was completely backless. Only two strings held that thing together.

I could see the entire line down her back, and it might be the sexiest thing that I've ever seen. My throat dried up, and I was pretty sure my jaw was hanging open. It was at that moment when she turned and caught me checking her out.

She raised her eyebrows.

"There's nothing in the back," I stupidly pointed out.

She laughed. "No shit, Sherlock."

"Aren't you cold?" I asked. She bundled up so much during classes. And here she was, tiny, backless blouse and no jackets.

She called me closer to her. When I bent down a little, she said, "I love my outfit. I'm not going to ruin it with a big, ugly jacket. I'm going to warm up once we start doing *garba*. And till then, the shot of whiskey I had at home will protect me."

She kept getting hotter and hotter, the more I looked at her.

She looked at me for a second and asked, "Where are your glasses?"

I touched the spot between my eyes, where I usually pushed them up.

I cleared my throat, trying to keep my eyes above her neck, and said, "I only need them while looking at a screen."

Akira stared at me for a second longer. I loved it.

"So, where's Luke? Is he not coming?" she asked.

Her friends were waiting around the subway turnstile. There were other guys around—guys who could see Akira's entire back. While I fumed in my green bubble, Akira asked again, "Sam? Is Luke joining us? Should we wait or leave?"

I hated that she had said Luke's name more than mine while wearing those sexy clothes.

"He's not coming. He had to go somewhere," I told her as I turned her to walk in front of me.

I tried to stay as close to her back as possible on our way to the station. Luckily, the train was just arriving as we climbed down the staircase to the platform.

The moment the doors of the train opened, we rushed inside, and I caught Akira's hand to make her sit in an empty seat that I found. This was oddly reminiscent of the first time I had held her hand while dragging her out of the subway.

I stood over her seat, our legs touching.

"Let's just go stand at the door. We'll be able to talk comfortably," she offered, as she tried to stand back up.

"It's fine. Just sit. I know you'll have to be on your feet for the entire evening. Take all the rest you can get." I was pleased I'd been able to come up with a logical response on the fly. All I wanted was to hide her back from the rest of the world.

God, I was getting more ridiculous by the second.

"How'd you know that?" she asked with a smile on her face.

I tapped her nose from where I stood and answered, "I googled it."

"You did?" Her entire face lit up.

"I'm very excited to see you do your *garba*," I told her.

At that, she gave me a devilish smirk that seemed to say *You haven't seen anything yet, boy*. And I won't lie. It scared me.

As we reached the station to change our trains to go to New Jersey, Akira's excitement had gone to a crazy level. The rest of our classmates met us near the station for the next train to Jersey. They were all dressed in traditional clothes like Akira and her roommates.

I had no idea when all of them managed to put together all

the outfits, but it was so heartening to see Americans, Chinese, Ethiopian, and Indians celebrating a festival together. Not just a festival, but celebrating the culture, celebrating the diversity, rejoicing in the chance to experience this moment that we would never have had, had we not been open to other cultures.

Akira made quick introductions of our classmates with her Indian friends, and we again jetted off for the next train.

But this time around, when we entered the subway, Akira grabbed my hand to stand near the closed side of the subway doors. We stood facing each other, her back to the entire subway.

Keeping my hold in her hand, I turned us so that we stood the other way around. She gave me a knowing smile, but I didn't care. There was no way I was going to tell her to hide her back from others. I had no right to her body, and I knew it.

But seeing that sexy back of hers, I just wanted it to be for me. I had never seen this possessive asshole side of me before, and it wasn't pretty. But apparently, I didn't care. Every time I saw that sexy line running down her back, all I wanted was to follow that line with my tongue. I was desperate for a bite. A taste. A touch. And for the entire ride, Akira held my hand.

I didn't know what had happened to bring about such a change in Akira, but I did not complaint. I was starved for her touch.

I ignored the looks that we got from her friends, and focused on Akira. She talked about how she celebrated Navratri back home, while I listened and tried not to step even closer to her. Before I could get more lost in her eyes, her smile, her lips, her clothes, Akira pulled me out of the subway.

I felt like the train had led me all the way to India. Everywhere I looked, I saw people dressed up in traditional clothes.

Akira took off her dupatta that was draped on one of her shoulders. Before I could panic, I saw that she already had another underneath it.

That's when she came forward to me and draped the thing around my neck. My breath hitched as her hands touched my shoulders and she arranged the thing the way she liked. She gave me a shy smile, and I couldn't stop staring at her.

Once she was done, she gave me an appreciative look over. I couldn't help getting excited at that, and I was glad about my loose shirt hiding the evidence of my excitement.

We walked down the street, hand in hand, to reach the festival location. Every person we passed talked in their local dialect. While I didn't understand a word of what people were talking about, Akira had a smile on her face.

A smile that said she remembered this.

That she missed this.

I had no idea that Jersey had such a large Indian community. I gave her hand a little squeeze. She squeezed it back. From about three blocks away, all of us could hear the music. Excitement filled the air.

Akira's grip tightened around my hand, and she walked faster.

After a short walk, we reached a street entirely closed off for vehicles. A police car sat at the end of the street to redirect people. But just beyond that, a whole new world opened up.

Thousands of people dressed in traditional clothes danced on the street. People had formed a vast circle that stretched across the entire avenue. Every single person did the same dance, and the whole formation looked like a magical symphony.

Thousands of ladies in their flowing skirts going in circles, the colorful skirts swaying in the same rhythm, resembled angels dancing in heaven. Some people had formed smaller circles within the big circle where they danced with their friends, creating unique dance forms.

Our entire group stood there, gaping at the scene. A loud song full of energetic beats played through the speakers. As the song changed, the beats changed, and consequently, every person changed their dance steps.

Every Indian person in our group had a maniacal expression of joy on their face. Akira's grip on my hand had tightened to a painful degree, and I'd never been more excited. It seemed as if she was physically stopping herself from joining the group.

I nudged Mo, who was looking at the dance, and indicated her to look around at our group. She laughed out and nudged the rest of our classmates. It was so endearing to see the borderline crazy delight on our Indian friends' faces. All of them seemed to be in a trance.

I finally nudged Akira. She came out of her trance and gave me an excited smile. Both of her hands encircled my arm, and she screamed, "Are you seeing this, Sam? Holy Shit. I can't believe it."

I couldn't help but give her an equally big smile. "This is so fucking awesome, baby. Now, when are you going to join in? I want to see you dance."

She turned around to her friends and shouted, "Let's go, guys!"

And everyone jumped into action.

"You're coming along too, Sam."

Akira dragged me inside the bigger circle with everyone. Akira and her roommates suggested that we form a small circle so that us non-Indians could learn some steps and have fun.

For the first half hour, Akira, her roommates, and the guys picked each one of us non-Indians and taught us some steps and how to pick the beat. Eventually, we formed a circle and started something called *Bey Taali,* which essentially meant *two claps.*

Apparently, that was the easiest step that ever existed.

So not true.

As we learned the dance form, we moved in half a circle in one direction, clapped once, and then we turned a full circle in another direction and clapped, and we repeated the same thing.

Once all our steps started to coordinate, we started moving in a steady circle. Soon, all of us moved in a decent rhythm without stepping over each other's feet. And then the magic happened.

It didn't seem like a dance form anymore. It was a pulsing, living art. The music and the beats surrounded us and carried us along. We dipped and clapped and jumped. Every one of us had a big smile on our faces as we turned in circles and clapped together. That's when my eyes met Akira's across our circle.

And my world stopped.

She became the focus. Just her. She'd never looked happier.

Her long ponytail swayed with her, her hair sometimes coming on her face. Her lips stretched into a big smile as she clapped her hands. Every time she turned in a circle, her long skirt flowed and followed her hips. Her waist moved in rhythm with the songs.

As it twisted and turned, her hips followed, her arms moved in sensual turns as she clapped, and her entire body was consumed in the music.

Every turn gave me a glimpse at her back.

And every time, I lost my footing and missed a step.

I was so fucked.

I was so glad about Akira's dupatta and my shirt, both of which helped me hide my ever-increasing desire for her. Every turn of her waist, every twist of her hips, every glimpse of her back, made me harder and desperate for her touch.

It was getting so much more difficult to hold myself to just looking at her and not touching her. The more she danced, the more sweat lined her back and her neck. I got out of the circle and moved behind Akira.

I needed to be near her, and if she noticed, she didn't mind.

She got more energetic. At a closer look, I could see her

entire blouse was stuck to her boobs and sweat dripped down her neck. Her back had a sheen of wetness. I was hard as a rock, and it was incredibly difficult for me to move.

I got lightheaded as she altered her step and instead of clapping at her side, she bent over to clap her hands.

And Holy. Fucking. Hell.

At every clap, her blouse gave me a clear view of half of her boobs. I could see the small gap between them, and they heaved and bounced every time she got up. If I had to see her dancing like that one more second, I didn't know what I would do.

She knew she was driving me crazy. I could see it in the glint of her eyes every time she looked at me. I knew my gaze on her affected her. I could see it in every breath that she took. She was clearly putting on a show for me.

Something had changed after our almost kiss. She had become free in expressing her reactions to me for about a week now. She had started initiating touching me. I'd stopped seeing the nervousness that my touch brought in her eyes. But now, I had reached my limit.

I wanted to touch her.

Desperately wanted to run my tongue along her back.

Bite her neck.

Taste her.

Kiss her.

Before my dick could push out of my jeans, I turned around. I had to get out of here. But as I tried to move out of the bigger circle, Akira grabbed my hand.

"Hey, where are you going?" she asked, a frown creasing her pretty brow. It was difficult to hear what she was saying over the loud music.

"I need to go," I shouted, avoiding her eyes.

Something changed in her demeanor. She looked me over. She met my eyes. And she understood. I could see the understanding in her eyes. She knew I had reached my limit. She could see it in my clenched fist, the way I faced my body away from her, and the piercing stare I directed at her lips.

She signaled at me to give her a minute, and she collected her wallet and told everyone that she was leaving. Everyone else was having a blast, and they decided to stay.

Even though I felt like an asshole for taking her away from the dancing, I couldn't help but almost jump for joy that she chose to get away with me.

We walked in silence as we passed the bigger circle and continued walking in silence, not touching each other, as we moved away from the noise. Out of sheer courtesy, I said, "You don't have to come with me."

She softly replied, "I want to."

There was nothing else to be said. The moment we were out of the noise and near the subway station, I took her hand in mine. She held mine back. If I had to look at her, I knew I'd kiss her. I was pretty sure she knew I'd kiss her too.

Nothing was said as we took the train back to Manhattan. The more my desire grew, the tighter I held her hand. She started rubbing her thumb across my hand, slowly, as if she wanted to soothe me with her gentle touch. All it did was make it harder.

Nothing was said as we changed the train from Manhattan to the university campus. We continued holding hands, and I had to consciously loosen my grip on her to make sure I didn't crush her hand. She soothed and ignited my body all at the same time.

Nothing was said while I walked her to her place. The world moved around us as we got lost in the heady sense of desperation. Our hands clutched together, her shoulders rubbing against my arm, her breaths shaky.

And as we reached the door to her building, she turned

toward me. Our eyes met. I took a step toward her. Instead of the nervousness I'd seen the last time, I saw desperation.

Hunger.

Desire.

Want.

And I lost it.

I kissed her.

I crushed my mouth against her.

I fucking *devoured* her.

CHAPTER 9

"We all live with the objective of being happy, our lives are all different and yet the same."
- *Anne Frank*

Akira

Sam was kissing me.

Finally.

One moment, we were walking to my apartment, and in the next, Sam had his arms around me, one hand holding my waist and his other hand firmly cupping my face as he gave me his all.

I've wanted him for so long.

Every little thing he did made me want to jump on him. But I was too afraid. Too afraid to take that step. Too afraid of our differences. Too afraid to kiss him. But after talking to Ria, I knew I could do this.

Kiss him. Date him. Get to know him.

And I wanted Sam. Desperately. Beyond any reason.

Sam kissed me with a passion I'd never known before. He kissed. Licked. Bit. He soothed. And I took it all. I gave myself to him, finally surrendering to my heart's desires. All I could do was clutch his shirt as tightly as I could and kiss him back.

With one kiss, I crossed the line that I was too afraid to cross.

There was an urgency in Sam's kiss, like he was afraid I would change my mind. With each passing second, he clutched me tighter. His kiss got firmer. When he ran his tongue along my lips, I eagerly parted them, wanting more.

The moment our tongues brushed, we both moaned.

"Fuck, Akira. I've wanted this for so long." Sam's voice came out in a rushed whisper, his mouth so close to mine I could almost taste his words.

His lips grazed mine, and I reached for his mouth. He stopped kissing but held me tighter than before, almost as if he was afraid to lose this moment.

He rested his forehead on mine, and whispered, "Akira."

Hearing my name being whispered so lovingly, so desperately, I couldn't help but moan, "Sam."

We breathed each other in.

"What changed?" he asked.

I needed him to kiss me again. I needed to continue what we had finally begun.

I ran my thumb along his jaw, and he nuzzled his face in my palm, breathing out.

"I finally agreed to listen to my heart."

Before I could change my mind, I whispered, "Will you come inside?"

His hold on me tightened, and he brought me even closer to his body. So close, I could feel his heart beating with mine and his desire poking at my stomach.

"Are you sure?" he asked. And I understood the implication.

I pressed myself tighter to him, putting pressure where he throbbed. He moaned. "Akira. Tell me."

I looked at him, noticed the burning desire in his eyes, and nodded. "I'm sure."

He quickly maneuvered us so that he was pressed along my back and guided me to my building's door so I could lead us in. As I opened the door, I turned around and warned him, "It's three flights of stairs to my apartment."

His face screamed sexual frustration, and I couldn't help but laugh. He ran his hand in his hair and said, "Get climbing, baby."

Every step I climbed, Sam was right behind me. Every few steps, he ran his fingers along my open back, top to bottom, making me squirm.

Brushed his hand in my ponytail and gently pulled it, making me gasp.

And when the touching got too much, he held my hand tightly, as if that would stop him from taking it too far.

It took an eternity to reach my apartment. I kept fumbling with the keys, trying to open the door while Sam held my waist and nuzzled at my neck, softly kissing it.

"Sam," I moaned and rested my head on his shoulder, giving him more access to my neck.

He gently placed two kisses on my neck, and whispered, "Open the door, Akira. Now."

He then promptly moved away, letting me focus on the challenging task of fitting the key into the tiny hole. Sam stayed afar as he told me to take him to my room.

We walked down the hallway, not touching.

The moment we stepped inside my room, he had me pinned to my door. He kissed me with a wild abandon, and I reciprocated with equal fervor. I clutched his hair and ran my hands all over his back. Every time I dragged my hand on his lower back, he reacted by thrusting wildly, moaning my name.

Every. Single. Time.

I got high watching Sam lose control.

His hands were everywhere. He dragged my skirt up from behind and grabbed my ass. He rubbed himself on my hips while I moved mine trying to put some pressure between my legs.

He soon realized what I was trying to do, and quickly picked me up by my ass, pushed me against the door and started thrusting where I wanted. Where I needed.

With one hand under my ass, he ran his fingers along the open portion of my blouse at my back. Breathing heavily, he slowly opened the bottom string of my blouse, waiting for me to stop him.

I didn't.

He whispered, "Akira."

I clutched him tighter. "Sam."

He moved in to kiss me again, and we got lost.

He opened the top string of my blouse and splayed his hand on my now naked back.

He moaned, "Fuck, Akira. What're you doing to me?"

My open blouse was barely supported on my shoulders. His one hand clutched my ass, while his other hand ran along my back.

"This thing has made me crazy the whole night, sweetheart."

We were still fully clothed, yet the sensation of our bodies pressed together and his skin on mine was overwhelming.

Sam clutched my waist, and I wrapped my legs around him.

"Yes," he hissed and pushed deeper into me.

God, I was so close.

I needed him closer. Closer than we were.

"Closer, Sam. More," I moaned.

"Fuck, Akira. Need you so much." He pulled down my blouse a little more, dragging it slowly, exposing my shoulder.

His thrusts got wilder. My hips couldn't stop moving with him. I clutched his hair as he nuzzled at the spot between my neck and shoulder. He took a deep breath as he ran his nose along my neck and sucked me there. Hard.

I whimpered.

He growled.

"Sam. More, please."

"Just a little closer, Akira. You trust me?"

I hurriedly nodded. I was willing to do anything if only he could get a little closer.

He dragged my skirt up from the front, and his denim-covered hips touched my underwear. I inhaled sharply.

"Can I just open my jeans, sweetheart? Please. No sex. Just let me feel you. Need you so much..." Sam panted.

I nodded. "Yes, please. Hurry, Sam."

He kept his hold on me against the door, while he fumbled with his jeans. He quickly pulled down his jeans a little and closed the distance between us, notching us back together like two pieces of a puzzle.

The smell of our mutual arousal filled the air around us.

The rising heat.

The sweat.

"Fuck. Fuck, Akira. You're soaked, baby."

Sam growled, his movements frantic.

Even with his briefs on, I felt his entire length—every throb, every jerk, every twitch. With every thrust, he took me higher. We were burning. He dragged his hardness through my bundle of nerves, causing sparks to fly behind my eyes. He thrust again, almost pushing himself inside.

The fact that we were so fucking close to each other, and yet we refused to cross that line, turned the heat to a crackling pleasure. I never wanted it to end. I could burn in this heat for all of eternity.

But the moment Sam put his lips back on my neck, all the while thrusting, I erupted. Wave after wave of ecstasy racked my body. My thighs clenched tight around Sam's hips, my opening throbbing and pulsing against Sam's hardness.

He growled my name and pushed hard one last time before he let himself go. I wrapped myself tightly around him as he shuddered, feeling the dampness spread where we were joined.

He kept his hold on me as we caught our breath, his forehead resting on mine.

I ran my fingers along his jaw and said, "That was so fucking hot."

A laugh burst out of him. "It was. The hottest experience of my life. I literally came in my underwear."

I made an appreciative noise and gave him a quick peck. "That was my favorite part."

He kissed my nose and slowly put me down, keeping his hold on me until he was sure I wouldn't fall on my jelly legs.

I dropped myself on the bed, my blouse still hanging on my shoulders. He pulled up his jeans and asked me where the washroom was.

"It's out in the hallway."

I laughed out loud as Sam hobbled to the bathroom with his thighs apart.

While he washed up, I changed into a soft, old T-shirt and silk shorts.

Once I got comfortable and returned from the high of Sam, I allowed my mind to come forward with the questions it had.

What now?

Is he my boyfriend now? Or are we still just friends now?

Do I want him as my boyfriend? *Yes*, my heart screamed.

How would this even work?

Would I hide it from my family?

I was in the middle of panic when Sam returned. He had his ruined underwear balled up in his hands which meant he was going commando, and that made me hot all over again.

"Stop staring there, Akira," Sam groaned.

That made me smile. Sam must've noticed my mood because he sat beside me and started rubbing circles on my back.

"What's wrong, sweetheart?"

Before I could stop myself, I blurted, "What now, Sam?"

He frowned. "Now, as in right now? Or now, as in, now that we've kissed and made out, where is this going?"

Wasn't he suddenly the talker?

"Both?" I asked.

He turned me toward him on the bed and put his hand on my knee. "Now, I would like to kiss you and hold you. If you want me to stay, I'll stay. If you want me to go, I'll go. And for the 'where is this going' now, I have been dreaming about you for months. And I would like to do this again. Touch you. Kiss you. Hold you. Date you."

I really wanted him to kiss me again. I moved on to his lap and kissed him. He kept kissing me as he moved us back to the headboard. I wanted him to stay. I *needed* him to stay.

I would like to do this again. Touch you. Kiss you. Hold you. Date you. As if it was that simple. As if I could truly have him if only I wanted him.

Couldn't he see us? How would I even explain this to my family?

My thoughts were so consuming I didn't even realize that I had stopped kissing him. And Sam was looking at me. Like, *really* looking at me. I squirmed on his lap to get off.

But he kept his hold on me. He pushed some of my hair behind my ears, cupped my face and gently said, "Talk to me, sweetheart."

I couldn't stop my outburst. "This. You, calling me sweetheart, baby. How can it be so simple for you? You must know how different we are. Not just our personalities, but even our race and religion. And what are we going to be now? Girlfriend and boyfriend? Friends with benefits?"

I so didn't want to ruin the amazing moment we had shared. "I'm sorry for ruining our first kiss and our first orgasm. I really didn't want to bring it all up right now. But my mind is shouting too loudly at me. *Why are you smiling!*"

His smile grew wider, which made me glare at him.

He kissed me. Just a small peck. And proceeded to tuck us under the blanket, with me being the little spoon and him the big spoon.

"Sleep, Akira. I've got you." He held me as he placed small kisses on my neck.

"You didn't answer my questions," I grumbled.

He placed one more kiss on my shoulder and said, "I heard you. And we're going to talk about it tomorrow. I've waited too long to be with you like this. So, right now, I'm going to enjoy this moment. Just know—I'm here. Stop worrying about every-thing and be with me."

And I melted.

I turned so that I could face him, put my leg over his hip, and tucked myself as close to him as I could and said, "If you put it like that. I, too, have wanted you for so long. Why do you think I came to the studio every day?"

Sam looked impressed. "You really came every day for me?"

I laughed. "I do have my laptop, and I hardly use the library. I could easily work from home for most of the days. So, yeah, I came to the studio every single day to spend more time with you."

Sam growled and rolled on top of me. "Fuck, Akira. I thought I was the only one. I even have a space set up in my room to make models and everything. I just needed to spend time with you and be near you."

He proceeded to kiss me. Again and again. Before I could lead him to repeat the earlier performance, Sam moved away. "No more, Akira. I only had that one pair of underwear." He looked down at himself and asked, "Umm, do you have some clothes I can borrow? I can't sleep in jeans and this shirt."

Poor guy had to be uncomfortable wearing the clothes we danced in and then made out in.

I jumped off the bed. "Of course. Let me see what could fit you."

I opened my closet and surfed through my pajamas and said, "Your ass is clearly smaller than mine."

I turned to look at Sam and found him checking out my ass. When he saw me staring at him, he met my eyes and said, "I agree."

"I don't have a shirt that can fit you, but I can give you some silk shorts."

Sam raised his eyebrows at that and said, "Anything will do. You mind if I sleep without a shirt?"

My cheeks turned red at seeing Sam naked for the first time.

I quickly shook my head and handed him my favorite pair of silk shorts, as I got under the covers.

"Thank you." Sam got out of the bed, and shamelessly, removed all of his clothes.

And I couldn't stop staring at his butt as he folded all his clothes and carefully put them on an empty spot on my desk in the opposite corner. All the while being naked.

He clearly liked his things organized, even when he was naked, about to wear my shorts and sleep with me for the first time. I'll have to ask him about it someday.

He wore my shorts, and I couldn't help but stare at his ass.

"I was right about your ass, after all," I said, my eyes stuck on his cute, little butt.

With an amused voice, Sam asked, "And you gave me the most girly shorts you own, didn't you?"

I couldn't stop the laugh when Sam turned around to face me. He looked so freaking hot in my silky yellow shorts with tiny suns printed all over them. I could clearly see the outline of his dick, and the shorts didn't even cover his thighs.

"You totally pull it off."

Sam chuckled and unconsciously slid his finger at the bridge of his nose, an adorable blush spreading on his ears and cheeks. He remembered that he wasn't wearing any glasses, so he shook his head, turned off the lights and got under the covers with me bare-chested.

I rolled over, and he tucked me to his front. I could feel the warmth of his chest, and our legs tangled under the covers. Our silk shorts rubbed against each other, and Sam couldn't stop moving his hips against my ass.

I giggled and asked, "What's up, Sam?"

He groaned and moved his hands over my waist and said, "Your shorts. God, they're so fucking soft and they rub against me every time I move."

I couldn't stop laughing out loud.

"You're so evil," he grumbled.

But just to mess with him more, I reminded him, "Sam?"

"Hmm."

"You know, I had the best orgasm of my life without even having taken my clothes off. What do you think will happen when we actually get naked?"

Sam groaned, and I felt something poking at my ass. "Akira, quit it already, baby. You're making it hard." He poked me with it again, making us both laugh.

"All right, I get it. Just so you know, you're making me wet too." I couldn't help it. He looked so cute when he got frustrated.

He let go of me and turned the other way, grumbling, "So cruel. I'm not holding you anymore."

I laughed and molded myself to him, becoming his big spoon. I kissed his neck and rubbed my hand along his chest.

"Okay, okay. Let's sleep. No jokes about hardness and wetness. I promise."

As I rubbed my hands along his chest, my hands couldn't help but move lower. Right before I could touch his dick, Sam took hold of my hand, joined our hands and said, "Sleep now, baby, or we'll be staying up the whole night."

"So uptight," I teased.

At that, he quickly took my hand to his dick and dragged the back of my hand to his hard dick.

"It's certainly up and tight." I could hear his smirk. Asshole.

"Fine. You win. Let's sleep," I grumbled and hugged him tightly, rubbing my boobs along his back, pretending to get comfortable.

He kept my hand in his as he fell asleep muttering, "Cruel. Cruel. Cruel."

CHAPTER 10

Sam

Soft hands ran through my hair. I roused from sleep to those magical hands running along my lower back. Who knew that was my sweet spot? When Akira ran her fingers there, I seemed to lose my mind.

"Sam," Akira whispered as she kissed my ear, all while she kept her hands on my back.

I moaned, wanting more of it but also wanting to stay here forever.

"Sam, wake up," Akira said again, nudging my shoulders.

Last night flashed in my mind and my eyes flew open.

There she was. Akira. How many times had I imagined waking up to this?

Her hair was in a bun at the top of her head, and she was dressed in a big, cream-colored sweater, her silk shorts, and fluffy socks, with a mug in her hand. She sat beside my head and threaded her fingers in my hair. I turned and put my head in her lap.

The fantasy didn't even come close to the reality.

Heaven. This was what heaven would be like.

"I could stay here forever," I mumbled in her lap.

"Oh, Sam, me too," Akira said and bent down to kiss my cheek.

I turned my head and offered her my lips.

She jerked back. "No, no. Not before you brush your teeth."

I laughed and said, "If I had to choose between your lips and your lap, good luck resisting my pretty lips."

"Sam," she whined and punched my shoulder. "You better wake up. I made some hot chai for you. It won't taste as good if you have to reheat it."

Oh, man. She was the cruelest little thing. She knew how I loved the chai she brought to the studio each morning.

"You're brutal, baby," I grumbled as I sat up and put on my shirt from last night. It was long enough to cover Akira's silky shorts. I had no intention of flashing them to Akira's roommates.

She quickly kissed my pout, but before I could slip her the tongue, she jerked back and said, "Now go freshen up, and I'll get your chai. I've put a new toothbrush at the sink for you."

I went into the hallway, and thankfully, didn't encounter any of her roommates. Once I had freshened up and returned to Akira's bedroom, she handed me the chai. Sitting beside her against the headboard, her hand in mine, we sipped from our cups.

Akira quietly sipped her chai as she played with my fingers. Every moment that I'd fantasized about us paled in comparison to the real thing. Kissing Akira had shifted my priorities. I didn't want to be afraid of losing Akira as a friend. I wanted her. Like I told her last night, I wanted to hold her. I wanted to kiss her. Make love to her. Call her my girlfriend.

Akira was lost in her own thoughts. Probably opposite to mine, considering her worries last night. Before she decided to blow me off, I needed to lay everything out.

I turned to her and said, "Akira."

She looked at me with a jerk. "Yeah?"

I entwined our hands and brought them to my lips. Akira's eyes softened and warmth radiated off her.

I placed our joined hands on my lap and said, "I know you have a lot of thoughts about us. But I need you to know that I regret nothing. I've been dreaming about kissing you for so long, and I don't want to stop. I want to be with you. I was always too afraid to ask you this because everything was going so well between us, but would you like to go on a date with me?"

Tears glistened in her eyes. "Oh, Sam. You have no idea how much I want that. But yes, I have a lot of thoughts too."

I squeezed her hand and ran my thumb over hers—just like she'd done when we were returning from Navratri all the way to her home—and said, "And we can talk all about your thoughts on our date. So, what do you say?"

She chuckled. "My thoughts aren't exactly an appropriate date conversation."

"Who cares? We already know each other enough to skip through twenty date conversations. C'mon baby, give me the chance to see you outside of school."

She looked at me, our joined hands on my lap, and while impatience tried to claw out of my skin, she said, "Okay. Let's do it. When do we go?"

"Yes. Yes. Thank you, Akira." I put my empty chai mug on her side table, put hers there too, and had her under me in seconds. I kissed her. And kissed her. And kissed her some more.

I had no intention to give her enough time to back out of this date, so I said, "We'll go tonight. Seven o'clock."

She laughed, knowing my intention. "Okay. Where will we go?"

"Don't worry about that. I'll make the arrangements and let you know. I'll pick you up at seven."

I tried to get up from my spot nestled on top of her, but she pulled my shirt to hold me in place. So hot. At my raised eyebrows, she said, "Wait. You're leaving?"

I tucked a few strands of her hair behind her ear and said, "I have to arrange our date. And if I spend any more time here, we're not getting up for a date. It's already noon."

I kissed her once more. God, how I loved to kiss her. After one more kiss, I got up and changed into my jeans. I neatly folded the silky-as-hell shorts Akira had let me borrow. I should see if there's something similar for men.

Akira sat up on her bed and stared at me with a small smile of possibly disbelief. Even I was surprised by my spontaneity, but I wasn't going to lose my nerve and slow down.

I was going all in.

With a last peck on her lips, I ran out her door.

∿

Akira

At 6:50 p.m. sharp, Sam called, asking me to open the door to my building. When I told him I could just meet him downstairs, he said, "It's a date, Akira. Let me in."

I could barely contain my smile when I buzzed him in.

I stood at the closed door as he climbed the three floors.

The moment I heard him reach my floor, I opened the door before he could knock.

And my jaw hung open.

Sam was wearing a black leather jacket. A. Leather. Jacket.

"Akira, eyes up here, baby."

It was when he closed my mouth with two fingers that I realized I was still gaping at him.

When I looked at him, he quirked his eyebrows at me. "Like what you see?"

I blushed but blatantly checked him out again. "Very, very much, Mr. White."

A loud laugh burst out of him, and he slid his hand behind my neck, pulled me forward and bit my lip. "That was so hot."

He kissed my lips once more. "I missed you so much."

I shivered as he rubbed his thumb along my jaw. "I missed you too."

He stepped back a little and checked me out. I was wearing a black, knee-length dress with lace at the shoulders and the sleeves. We matched. The intensity of his stare burned me. Goose bumps lined up across my arms, and I blushed at his perusal.

He came back closer to me, so I had to look up at him. He pushed my hair behind my ears and said, "You look gorgeous."

I giggled. I couldn't help it. My giggle turned into a laugh.

With an amused smile, Sam asked, "What'd I say?"

I shook my head and said, "It's so weird to hear you say that. For weeks, we haven't said this kind of stuff, and now you're being all romantic. It's...how do I say it...too thrilling to process."

"The good kind of thrilling?" he asked.

"The best kind of thrilling."

A huge smile lit up his face, which turned into laughter.

"You're right. Hearing such things from you sounds weird, but it still makes me want to fly."

My heart fluttered and butterflies took flight in my stomach, wanting to fly with him, and all the while we stood still at my front door, smiling like loons at each other.

Sam quickly dropped a kiss on my lips. "Let's go before I drag you to your room and say all the romantic shit to you till it stops sounding weird."

I laughed and punched his arm. "I'm loving this weird. Let's go."

I put on my heavy jacket and locked the door.

Sam took me to the Upper West Side, to a restaurant across Central Park. Since it was evening, I couldn't see the park at all, but the streets were full of tourists and locals. We walked hand in hand to the restaurant—Sam hadn't let go of my hand once since we left my place—talking about nothing and everything.

"This is us," Sam said, and led us inside an Italian restaurant.

The moment we stepped in, the heavenly smell of tomatoes and garlic made my stomach growl and my mouth water. The place was decorated in a rustic theme, and the lights were dimmed to low.

All the tables were intimate and candlelit, making it a perfect place for a date. As if I could ever doubt Sam's taste. He was a perfectionist, after all.

As I stood there gawking at all the wonderful dishes that people had on their table, Sam came back from the hostess stand.

"Let's go, Akira. Our table's ready."

Once we were seated, the server brought our menus and water. They put some garlic bread and butter on the table as we looked through the menu.

"So, what's good here?" I asked Sam.

"I haven't been here before. I've heard about this place, so thought we could check it out together."

"Really? So, what should we order?"

"Since you don't eat meat, should we order one veggie and one normal pizza?" he asked, smirking his little smirk.

"Hey! Vegetarian pizza is normal pizza. Margherita is the classic, and it's veg."

He laughed and squeezed my hand. "I was just kidding. You have any preference for wine, or should I order?"

His hand gave me all the warm fuzzies. "You order it. I'm not that knowledgeable in wine."

Once our server was here, Sam ordered a Margherita pizza,

one with meat, and some sort of a red wine whose name I didn't register. I was busy thinking about the serious conversation that we were supposed to have.

But I didn't want to ruin this date with tense conversations. I would keep our conversation light for now and talk to him about my concerns on our way home. Yes. I was on a date. With Sam. *Sam.* I couldn't stop the giddiness that bubbled on that thought.

"What's the smile for?" Sam asked, and I came out of my musings. I didn't even realize I was smiling.

"I still can't believe we're on a date."

Sam entwined our fingers on the table. "Me too. For so long, I've wanted to know you outside of school. Tell me what you do when you're not at the studio."

I rubbed my thumb over Sam's, where our hands were joined. "Well, I do watch a lot of Bollywood movies in my free time. My roommates and I often go and watch a Bollywood movie in a movie theater. Thankfully, theaters in Manhattan and Jersey City do screen Bollywood movies. And I talk to my family once or twice a day. To be honest, I'm not home much. Most of my days are spent with you."

"You have no idea how happy that makes me, as bad as it sounds."

"It doesn't sound bad at all. I love spending time with you. What about you? What do you do when you aren't with me?"

"Well, I sketch sometimes. Buildings mostly. And if I have some more time, I help my dad in his business, doing construction drawings. Keeps me busy."

He'd told me about it before. I've seen him working on it sometimes in the studio too. "Do you plan to work for your dad after you graduate?"

"Yeah. I can't wait to start."

He seemed to want to expand but he stopped. Seemed like I'd hit a sensitive topic. So, I didn't ask further.

By the time I could ask him anything more, food arrived.

For the next few minutes, we ate, conversation limited to exclamations about the food. Thank goodness he folded his slices like a New Yorker. I'd have lost it if he had pulled out a fork and a knife.

As I was pulling a slice of pizza from its dish, Sam asked, "So, Akira, if you don't mind me asking, do you not eat meat for religious reasons?"

I put the slice on my plate and said, "To be honest, I'm not that religious. I don't go to temples or do fasting like my mom and aunts do. But my parents are religious. They've never cooked meat or eggs in the house, so I just never developed the taste for it."

Sam nodded. "Makes sense. So, you celebrating your festivals like Navratri isn't for religious purposes?"

I chuckled. "Umm. It's both? In India, I would sit for daily prayers for the nine evenings of Navratri, and if there was an important fasting day, I would do it. But I wouldn't feel bad if I skipped it either. But my *love* for my festivals is all because of the clothes, food, and the celebrations. You've seen one now. You know how it is."

Sam's eyes darkened in arousal. "If they're all that *exciting*, I can't wait to celebrate your other festivals."

Blood rushed my cheeks at Sam's heated words. After having a few bites of my pizza, I cleared my throat.

When Sam looked at me, after taking a large bite of his pizza, I asked, "Can I ask you something? You don't have to answer if you don't want to."

He frowned at that and put his slice back on his plate. "You can ask me anything, sweetheart."

I blushed. His *sweethearts* had some serious superpower. "I've noticed that you're very organized. And neat. And kinda don't like it when other people's stuff gets on your desk."

A light blush coated Sam's cheeks. "You've noticed, huh?"

I ducked my head a little. "Yeah. The other day, you glared so hard at my purple highlighter that had gotten on your desk, I thought you would dry out its ink with the lasers you were shooting at it. Is it OCD?"

Sam chuckled at my poor joke and shook his head. "I'm definitely compulsive about certain things in my life. I like my things to be properly organized and everything to be at their right spot. But I don't get anxiety if it isn't. Sure, it irks me a lot. But it doesn't give me anxiety that stops my normal functioning. So, to answer your question, I'm not OCD. I'm just more of a perfectionist or even particular about certain things."

I placed my hand on top of Sam's across the table. "Thank you for explaining that. I didn't want to offend you or anything. I just want to know you better."

Sam picked up my hand and placed a soft kiss on my palm. "I know. I love that you care, baby."

He let go of my hand, and once we were done eating, the server asked if we wanted a dessert. Sam asked me if I'd rather have an ice cream from a cart outside. I agreed. It would give us a good time to talk about more serious topics.

Once Sam paid the bill—I insisted on splitting it, but he glared at me—we walked out in the brisk, cool air. Sam blew my mind when he held my hand and put our joined hands in the pocket of his jacket. I had always seen people do that on the street, and my day was finally here. I wanted to skip down the sidewalk with joy.

When Sam raised his eyes at my big-ass smile, I shrugged and squeezed his hand in the pocket. "I always wanted to do that."

He laughed and kissed the side of my head as we walked.

I'd died and gone to heaven. I swayed on my feet and mock fell on him. He caught me, and I had to say, "I just swooned."

He laughed and shook his head. "You're crazy."

"Made you laugh, didn't I?"

This time, he kissed me on the lips, out in the street, in front of the world.

"That you did," he said, and led us to the ice cream cart nearby.

I got my ice cream in a cup and insisted Sam get it in a cup too. I was worried we wouldn't be able to have a serious conversation if we were too busy keeping ice cream from dripping. I asked him if we could walk for a while. He frowned at all my requests but went along with it.

Once we had our ice creams—that I paid for—I led Sam to the edge of Central Park to walk. We ate a few spoonsful in silence before he broke the tension.

"You're not going to make me laugh now, are you?" Sam asked.

I chuckled, disappointment heavy on my chest, and shook my head. "We need to talk."

CHAPTER 11

"Bring the pure wine of love and freedom. But sir, a tornado is coming. More wine, we'll teach this storm a thing or two about whirling."

- Rumi

Sam

"Okay. Tell me what's been bothering you," I said.

Her silence made me angsty. I scooped some cold ice cream and put it in my mouth to stop any further questions from spilling out.

She sighed, preparing herself. She stuck the plastic spoon in her cup and said, "Sam, I'm going to sound crazy to you for a while, but please bear with me. Okay?"

She looked scared, and I couldn't help but hold her hand. "Baby, I love your crazy. So, talk to me. I'm here."

As terrified as I was of what she had to say, I think she felt worse. We walked for a minute, listening to the cars zooming past us, and people occasionally walking around us.

She blew out a breath as if preparing for a fight and started,

"Okay. Here it is. We are from two different countries, Sam. I am an Indian. A Hindu, Gujarati girl, which probably means nothing to you. And I just came here. Do you know what my dad told me before I came to New York?"

She waited for me to ask her, as if she wasn't going to continue if I didn't ask. I complied and asked, "What?"

Imitating her dad's voice, she said, "He told me *Akira, I know the times are changing, and I'm aware that someday, you might bring home a boyfriend. I just have one request. Please, don't bring home a BMW*."

I frowned. As far as I know, a BMW was a car. And if Akira brought home a guy with a BMW, I didn't see the harm in that. "What's a BMW?" I asked, just to confirm if her dad was indeed talking about the car.

Akira exclaimed, "I asked him the same thing. And you know what he said? BMW stands for Black, White, and Muslim. His only request was for me to not bring home a guy who is Black, White or Muslim."

Shock.

Horror.

Disgust.

Disbelief.

A mirthless laugh burst out of me, causing me to accidentally squeeze the plastic ice cream cup. Surely, her father couldn't have said such things. But Akira remained silent. Embarrassment coated her cheeks red, and shame curled her shoulders inwards.

I let go of Akira's hand. I ran a hand through my hair, tugging as I went, and the little sting of pain helped me think.

"What does this mean?" I asked Akira. I needed more. There had to be an explanation for this.

We found a bench and a garbage bin near it. I threw in my ice cream while Akira sat on the bench, her ice cream cup in her lap. "There's nothing so shocking about this, Sam. India is still a conservative country. Our cultures and traditions are far different than here. It is still a country of arranged marriages. Parents are fine with a love marriage so long as the man and woman are of the same caste, not even the same religion. So, when my father says that he is fine with anyone but Black, White, or Muslim, that is a big deal in terms of Indian standards. There are a lot of parents who don't allow their daughters to marry the guy they love just because she chose him herself, or because his family believes in a different god, or just because he doesn't conform to their definition of a husband."

Did she say a husband? I had no words. This was all too much information, and my knees went weak. I went and sat beside her on the bench. Akira's words were like a bucket of cold water dropped on my head. What did this mean for us? A bigger question, was there an us?

Akira realized that I wasn't going to say anything yet, which prompted her to continue. "Do you realize where I'm going with this, Sam? Dating me comes with a lot of consequences for you. To be honest, dating you comes with even more consequences for me. Sam, you look like you're going to barf."

I felt like it. But I understood Akira. I knew she was terrified. She was, in her roundabout way, questioning the same thing that I was.

Are *we* worth going through all this trouble? But I refused to consider not dating Akira. I wanted more. I needed more. I just got Akira, and I wasn't going to give her up just like that.

So, I gave her my truth, "I like you, Akira. I like you too much to consider you just a friend. I just got you, sweetheart. I am not giving you up. You fill my life with so much light and laughs. And I don't want to spend another day without you in my arms. But I don't think I can give you a forever commitment after one kiss. We hardly know each other as a couple."

Her face crumbled at my words. I dropped to my knees on the dirty pavement and held her hands in mine. "Akira, please, don't think that you're not who I want. I'm crazy about you. Crazy enough to ask you to give us a chance to get to know each other. I want us to date, baby. I want you to give us a chance to grow as a couple. I want to know your likes and dislikes. Your passion. Your dreams. I want to become an important part of your life. I want you to know all of me, not just a version of me, before you decide whether I'm worth the trouble you'd have to go through. I know this doesn't define our relationship, but all I can ask is for you to give us a chance at a real, exclusive relationship where we take one day at a time. Do you think we could do that?"

Akira's eyes filled with tears. She squeezed my hand with both of hers and said, "You don't know what you're asking for, Sam."

How could she not understand? Us not being together was not an option for me. She looked so heartbroken. I couldn't stop myself from taking her in my arms. I wish we were having this conversation in Akira's room so I could hold her better. She clung to my arm, as if she feared I would agree with her and give up on us.

"This is the first time we've sat like this," she murmured in my chest.

"And I don't want this to be the last time," I murmured back. I couldn't completely grasp the reasons for her fear and uncertainty, but I was starting to realize that there were going to be a lot of consequences on her end.

"Me neither," she said and held on to me tightly.

"Then give us a chance, baby," I whispered in her hair. I was willing to resort to begging if I had to.

We sat together like that for a long time as I waited for Akira's answer. Minutes passed as I ran my hands in her hair and down her back, soothing her. The sounds of the traffic fluctuated with the changing traffic signals. And Akira stayed still. Thinking. Chewing her lip. Not looking at me.

People went in and out of different restaurants, some laughing and smiling, some walking silently. And I kept looking at her, my heart beating out of my chest.

She looked at me, and her chest rose and fell. She took a deep breath in, as if mustering all the strength to tell me no, and whispered, "Yes."

My heart stopped and roared. I clutched her hand, not quite sure I heard her correctly.

And then in a stronger voice, she cemented what she'd whispered. "Okay, Sam, let's do this."

She gave me the warmest smile that she could muster on her anxious but determined face.

Relief and happiness flowed through every vein of my body. Before I could sweep her in my arms to celebrate, she held up her finger between us to stop my advance. "I just need to warn you, Sam. I can't let my family know that I'm dating you until we are absolutely certain about each other. A war is going to break out when I tell my family that I'm dating an American guy. And I don't want to get into this battle if we're going to end up breaking up later. Is that okay with you?"

As much as I wanted to say yes, it didn't feel okay to me. It felt as if we were doing something wrong. And I despised feeling guilty when I had done nothing wrong. Akira saw the doubt etched on my face.

"Please, Sam. Please understand," she begged.

She clutched my hand in both of hers. I couldn't stand the fact that she had to beg me for something she knew wasn't right. And it felt so right to be with Akira. Holding her. Kissing her. I was fine with her not telling her family about us. But the fact that she was just waiting for us to break up was an insult to what we shared, and I was not okay with that.

"Akira, it feels as if you're just waiting for us to fail."

She flinched at that. "It's not like that, Sam."

She held my face.

"Then what's it like, Akira? Because I'm fine with you informing your family about us whenever you feel right. But already planning for us to break up when we're just trying to get together is an insult."

She jerked upright at that, dumped the ice cream in the garbage can and started speed walking away from me. Fuck. I caught up to her and walked beside her. She looked at me and said, "Insult? Do you think it's an insult to try to save our relationship? To save *you* from trouble?"

"You are not trouble, Akira. Why can't you believe me?" I shouted.

"Because you don't know my family!" she shouted back. A sob broke free that she tried to contain, and she looked anywhere but at me as she said, "You don't know my family. Do you know, in most of the Indian families, there is no such thing as *dating*? For them, a boyfriend is a future husband."

I knew my eyebrows had gotten lost somewhere in my hair. Husband. Again with that word. It had been thirty minutes since Akira became my girlfriend.

Although, girlfriend seemed a little too light for what I felt for her. She was much more than my girlfriend. Or a partner. She was just my Akira. Mine.

I wasn't afraid of marriage. I wanted to marry—someday. And as much as I liked Akira, I wanted to be with her, get to know her, in all the different ways, see what made her happy, what made her sad, and I wanted to fall in love with her. Not that I was very far from that, but I wanted to take my time.

Akira must have seen my worried face, because she continued. "And that's the best-case scenario. Worst-case scenario, they make you choose between the family and the boyfriend. I'm terrified that I'd choose you and lose my family. And I'm even more terrified that I'd choose them, and we'll never get the time and the chance to be together."

And she broke down. I finally understood. She needed this time for just us. Because if we didn't get this time to be together, just us, she wouldn't be able to choose us. She was giving *us* a chance. And she was asking me to do the same.

I realized the gravity of what we were dealing with. We were fighting the wall between two countries with two different values.

All this time that we were skirting around each other, Akira was thinking about these consequences she'd have to deal with, the sacrifices she'd have to make and the choices she'd face, without ever telling me.

She dealt with all of this, alone, yet with a smile on her face. And she still took the chance to be with me last night. The least I could do was tell her she wasn't alone anymore.

I gently lifted her chin with my finger, so she looked at me. I kissed her forehead and held her. "Thank you for giving us a chance, Akira. I'm sorry for losing my temper and doubting you. I'm very sorry. And if you'd still have me, I would like to explore this for us. Let's get to know each other, and be with each other the way we want to. Because as much as I want you to choose me in the end, I want you to not have to choose at all. What do you say?"

And she kissed me.

No—she crushed her mouth against mine.

She fucking *devoured* me.

After kissing for what felt like a lifetime, I asked Akira the most crucial question, in the middle of the street, in front of the world. "When will you wear your Navratri outfit again?"

She let out a bark of laughter, grabbed my face, and answered, "Next weekend, and then next year."

"What? Next year? How can you not wear those wonderful clothes all the time? You break my heart, baby."

She laughed and said, "If you want, I can wear it in private, just for your eyes."

I clutched her hand and ran to the nearest subway stop, taking her back to her place to show her how grateful and happy I was.

CHAPTER 12

"Love is a friendship set to music."
  - Joseph Campbell

Akira

The next morning, Sam hadn't even had time to get all the way out of the building before the door of my room burst open and my excited roommates crowded onto my bed. I'd hoped they hadn't seen Sam as he left, but guess I was wrong.

"Yes?" I tried being oblivious.

"Oh, don't even pretend, Akira. Sam literally greeted us in the hallway. So, fess up," Megha said as she raised her eyebrows at me.

"He spent the night again, didn't he?" asked Shruti, with a big smile on her face.

"Well..." I didn't even know where to begin.

"Well...go on," Megha encouraged, her eyes twinkling.

"Well, Sam and I are sort of together now," I said.

I was met with some gasps and some excited squeals.

"Oh my God. Wow. Tell us everything. I knew Sam liked you when I saw him watching you do the *garba*. He just kept staring at you the whole time. Didn't I tell you, Megha?" Shruti asked, her smile wide and her ponytail bouncing as she looked between Megha and me.

"Yeah, and Akira wasn't far behind. She kept looking at him constantly too. Did you see her putting her dupatta around Sam's shoulders? That screamed *He's mine.* What was that about, Akira?" Megha teased.

I knew I had turned red.

"Well, now he is. Mine that is," I admitted.

"Ooohhhhhh!" they all teased.

"I saw both of you leaving quite early on garba night. And how was your date last night? Boy, he works fast, doesn't he?" Shruti waggled her eyebrows.

"Well, we kissed. A lot. And last night, after dinner, I informed him that if he was serious about dating me, and if he really wanted to be in a relationship with me, then he needed to know my family would be a problem. Well, you know how our parents would react if we got some non-Indian person."

Every one of them nodded.

"My parents might disown me. And not just non-Indians. I would have to fight them even if I bring some guy who was not of our caste," Vidya said, rolling her eyes in defeat.

"So, what did he say?" asked Megha.

Afraid of their judgment, I stared down at my fingers as I said, "He asked me to give our relationship a chance."

Shruti squeezed my shoulder in support, and I sighed in relief. She added, clearly considering the circumstances herself, "He has no idea how dirty our Indian parents can fight, does he? He has no idea what he is dealing with."

"I know. That's what I'm worried about. That's why I told him that I'm not going to inform my family about us until he is certain about us."

I relayed our entire conversation to them.

"Makes sense. No point in putting yourself and him

through all that drama," Shruti said with a nod. She then proceeded to hug me and said, "I'm so happy for you though. You, dating an American guy. It's so exciting. And don't you worry. We'll all train him on how to deal with Indian parents. He'll be an expert in no time." Shruti certainly brought my hopes up.

"You think so?" I mumbled.

"I know so. Who else has had a lifetime of experience in dealing with Indian parents? And if we can convince them to send us to New York to study, I think we can convince them to let us marry a guy of our choice. It would be a little difficult in your case. But we'll do it," Shruti said with conviction.

"You can always tell your parents that you'll become a citizen of the States once you marry him. That'll convince them," Vidya suggested.

My stomach dropped at that. I had never thought about the status of my citizenship in the course of my dreams of Sam. Not once did it cross my mind.

But it would cross others' minds.

People would call me a green card girl.

People would call Sam a sucker for being duped by an Indian girl.

Oh, this was bad. I was so worried about my family's reaction that I never even considered how everyone else would react to our relationship.

I suddenly lost my ability to speak.

"I...I don't. I don't want to be with Sam for citizenship," I said out loud, feeling compelled to justify my feelings for Sam.

Vidya must have noticed the hurt on my face because she instantly sat up from the chair and came beside me.

"I didn't mean it in a bad way, Akira. I know you don't want him for his citizenship. But this is a perk, and it might be the only thing that could convince your family."

"I don't want to be known as the girl who married for citizenship."

All the girls gave me sympathetic looks.

Shruti placed her hand on my knee and said, "There will be a lot of people who would say that. And they won't be just Indians. Literally every immigrant who wants to settle in the States would say that. And you will have to learn to ignore it if both of you get serious."

How was it fair that our relationship had more battles to fight just because we were from different countries?

"Are you sure this thing with Sam is worth going through all this?" Vidya asked, ever the practical.

"That's what we are going to figure out. We owe it to us. And if we are worth it, I'm going to give one hell of a fight," I declared.

"That's the spirit. And we'll help you prepare. Starting from training Sam in all things Indian," declared Shruti with a clap of her hands.

"Hell yeah," everyone cheered, filling our little room with excitement, hope, and anticipation.

"Well, I will inform my cousin Ria about this development. She'll surely start plotting the means to handle my family," I said.

Once everyone retired to their rooms, the only thing that kept replaying in my mind was our first kiss. That moment when he finally let go of all his restraint and just kissed the hell out of me. The raw, primal, inexplicable urge to drive Sam crazier and wilder rose within me.

I wanted to see him at his most vulnerable.

Wake up in the middle of the night and hug him closer.

Talk to him until the early morning sun washed over us.

Walk around the city listening to his endless, passionate stories of buildings.

Hold his hands and feel his skin.

Laugh with him.

Kiss him.

Touch him.

And do everything that I couldn't do before he kissed me and convinced me to give us a chance.

~

Sam

Happiness.

I never thought that happiness born out of the sheer gift of companionship could exist for me.

I have seen the love my parents share. The openness and honesty between them have been my lifelong goal.

And to see my life taking the same direction brought me joy like nothing ever had.

Everything seemed more beautiful as I walked back to my place. I couldn't stop replaying the moment when I woke up to Akira playing with my hair. I never wanted to move out of her lap. I had dreamed a lot about kissing Akira. But none of those dreams came close to reality. Akira had the power to bring me to my knees.

I entered my apartment in a daze, forgetting that Luke might be home on a Sunday morning. I forgot to keep my face neutral, and unfortunately, Luke saw the joy on my face as he was quick to point out, "What's with the smile, dude?"

I wasn't quick enough to remove the smile as Luke continued. "You got laid, didn't you?"

"That's none of your business, and no, I didn't get laid," I said. Technically, we didn't have sex. What we did had been hotter than any of my other sexual encounters, but I stood correct in my answer to Luke.

He frowned at my answer, and prodded more. "Then what's with the stupid smile?"

I couldn't resist sharing this with Luke. So, I openly smiled and said, "Well, Akira and I decided to be together."

"No shit, dude. I love her," Luke blatantly declared.

At my severe frown, he added, "For you. I love her for you."

"You don't need to love her for me. Stop saying love and Akira in the same sentence. She is mine." I didn't care if it sounded crazy, but I had worked hard to get Akira to agree to give us a chance.

Luke quickly said, "Chill out, dude. I am not interested in her like that. She's all yours. Although, I would advise you don't behave like a caveman in front of her. Or she won't stay yours for long."

Hmph. He did have a point.

"Yeah, yeah. I'm sorry for snapping. Last night was a little rough."

"Already trouble in paradise?" Luke chirped from his seat on our couch.

I didn't even have the words to explain everything to him. But I needed some advice and an ear to listen. So, I took a seat on the chair of the dining table, and I told Luke about my conversation with Akira.

Akira had become my best friend before she became my girlfriend. I admired her tenacity to work hard for what she wanted and achieving it with humble grace. She had a loud personality but a peaceful mind. She had an innocent smile but a wicked sense of humor. She was one of a million Indian girls in New York, but she was just one in a million for me. And I wanted her with a passion and equal desperation.

I wanted to be the one she spoke to. I wanted to be the center of her attention. I wanted to be the one she shared all her joys and sorrows with. And I truly wanted her to want just me.

I didn't say all of that to Luke, but I told him what I could. "I want her to want this. I think we are great together, and I don't want her to give up on us."

Luke patiently listened to my entire story. Even though he usually joked around, he was one of the most sensible men that I knew. His passion for his work was proof of that. So, when he talked, I listened.

"Sam, she is right to be concerned. You do have the luxury to choose your partner, to an extent. I know you would want your parents to be pleased with your choice, but if they aren't impressed by Akira, would you leave her?"

"No. Of course not."

"And if they made you choose? I know they never would; I love your parents—but if they asked you to choose between them and Akira, who would you choose?" Luke pressed.

I stood up from the chair and walked across the room. I straightened up the stray drawing sheets on the table. I would not want anyone to face such a choice. I loved my family. But there was Akira. Fuck.

"I don't want Akira to have to make a choice. It would break her. And if I allow her to put herself in that position, what does that say about me?" I asked the question that had been troubling me since Akira admitted to how her family would react.

"It is her choice, Sam. Just like her parents don't get to make her choose, you too don't get to make a choice for her. If you make decisions for her, you are no better than her family."

I flinched at his words.

"I am trying to save her from regret in the future."

"Oh, I think her family would say the same thing," Luke remarked.

"Fuck!" I almost punched the wall. I wouldn't. I'm not that strong, and I needed my hands.

As harsh as Luke was, he was right.

I had to have faith in Akira's choices. She knew the risks she was taking by getting into this relationship—by giving us a chance, by choosing me.

But it was the guilt that came with it that was so hard to deal with. Even though I wasn't the one who might eventually have to make a choice, I was the reason that required Akira to make any choice at all.

"How can I bear to be the reason for her to choose between me and her family, Luke? What if she regrets it—regrets me—in the future? She would never be able to go back. Am I even worth it?" I admitted my worst fears.

Luke was somber as he said, "She knows that, Sam. And you have a choice too, you know? Do you want to be involved in the family drama, and deal with racism here and the inevitable religious complications? Is she worth it to you?"

I didn't even have to pause to think before I admitted, "Yes."

Luke smiled with genuine happiness. "Then go get your girl, man. And if Akira feels the same for you, you have your answer." He winked and got back to his sketching.

"Huh. That simple, huh?" That did relieve me a bit.

"That simple," Luke murmured and got lost in his work.

I walked into my room hoping Akira felt the same for me.

As I plugged my phone in the charger, I saw that I had a message from Akira.

> Akira: Hey, boyfriend. :-*

That brought my stupid smile back to my face.

> Me: Hey... ;-)

> Akira: You were supposed to say "Hey, girlfriend" X- (

> Me: I know... ;-)

Akira: Jerk

Me: LOL... Don't be mad, sweetheart... :-*

Akira: Aww...I love it when you call me that...

I'd be lying if I said my face wasn't blushing too.

Me: I miss you

Akira: Me too, Sam. See you tomorrow?

Me: Can't wait.

Akira: Studio at 6, and lectures before that?

Me: Yeah. What are your plans today?

Akira: I talked to my roommates. We are going to train you in all things Indian. To prepare you for the war. ;-) And I was going to tell Ria about us. She'll be our man on the inside.

Me: Go, Commander. What do you need me to do?

Akira: Just be with me. And we'll conquer the world, baby. :-*

Damn, this girl!

Me: If you were here right now, I would've ravished you twice by now.

Akira: Promises, promises... ;-)

Me: I'm coming back to your place.

Akira: No, no. I need to call Ria and talk to her. And then talk to my family. Clean the house. Prepare for the class tomorrow. Now that the midterm is over, I'm a little worried about the finals.

Me: You've done great so far. This is not going to be any different. It's certainly going to be easier than dealing with your family. ;-) If that doesn't scare you, this should be a breeze for you.

Akira: As non-hilarious as that was, it helped. Thank you. TTYL. Calling Ria.

Sam: Call me before you sleep. We'll talk... ;-)

Akira: Can't wait!!! :-*

CHAPTER 13

"A nation's culture resides in the hearts and in the soul of its people."
- Mahatma Gandhi

Akira

Two weeks flew by with Sam, and I'd never been happier. This was the first free weekend we got after two weeks of constant assignments but also the constant joy of being with Sam.

Today, my roommates and I finally got the time to start teaching Sam some "Indian Relationship Tutorial." We arranged our small living room to accommodate all four of us plus Sam and Luke. Megha was ready with snacks. Shruti had her speech in hand. Vidya read her book, while I tried to stop my bouncing leg as we waited for Sam and Luke to arrive.

While nothing much had changed since Sam and I got together—we still sat together and worked, we still bickered constantly, and we still hadn't had sex—there were little things that had rocked my world.

Now, we held hands in the middle of work. Sam kissed me to end our bickering, and even though we hadn't had an opportunity to have sex yet, we did a lot of other things.

Now, when Sam got near me to discuss my designs, he gave me a quick peck before he leaned back. Every few hours, we took a small coffee break, where we talked about the things that you don't talk about with your "friend." I asked him how many girlfriends he'd had before me.

"Two meaningful relationships," he'd said. They didn't work out because they wanted different things in life, and neither was willing to compromise.

He asked me the same, and I told him about my ex in India. The guy was decent, but his family was not. My ex had informed me that his family wanted a girl to stay at home and be the good daughter-in-law, a show pony for the society. Things didn't last with us after he refused to go against his family for me.

When I'd asked Sam about his "meaningless" relationships, he'd replied with a stiff "I don't spend time in meaningless things."

That was so Sam.

Doing nothing meaningless.

Even his favorite shows on Netflix were Amazing Houses and Amazing Hotels. While I admit that the shows were terrific —Sam made me watch it during a lunch break—he didn't watch the kind of shows where we could cuddle up in front of the computer or get hooked into watching an entire series. I did manage to show him and Luke one of my favorite Bollywood movies. They wouldn't admit it, but I did hear a few sniffles during the movie.

The loud doorbell had me jumping out of my seat.

The moment I opened the door, I was greeted by Sam, who looked ready to take over the world in his crisp shirt and black jeans, his glasses sparkling, and a determined gaze that formed two lines between his eyebrows.

I smiled.

Only he would get that ready to talk about my family at 10 a.m. on a Saturday.

As our eyes met, he came over and dropped a kiss on my lips. My hand went to his chest, holding his shirt, creating a few wrinkles in it.

"Hey, sweetheart."

He pushed my hair behind my ear and kissed my cheek.

I sucked in a sharp breath.

"Hi," I said, my voice more of a gasp.

A throat clearing had me jumping away from Sam.

"Hi, Akira," Luke said.

And I laughed.

He looked like someone had dragged him right out of bed despite many protests. His hair was sticking up in all directions, he was wearing sweatpants and a T-shirt, and the only thing keeping him standing was the giant coffee in his hand.

"Good morning, Luke. You sleep okay?"

Luke glared at Sam, and answered with clenched teeth, "I would've if someone hadn't dragged me out of bed."

Sam shrugged. "He's here to take notes in case I miss something."

And I burst out laughing. I laughed more at Luke's exasperation and Sam's sincere yet evil expression. I quickly kissed Sam and invited them inside. They handed me their coats that they must have removed on the three flights up, and I quickly hung them on the coat rack and led them to the living room.

I officially introduced Sam as my boyfriend to my roommates. Most of them wished him good luck, not for being my boyfriend, but for taking up an Indian girlfriend.

Now, all of us were gathered in our living room. Luke and Sam had been seated on the couch right across a whiteboard, while us girls took a seat on the chairs. I sat on the chair that I'd put right beside where Sam sat. Since it was Shruti's idea, we let her begin.

"Sam, we are so glad that you've decided to embark upon this journey, which even Indian guys hesitate to do, with such enthusiasm and fervor. Luke, I'm sorry you got roped into the Indian lessons, but I hope you learn something new."

While Luke gave a dopey smile, as if amused by everything, Sam had already opened his book, his glasses perched atop his nose and ready to take notes.

"Of course, thank you so much for your time and effort," Sam replied in complete sincerity.

And I couldn't hold my laughter. And neither could the rest.

Sam glared at us all and said with his teeth clenched, "This is serious. Let's get to it, shall we?"

I couldn't help but snicker. As Sam glared at me from his seat, I blew him a kiss. Finally, he smiled.

"Let's begin," I declared.

Shruti began. And Sam got on the edge of his seat with his pen ready to fly.

"So today, we will talk about being in a relationship with an Indian girl. It's going to be challenging, Sam, but it's going to be worth it. Now, there are a few rules for dating an Indian girl.

"Rule number one: if the girl is talking to her mother or any other family member, do not do anything that might indicate your presence in her vicinity. The moment the family finds out that their daughter has a boyfriend, one of two things might happen. Either you'll be married to her within a year, or she'll be married to someone else within a year. Considering your relationship situation, I wouldn't risk it."

Sam and I nodded obediently, looking at each other.

Shruti continued.

"Rule number two: a girl living in India usually has many more restrictions than we all do. Obviously, our parents were cool enough to send us to the US to study. But occasionally, the parents ask us if we found a boy in the US. Well, Akira might be having similar phone calls with her parents too."

I nodded and admitted, "Usually once a month, my mom asks me if I've found a well-educated Indian man here."

"What?" Sam barked.

I cringed. "I just tell her no and divert her attention to Aakar. It's not a big deal, Sam. My mom has been asking me this for two years."

Sam looked a little unsettled, but once Luke slapped him on the back, Sam pulled it together.

Shruti continued. "Mothers will often send photos of different guys for arranged marriage options, along with information about the men. Don't let that spook you too much. Use the information that her mother sends for your benefit."

I had no idea Shruti was such a cunning devil. Looking at us frown with confusion, Shruti huffed a sigh, as if we weren't smart enough for her. "When your mother sends you information on other guys, it will help you understand the kind of guy that your family is expecting for you. In the future, if you guys ever decide to come out to Akira's family, you can list down how Sam is better than the other guys that your mom has shown. Then logically, they wouldn't have any reason to oppose your relationship."

"You clever woman," Luke exclaimed in awe.

As much as I loved Shruti's idea, I already knew what my parents were looking for, or rather, *not* looking for, in a guy. Their BMW list. Ugh. As much as I hated admitting to it, I owed the truth to my friends, who were so excited to help us out.

I looked at Shruti and the rest and admitted, "My parents wouldn't mind any Indian guy. Their only condition was to not choose a White guy, a Black guy, or a Muslim guy."

I couldn't meet anyone's eyes as I finished speaking.

"That's as cool as it is disturbing," said Shruti.

When Luke raised his eyebrows, she shrugged. "Her parents are relatively cooler than mine. I wouldn't even be allowed to marry a guy who didn't belong to the same caste as ours."

"Wow, this is a little fucked up," said Luke.

"To say the least," added Sam.

We talked some more about Indian families, and soon we all had started watching a Bollywood drama film for "research purposes," which was Megha's idea. She was the Bollywood queen of our house and even after coming to the States, she stayed up to date with the latest Bollywood movies and gossips.

It was late at night when we were done with the movies and dinner.

To say that deciding the sleeping arrangement was awkward was putting it mildly. Sam usually ended up staying at my place every night since he came to drop me off.

But it was a little awkward to not let Sam leave my place with Luke, since they came together. It was even more awkward since all my roommates were present in the room when it was time for the guys to leave.

Sam must've noticed my dilemma, because he came near me and asked in a voice that seemed personal but could be heard by all, "Come for a dessert with me?"

And then he whispered in my ear so that no one could hear him, "And then come home with me?"

I was pretty sure everyone could see me blush when I nodded. I went into my room to get my tote packed with some essentials and changed into something comfortable.

That was a clear indication of my night's plans, but there wasn't any point in pretending otherwise. I put on my heavy winter coat and a scarf as Sam and Luke put on their respective coats.

Luke parted ways from us right as we left my place. Sam and I went to the West Harlem Pier, a ten-minute walk from my place, after we left.

After an entire day of discussing Indian culture and

watching two loud Bollywood movies, Sam needed a little quiet. The pier was one of my favorite places near my house. You could see the Empire State Building and most of the downtown when you stood at the edge of the pier. Sam stood with his arms around me, us facing downtown Manhattan.

Every time I looked at the view, I felt how incredibly fortunate I was to be able to come to New York City to study something I loved. Very few people got that chance. And to be able to find someone that I could share this part of my life with...it was humbling and exhilarating.

"What are you thinking?" Sam murmured in my hair.

"Just thinking how lucky I am to be here," I said as I leaned back in his arms.

Sam nuzzled my hair and neck as he held me tighter.

"How do you feel?" I asked him. I needed to know how he felt after hearing so many stories of my culture.

"It was." He paused for a few seconds before he continued, "Um...enlightening."

We burst out laughing.

"You still sure about us, then?" I inquired, pretending to be casual while my heart raced, and my stomach churned with a million butterflies.

"More than ever, Akira. I'm glad that we're different people. Every day, I learn something new. Not everything makes sense to me when it comes to understanding your culture, but you make me see the world differently. And I like seeing this world with you."

I was glad Sam stood behind me, because, for the life of me, I wouldn't have been able to hide the few tears that slipped out of my eyes at his sincere declaration.

After I got my emotions under control, I put my hand on Sam's, which was wrapped around my waist, and leaned into him as I admitted, "I like seeing the world with you too, Sam." *And I don't ever want to stop*, my heart said, but my mouth didn't.

"Let's go home," Sam said.

We held hands all the way to Sam's apartment. Once we reached his bedroom, he turned on the night lamp and took my tote. He gently placed it on an empty space of his desk. His bed was a simple queen size with immaculate navy-blue sheets tucked perfectly with a matching comforter arranged just like they do in hotel rooms. I almost didn't want to get into the bed with him. It would totally ruin the sheets.

I turned around to Sam, who stood near his desk, watching me with raised brows and a small smile.

I shook my head and him and said, "You sure you wanna ruin those sheets? I've never seen something so perfect."

Without looking away, Sam came closer to me and opened the zip to my coat. "I'm starting to see something more perfect."

My breathing turned rapid as I got my words out. "Oh, you're good."

The only sound in the room was our hard breathing and the loud zipper. After he put the coat on the little coat rack in the corner, he removed the scarf I'd wrapped around my neck.

Slowly.

At every turn around my neck, he grazed his thumb to my jaw or my cheek. And every time he did that, I shivered. I clutched his coat so I would stay upright.

He stood close enough for me to feel his hardness at my stomach. I couldn't help but arch my back. He groaned. His eyes burned me. I wanted him closer. Needed him to surround me with his heat, hold me with his beautiful hands, and show me how much he wanted me till I forgot all the consequences against us.

Heat sizzled between us, an invisible string joining us together.

Sam's hands were clenched in a fist, as if stopping himself from dragging me to his bed and ravishing me. As he stepped closer, I moved back till my back hit the door.

Sam neared and stood against me, all of him touching all of me.

I so badly wanted him inside; I ached for it.

The tether that had held me from giving in to having sex had weakened. It was barely hanging there.

With every kiss, Sam made me believe in us more. Every time he held my hand, I was a little less afraid. Every time he called my name, I got more ready to shred all the tethers stopping me from becoming his forever.

Sam's faith in us gave me the courage to fight anyone who dared to separate us.

His fingers pushing my hair behind my ears had me looking into his eyes.

The heat in them, the warmth of his body called me forward.

I swayed toward him, and before I could blink, he'd caught me in his arms.

He grabbed my waist and held my hair.

Our foreheads touched, our heavy breaths fogging his glasses.

I placed my hands on his chest. I could feel his heart pounding, matching the beats with mine.

"Akira." He moaned my name in anguish, in heat, in frustration, in want, in possession.

And I fought the tethers holding me away from him...that stopped me from taking this final step. I fought my mind that was too afraid of the risk while my heart had already made a home in his.

His hips moved, almost unconsciously, and my legs opened on their own accord.

Sam closed the distance between us, and we fit perfectly. With my mind loosening its hold on my body, I brought my leg around Sam and pushed him closer.

"God, Akira. I need you so much," Sam moaned, his lips sucking my neck.

And with his call of my name, his need matching my hunger, every tether broke.

I clutched his hair and kissed him on the mouth.

Sam groaned and kissed me back until our lips were swollen. Till his glasses were smudged by my nose and he couldn't see anymore. Till his arousal rubbed against mine.

"Sam," I gasped. He pushed my sweater to the side and sucked my shoulder.

Sparks lit up my insides, crackling energy zapping through my veins. So much so that I was grinding on his thighs and I didn't even realize it. Sam groaned in my neck and pushed his erection against my hips.

"I need you, Akira," Sam rumbled in my neck and kept rubbing against my hips.

I was dying to feel him. Desperation had me arching my back.

"God, I need you too. Want to feel you inside me," I gasped and I thrust my hips, trying to get closer.

All of Sam's restraints collapsed, and he let himself go.

I didn't even realize we'd reached his bed, but Sam had me lying on it in no time.

"Are you sure?" he asked. He was panting above me, and I knew if I told him to stop, he would. And that had me wanting him even more.

I nodded. "Yes. Yes. Very, very sure. I want you so much."

He groaned and kissed my neck, my chest, my boobs.

I was desperate to feel his skin. I removed his jacket and flung it somewhere. I then grabbed his shirt and tried opening the buttons. But they were the little devils that refused to budge. All I could do was drag his shirt over his head.

Once I had the shirt removed, Sam got his jeans off and

placed his glasses on the nightstand. We then quickly got my clothes off.

We were both panting as we got naked, and we couldn't hide the big smiles on our faces. I dragged my hands along Sam's chest, his neck, his hair, as my lips followed the path. Sam had my ass held tightly in his hands while he dragged me along his hardness.

"Akira," he groaned.

"More, Sam," I moaned.

Sam laid me back on the bed since I'd climbed onto his lap in my desperation. He got a condom from his nightstand, tore the wrapper with utmost care, got the sticky thing out, pinched the tip, and rolled it on. I couldn't help but giggle at his meticulous process.

With a mock frown, Sam said, "Do you want me to go careless here?"

With a laugh, I shook my head. "Not at all. Now come here."

And he didn't need to be told twice.

The moment our naked bodies touched each other, we both sighed.

Sam's delicious weight on me had me writhing for more. More. More. More.

His entire length rubbed against me in the most delicious rhythm, and I twisted my hips for better contact.

Sam's eyes were pools of hunger and desperation. He groaned as he held my thigh in one hand and my neck in another and planted his lips on me.

He kissed me as if there was no tomorrow.

He touched me as if he could mark me his forever.

I held his back and felt his body move over me.

"Now, Sam. Please," I moaned and sucked his neck and grazed my hand along his lower back.

His entire body jerked violently. "Fuck. Yes."

He raised himself on one arm, took hold of himself and slowly pushed inside me.

Gasps filled the room the moment he was inside me.

"Hold still, sweetheart. Just a minute." He groaned, and took a few deep breaths in my neck, his arms trembling.

The fact that Sam still had a strong grip on my ass and my neck, in an attempt to keep me from moving, made me wild with want. I wrapped my legs around him which pushed him in deeper and made him jerk and hiss out a curse in a way I found absolutely thrilling.

My motion did him in, and he began to move within me. With every push in, he chanted my name. My name from his mouth had me seeing stars, and I couldn't stop my hips from moving with him.

It felt as if we'd been doing this for ages, but I'd never experienced this mindless intensity in my life. I wanted this to never end. Never wanted to lose the feeling of us being so close together.

Nothing mattered at this point.

We were simply two people trying to experience love in its purest form. In its most naked form.

We were at our most vulnerable, and I'd never felt safer or stronger.

I wanted more. With every thrust, I got greedy. I clawed at his back and grabbed his hair. I led his mouth to my neck, and Sam understood what I needed.

The moment he sucked my neck and squeezed my nipples hard, I exploded. Sam slowed down his thrusts till I finished, but the moment I was done, he grabbed my ass and gave himself to me. He kept pounding into me until he was screaming his orgasm in my neck.

Minutes passed, and we lay there, Sam still inside me, as we floated down from the high.

"Well, now you have the answer." Sam's gravelly voice

murmured in my ears as he placed gentle kisses on my cheeks, ears, and neck.

"What answer?" I asked, my voice hoarse.

"The first time we gave in to each other, you asked me how it would feel when we have sex, rather than just humping each other. Well, there you have it."

"Hmm..." I smiled, remembering our first night all over again.

"Hmm? Give me your words, sweetheart." Sam chuckled as he swept my hair behind my ear and kissed my lips.

"Keep doing that and I won't be able to say anything for a week. And to answer you, I haven't felt anything like this before. It was so much more than just an orgasm."

I ran my hands in Sam's hair and kissed him.

Sam was quiet while I kissed along his neck. His sex-soaked smell renewed my arousal, and I kissed him more.

I don't think I can feel this with another person ever again, I thought. It was both terrifying and utterly exhilarating.

I might've verbalized my thoughts because Sam growled and said, "You're not going to experience this with anyone except me, Akira."

"Only if you're not going to experience this with anyone except me. You're mine."

"And I don't ever want to. Now tell me you're mine too, baby," Sam said, as he took my heart.

"I'm yours." I barely had the words out before Sam was kissing me and showing me how we belonged to each other.

We slept when the room was washed with the early light of dawn, after exchanging a promise to make us work, no matter the odds against us.

CHAPTER 14

"I saw that you were perfect, and so I loved you. Then I saw that you were not perfect and I loved you even more."
  – Angelita Lim

Sam

It had been a week since we first had sex. And life had again resumed its routine. Well, not the old routine. A routine with a heavy dose of Akira.

We spent our days in the studio, attending classes, working on our projects and papers. The workload was so intense that we spent ten to fifteen hours a day in the studio.

And we usually spent our nights at my place, sometimes too exhausted to do anything but sleep, reconnecting with our bodies when we could steal the time.

Now, in the early morning, after spending the night without Akira, I missed her. She was back at her place after five nights of staying with me, since she ran out of all her fresh clothes. Even after spending all that time with her, I missed her.

I'd missed her through the night.

I'd missed having her in my arms, her presence in my bed.

I'd missed cuddling with her in the early mornings, sliding my legs between her cold ones.

I'd missed watching her make chai in my kitchen, wearing my T-shirt and her fuzzy socks.

I missed her even though she'd turned my life upside down with her colorful clothes, loud personality, and big heart. I still remembered the first time I saw Akira, my colorful girl, introducing herself and sharing her passion more than three months ago.

I had come to Columbia to learn about architecture, priming myself to take over my dad's business and let them enjoy their life together. Little did I know that I would be spending a lot more time learning about myself and what I truly wanted out of *my* life.

I hadn't even realized when my priorities had started to shift, but every day that I spent with Akira made me want to have more. Not only did I want to succeed in getting my degree and start running Wilson & White Construction, but I also wanted Akira by my side.

I wanted to be successful with her. I wanted to see her succeed in every aspect of her life and share them with me.

I was terrified of what spending her life with me would do to her relationship with her family. I wouldn't be able to handle seeing Akira regret choosing me. To regret me. To regret us. And it was my only prayer for our relationship—to not let Akira suffer the loss of her family. I didn't want to be the reason for that loss.

The moment she arrived in the class, I couldn't stop touching her the whole day. I couldn't resist dragging her in a supply closet and making out with her.

Akira still got a little shy every time I kissed her in public. Apparently, in India, you don't kiss in public. So, every time I gave her a peck on the lips in front of people, she got shy and equally aroused.

And she showed me how much she liked our public kissing in the bedroom. Just for that, I'd started showing a lot more affection in public than I normally would.

Right now, we were working on our design in the studio after a long day of classes. I was writing my research paper while Akira had gone with her friends to get some coffee. About fifteen minutes passed before she arrived, a coffee for me in her hand. As soon as she handed me my coffee and took her seat beside mine, my phone rang.

Mom calling...

"I need to get this. It's my mom," I told Akira as I got out of my seat, kissed her on the cheek and took my phone out of the studio. I turned around on my way out to see Akira blushing and trying to hide her smile.

"Hey, Ma," I said as I picked up the call.

"Sammy, honey. How are you?" Mom asked. We talked once or twice a week, and she would always start her conversation with this.

"I'm good. How are you? Your work okay? Dad?"

"Everything's fine. Your dad's good. Now, Sammy, Thanksgiving is in two weeks. And I just called to remind you of that. Do you know when you'll be coming home?"

Just two weeks. Wow. I didn't even realize how quickly time passed. What was Akira doing for Thanksgiving? And if she wasn't doing anything, I didn't want to leave her alone.

"I don't know, Ma. I might arrive the evening before Thanksgiving. And leave the next day. That work?" I asked, preparing myself for my mom's reaction.

"No! Why would you come all this way and go right back?"

I usually stayed home for a week. But maybe if Akira wasn't doing anything, I could invite her to join me.

"Umm. It's not that, Ma. But—umm, do you think I could maybe...uh...bring someone with me?" I cringed at my poor delivery.

She took in a sharp breath. "Oh, Sammy. Of course, you can bring someone. Who is she? And since when have you been dating?" Her voice rose with each question, and I tipped my head back in despair. I'd never invited a girl for Thanksgiving before, and this was going to send my mother over the top.

"It's Akira, Ma. Remember, I told you about her the last time we talked? She's my Indian friend," I rolled my eyes at myself for having to describe Akira as "Indian friend" as I continued. "And we're together now."

"Aww, Sammy. I'm so happy for you. And I had a good feeling about Akira. I told your dad that there might be something more between you two, with the way you were talking on and on about her. I'm so excited to meet her. You have to bring her with you."

"About that," I sighed. "I haven't asked her yet. I don't know if she has other plans. But I will give her the invite. I'll confirm with you if she is coming once I get a chance to invite her. Is that fine? And don't get your hopes up."

I didn't want to break my mom's heart in case Akira couldn't make it.

"Okay, honey. But do tell her that we would love to have her. Okay?"

"Yeah. I need to get back to work now, Ma. I'll call you later. Okay? Bye."

"Okay, honey. Bye. Call me soon. We'll talk more," she said, and I dropped the call. I knew what she wanted to talk more about.

I entered the class with a smile and sat beside Akira.

I ran my hands along her hair. I loved her hair. It was so black it glinted blue in the light of the studio.

She smiled at me and asked, "All okay with your mom?"

"Yeah, all good. What are you working on right now?"

"Oh, good. I'm done revising the drawings in Revit, so I'll convert the 3D into elevations and sections. If I still have time today, I'll probably start with cleaning up the lines and start making the drawings look presentable. You?" she asked, as she shifted in her seat.

"I'm working on my paper, but I still need to revise some of my drawings and work on my public amenities. I'll do the elevations tomorrow."

Akira frowned as she shifted again. "It's a little weird that I'm ahead of you in work. Am I missing something? Or are you doing some awesome designing that I don't know about?"

I smirked and said, "You'll see." She hated my vague answers. It got her all worked up.

Right on cue, her eyes flared. "You're an asshole."

I laughed and shook my head. "Last week I had a lot of work for one of my dad's projects. I'm just catching up."

That calmed her a little. So, I added, "Doesn't mean I'm not doing some awesome designing."

She fake-laughed as she turned to her computer and gave me the finger without looking at me. She shifted restlessly again.

"You alright?" I asked.

She turned red at my question and blurted, "Oh. Yes. I'm fine. Just thinking about my design."

That was weird. Akira usually thought loudly, murmuring incoherent things, generally in Gujarati, and listening to songs so loud that I could hear them through her headphones. But right now, she was way too quiet and restless.

"You sure, baby?" I asked again, hoping to get some answer out of her.

But she seemed to decide something mentally and stood up, murmuring, "I need to go. I'll be back in a bit."

Ever since the day we sat together and started working, Akira had started leaving for several minutes in the evening. Some days, she brought back some dinner or chai with her. Those days, I concluded that she'd gone home for some reason.

I wasn't going to pry into her personal matters then. But occasionally, she showed similar symptoms like today—blushing, restlessness, quietness, and abruptly leaving the studio for several minutes with an embarrassed or guilt-ridden look on her face.

I never asked where she went. It wasn't my place then.

I had my theories though.

My initial assumption was that she went to meet a boyfriend.

But once I got to know her a little, and she informed me that she wasn't seeing anyone, that theory was disproved.

Some of my unproven assumptions were:

1. She went to smoke
2. She went to free wine tastings that happened near our university
3. She had to tend to girl problems.

This hadn't happened in a while, and I had forgotten entirely about Akira's mysterious disappearances.

But I was her boyfriend now, and I think I had the right to ask her where she disappeared to for several minutes and *always* came back happier than usual. I wanted to know, dammit, and I wasn't going to back down this time.

While Akira logged off her computer and made a move to go outside, I asked, "Akira, would you mind if I join you?"

She stared at me for what felt like forever. My heart pounded and my palms turned sweaty. But I was determined to wear her down this time and find out what she has been hiding.

Either she noticed my determined face, or she finally decided to share her secret with me, but she eventually nodded.

We packed up our bags, switched off the class laptops, and

left the studio. I didn't even know where we were going, so I stayed behind her.

"Thanks for letting me join you," I said. I was genuinely grateful that she felt comfortable enough with me to share her secrets. *You cornered her and literally forced her to take you with her*, my mind screamed in disbelief.

Guess I was already listening to my new best friend, Heart, and Mind could take a back seat for now.

We walked toward the campus exit.

"It's no big deal. It's okay. I don't have anything to hide as such." Akira's rambling had me a tad worried.

Well, clearly, she did have something to hide.

"So, where are we going?" I asked her, as we neared the exit of the campus.

"My place," she mumbled.

I felt bad for being an insensitive jerk. She didn't have to tell me anything if it made her that uncomfortable.

"Hey, Akira, you don't have to take me with you. I have been wondering where you go, and what you do every time you leave in the evenings. If it's too personal, I'm really sorry. I shouldn't have forced myself upon you."

She struggled to look into my eyes.

She kept walking. And I followed her.

"Sam," she said, finally, "you don't have to apologize. I'm not hiding anything as such. I just feel weird explaining about where I go in the evenings."

She snickered, embarrassment coating her cheeks, as we walked toward her home. I went ahead and held her hand.

I decided to ask her for Thanksgiving dinner before she could tell me her secret. Not only would it convince her that it was safe to tell me anything, but if she decided to say yes to join me, she wouldn't be able to back out in case I screwed up my reaction to her secret. Well, technically, she could back out, but I'd at least have a chance to talk to her.

"Akira, remember the call I got from Mom a few minutes ago?"

She frowned at the direction I was taking the conversation.

"Yes...?" she asked, as lines pulled between her eyebrows.

"Well, she invited us for Thanksgiving dinner at their house."

I cringed at the horror on her face.

"That is, if you don't have any plans and would like to join me. I would love to have you with me. But if you have plans, I completely understand." *Stop talking, Sam.*

"You want me to meet your parents?" I couldn't tell if she was more nervous or horrified.

"Yes. I would love it. Akira, sweetheart, I really like you. And I want to be with you. Long term. I love learning all about Indian culture, food, movies, your family, and every little thing. I would love for you to meet my family and experience a little of my culture, of our holidays. Would you like that?"

I had to make her understand that I was in for the long haul.

Her secret wasn't going to change my feelings for her.

Akira's eyes glistened. She looked into my eyes and whispered, "I would love that."

We'd stopped in the middle of the street and hadn't even realized until someone's shoulder bumped into mine. He gave me a sour look, but nothing could deflate my joy at her answer.

I put my arm around Akira's shoulders and started walking toward her place before I voiced my question, "So, you'll come?"

She looked nervous, not horrified anymore, and asked, "You sure your parents wouldn't mind?"

I placed a kiss on the side of her head and confirmed, "Not at all. My mom is very excited to meet you. I promise."

She finally smiled at that. "Then, I'd love to join you. Thank you for inviting me."

And I couldn't help but kiss her, right there in the middle of the street.

She blushed all red and took out the key to her building.

We climbed the three flights of stairs up to her apartment. I couldn't stop sliding my arms down her back or in her hair. She laughed and shook her head. "Just saying, Sam. You have come here for literally no big reason. I'm, as such, not hiding anything from you."

"Well, you've said 'as such' every time you said that you aren't hiding anything from me. So, let's find out what's making you say 'as such' so many damn times. And besides, you can tell me anything, Akira."

She laughed nervously. "I know. Well, okay. But you can't laugh at me." She warned me and followed it with a fierce glare that made me want to laugh and also run back to the studio.

I tried to hide my smile and raised both my hands in surrender. "Fine. I won't laugh if your secret isn't funny." I winked and nudged her shoulder while she tried unlocking her door.

She pushed me away with her hip and said, "Ha. Ha. Very funny."

I quickly pulled her in for a kiss.

After I gave her a kiss that loosened up the tension a little and tightened up my pants a lot, I let her open the door to her apartment.

We walked to her room and put our bags on her desk. She started removing her boots and socks and got into flip-flops.

She walked in circles around the room twice before I stopped her. "Akira, just tell me. Obviously, it's something you are embarrassed about and might make me laugh. Don't stress over it so much, sweet—"

"I need to poop," she said, before I could complete my sentence.

"Oh," I stupidly blurted. She had to poop. Okay. Yeah, that's more important than our conversation.

My silence seemed to embarrass her, so I quickly composed myself and told her, "Please, go ahead. We can continue after you're done."

She frowned. I pointed to her bed as I took a seat. "I'll just wait here, baby."

She smiled and rolled her eyes. "Sam, I have been coming home every time to poop."

What? That's it?

All my agony over the past few months—where she was going, who she might've been with, what could she be doing—was over poop?

And she had warned me not to laugh.

I didn't laugh. I downright howled. Joyous relief burst free.

Before she could glare at me, I said in my defense, "Baby, so much mystery over poop. What's there to be embarrassed about? So, you poop. I poop, too. You didn't have to hide it from me."

She glared at my chuckle and said through her clenched teeth, "I wasn't hiding. I was just not announcing to everyone that I was going home to poop. It wasn't anybody's business. My shit is my business, pun intended."

She giggled at her own joke, setting me off again into fits of laughter.

"But why go home? We have a lot of great toilet facilities in Columbia, you know?"

I was so fucking glad this was her secret. My laughs were more of the joy at finding the innocence of her "not secret" as she mentioned it, and less at the hilarity of the situation.

"Well, they don't have a bathroom mug there, you know," she mumbled, and looked everywhere but at me.

"Bathroom mug?" I asked, because honestly, I had no idea what she was talking about. Why would someone want a mug in the bathroom? I couldn't even picture the stuff that she was talking about.

"Yeah. How else am I supposed to..." And then, she whispered the next words, "Wash, you know..." and trailed off with a waving motion around her butt.

"Wash your hands?" I asked, confused again.

"Sam," she whined and ran to the bathroom. But before I could follow her, she yelled from outside, "Stay there. I'm coming."

She was back in a minute.

And she held a small plastic container or "mug" in her hand.

"This"—she emphasized the mug—"is the bathroom mug." She then looked me in the eyes, took a deep breath, and said, "And I use this to wash my butt after I poop."

She waved the cup near my face—*the same cup she regularly used to wash her poopy butt.*

I jerked back out of range. "I think I threw up in my mouth a little bit."

She might've mistaken my disgust of the mug's proximity for disgust of washing her butt, because she reacted like a cornered animal.

"You think it's disgusting that I wash my ass after I poop?" she accused, hurt and anger warring on her beautiful face.

"No, baby," I snorted and laughed. God, the conversation we were having was mind-boggling.

But again, my laugh enraged her, which consequently made me laugh harder.

"What?" she yelled.

I laughed, "You look so grossly cute talking about your poopy ass and washing it."

She relaxed and snorted, "Fine. But consuming all that hot coffee and tea in the evening gets my motor running sometimes. And Columbia doesn't have a mug that I could use to wash, and I refuse to only wipe my ass. So, well, now you know what happens when I leave in the evening."

"Wait, what's wrong with wiping your ass?" I asked, now a little affronted myself.

"How can you even say that with a straight face? It's so gross."

"It is not gross. It is normal. And I can tell you, I've been doing that my whole life, and I'm a neat freak, remember? Touching your poopy ass is grosser."

"Huh. Let's say a lot of your poop got on your hand. Would you rather wipe it with a tissue or wash it with soap and water?" she asked, her eyes full of challenge.

I imagined the scenario.

My poop. On my hand.

I needed water, damn it.

Fuck.

"Ass is not the same as hands," I argued back.

She knew she had me by my weak argument and my green face.

"What did your ass do to you? Why not give it the same treatment as your hands?" she volleyed back, smiling.

I narrowed my eyes at her. "I don't use my ass for the same purposes as my hands."

She nodded along, pretending to understand. But I knew her. She was going for the killer blow. "Well, that may be so, Sam. But while we're naked and having hot, wild, dirty sex, and when I want to grab your ass to push you in deeper, I'm not going to be able to do it when you've not washed your ass. Such a shame, no?"

"You've never grabbed my ass while we've had sex. Ever," I remarked, shell-shocked. Fuck. How did I not notice?

"Well, of course. I couldn't risk getting your possible mistakenly unwiped poop on my hand."

She was gross as fuck. But fuck if I didn't find her arguments cute.

"You little—" But before I could grab her, she ran off to the bathroom shouting, "If I hold my poop any longer, it will slide back in and then I'll have constipation."

And I laughed so hard I had to sit down on the floor.

Fuck, I loved her.

Fuck.

Fuck.

Fuck.

I. *Loved.* Her.

I. Loved. Akira.

And I said that a hundred more times in my head, sitting on my beautiful girl's bedroom floor, dazed and crazed out of my mind.

I love her.

Her cute mannerisms and soulful eyes.

Her inherent openness to everyone and everything.

Her strength for moving to a new continent all alone.

Her ability to adapt to a whole new country, while still following her culture and traditions, even making me fall in love with them.

Her quick remarks and her laughs that came so easily.

Ever since I met her, I didn't even realize when my world started to revolve around hers. I never had a female friend before. And here was this girl, talking about the grossest of things and the most beautiful things with an openness that I'd never encountered before.

She made me want to talk *more.*

She made me want to live *more.*

Do *more.*

Be *more.*

I never really had a chance, did I?

I was in love.

And it was terrifying.

CHAPTER 15

"I am free, no matter what rules surround me. If I find them tolerable, I tolerate them; if I find them too obnoxious, I break them. I am free because I know that I alone am morally responsible for everything I do."

- Robert Heinlein

Akira

I was so nervous I might faint.

Sam and I were driving to his parents' house in upstate New York. His firm hold of my hand barely curbed my anxiety.

"Relax, sweetheart. It's going to be fine," Sam said, squeezing my hand.

I squeezed his back and didn't let go.

"Tell me about your parents," I said, trying to distract my mind from making up imaginary scenarios where I fail to impress his parents.

Sam squeezed my hand again, knowing how I felt. "Well, they are as in love with each other as they were when I was young. My mom is the talker of the house, sometimes embarrassingly so. They had me when they were forty-five."

I couldn't stop the shock on my face. That was really late.

"Is it safe to have a kid at forty-five?"

Sam shrugged. "Well, my parents tried for a kid for years. No success. They'd given up after trying for more than fifteen years of their marriage. They'd married young, at twenty. And on their twenty-fifth wedding anniversary, they found out that Mom was pregnant. And despite the doctors' warnings, Mom was adamant. Dad tried to reason with her, but you don't win an argument against Mom."

"That's amazing, Sam. I'm so glad your mom decided to have you. And now, I can't wait to meet her."

"You'll love her," Sam said, adoration and relief evident in his eyes.

"So, what do your parents do?"

"My mom is a history teacher in the district school. And my dad is the co-founder of Wilson & White Construction company. Luke's dad is his partner."

"Oh, so you've known Luke since you were kids?"

"Yeah. And I can't wait to start working, so Dad can finally retire. He's seventy-two. And he's still working. He's finally started staying in offices instead of going to construction sites. All the dust and construction materials were affecting his health."

I held his hand tight. "You'll be able to work full-time in your company in five semesters."

Sam held my hand tighter, his other hand white-knuckling the steering wheel. "I hate that he works. He needs to relax. Travel the world with Mom. And it kills me that I'm not already there. I try and help out as much as I can. I spend my summers working, and draft up designs and details every chance I get. But I really wish I was doing more."

"That is more, Sam. You are doing your best, and that's what matters. If you want, I can help you out in drafting too. Only if you want. I'd love to help out."

I couldn't bear to see him so disheartened. I'd do anything to help him out.

Sam looked at me, taking his eyes off the road, his eyes glistened. "You'd do that?"

I touched his jaw. "You even have to ask?"

He shook his head, as if stopping himself from saying more, and focused on the road.

After a few minutes of driving, Sam cleared his throat and asked, "So, what does your life look like after five semesters?"

A smile tugged at my lips. "Are you asking me if I plan to stay in the States or go back to India?"

Sam squeezed my hand and, without meeting my eyes, said, "I've been thinking about it for a while now."

"Well, ideally, after graduating, I would like to work in an architecture firm in New York. Get a work visa and continue working here for as long as possible. It wouldn't hurt if the company I work for sponsors me for a green card, so that I can be free to work for whatever company and in whatever field I want to work in. And in my ideal world, you would be with me all along. How does that sound?"

Sam's chest was rising and falling, and with a rough whisper, he said, "Sounds perfect."

He placed a kiss on the back of my hand and put them back on his thigh.

We were silent for a while. Seemed like we both needed to catch our breaths. A weight seemed to have lifted off my shoulders. Sam liked the idea of us being together in years to come. It was exhilarating yet calming. I couldn't wipe off the smile on my face even if I tried. And looking at Sam, he was in the same boat with me.

"So, how far is your parents' house now?"

"Just a few minutes."

"What if I offend them in some way?" I asked, as we seemed to get closer.

Sam tried to hide his smile and failed. I glared at him. But I was so glad to see his smile.

He chuckled. "My parents don't get offended too easily. My mom is really looking forward to meeting you."

As if I wasn't nervous enough already. "She is?"

He let go of my hand and maneuvered a turn on the road. "Yeah. She has called me twice to confirm if you have any allergies, what foods you like, what you don't like, that sort of thing."

That didn't sound bad. It was the first time I was meeting a boyfriend's parents. And I had absolutely no idea how to make a conversation with a boyfriend's parents. Also, I wasn't exactly an expert in middle-aged American people. I've never had a conversation with that generation of Americans, outside of a few professors.

"Hmm. What if they don't like me?" I asked.

Sam snorted at that. Snorted. "What happened to my bold, outgoing, I-don't-give-a-shit-about-what-others-say Akira? She would never question herself. But, to answer your question, I am the toughest person to please in our family, and you have managed to make me fall—" He paused, shook his head, and continued. "Managed to make me like you very, very much."

Before I could comment, Sam took a turn into a gated community, and we entered a street lined with beautiful houses and gigantic trees.

The houses were a beautiful mix of historic and contemporary architecture, glass fighting with terracotta. Concrete making love to wood. And stone and bricks creating elegant and sturdy walls and columns.

Sam took a few more turns and we finally reached a gated entryway. He rang the bell and the door automatically buzzed and started opening.

He gave my hand a quick peck on the knuckles and parked the car under the covered parking space at the side of the house. We got out of the car, and the fine piece of architecture that he got to call "home" stood tall in front of me. The entire house had exposed brick and gigantic windows. As we climbed the steps to the highly decorated entrance door, Sam rang the doorbell.

"You didn't have to change your dressing style for today. I love your colorful clothes," Sam whispered as we waited for the door to open.

"I just want to impress your parents," I admitted, a little embarrassed, as I looked down at my new, light blue dress and nude heels. I carried a present in one hand and clutched Sam's hand with another.

"You look gorgeous. But don't change yourself for anyone. I love the way you dress," he said, and I noticed the slight blush that appeared on Sam's cheeks at the L-word. I was pretty sure even he could see the same blush dotting my cheeks.

We didn't even have to wait a whole minute after our conversation before an older version of Sam opened the door. A *much* older version.

"Sam! Son, come here." Sam's dad pulled him in for a hug.

"Happy Thanksgiving, Dad."

"Happy Thanksgiving, Sammy," his dad said, his face brightening when he saw me behind his son.

"Ah, who do we have here?"

Sam came and put his arm around me. "Dad, this is Akira, my girlfriend. Akira, that's my dad."

I pushed my hand—hopefully non-sweaty—forward. "Hello, Mr. White. Happy Thanksgiving."

His dad's eyes warmed, and he smiled at me, the same smile that Sam gave me when he thought I was funny. "Happy Thanksgiving, Akira. And please call me Daniel."

Daniel put his arm around me and led us inside. "Let's go sit in the kitchen. Sam, your mom is almost done with the cooking. Let's see if she needs anything."

Sam's father, or Daniel—it was so weird to call my boyfriend's father by name instead of "uncle" because, in India, every man older than you was addressed as an uncle or a brother—went ahead of us to the kitchen, while Sam and I removed our coats.

He held my hand, kissed me softly—I blushed every freaking time—and led me into the main living space.

I couldn't believe I was looking at Sam's childhood home. Even though the house was big, it felt warm.

The living room had a fireplace along one wall, with leather couches and one gray couch with colorful pillows arranged in a C-shape across it. Enticing aromas carried us toward the kitchen, where Frank Sinatra sang in the background.

Soft murmurs and hearty giggles floated around the space.

The moment we entered, Sam's mom rushed toward us and engulfed him in a tight hug. She held him for an entire minute, and Sam held her back as fiercely. Their warm affection and embrace reminded me of my own family and almost brought me to tears.

But before I could get lost in my memories, they let go of each other, and Sam's mom stood before me in all her glory.

"Mom, this is Akira. My girlfriend."

"Hello, Mrs. White. Happy Thanksgiving. I brought—" I was engulfed in a hug before I could offer her the wine that I'd gotten her.

Sam and Daniel laughed, and I tried not to cry at the warm feeling at being hugged by a mother. I missed my mom.

"Rose, let the poor girl go. You're crushing her present," Daniel said.

Sam's mom gasped. "I'm so sorry, dear. And please call me Rose. I'm so glad you could make it."

"Mom," Sam warned.

Rose laughed. "Oh, hush. Could you please help your father

prepare the salad? And please set the table, dear. I'll give a tour of the house to Akira."

Clearly, the men of the house adored her and were used to helping in the kitchen because both of them took up the knives and got to work.

Rose showed me hundreds of pictures of baby Sam and told me all the embarrassing stories. The more we talked, the more we laughed. After about half an hour, we made our way back to the kitchen, which opened into the dining room. Sam and his dad had set up the table in spectacular fashion with some candles, the bottle of wine that Sam and I had brought, and all the food.

I couldn't help but compare them to the men in my family. Not once had I seen any men in my family help the women. I had never seen my father or uncle make even a cup of tea on their own.

Seeing such glaring differences in culture opened my eyes to how different and normal and wonderful it could be when a man and a woman shared their life instead of living a shared life.

As we took our seats, Sam and I on one side of the table and Daniel and Rose on the other, everyone said a small prayer— even my parents and grandparents do that in India—and started filling up the plates.

Dinner was a somewhat quiet affair, all of us scarfing down the mouth-watering delicacies that Rose had made.

Since I was a vegetarian, she had prepared some great vegetarian sides for me like mushroom risotto, mashed potatoes, green beans, roasted vegetables, and freshly made pumpkin bread. Most of these dishes could be a little spicier but well, I wasn't going to complain. It was still delicious.

The rest of them had some more sides and, of course, the poor turkey. Sinatra was our soundtrack. The entire time, Sam had his hand on my thigh, that he occasionally squeezed, ran his hand along my leg, and, once in a while, he simply held my free hand.

Once the dinner was done, Sam put on a pot of coffee for all of us, and Rose got the pie out. Daniel led me to the living room, where he turned on the electric fireplace and the blaze came to life with the flip of a switch.

He sat on the brown leather couch, and I settled on the gray love seat, with a turquoise pillow in my lap.

"So, Akira, how is America treating you?" Daniel asked.

I often got this type of question from professors and my classmates. Overall, I had the best of times in the States. But, when someone asked such a broad question, I could either give a very verbose answer or just give a very "American" answer.

I chose the latter. "Pretty good."

Daniel raised his eyebrows at me and said, "Don't you be vague, Akira. Sam has already informed his mother that you are a talker. Don't hold back for us. I would love to know about your experience."

"That tattletale!" I burst out. Daniel let an amused chuckle escape.

It was right then that Sam and his mom entered the living room with coffee and pie. I went and took the tray of pie from Rose.

"Rose, please, take a seat. Sam and I will serve it."

She smiled at me and got settled beside Daniel.

My eyes found Sam, and I couldn't stop staring at him. He looked so relaxed and carefree. He placed the tray of coffee and cups beside the pie and ran his free hand in my hair with a loving smile, right there in front of his family. We would soon need to talk about this when it came to PDA in front of my family.

We served the pie and coffee to Rose and Daniel, fixed our dessert, and sat on the love seat.

"So, what were you laughing about, Dad?" Sam asked, and took a bite of the pie.

"Well, Akira was going to tell us about her experience in the States," Daniel answered.

~

Sam

Interesting. I never thought to ask something so simple to Akira. Every day, she got excited by "American things" and I just assumed that she was having a blast experiencing this country. It never occurred to me to find out how my country treated her. If she had an opinion on how we did things here.

Every time I thought I'd gotten sensitive toward Akira's culture and her being new to the country, something happened that reminded me how naive I was.

Thank you, Dad.

Akira looked at me for help. Poor thing got roped into a tough spot. Her voice was silent, but her eyes screamed passionate sentences. I squeezed her hand in encouragement and nodded at her. "Tell us. I really want to know too."

She smiled, took a deep breath, and on an exhale, she looked at all of us and started, "Well, Daniel, honestly, America has truly treated me well. I love the architecture here, the university is amazing, the desserts, the weather, and the fact people from all around the world can be found in one city is awesome.

"Mind you, India is also a highly diverse country with people of different religions, castes and sub-castes. But all of them are Indian. Like, back home, I wouldn't have to think twice before guessing whether someone around me is Indian or not. But here, I can never guess which country the next person might belong to, you know. And that is just mind-blowing."

Always trust Akira's mind to surprise the hell out of me. It's innocent, yet powerful. Or maybe every person from another country feels the same for America. I'm sure I looked enamored by her. Mom looked utterly fascinated too, and my dad had switched his position on the sofa from lying back to leaning forward.

"You'd never look at the people that way if you've lived here your whole life. With the political scene right now, you've not had to deal with racism or hate crimes, have you? If there's anything, just let me or Sam know, and we'll be there for you, okay, honey?" Dad said.

As far as I knew, Akira spent most of her days in the studio with me. And other than that, she spent her time with some class friends and her roommates. Our lack of a social life might have been disappointing, but with the workload of the university, we didn't really have the time to think about much beyond our little world.

Akira shook her head. "No, no. Nothing like that, Daniel. To be honest, I was prepared to face some form of racism. But I guess, most of my time is spent between the five blocks from Columbia to my house. And even at school, I'm mostly hanging out with Sam and some of my international friends. It helps to hang out with people facing similar challenges, you know."

"Absolutely," Dad said.

She nodded, and continued, "What saddens me is how some white people treat their fellow Americans. As a developed country, I expected better. But here I come to *America* and find that so many white people behave in the same manner as a lot of majority group behave toward the other minority groups as they do back home."

Mom frowned, and asked, "Oh, is it that bad in India? Forgive me, but I am not aware of the political scene in India."

Akira gave a short, mirthless laugh. "Oh, it's bad. And getting worse. Religious intolerance, Casteism, Colorism, India getting downgraded from free to partly free in democracy. I mean, you guys are seeing similar things here in violence against Black and Asian Americans, and other problems in the name of religion."

Dad nodded. "Yes, and it's horrifying."

Akira nodded, and said, "It is. Fortunately, it hasn't been too bad for me. But, you know, I think second generation immigrants have worse than me right now."

Dad took a sip of his coffee, and asked, "How so?"

"I mean, for instance, imagine the situation of a Desi American. You know, an American born to Indian immigrants here. For so many white people here, they're not American enough, and for us who're born and brought up in India, I would never be able to connect with them. They are the epitome of privilege for immigrants like me."

Akira looked at me, and at my nod, continued. "Growing up as an American, they never have to worry about immigration. Less tuition fees. And yet, I feel like they have to constantly battle between being American while embracing their culture.

"And as if that wasn't enough, Black and Asian American people are facing such brutal violence. They might be feeling so betrayed. Your own countrymen stabbing you, killing you, treating you like you don't belong. I *know* I don't belong, and I am not an American. But they are. They are as American as Sam, you know. It's just sad. And all because we look a little different and have different amounts of melanin."

"I hear you," said Daniel.

Everyone was quiet after that. Mom and Dad sipping their coffees, lost in thoughts.

Akira turned to me, and asked, "Did I totally ruin the happy mood?"

Before I could deny her, Mom jumped in. "Not at all, Akira. We asked. And I am so glad that you talked to us."

"Absolutely, Akira. More often than not, we forget the privilege we have in the smallest of things. And we must do better."

I rubbed by hand along Akira's back, trying to show my support. Because what else was there to say? I would always be there for her. Listen to her.

She turned to me and squeezed my knee in thanks.

Dad got up from his seat and took the tray of empty coffee mugs toward the open kitchen. When Akira got up to help with the tray of empty pie dishes, Mom told her to stay put. She gathered the plates and followed Dad.

Akira and I watched as my dad pulled Mom in his arms for a dance, as one of their favorite songs played in the background.

We sat on the love seat, staring at my parents, who were slow dancing to the tune of "Strangers in the Night." Akira laid her head on my shoulder. I pulled her back on the love seat so that I could put my arms around her.

I could smell her fresh citrus scent, and I couldn't help taking another deep breath, taking her in as much as I could. I placed a kiss on her forehead, and she snuggled deeper.

The slow tune of the song took me back to the beginning of *us.* How irritated I used to get with Akira's bubbliness. Her qualities that once used to make me wonder about her sanity had now become my favorite quirks. Her beautiful thoughts, her inquisitive mind, and her unfiltered words had uprooted my once-silent, comfortable life.

Life with Akira looked a lot like her festival of Navratri—full of music, colors, and heart-throbbing beats of happiness. And I wanted all of her and everything that she had to offer.

Could she hear my rapidly beating heart?

Did she feel the same?

We were together yet lost in our thoughts when the next song brought all my feelings to the surface. The opening notes of Sinatra's "I Love You, Baby" started playing. And when Akira turned in my arms and met my eyes, my world again shifted on its axis.

She didn't take her eyes off me. Not once.

Neither did I.

And I knew.

Her eyes shone with unexpressed emotions—emotions so strong, Akira couldn't speak.

But I didn't need the words right now.

Just the knowledge that she felt the same way about me was enough for today.

All I needed right now was her.

Just her.

Before I did anything stupid and kissed her senseless right in front of my parents, I gave my beautiful girl a quick peck on her lips to bring her out of the daze and got up. I needed to go home with Akira. I desperately wanted to show her what she was doing to me.

I headed to where Mom and Dad were dancing and putting the dishes in the dishwasher. Mom saw me approaching, and she exchanged a look with Dad. Dad left and headed to where Akira was sitting in silence.

I had spent enough time with Akira to know that when she went silent, it was because her emotions overwhelmed her. It happened during Navratri when I first kissed her. The next time it happened was when she was going home to do her business most evenings. I might've been staring too long at Akira and Dad making conversation, because Mom tapped my cheek.

"You all right, Sammy?" Mom asked.

Was I all right? *No.*

Try terrified. Overwhelmed. Falling at full speed without a parachute.

Only a heavy sigh came out of me at this point.

"I don't know. So, what do you think about Akira?" I inquired, as I started helping Mom with the cleanup.

"I love her, Sammy," Mom exclaimed.

"Yeah. Me too," I blurted out. Accidentally.

My eyes widened.

So did Mom's.

Mine in horror and embarrassment.

Hers in delight and excitement.

"I know, my sweet boy. It makes me so happy you've found someone," Mom said, hugging me.

"I haven't told her yet. What if she doesn't feel the same?" Just great. All my vulnerabilities had to pour out at the same time.

"That girl hasn't stopped looking at you or talking about you once. She looks at you like you hung the moon, Sammy. I'd say she loves you too," she said gently.

If only it were that easy. "It's not that simple, Ma. Things are a little complicated on her family's end. They might have some serious issues with this relationship."

"How serious are we talking here?"

"There is a possibility that Akira's family might marry her off to someone else, or worse, make her choose between them and me. And I would hate myself forever if she had to make a choice, because she loses in every scenario. It makes me so mad to just think about that." My voice cracked toward the end, in anger and sadness.

Mom ran soothing hands on my back. "Oh, honey. She must be so brave to stand up for herself, despite the consequences. And, Sammy, if that girl is ready to fight her family for you, that itself screams her love for you. Who would be willing to give up their family?"

"I know, Ma. My admiration for her far exceeds my love for her."

"I'm so proud of you, Sammy. You both might have tough days moving forward, but remember, you do have us. Always. Akira now has a family here too."

I choked back the lump in my throat and hugged my mom with all I had. What if Mom had reacted in a different way? What if we didn't have her support? What if she had refused to accept us? I would've never realized the importance of acceptance by family if I wasn't facing this battle with Akira.

"Mom, I know I usually stay for a few days, but I need to go home tonight. Is that okay?" I asked as I kept my arms around her.

"Of course, sweetie. Go get your girl. If I'm not wrong, your dad might be laying on all the charms to get her back soon."

We laughed, and I kissed her cheek as I went back to drag Akira home with me.

I needed her.

As I went to the living room, I asked her, "You wanna head home, sweetheart?"

She frowned for a second. She knew we had planned to stay for the weekend. Our bags were in the car. But she might be desperate, too, because she just nodded and got up.

My parents gave us hugs and ordered Akira to be back soon.

She agreed and thanked my parents.

I held her hand as we got into the car.

Just like the first time I kissed her, just like all the other days after that, I held her hand all the way home.

CHAPTER 16

"Love is of all passions the strongest, for it attacks simultaneously the head, the heart, and the senses."
   - Lao Tzu

Akira

It was past midnight when we reached Sam's place. The entire way home, I was lost in thoughts. It started when Sam and I had watched his parents dancing in the kitchen.

All I could do was imagine myself with Sam. Hoping. Wishing. Dreaming. To be with him like that. To be able to share such a moment of sweetness with him, without any fear of my parents' approval. Without any prejudices. To have a love that is so simple, yet so powerful.

At that moment, I realized the feeling coursing through me. Love.

But it wasn't just love.

Loving Sam was my truth. A truth that I accepted every day ever since we got together.

Not being able to love him *freely* was my reality. A reality that had been slowly creeping on me while we grew together.

It was this reality that kept me from telling Sam the truth.

I loved Sam.

I loved him so much it terrified me.

Courage to face my family, my world, had started gathering in my heart. Every day, that courage grew stronger. It pushed me to open up. It screamed at me to spit the words out. But I knew. I knew that the moment the words were out in the universe, it would mean I was ready to face my family. It would mean I chose Sam over them.

My parents had not married for love. They had an arranged marriage. I've seen my parents respect each other. I've seen affection between them. I've seen the humor. Never love.

I'd never known what love looked like between two people in real life. The only love I'd known and seen was in Bollywood movies, between friends and people I knew.

But watching Sam's parents, for the first time in my life, I saw what love looked like between parents.

It wasn't the hyperbolic version shown in Bollywood movies.

Love was just a state of being. To simply exist with a person in a harmony that was perfect just for them. To feel settled and calm by their mere presence in your life.

And I wanted it. Desperately.

For myself.

With Sam.

Only him.

He was the only one I could think of every time I conjured up a dream of my life in the next ten years, or the next twenty years, or the next fifty years.

It was Sam who I saw. Holding me. Dancing with me. Marrying me. Having kids with me. Doing the boring, adult stuff every day with me. Getting even crankier in his old age and snapping at the nurse as we rested on separate beds when we were ninety.

With all these images swirling in mind, the moment Sam led me to his room, I stopped him with a squeeze of my hand. He turned with a worried frown.

"You okay, sweetheart?"

His "sweetheart" got to me.

Every. Damn. Time.

This time, though.

It only fueled me.

"I love you."

The words flew out of me. I couldn't have contained them even if I wanted to. Sam had slowly become my world. He had taken over my dreams. A forever with him was my only prayer. And my heart was hell-bent on making it a reality.

Tears blurred my vision. "I love you so much. I can understand if you aren't feeling the same..."

Sam's solid warmth enveloped me in a fierce hug.

"Oh, Akira. I love you too, baby. So fucking much," he said, resting his forehead on mine.

Tears welled in my eyes. One or two slipped out.

"You do? You're not saying it just because I said it?" I confirmed, too scared for the answer.

"You kidding me? I've been dying to tell you how much I love you," he admitted to my shock and utter relief.

"Then why didn't you?"

He held my face in his one hand, so much love shining in his eyes. It made my heart pound.

"I never wanted to put that burden on you. I didn't want to be the reason you had to choose between your family and me. I still don't. I was worried that if I said something before you did, you would've been forced to decide whether you wanted to fight for an 'us' before you were ready. I couldn't do that to you, Akira," Sam said, wiping my tears that steadily ran along my cheeks.

"Oh, Sam. Have I told you how much I love you?" I cried.

"You might've mentioned it before. Could you refresh it for me?" He kissed my cheeks, my neck, and gently bit my ear.

"I love you, Sam. God, so much. I am going to fight so hard to be an 'us.' Just wait and watch."

And I kissed him.

I kissed him with all the love I had for him. With every kiss, Sam groaned. His hands were all over me as he lifted me against the door. The more we kissed, the hungrier we got.

I couldn't stop kissing him. His neck. His jaw. His collarbone. I clutched his shirt and pulled it across his body to get more access to his shoulders and chest. All the while, Sam rocked into me.

The moment I rocked against him, all bets were off.

Sam carried me to his bed and threw me on the perfectly made bed. He pulled off the sheets from all the edges in one sharp tug. I went under the sheets and Sam was on me, grabbing at my dress.

"Off. I want it all off," Sam groaned, quickly taking off my dress. I was so glad I had worn a dress and not pants.

The moment I was naked, he was on me, placing hungry, biting kisses all over my neck, still fully clothed.

"Sam, take off your clothes. Please," I moaned, urgency rushing through my veins. The need to have him closer. Every brush of his clothes on my naked skin had sparks lighting up my body. I grabbed his shirt and pulled him even closer to me so that all of him rubbed against me.

I dragged his shirt above his head. He quickly got out of his remaining clothes and got a condom on, slowly, all the while I burned. His eyes trailed over my body while I watched him touch himself and roll on the condom.

The moment he re-aligned us, naked, we moaned loudly.

The closeness. Sam's hot skin against mine. His touch.

Everything intensified my need for him.

I moved my hips to get closer to him.

"Yes," he hissed.

He licked me.

He kissed me.

He sucked me.

Every inch of me burned with pleasure.

For every kiss and every bite, he told me how much he loved me.

With every thrust inside me, he recalled every moment he loved me more.

"Remember when you wore that Navratri dress? I wanted to bend you over the bed, pull up your skirt and just fuck you." *Thrust.*

"Every time you fucking laugh, I get hard." *Thrust.*

"Fuck, I love your boobs." *Thrust.*

With every sweet line and crude word, he got me higher and higher. I felt like I could touch the moon, and he was the only one grounding me. He took me higher and pulled back. Back and forth. On and on he went, making me crazier and wetter.

He groaned when I squeezed him tight.

I moaned when he thrust especially hard.

I wanted to come. So fucking much.

"I don't ever want this to end," Sam moaned.

Oh, the fucking irony!

I knew he was close. His thrusts turned frantic, no rhythm whatsoever. He was unraveling, and I was so fucking close. I needed him to go harder and faster, and fucking lose control.

I knew he was going to pull back but no more.

I grabbed his ass with both of my hands and jerked him inside. Hard.

He yelled.

"Akira, fuck! Don't stop." And I remembered.

I jerked my hands from his ass and asked, "Did you wash your ass today?"

He groaned loudly and put his head at my neck. "Akira, I swear to God. I had a shower later. Now fucking squeeze my ass like before."

I didn't wait another second.

I grabbed his ass, and Sam whimpered in my neck, all the while thrusting.

"Harder. Squeeze harder, baby," he groaned.

His desperate need took me over the edge and had me coming so hard, my eyes rolled back, my body locked up, and I squeezed Sam's ass so hard he would have the imprint of my nails on his ass for days.

But Sam loved it all, because he fucking lost it. His thrusts became frantic, sweat gathered between our bodies, and he groaned so loud in my neck as he came that I almost had another orgasm.

Everything fell silent around us as we came down from the high, like the silence after a storm.

Sam was still inside me.

He kissed my neck, eased out of me slowly.

He had just thrown the knotted condom in the garbage when I got the words out. "So, you like your ass squeezed, huh?"

"Shut up," he grumbled, redness coating his cheeks.

I laughed, he was cute. "I love your ass."

He groaned in embarrassment and pulled me in his arms.

I laid my head on his shoulder and laid my hand on his chest, feeling his warmth, his strength. "I love you, Sam. I can't believe I get to have you."

Because I truly couldn't believe it. I felt incredibly lucky to have found someone who loved me and respected me.

"Oh, baby. You've got it the other way around. I am the lucky one. Even my mom says so," he admitted, kissing my hair.

"Really? Your mom liked me?"

"Of course, she did. Have you seen you? And both my parents loved you."

"Well, one family down. One more to go," I said.

Sam noticed the sadness in my tone. He gently lifted my head and kissed me on the mouth. "We're going to get them too. You just see."

His use of the word "we" brought me a renewed sense of hope.

We will get my parents too.

We will win them over.

The only question was "How?"

CHAPTER 17

Sam

Akira loved me.

Hours passed.

And she loved me.

Days passed.

And she loved me.

We told our friends about us. I told Luke. Akira told her roommates and her friends in the university.

We all started hanging out together.

Luke and I occasionally had dinners at Akira's place with her roommates.

Our worlds came together.

And Akira still loved me.

Together, we celebrated Diwali. Akira described it as a festival where friends and families come together, have dinner, enjoy fireworks, and make some rangoli—making colorful designs with colored powder at the entrance of the house.

This had been Akira and her roommates' first Diwali away from home. So, we'd organized our own little Diwali party. Akira had dressed up in a long, backless kurta, tight pants, and her gorgeous, flowy, dupatta that had made me lose my mind.

The girls had decorated their place with lots of lights, candles, and colors. We had invited all our friends. Even my parents had shown up for a while. Akira and her roommates had prepared some homemade delicacies, and we'd ordered some Indian food from Akira's favorite place.

Akira had video-called her family and shown everyone the festivities. No introductions were made when she had shown the house full of people. All of us were introduced as friends to her family. All fourteen of her family members had been present, and the conversation had been indecipherable on the other side of the phone.

When everyone had left that night, and it was just the two of us in her twin-sized bed, Akira had apologized to me for putting me in the "friends" category when she had introduced us to her family.

"I don't want you to think that I'm not proud of us. I love us so much," she'd said, snuggling deeper into my arms.

"There is no need for you to apologize. I understand. I wasn't expecting you to introduce me as a boyfriend."

And it was the truth. I hadn't expected Akira to introduce me as a boyfriend. I'd been prepared, considering our situation. But it had still stung. Not because she had introduced me as a friend. But because she *had to* introduce me as a friend.

That had been just the first of many more times that Akira had apologized to me for hiding our relationship. Every time one of her family members video-called her, which was every single day, I had to leave her bedroom, or her vicinity, for her to talk. Every time, she hadn't been able to meet my eyes later.

Hiding us from her family had started to weigh on my girl. And I didn't know what to do. I would not force her to admit anything before she was ready, and the time was right. But I didn't even know when that time was.

I was still coming to terms with the fact that I was in love with a girl who wasn't of my own country. She was from India. A fucking whole new country that I knew nothing about.

Right now, I sat in her living room, while she talked to her mom and younger brother in her bedroom. The three of them were apparently gossiping over the girls that her mom was considering for their older brother, Aakar. Arranged marriage conspiracy was going on right across the room. Something completely antiquated for me, while completely normal for Akira.

Akira came out of the room after a few minutes. I put aside the design I'd been working on for Dad, and opened my arms for her. She quickly came on my lap and rested her hand on my shoulder.

"You know, our generation in America would never agree to an arranged marriage," I said.

She looked up at me, and finally met my eyes. With a frown, she asked, "What if someone doesn't find anyone till they're forty? Won't their parents find someone for them even then? Even if they're alone?"

So innocent, the poor thing.

"Sweetheart, most of them would rather be alone than trust their parents' choice of a partner."

With a frown, she mumbled, "Huh. My parents would be on my case the moment Aakar decides on a girl to marry— arranged or not."

Now that was news. Disturbing, to say the least.

I turned her to face me. Up until now, she had been sitting with her face in my shoulder, trying to get back to normal after feeling guilty about the video call.

"What do you mean 'on your case'?"

She rolled her eyes at me as if I was overreacting. I didn't think I was.

"Explain, Akira. Has your mom talked to you about

marriage, to specific guys, before? Or are you just predicting that she would get on your case after Aakar's marriage?"

"She might've sent me a few photos of some guys she's looking at," she mumbled, not able to meet my eyes.

"What?" That was news.

"I rejected every single one of them, Sam. Without even looking. Where are you going?" she called after me as I got up from the couch. I needed to move.

How did I not know that Akira was still looking at other guys? I had come to know that her mother sent her photos of guys when she mentioned it during the tutorial session with her roommates. But I thought that was occasionally.

And I had just assumed she would've refused to see those guys' photos ever since we got together.

"Sam, just listen to me for a second, will you? At least let me explain. Please, baby?" she pleaded. And she called me "baby." Of course, I was gonna listen now. How did my life go from discipline and order to chaos and surprises?

"Well, go on, then," I said, and pulled her into her room. I got the chair from her desk, placed it across from her bed and took a seat.

"Where do I start?" Akira asked, sitting across me on the edge of the bed.

"How long has your mother been showing you pictures of guys for an arranged marriage?" I asked my first question, the most important one.

"She has been looking for about two years. Showing me maybe the past nine months," Akira answered in a somber tone.

Two years. Nine months.

"Are you in a rush to marry?" I asked. What if getting married was her priority? What if someone better came along? What if she changed her mind to fight for us?

Every question brought a sharp stab of pain in my chest. I had to keep rubbing along my chest to hold myself together.

"Oh my God. No, Sam. I am in no rush to marry. This is so complicated to explain. Ugh... Can I start from the beginning?" she asked, frustrated and oddly annoyed.

God knew what she was annoyed for. I was the one potentially getting ditched for some guy she'd never even met.

"Please," was all I could get out.

She took three deep breaths, likely collecting her thoughts and trying to put them in words. Once she was ready, she looked at me, gave a tiny smile, and said, "So, in India, most parents start looking for a guy for their daughters once they are done with undergrad. Some even before that. Arranged marriages are very much normal in India, maybe because most of the cities don't have a dating culture. Or because that's all the parents of our generation know. Or maybe because people don't want to expand beyond their caste."

I nodded, trying to understand. It all sounded very archaic to me but who was I to comment on her culture. She saw the baffled look on my face, and with a softer tone, kept going.

"But, just know that it's normal for daughters to start getting proposals from different families once we have graduated. It was the same for me. Mom didn't consider any proposals before I was done with my undergrad. But after that, while I was working in India, she started considering the proposals. and kept asking me if I was ready. But every time I said no, she stopped the conversation."

When she spoke next, she clutched my hand in hers, her eyes pleading with me to understand her. "But when I decided to come to the States to study, she got a little worried. Either she was afraid that I might find someone here, or that I might not find anyone at all, and that made her take action. She started showing me some guys, and I kept rejecting them."

I believed her. I was entranced by Akira's life in India. I kept forgetting that she had a whole other life in India.

We talked a lot about India. Sometimes funny quirks and lifestyle stories. And sometimes the sad and unforgiving nature of the overpopulation in India.

But we rarely talked about her life with her family. Akira hadn't been able to be open about her family as much as I'd hoped.

The fact that she had to create a wall, or rather *be* a wall between her family and me, restricted her from sharing intimate details about her life with her family. But the more she opened up, the clearer our circumstance appeared to me.

Akira had opened a small door in her wall, and I wanted as much as I could get.

I was glad she had rejected every guy she saw.

"Go on." I encouraged her with my words and pleaded with my eyes.

She smiled and squeezed my hand. "Since I've come here, in every other phone call, Mom asks me if I've found any good Indian boy."

The sharp intake of my breath had her looking up at me with worried eyes. "What do you tell her?"

She shrugged, a little defeatedly. "What do I even say? It's not like I'm going to say yes to any guy that Mom shows me. I love you, Sam. But I can't just tell my mom that I don't need a nice Indian boy because I've already found a nice American boy. Silence has been my only choice."

Fuck, I loved her so much. As angry as it made me that she was looking at other guys' pictures, it made me much sadder that Akira had been suffering in silence. And I had known nothing.

I loved Akira. I couldn't imagine not spending the rest of my life with her.

Fuck.

Did I just imply that I would marry Akira? *Yes, you did.*
Of course I did.

When did I fall so fucking deep?

Was I terrified? *Yeah.*

Was I okay with it? *Hell, yeah.*

Fuck.

I didn't even know that she had all this going on in her life. I had been blissfully unaware in the happy bubble I had created around myself. All along, I thought Akira was in the bubble with me, but she had been right outside it, protecting *my* bubble from bursting open.

Not anymore.

"Why didn't you tell me, baby?" I had to understand.

She let out a sad, hopeless laugh, one I hated to my very bones. "How could I have possibly told you that my mom has been looking for a guy for me to marry? Even right now, it sounds like I'm saying, 'Sam, marry me or someone else will.' And I don't want to assume the status of our relationship or force you into something that you don't want."

I almost laughed. This girl. This sweet, beautiful girl.

"I'd marry you in a heartbeat, sweetheart. I can't imagine not spending the rest of my life with you. You're it for me," I said, holding her cheeks, my forehead touching hers. I had never been in love before. Never felt someone so deep in me that they felt like a part of me.

"Don't say the M-word so lightly, Sam. You can't even begin to understand what we would—what *you* would be facing," she explained, her eyes closed, in the same spot.

I squeezed her neck and said, "Then explain it to me, Akira. What are we facing? And I'm saying 'we' because we damn well are a 'we.' I don't even know what you consider the right time to tell your family about us. Are you waiting to tell them face to face? Or are we not there yet in our relationship? I'm not trying to rush you, but I would really like to understand better."

"Oh, Sam," Akira began, "that's a whole lotta questions for me. But well, let's see. I am worried that there are going to be so many people who won't believe in our relationship. You'll always have to prove your love for me, because I'm from a different country. I'll always have to prove my love for you, because there will be a lot of people who would claim that we got together so that I could get a green card. People will always make up stories on why we got together. I don't want you to face that."

My eyes bugged out at the mention of a green card. That hadn't even crossed my mind.

She continued. "I don't want you to resent me in the future if or when people keep saying mean things about us. And I guess, subconsciously, I'm just waiting for us to fail. But truly, Sam. I don't want us to fail. I just want us to *be*."

"Oh, baby, I'm not going anywhere. Do you understand me?" I dragged her on my lap and held her by her waist as tightly as I could. "I love you too much. I don't want to spend my life without you in it. And if I have to hear mean comments from everyone to be with you, I'm all ears, baby."

A tear rolled out of Akira's eye, and I grazed it off her cheek with my thumb.

"I feel the same, Sam," she said and kissed me. A few more tears slipped out of her eyes, and yet she did not stop. I tasted the salt on her cheeks and the sweet passion with which she kissed.

I tightened my hold on her and showed her my will to fight for us through my kiss. I poured all my strength into the kiss, and I did not stop.

After a few minutes or hours of kissing, Akira had her happy shine back in her eyes. I felt so much lighter after admitting the true extent of my feelings for Akira. And it felt down-right humbling to know that those feelings were reciprocated by the most important person in my life.

Akira ran her fingers through my hair. After placing three more pecks on my lips, she said, "To answer your other questions, about when I planned to tell about us to my family—a girl usually doesn't introduce a guy to her family unless she plans to marry him."

At my shocked expression, she held up a finger to let her continue and said, "Most of the cities in India do not have a dating culture. There are very few parents who are cool with their kids dating. My family is not one of them. No one in my family has dated. Most of us have had a few relationships. Nothing serious enough to tell our family. But typically, in India, if you tell your family that you're seeing a guy, all they hear is *I plan to marry that guy*. There is no in-between. For Indian parents, you are either single, or you are going to marry your boyfriend, if and only if they approve of him."

"And what if they don't approve of him?" I asked, almost afraid to hear the answer, given our circumstances.

Akira blew out a breath and continued running her hand in my hair and said, "Well, some parents either get you married to someone else within a year or some force you to break up with your boyfriend."

My hold on Akira instinctively tightened. "Like hell I'd let anyone else marry you." *Wait a minute.* With a stark realization at what Akira said, I asked, "Is that why you haven't told your family about us? You don't want to marry me?"

Fuck!

My eyes widened at my own words. So did Akira's.

Did I just say that out loud? *Yes, you did.*

Akira was silent for too long. Heat rose high on my cheeks. Before I could retract my question, Akira mumbled, "It's the other way around."

"Can you elaborate a little for me, Akira?" I asked, hoping like hell that she felt the same way as I did.

"I haven't told my family about us for two reasons actually,"

Akira said, avoiding my eyes as she played with the buttons of my shirt. I raised her chin with my finger so she met my eyes.

"Well, now that you know what it means when you introduce your partner to your Indian family, you'll understand that I didn't want to assume what you expected out of our relationship. I didn't want to drag you into any drama if you didn't plan to, you know, uh, marry me," Akira explained as she furiously tried to control her blushing. But, in vain.

I couldn't *not* kiss her right now. I gave her a few kisses—her lips, her cute, pointed nose, and her forehead. She still kept thinking about what I wanted. I wanted to know what *she* wanted. I asked her, "What do *you* want, Akira? Do you want to marry me?"

She gasped, "You can't. This doesn't count as a proposal. You're not proposing right now, right?"

I scoffed. As if I'd be that lame at a proposal.

She frowned and asked, "What? Is it or is it not?"

I laughed and answered, "It definitely is not. Don't get me wrong. I do want to marry you. Very much so. But I need to know if you'd want to marry me someday too."

"Of course, I do. You think I'd just willingly take upon the wrath of my family and possible disowning for just anyone?"

The mood again sobered a little. I was having the same thought as Akira when she voiced them out loud. "And that's the second reason why I haven't told my family about us. I'm too scared to lose any of you. And if you didn't want to marry me, and I told them about us, I'd lose all of you. Every time I talk to my family, the lies weigh me down. But if you are with me, I'm ready to tell my family about us."

And what did I gather from that?

"So, you want to marry me, huh?" I asked her, almost giddy.

She laughed and rolled her eyes at me. "That's all you got from the entire explanation? I said I'm ready to tell my family about us."

"Because you want to marry me," I stated, elated. I was hopelessly stuck at that. I'd never felt so much peace and happiness at the same time before. Not when I got into Columbia. Not when I first kissed Akira. Not even when she told me "I love you."

Just the fact that she wanted to marry me, spend her entire fucking life with me, humbled me to my core. My heart felt so full it could burst any second.

"Feels like we're engaged," I admitted, embarrassed to say that out loud.

"It does, doesn't it?" Akira agreed, to my utter delight. To my disappointment, she continued, "But, we're not. Not until we get the approval and blessings from my family. And you do things right."

"I know," I grumbled.

And she laughed.

As if that wasn't worse, Akira was kind enough to say, "You know, in Indian terms, we won't be considered engaged even if you proposed to me and I agreed."

"What the hell, babe? How do we decide that we want to get married?" I groaned.

"Didn't we just do that?" she asked, and continued, "We just decided that we would eventually get married. And I'm pretty sure it will take us months to convince my family. So, I hope we would be ready to marry each other then. I, personally, would marry you any day."

Huh. So, if we both were willing to marry each other, how was that different from being engaged?

"I can't think of you as 'girlfriend' anymore. That term is too insignificant for what I feel about you. And I'll be honest here, sweetheart. You're my girl now. And I'm going to think about you as my almost fiancée. Because if it weren't for your family's permission, you'd have a ring on your finger," I explained to her and kissed her with all the love I could pour into that kiss.

"Really?" she asked, tears filling her eyes.

"Really," I said.

I got up from the chair, kept a hold on Akira by her hips, and laid us down on her bed.

Akira wanted to marry me.

It made me feel like a king.

Her arms around my neck and her kiss on my neck had me losing my mind.

I needed to feel her.

Needed to know this was real.

Needed to make her mine.

This sense of possessiveness zapped through my body the more I thought about Akira and marriage in the same sentence.

Before I could proceed to show her how much I liked the idea of her as my almost fiancée, Akira had other ideas.

Like me, she was lost in thoughts too.

Her thoughts were in a completely different direction than mine.

"You know," she began as I started to pull off her clothes.

"What?" I asked as I placed kisses along her hips.

She moaned but continued, "Would you want me to take your last name when we marry?"

She was in her undergarments now, and I all but stopped pulling off her clothes. Just thinking about her taking my last name brought out the caveman in me, but I refrained from showing that trait outright. "Would you like to? I'm happy with whatever you choose to be, baby."

I would be. Akira was already ready to give up her whole world for me. I tightened my hold on her waist and kissed her across her exposed neck. She could damn well keep her name. Hell, I'd take her name, if that's what she asked of me.

She snorted loudly and started laughing. It jerked me out of my thoughts, and her neck. "What?"

"If I take your last name, my name would be Akira White," she said, and snorted again. "The fucking irony."

A loud laugh burst out of me.

She again mumbled "Akira White" and snorted.

Mumbled.

Snorted.

Mumbled.

Snorted.

"Oh my God, I won't be able to say my full name without snorting. How would I ever properly introduce myself without making a fool of myself?"

And I laughed, a deep belly laugh, like I hadn't had in a long time.

Tears streamed down my eyes. Her partial nakedness was all but forgotten.

The joy that Akira gave me was something I never imagined I could get in my life.

And to think she was considering taking my name made me want to protect her from anything and everything that could dull her brightness.

As I pulled off her undergarments, I asked, "So you still wanna take my name?"

Akira smiled widely and nodded with so much love and excitement, I let go and slipped inside her.

We both groaned loudly.

And for the rest of the day, I showed her how much I loved being her almost fiancé.

CHAPTER 18

"I love you and that's the beginning and end of everything."
  - F. Scott Fitzgerald

Akira

Sam loved me.

Every time I thought about him, butterflies took flight in my stomach. Every time he looked at me, my heart skipped a beat. Every time he called me "sweetheart," my knees went weak.

He became the center of my universe. As the days passed, he became an important part of my world. So important that I was ready to fight my family to be with him. He had my heart.

I didn't want to choose between Sam and my family. I couldn't have been who I was today because of one, and I couldn't be who I wanted to be without another.

My only choice was to have faith in my family. And I did.

I just had to make them believe that Sam was the only guy made for me. I still couldn't believe I had the marriage talk with Sam and he didn't bolt.

But to think he loved me enough to consider marrying me made me dizzy with thoughts of a future life. The life where I woke up in Sam's arms every morning, where we got ready for work in a rush because we were late getting up, then rushing home where we spend our time cooking dinner—sometimes watching his boring documentaries and sometimes enjoying Bollywood movies with subtitles on Netflix, and then making sweet, sweet love or having crazy hot sex before sleeping.

That would be a good life.

And I was so ready to get it.

December was near. The semester was coming to an end. We were scrambling to get our research papers done and designs ready.

Well, I was scrambling.

Sam had everything ready. He was still his competitive self and almost done with all the assignments. We spent most of our time together. So, I had no idea how he managed to get everything done. *Maybe because he spent his free time working and not gossiping with his roommates, siblings, and family, Akira.*

Like right now.

I was in a group video call with all the ladies, including my cousin and Sam supporter, Ria. Our conversations mostly went from what I was eating and cooking to the different places I visited. I'd gotten used to telling the stories of my different adventures without including Sam.

"Did you wear that top that I'd gifted you when you went to America?" my aunt asked.

"Yes, *kaki*. I recently wore it to a get-together we had at a friend's place," I lied. In truth, I wore it on a date with Sam last weekend.

"*Beta*, how often do you get to eat Indian food?" Mom asked, out of nowhere.

"Not often, Mummy. I don't have much time to go to a good Indian restaurant. I have so many assignments I need to submit," I lied, again. In truth, Sam and I often made plans for Indian food. Just last night, we'd gone to have *pani-puris,* an

Indian delicacy full of sweet, spicy, and tangy flavors. Sam has been determined to develop a stronger tolerance for Indian spices despite my pleading not to give himself a stomachache.

"So, what's your plan for today?" Ria asked.

"Nothing much. Working on my assignment," I lied. A-freakin'-gain. In truth, Sam was right outside my bedroom door, and we were going to go to the studio together and work there. So, maybe it was a partial lie.

"I'm so excited you're coming home, Akira. Just two more weeks, and you'll be home," Mom gushed, her eyes glossing over.

"Time flies so fast, no, *didi*?" my aunt asked.

"Aren't you excited, Akira?" Mom asked.

"Of course, I am. So excited," I lied. I was so going to hell. In truth, I was beyond terrified.

Every single lie to them rested heavy on my heart. Each lie was a painful stab to the love for my family. And every minute of talking to them was emotionally draining.

By the end of every conversation with my family, I needed to look at Sam to convince myself that he was worth it. And he truly was. Despite all the guilt I felt for lying, I never felt regret for loving Sam. Not once.

And that's how I knew that I wasn't doing anything wrong.

I loved Sam. And I was keeping him.

However, soon after the call with my family ended, Ria called me back. This time from her personal phone.

It was right at that moment that Sam returned to my room.

"Your phone, babe," he said, raising his eyebrows at my phone.

I sighed. "Yeah, it's Ria," I informed him tiredly.

As soon as Sam got settled on my bed, he opened his arms for me. I readily fell into his hug and nuzzled into his neck.

This. Him. It was all worth the lies. At least that's what I told myself.

"Are you going to take that?" Sam asked, his fingers running in my hair. All the thoughts disappeared from my mind, including the phone ringing in my hand. I just wanted to spend my days doing this—pass my days in Sam's arms, getting lost in the love that he showed me in his every touch, every conversation, and every laugh.

But, life.

"She'd want to talk about our group video call," I mumbled in his neck.

He placed a gentle kiss where my neck meets the shoulder. I shuddered. Every single kiss sent sparks flying down my system.

"I thought she knew about us."

I had informed Ria when we decided to start dating. I had even kept her in the loop when things went further. But she has no idea Sam and I had the marriage talk and we were 'almost engaged.' "I haven't had the chance to talk to her about our 'almost engagement' but I'll be talking about it with her today."

I was too tired to deal with all that came with my huge-ass family. As grateful as I was about Ria being on our side, her knowing everything made me feel even more guilty for hiding such a huge part of my life from my family.

"You want me to tell her that I plan to marry you someday?" Sam asked casually, as if the words "marry" and "you" in the same sentence didn't simultaneously exhilarate and terrify me. Sam has had random conversations with Ria a few times. So technically, he could pick up Ria's call, the one that had stopped ringing a while ago. She knew I'd call her back.

Ria had been skeptical about our relationship when I'd first informed her about Sam and me. But she'd given me her heartfelt approval once she started talking to Sam—video call as well as phone calls.

"His calmness balances your constant chatter," she'd said. I had snorted. As if I didn't know how chatty Sam was with me.

To answer Sam's question, "Thanks for offering, honey. But I need to do this on my own. I just...I'm just so tired of all this. The lies. The bullshitting. Needing Ria or anyone on our side for us to be together."

I didn't realize how close I'd come to crying. But when Sam grazed his thumb over my jaw, I couldn't stop my lips from wobbling. I bit it hard to stop the sob that threatened to come out. But the moment Sam pressed his lips to my forehead, a sob broke free.

"I'm here, Akira," Sam murmured, as he pulled me into his arms.

He was, wasn't he?

And he would be. I knew that.

I didn't let another sob break free. I refused to cry for loving him.

I wasn't crying for loving him though. I was crying for having to hide it from my family. It wasn't uncommon to lie to parents to get what you want. It wasn't my first time lying to my family either.

But before, I used to lie about grades or going on a date with my ex. Those lies didn't revolve around a fundamental part of my life. Like Sam.

I was going home in two weeks. And I was pretty sure I would be informing my family about Sam. I had to. It wasn't fair to Sam, who had been so open about our relationship with his family.

"You know this is just the beginning to what we'll have to deal with, right?" I asked Sam, taking his hands in mine.

"I feel as if you're the only one having to deal with all the lying and hiding and struggling with protecting our relationship. I can see the guilt building, sweetheart, and I can't do a thing," Sam said, his jaw ticking, deep frown lines etched between his forehead.

"Not for long, Sam. Not for long," I said, trying to lighten the mood.

After a moment of thought, Sam asked, "Are you sure you're ready to tell your family? I don't mind waiting, babe. I just can't lose you."

We had been talking about the right time to tell my family. Even though we were sure about each other, my parents might need more time to come to terms with the fact that their daughter was planning to marry an American guy.

"Yeah, I'm sure. The sooner we tell them, the more time they'll have to process. Which means the more time we'll have to convince them that it's the right decision," I explained, and just to lighten the mood, I added, "As if *intercaste* marriages in India aren't controversial enough, I'm giving them interracial marriage."

Sam chuckled.

Still, I couldn't be happier with my life and my decisions, minus the lying.

So, for the next hour, I talked to Ria, informing her about the latest development in my relationship status. Sam interjected at a few instances, assuring Ria of his feelings for me and his readiness to inform our parents when I went home.

Thankfully, Ria was on board with us and prepared to fight on our side. I could not have asked for a better sister.

Sam

The semester was over. The assignments were submitted. The bags were all packed. Akira was all ready to leave. But I wasn't.

It was the first time we were going to be apart for more than a day since we'd gotten together, and now she was going away for an entire month. Just the thought of her absence had my heart pounding.

She was busy rechecking her carry-on bag, on my insistence.

"All there," she said as she turned toward me.

"You sure? Maybe you should check once more," I insisted, any way to extend her stay. I was trying to let her go. I really was. But it was difficult. Akira was my constant. My best friend. My love. And I'd forgotten what it felt like to be without her.

"I already did, baby. Four times," she said with a tiny smile and raised eyebrows. I was glad it was difficult for her too.

"Let's go, then. You've got to be there two hours before the departure."

I moved closer to her to get her bags. I didn't make it, though. Akira was in my arms, kissing me. She poured every emotion in her kiss. And I hungrily swallowed them up.

Warmth.

Home.

Love.

Miss me.

With every kiss and every moan, I conveyed every emotion that I felt but couldn't let out.

Hunger.

Possession.

Love.

Come back to me soon.

After some minutes of kissing and a few unshed tears, we got her bags down her three floors. I kept her hand clutched in mine in the cab throughout our way to the airport. She kept her head lying on my shoulder, occasionally kissing my hand or my cheek.

My jaw hurt from keeping it clenched to stop the emotions. I couldn't get weak right now. Akira needed me to be strong.

She needed to see that if she fell, I'd catch her. I had no idea how I'd do that from across the world, though.

No words were spoken.

We knew what was coming.

We knew what needed to be done.

We held hands all through the check-in line.

We walked slower as we neared the security gate.

We had to let go here.

Anytime now.

But we couldn't.

Ten feet away from the security check-in entry, we stopped.

People passed around us. Announcements played through the overhead speakers. Children ran down the passage, mothers shouting after them.

We moved to the side to let the crowd pass. I couldn't imagine how those people could laugh when our hearts hurt so much.

Was I overreacting? Possibly.

Was I terrified of how her parents were going to react? Absolutely.

Did I want Akira to go? Never.

Did I have a choice? No.

So, I clenched my jaw to stop the words "Don't go, Akira" from coming out of my mouth, and took Akira in my arms. Her arms wrapped around me and she kissed my neck.

"Wish me luck, Sam," she whispered in my ear.

"Come back soon, sweetheart," I whispered back. I didn't trust luck. I trusted her.

I felt her nod, and a shudder racked her body as she sniffled. I felt wetness at my neck, and I held her tighter. Not even my clenched jaw could stop the tear that fell in Akira's hair.

"Don't cry, Akira." I loosened my hold on her and held her cheeks.

I looked into her eyes, and with as much strength as I could gather, I said, "I love you. And all I care about is your happiness. I never wanted you to have to choose between your family and me. But, if choosing your family makes you happier, I'll be happy for you. Do not choose anyone over guilt or obligations. You hear me?"

Tears slipped out of Akira's eyes. And she kissed me.

It was a kiss of desperation. Need. Consolation.

Akira looked at me, determination shining in her eyes. Her words were steel as she spoke. "I love *you*, Sam. I choose *you*. I love my family, but I want to spend my life with *you*. I may be the one who is physically going to tell everything to my family, but you are the one who will face the consequences with me. In fact, you are already facing the consequences. Don't you see? We're in this together. Always."

I clutched her as tight as I could and kissed her as deep as I could. I could taste the saltiness of the tears. I moaned as Akira ran her fingers in my hair.

"I'm going to miss you so fucking much," I mumbled, placing kisses on her cheeks, forehead, and neck.

"Me too, Sam. Me too."

An announcement of her flight brought us back to reality.

"I need to leave," Akira said, fumbling with the strap of her bag and looking everywhere except at me.

"Yeah," I said, lightly running my thumb on her hand.

No sooner had she walked three steps, I said, "One last thing, Akira."

She quickly turned around with red-rimmed eyes and a frown on her face.

I walked to her and took her hand in mine.

I slid the ring on the ring finger of her right hand, so it doesn't draw attention.

She gasped, "Sam...it's...what...how?" Akira looked back and forth between the ring and me. Once. Twice. Five times.

I didn't know if she was happy or sad. I could feel my

cheeks burning. "I know it's just a silver band. I didn't want it to draw attention. I know you said engagement through proposal wouldn't count. But I needed to show you that I am right there with you. Always, sweetheart. This is just a promise ring. I wanted you to have it. Whenever you have any doubt about us —and I know it's bound to happen when you go home and spend more time with your family, God knows I'm terrified of that—I want this to remind you of us. And since we are just telling your family that we're together, I didn't want anyone to question you about any ring."

She looked at me, stunned. Her eyes filled with tears. I grazed my thumb along her cheeks, savoring the satiny skin and soulful, black eyes.

I continued, "If you don't want it..."

"It's mine," she finally said. And her words were the relief and assurance my heart needed.

"Good," I mumbled, wiping the tears that finally ran down her cheeks.

These weren't the sad, goodbye tears that we shared earlier.

These were the happy, hopeful tears that I gladly captured.

"Good," she said, a big smile on her face.

Akira's smile was the brightest I'd ever seen. She wiped the stray tear that had managed to escape my eyes.

Her happiness was the only thing that mattered to me.

I watched her walk into the security gate with the biggest smile on her face.

Her smile shone with hope, and my heart believed it.

PART II

CHAPTER 19

"Being a family means you are a part of something very wonderful.
It means you will love and be loved for the rest of your life."
  - Lisa Weed

Akira

Chaos welcomed me.

Thousands of Indians were all around me. Children shrieked through the airport, their mothers following right behind them. Constant chatter and loud laughs made it difficult to interpret the blaring announcements. I used to be able to make out such announcements before.

> Me: Landed safely. Going to baggage claim right now. Love you. :-*

> Sam: Good. I miss you, sweetheart. Love you too :-*

Someone slammed into me as I tried to read Sam's text and walk simultaneously. Before I could look up at the person, he or she was already lost in the crowd.

Me: Can't text while I walk. Too crowded. TTYL?

Sam: Okay. Keep me posted

My phone started ringing as I stopped at a barely open space at the baggage claim. JFK airport had a lot more open space than Ahmedabad airport.

Aakar calling...

"Hey, bhai." *Hey, big brother.* I couldn't stop the smile stretching across my face.

"Akira, where are you? We've been waiting outside for an hour. We had to wake up at five a.m. to get here," Aakar said in Gujarati, our native language. My family and I only talk in Gujarati with each other, except for a few English words like please, sorry, thank you and similar perfunctory words.

Aakar's excitement had me bouncing on my toes. "Who else is here?"

"It's a surprise. Now, will you hurry up?" I could hear the *umph* before I heard the phone being shifted around and a few familiar voices arguing.

Oh, I'd missed this.

As soon as I got all my luggage, I tried running out with my trolley. Alas! There was a line of fifty people before me to do the same. So, I got in line and waited for more than half an hour to get out of the airport.

The moment I was outside, I was tackled into the ground by my younger brother, Abhi.

"I missed you, Akira," he mumbled into the bear hug we were in.

Before we could disentangle ourselves, two more people were on top of us, right outside the airport door.

"Oh my God, you guys. I missed you all so much," I screamed into the tangled mass of arms and legs.

A lump formed at the back of my throat. Happiness and

sadness waged war in my heart as tears threatened behind my eyes.

"Children," my dad's voice boomed over us.

All of us scrambled to right ourselves. As we all stood up, I saw that it was Ria and Aakar who had jumped our bear hug.

The moment I saw my dad, tears ran down my eyes.

"Pappa," I whispered.

"Akira!" Dad came toward me, and I lunged into his arms.

Home.

It felt like home.

Arms wrapped around me from the other side and warmth engulfed me.

Mom.

I was sandwiched between Mom and Dad, and I couldn't stop the tears.

"I missed you all so much," I said into my father's hug.

"We missed you too. Video call is not the same at all," Mom said, tears running along her cheeks.

As I looked behind Dad, the sight almost brought me to my knees.

I didn't know whether to laugh or cry.

I did both.

My entire family had come to welcome me. All. Fourteen. Of. Them.

I ran and hugged all my aunts, uncles, grandmother, grand-father, and the kids.

Questions bombarded me from different directions.

"*Didi*, what did you get us?" three kids yelled from one side.

Before I could answer, I was pulled into the circle of my aunts.

"You've become so thin, Akira. Don't you eat properly?" Radhika *kaki*, my elder aunt, held my arm and turned me around. *Kaki* meant Aunt, who is the wife of one's father's brother.

"Look at your sweater. It's so soft." Ekta *kaki*, my younger aunt, rubbed my cardigan and examined the material.

"Leave her alone, everyone. Let me have a look at my grand-daughter," my grandmother shouted.

I went to my grandmother, who was sitting on a public bench with my grandfather. The moment I neared her to hug her, she had both her hands on my cheeks and turned it at different angles and said, "You look good, *beta*. A little thin. But good. Are you happy?"

Tears welled in my eyes when Sam's face popped into my mind. I nodded and said, "I am. Very happy."

A constant, excited chatter along with the repeated airport announcements almost overwhelmed me.

Almost.

"We had to bring three cars to pick you up," Ria said, coming up beside me.

When I met her eyes, a moment of shared knowledge passed between us. "*Later*," our eyes said.

"Akira is coming in our car," Abhi announced and dragged me to the "fun" car. The fun car consisted of Abhi, Aakar, Ria, and me.

We grabbed my luggage and were on the road in no time. The bumpy roads, the heat that burned my skin, the blaring horns from the vehicles around us, the endless traffic, the pollution, and the latest Bollywood songs playing in the car—I missed it all. I wished Sam could see all of it. He would prob-ably hate it.

"What are you smiling about, Akira?" Abhi asked from beside me. He had his arm wrapped around my shoulder.

I missed Sam.

"I missed this," I lied. Guess the lying didn't stop even when I was back home.

It wasn't a complete lie. I did miss Ahmedabad. There was

something about your home city that always stayed with you. I guess you never get rid of the essence of your city.

The smell of the air stayed the same, and the distant chatter from the streets was decipherable, as opposed to that in New York City, the fashion evolved yet felt the same, and the streets were still lined with a million two-wheeler vehicles, food carts, stray dogs, and occasional cows.

We were the first to reach home. The entire ride was spent talking about the current family gossip and teasing Aakar about potential brides. The moment the car stopped, I jumped out of the car and hugged one of the pillars of our porch.

"I missed you, home," I said, making my siblings laugh.

The rest of the family arrived just a few minutes after we got all the luggage out of the car. Mom came rushing out and held my hand. She gave me a few more hugs and kisses as all of us shuffled inside.

Our live-in, full-time helper Raju *kaka* rushed into the living room where all of us were gathered. *Kaka* is referred to an uncle (father's brother) as well as any elder man as a sign of respect.

With a gentle smile, Raju *kaka* announced, "I am making my special chai for Akira. Who else will have it?"

Ten different hands rose up.

Raju *kaka* laughed and returned to the kitchen, shaking his head.

I snorted.

At that, Dad said, "What? This is our regular teatime. And we have Raju's special chai every day."

"Yes, Akira. Savor it while you're here," Abhi added.

My entire family were tea enthusiasts.

And Raju *kaka* was the Chai Master of our house.

My phone vibrated.

Oh shit!

Sam.

I forgot to message him.

> Sam: You reached home?

> Me: Yess!! Everyone came to pick me up, Sam... EVERYONE!!

I could still feel the cool metal on my ring finger. Every time I ran my thumb along the ring, I remembered Sam's words, his fear that I might doubt our relationship once I was with my family. I don't.

My phone vibrated. Mom frowned at my phone.

Trying to be oblivious to my mom's reaction, I checked Sam's message.

> Sam: That's amazing, baby. What're you doing right now?

> Me: Waiting for Raju kaka to bring me his special chai...

> Sam: Raju kaka?

> Me: Our family helper.

> Sam: Family helper?

> Me: Um... He lives with us and helps us in cleaning and cooking and other chores.

> Sam: You have a helper? Full-time? Judging you so hard right now, babe.

I couldn't stop the smile on my face.

> Me: It's not like that. Having a helper at one's place is pretty common.

> Sam: Still judging you...

Me: Shut up!!

"Akira, who's making you smile so much?" Mom asked in front of everyone.

Dammit. I knew I shouldn't have started chatting with Sam right now. Stupid Sam, making me smile.

"Oh... Uh... It's nothing. Friends from the university. They're teasing me when I told them that we have a helper," I fibbed. And decided to stop replying for a while.

A few people snickered.

Navin *kaka,* my elder uncle, added, "I've heard people in America don't have any helpers. Is that true?"

I nodded. "Oh, yeah. Some wealthy families have someone come once or twice a week to get everything done. But not many people can afford a helper there."

"How would you survive there, Akira?" Aakar teased.

I might've behaved like a princess when I was home.

"Just like I've been doing up until now, *bhai*," I said.

Raju *kaka* came with a tray full of everyone's tea and some snacks.

"Here you go, everyone. Let me know if you need anything," he said.

The moment I took the first sip, my eyes rolled back into my head—absolute heaven, as always.

"You're the best, Raju *kaka*," I said with a grateful sigh.

He laughed.

The rest of the day was spent trying to stay awake to avoid jet lag, giving everyone the gifts that I'd gotten them, spending time with my family, and trying to sneak in some texts with Sam before he went to sleep during my lunchtime. He woke up during my dinner-time so I couldn't talk to him then.

But by 9:00 p.m., I was too tired to stay awake any longer. I wished everyone good night, told Ria that we'd catch up the next day, and headed to the room that I shared with Ria. She usually went to bed around 1:00 a.m., so I knew I had some privacy to call Sam.

The moment I was in my room, I video-called him.

He picked up on the third ring.

Relief washed over me the moment his face appeared on the screen.

I was talking through headphones so nobody would hear his voice.

"Hi," I said in a low voice. Just in case someone passed by my room.

Sam was on his bed, glasses in place, wearing his white sleeveless tee, running his hand in his mussed hair and yawning. He looked so freaking adorable. I just wanted to kiss his face.

"Finally, Akira," he groaned and adjusted his comforter over him.

"I want to kiss you so bad," I whispered.

"Me too," he whispered back and asked, "Why are we whispering?"

"I told everyone I'm going to sleep. If someone walks past my room and finds out that I'm talking to someone, they might drag me back out," I explained, still whispering.

"Okay. And did you sleep even a little throughout the day?"

"No. I'll sleep after this call. I just wanted to see you before I slept," I said and yawned simultaneously.

I leaned back on the bed and snuggled deeper into my comforter.

Sam did the same on the other side.

"Good. You've been awake too long," he said.

"Hmm..." I had no energy to say more than that.

"Fuck, I miss you so much, Akira."

"Me too, Sam,"

"How does it feel being back home?"

How do I explain something I didn't even understand myself?

"It's fine. Feels like I never left. But I feel guilty, too, knowing I'm going to disappoint them before I leave," I said.

I missed everyone. It was so good to be home.

"Oh, baby," Sam said. What else could he say?

I continued, "You know, Mom sat with me and made me give her an entire list of everything that I'd missed eating in New York and promised to cook one or two items off that list every day."

A nervous and disheartened look crossed Sam's face.

"If you don't want to tell everyone about us..." Sam began.

Before he could finish the sentence, I tried to glare at him with my sleepy eyes, and interrupted, "Now, now. No need to get all sacrificial and understanding and shit. We are doing this. I might be feeling guilty, but I can't lie to my family anymore. And lying to their face isn't as easy as it is over the phone."

Sam smiled and shook his head. "I love you, Akira. You can tell your family whenever and however you want. But now, you need to sleep. We'll talk tomorrow."

I was so tired. I'd been awake for the past thirty hours. So, I willingly agreed. "I love you too, Sam. I wish I was sleeping in your arms right now. And don't know about tomorrow. I will try and sneak in as much as I can. Okay?"

"Okay, baby. Sleep now. Good night," Sam whispered and blew me a kiss.

That brought a smile to my face, and before I could kiss him back, I was asleep.

DAY 3

"Akira, wake up, *beta*."

I woke with a start.

Mom.

I missed this. Mom was sitting on my bed and petting my hair. She used to wake me up just like that when I was little. Once I was old enough, she just shouted at me from whatever room she was in.

I moved my head from the pillow to Mom's lap so she could continue her petting.

"Are you happy in America, *beta*?" she asked in a soft voice, running her fingers in my hair.

I kept my eyes closed to just take in the bliss and said, "Yeah, Mummy, I'm happy."

"Good, good. That's all I want for you," she said and placed a kiss on my head.

I put my arms around her waist and stayed in the warmth of my mother's arms. Her familiar sandalwood smell and gentle hands had me almost tearing up. I didn't want to lose this.

"Now, get up. We have lots to do today. The weekend's over. Your father and uncles, and now Aakar too, need to be off to work soon. I need to help your aunts get the breakfast ready," she said and tried to get off the bed.

I held her by the waist, and at my protest, she just laughed and said, "C'mon, Akira, get up now. I'll tell Raju *kaka* to get your tea ready. Abhi just woke up. Come down and have breakfast with everyone. The men won't get to see you the whole day."

"Yeah. Give me fifteen minutes." I turned my head back in the pillow and drifted back to a snooze sleep.

I smiled in my sleep hearing my mom laugh.

Day 5

Breakfast in my family has always been a big affair. It's the only time the entire family had a meal together.

"Pass me the sugar," Navin *kaka* asked his youngest kid, Soham.

"Mom, I hate *haandvo*. Can I get something else to eat?" Abhi complained.

"It's your sister's favorite, Abhi. You can bear it today, no?" Mom chided.

Abhi mock-glared at me and asked, "When are you going back again?"

"Abhi!" Dad reprimanded, along with my mom and my aunts.

I snickered and answered, "Not for three more weeks."

"Three more weeks of Akira's favorite foods. If only her choices were any good," Aakar teased and took a ginormous bite of the said *haandvo* and made faces as he chewed.

If only he knew.

I could only imagine how well my choice of lover would be received when even my choice of food was controversial. And *haandvo* wasn't bad at all. It was like a savory cake made of rice, lentils, lots of vegetables like carrots, peppers, and its top layer of cake was full of crunchy goodness of sesame seeds and mustard seeds. And combined with chai, it was heaven.

"Give some more to Akira," my dad said to Mom, and before I could protest, he added, "You better finish it up, Akira. You've become too thin. And God knows when you'll get to eat all this home food again. *Eat it up, beta.*"

I ate three more huge pieces of *haandvo* and two cups of chai.

I wish Sam could be here. He would have loved the food. I'd have to ask Mom for the recipe.

I clicked the picture of my plate and sent it to Sam.

> Me: Having Hot Haandvo... ;-)

> Sam: Ignoring the alliteration and the weird-ass word of the dish, it looks interesting. Cook for me here, and I'll see if I like it.

Me: You'll love it.

Sam: Somehow, I doubt it. But we'll soon find out... :-*

Day 7

The sinful fragrance of fried *puris,* a type of an Indian flat-bread, and the overlapping gossip filled the air in the kitchen. Radhika *kaki* sat cross-legged atop the kitchen countertop and cooked potato curry on one stove. Ekta *kaki* stood at the other stove and fried the *puris* that Mom and I prepared. Mom and I sat on the floor across each other, rolling board and rolling pin in our hands. Preparations for our two-day trip was in full force.

"Whatsoever happened to that boy you were looking at for Ria?" Mom asked Radhika *kaki,* Ria's mom.

"I heard that their family is very conservative. Wants a housewife and the wife to not wear jeans. I'm not sending my daughter off to such people," my aunt said. Her glare itself could fry off all the *puris.*

If Ria knew the sort of proposals coming her way, she would rebel. Thank God she was at work rather than cooking *puris* with us.

Before I could voice my opinion on that, Ekta *kaki* added, "Good thing you found that out soon, *didi.* Ria would've refused to see any guys at all for one whole year. Again."

We all chuckled.

Remembering the incident, Mom said, "Oh God, she was so furious. When the family asked if she would take over doing accounts for their family business and leave her firm, I still remember the glare she'd thrown at the guy's mother."

Ria was two years older than me. And I was there when that family had come to our place to see Ria for an arranged marriage. The experience had been harrowing and amusing. "And when she said *I am a Chartered Accountant, not your family's bookkeeper—no offense to bookkeepers.*" I tittered at the memory.

Radhika *kaki* guffawed. "Yes, Akira. And then she'd given me the harshest glare and walked out of the house. I don't blame her though."

The amount of spices that Radhika *kaki* was adding in the curry was relative to Ria's glare at that time. The curry was going to burn everyone's assholes tomorrow morning.

Ria had refused to see any guy for a year as a punishment to the family for even considering a family like that as a prospect.

"Easy on the spices, *kaki*!" I cringed at the dollop of red chili powder that went into the curry with a forceful flick of her wrist.

"I had to save all the proposals for a year! Some of them were even taken away by the end of the year. Two were even good," Radhika *kaki* continued her lament. Her distress over the issue was being taken out on the poor curry vessel as she stirred the potatoes around.

I laughed and added, "No one is good enough for Ria. She wouldn't accept anyone with even a slight imperfection."

With a smile, Ekta *kaki* pitched in. "Radhika *didi*, Ria is forever going to stay home with us."

When everyone nodded, Mom looked at me and asked, "What about you, Akira? Should I borrow some of the proposal options from Radhika *didi*?"

Walked right into that one, didn't I?

The smile on my face was intact while I pieced together the half-lie in a frantic pace, "Oh no, Mummy. Let Aakar and Ria go first. I still have a lot to do."

Mom rolled her eyes at me and continued rolling the *puris*. "You can, at the very least, consider meeting the guys. I can even look for some in America. We have some relatives in New Jersey. What do you say?"

Oh God, this was endless.

I got up from the floor and handed all the rolled *puris* to Ekta aunt to fry. "I'll think about it. Now, tell me if Aakar saw any of the girls you've selected."

The rest of the afternoon was spent catching up to the latest news on everyone.

DAY 9

The cold water of Lake Pichola swirled beneath my feet as I sat on the steps of the Gangaur Ghat at the edge of the water.

A *ghat* is a series of steps along the bank of the lake, leading into the water. Ghats usually have a small temple and are used as a gathering space for the people of the city to celebrate festivals.

I cozied up in my warmest sweaters to battle the cold winter of Udaipur city. Vernacular songs of Udaipur enlivened the spirit of tourists passing through the Gangaur Ghat, one of the many ghats of the city. Street vendors sold colorful bangles, balloons, toys, and local crafts.

All the ladies of our family had gathered around a woman's handicraft shop selling traditional clothes. My brothers had gone off to try local food.

The family trip to Udaipur and Shrinathji temple had been refreshing yet tiring. Yesterday, we'd gone to visit our deity, Shrinathji, in Nathdwara in the state of Rajasthan. Udaipur was one of the most beautiful cities in the state, and our plan was to spend a day here.

The beautiful sun setting at the horizon of the still water of the lake reminded me of the nearing end of all my lies. My time in India was passing fast, and I had not gathered enough courage to say the truth to my family. Sam deserved a love where I proudly showed him off. I deserved to love him openly.

Someone moved in my periphery and took a seat beside me.

Dad.

Staring off at the lake, he asked, "You having fun on the trip?"

I turned to him and said, "Yeah. I missed our family trips. I'd forgotten how entertaining it is to see Abhi getting all competitive with Aakar."

Dad scoffed, rolled his eyes, and spoke. "That boy. He just doesn't accept that he is seven years younger than Aakar. Now that Abhi is twenty-one, all he does is compare the freedom he is given with that of Aakar."

Sounded like him. Abhi used to do the same thing when I was home. Every time I went to movies with my friends, he turned into a recalcitrant devil.

I laughed. "So, how is work going?" I asked Dad. Our family ran a textile business in the city.

Dad folded his trousers to his knees and dipped his feet in the cold water.

He hissed. "Do you even feel your feet?"

"You'll get used to it."

Dad nodded and said, "The factory's doing well. Especially since Aakar joined the business. He is adapting well too." Dad smiled and continued, "I am so proud of you two."

Guilt made it difficult to speak. Dad was looking at me like I'd fulfilled all his dreams. How would I tell him about Sam?

I didn't want to disappoint my dad. I didn't want to extinguish that proud glint in his eyes. The truth would crush him. Why was I afraid of telling him the truth?

Maybe because we, Indians, were brought up to believe that our sole purpose in life was to make our family proud. And by doing anything that went off that course—no matter if it led to our happiness—we were committing an unforgiveable sin that would be an ultimate demise for our family.

It wasn't true.

But we were so well conditioned that telling our parents that we've found something or someone that made us beyond happy made us feel so guilty that we'd rather suffer in silence.

In fact, right now was the best opportunity to just tell my dad about Sam. But were the words coming out of my mouth? No.

They were stuck in my throat, making it difficult to breathe. I wasn't afraid of my dad's anger. I was prepared for it. But I was terrified that disappointment would replace the pride in Dad's eyes.

I smiled at Dad but could barely meet his eyes. "You don't have to be so proud of me, Dad. I'm not perfect."

Dad shook his head in—dare I say—wonder, and patted my hand. "You are my brave daughter, Akira. It takes guts to leave your home, your country, and follow your dreams to a whole new country. It takes humility to make new friends. It takes so much work and adaptability to survive in a new environment around new people. It takes a very strong heart to miss your family and not run back home. So, don't tell me not to be proud of you, *beta*, because that is not happening."

The words that were stuck in my throat came out as giant waves of waterworks from my eyes. "Pappa," I sobbed.

How do I ever compete with that? How do I willingly break his notions about me?

Dad sat beside me and took me in his arms. The world disappeared around us. His strong arms around me were breaking my resolve to come out to my family. It was also breaking my resolve to keep lying to them. Everything was fucked up.

"Let's go, *beta*. We need to leave if we want to reach the hotel for dinner," he murmured.

"Yeah," I said, my heart heavy with guilt. We got our feet dry and slipped on our shoes, all the while not meeting each other's eyes.

"We only have a few days left with you. Hopefully, we'll see you in summer," Dad said as we made our way to the rest of the family, who'd gathered near our bus.

"Of course. I'm coming home every time I get a vacation," I added.

Dad nodded, his eyes glistening in the warm light of the evening.

Everyone dozed off in the bus on the way to the hotel.

I didn't sleep a wink the entire way.

Trees passed by. Roads passed by. The evening turned to night.

And I kept thinking.

About Sam.

My family.

My life.

Everything,

Nothing.

CHAPTER 20

"Nothing is better than going home to family and eating good food and relaxing."
   - Irina Shayk

Sam

Christmas was here.

I'd been staying at my parents' place for two weeks now, right after Akira left for India. And I was miserable. I'd forgotten what it felt like to be alone. I had been helping my dad at his construction company and trying to stay busy. But I missed Akira.

We tried to stay in touch as much as possible, but the time difference was shit. Akira kept sending me pictures of all her favorite food and the places she visited with her family. She looked so happy. I, on the other hand, sent her pictures of me and my mom decorating the Christmas tree and the home-made cookies that Mom baked. Were we cheesy and boring? Fuck, yes. Did I mind it? Not even a little bit.

The only thing that kept niggling at the back of my mind

was Akira's avoidance at talking to her family about us. It had been two weeks, and I saw no signs of her planning to tell them about us. No way was I going to rush her. Yes, it bothered me. But staying patient was my only job right now, and I was going to fulfill my duties silently.

It was the early morning of Christmas, and I was still in bed.

> Me: Merry Christmas, sweetheart :-*

Akira calling...

The moment Akira's face appeared on the screen, it finally felt like Christmas to me.

"Merry Christmas, Sam," she said, looking around her.

We haven't once had a proper time just to sit and talk to each other.

"Merry Christmas, baby. What're you looking at?" I asked.

She kept looking more around the screen than at me. It irked me a little.

"Oh, I'm hiding in my bathroom and talking to you," she whispered.

Before we could talk more, we heard Akira's name being shouted in the background.

"I need to go," she said, almost panicking, and continued, "I know we haven't talked properly in ages, and I miss you, but my family has not left me alone for a second. It's the first time we had been separated for six months."

She must have seen the disappointment on my face because her face was riddled with guilt. "Please don't be sad, Sam. I'm just really afraid that once they know that I'm in love, they'll be so mad at me. I guess, I'm also making the most of my time with them."

I didn't understand her need to please her family so much,

but I didn't want her to be sad or afraid. "I understand, Akira. Go spend time with your family. I'll be here for you."

She smiled, blew me a kiss, and cut the call.

After freshening up, I went to the kitchen to get some coffee.

The tantalizing aroma of freshly made muffins in the kitchen brought back childhood memories. The pot of coffee was already brewing and, just like the last ten days, I was happy to be home.

"Merry Christmas, Sammy," Mom murmured as she hugged me.

"Merry Christmas, Mom." I squeezed her back into my arms.

A few seconds passed as we let go of each other.

"Where's Dad?" I asked, filling coffee in my cup.

"In the living room, at his usual spot," Mom answered with a roll of her eyes.

"Did she roll her eyes at me?" Dad shouted from the living room.

Mom and I laughed.

We joined him in the living room, with the coffee pot in my hand while Mom carried the muffins.

"So, who's going to start?" Dad asked, filling his cup with the second round of coffee.

We had already piled our presents near the Christmas tree last night. We spent the next few minutes opening our presents. My parents gifted me a dark brown, wooden watch with a contrasting off-white dial. As I examined the dial, I felt a rough texture behind it. I turned the watch to find an inscription.

Don't stop until you are proud.

I got them a three-day trip to Budapest. They deserved a good holiday.

I was on my third muffin when Maa gave me a present for

Akira. My heart warmed to think she remembered her and included her..

"Thanks, Maa. She'll be very happy," I said.

"It's all right, son," Dad said and looked at my mom.

They seemed to be having a silent conversation, which instantly put me on alert.

"What?" I asked them.

"What what?" Dad asked back.

I rolled my eyes and said, "You guys just shared a look after I mentioned Akira."

"Well—" Dad started.

"Not today," my mom interjected, sending a sharp look to my dad.

Dad raised his hands in peace at that and shrugged his shoulders at me.

"Some other time, Sam," he said.

This was crazy. It was obvious they wanted to talk about something, and the fact that Mom stopped the conversation for "today" clearly meant it was something upsetting. As if I was going to be fine delaying something like that. Especially when it was about Akira.

"Not some other time. Now. It's clearly about Akira. So just say it," I demanded.

Dad looked at Mom, asking for permission.

Mom met my eyes, and I met hers. I didn't budge. She understood the determination in my eyes and waved her hand at Dad, relenting.

Dad shifted his position from relaxed to straight on the edge of his armchair. I braced myself. My arms on my knees, hands clenched tightly forward, and my breath held in my chest. Mom had guilt written across her face.

Before Dad could begin, she said, "Sam, before we say anything, you have to remember that we love Akira. But we love you more. So, we just had a few questions."

My jaw hurt from biting back my words. I simply nodded.

Blowing out a breath from his mouth, Dad said, "So, I happened to mention to my friends in the country club that you were dating a wonderful Indian girl."

Just great.

My eyes narrowed, and I nodded him to continue.

Dad already had a defensive stance as he said, "Everyone was very pleasant, Sam. But, remember one of my clients, Mr. Miller? Uh...he mentioned something to us, which got us thinking."

He looked at my mom. I could see that my silence was worrying them.

Good.

I could almost guess where this was going, but I wasn't going to make any guesses. If they had a question, they needed to look me in the eye and ask.

So, keeping my mouth shut, I nodded them to continue.

Mom took over the conversation, "Sammy, we just had a question. We love Akira. You don't have to worry about that. We just wanted to know how serious you were about her. And if you knew that by marrying you, Akira could gain citizenship."

I knew what they were trying to imply. I was not going to make it easy for them.

"Your point?" I challenged them to convey their doubts out loud.

Dad met my challenge and asked me, "Are you sure she is not using you to stay here and be a citizen of the US?"

And there it was. I knew my parents wouldn't have had that thought.

But, once they were informed, they wouldn't have been able to ignore it. I don't know why I expected them to dismiss this scenario without having to ask me something like that. But they've met Akira. Talked to her. How could they doubt her motive?

When Akira had warned me about it, I had prepared myself to expect such questions from people. But to hear such doubts from my parents...it broke my heart. They even got her a present for Christmas.

"Was your Christmas present to her just a means of softening this blow?" I asked patiently.

"No, Sammy. Of course not. We love Akira. She is wonderful. But you can't blame us for being concerned. If you tell us that you were aware of this and trust Akira, we would be with you," Mom explained, worry clear in her eyes.

"We just wanted to make sure you were aware of this, Sam," Dad said, reaching out to Mom and holding her hand.

I clenched my jaw, not wanting to let my angry words flow without a filter.

"Say something, Sammy," Mom said, concern clear in her eyes.

"You asked me if I was aware of what Akira would gain by being with me. I am. Did you consider what she risked by choosing me?" I asked.

Guilt and uncertainty shone in their eyes.

"Sam..." my dad started.

"Her family!" I cried out.

"Sammy," Mom said.

"Yes, Mom, she would become a citizen of the US if she married me. But she will lose her family if they don't approve of our relationship. And you know why she would lose them? Because she would choose me. Me," I thundered.

My eyes burned with hurt and anger.

I stalked out of the living room. I heard my name being called out, but I couldn't stop.

I couldn't.

I stormed into my room and called Akira.

She might still be awake.

After about five rings, she picked up.

Her face appeared on the screen. She had a huge smile on her face and a Santa hat on her head. She looked adorable. Just looking at her calmed me.

"What's wrong?" she asked.

Well, it didn't completely calm me. I was still furious.

"You have some time to talk?" I asked. Most of the time, she was snatched away by her family.

"Yes," she said, worry clear in her eyes.

"I don't want to hurt you, but I talked with my family today. *About* you."

Understanding dawned on her face. With a calm, patient voice, she asked, "What did you guys talk about?"

I told her everything that was said between us.

"It's okay, Sam. I'm glad they love you so much. That's the only reason they questioned you."

I groaned. I understood that. I did. But it wasn't fair. They wouldn't have questioned a girl's motives if she was an American.

"What about you? I'm sorry if I hurt you by telling you all this. But I wanted you to know."

She touched the camera with a soft smile. "I'm glad you told me. Now, I won't villainize my family too much when I tell them about us. All families would have apprehensions. And to be honest, if my family were to question me the same way yours did, I would've told them on the first day I came to India."

"When do you plan to tell them? I don't mean to rush you, but I just wanted to be prepared."

Worry lines creased her forehead. She sighed and looked at me in the camera. "Soon. I was thinking, maybe the last week of my stay. Umm...I was thinking..." She stopped talking, clearly a little afraid to finish her sentence.

"Sweetheart, what were you thinking?"

"Umm. Would you, you know, um...maybe stay with me on

the phone when I tell them about us?" she asked, not meeting my eyes anymore.

Fuck, this girl.

"Of course, Akira. If you think that would help you, I'll be right there with you. Though, I have to remind you that I don't speak or understand Gujarati. So, if you are—"

Before I could finish the sentence, Akira blurted, "Ria could be on the conference call with us, and she'll keep translating for you."

She seemed to have given it a lot of thought.

"You've thought all about it, haven't you, baby?"

"Of course. I know I haven't talked to you about it much, but I have been trying to figure out the best way, you know," she said, grabbing a fistful of hair and pulling it lightly.

I can't even imagine how terrifying it could be to tell her family about us.

"God, Akira. Do you think me being there with you would help? If there is even a slight possibility of the situation getting easier, I'd take the next flight and be there in India. So be very honest, Akira. Would it help you if I was there?"

She was silent on the other end.

"I don't know, Sam. I'm pretty sure it would make it worse. Seeing you there, they'll feel as if I don't care about what they feel, and that I'm rebelling against them. And before you say anything, I know that's what I'm doing, but I want them to be able to voice their opinions. And make them feel like I really gave them the chance to support me."

"I understand. Are you scared?" I certainly was.

"Terrified. But you and Ria being on the phone with me, it would help. And I would keep you on the line and put the phone in my pocket. So, remember, I won't be able to hear you guys."

Fucking great. So, I'd be just a bystander.

"Wow. Okay. Let's do this," I said, with as much determination and strength I could muster.

"In a week, baby," Akira said.

"In a week," I repeated.

CHAPTER 21

"Do you want me to tell you something really subversive? Love is everything it's cracked up to be. That's why people are so cynical about it. It really is worth fighting for, being brave for, risking everything for. And the trouble is, if you don't risk anything, you risk even more."

    - Erica Jong

Akira

Ever since I'd arrived in India, my time had been spent in doing three things: eating as much food as I wanted, meeting as many relatives as my parents wanted, and going to as many temples as my grandparents wanted.

And in the few moments that I could spare in between, I talked to Sam. I missed him. Anything I ate, I wished Sam could taste it. I wondered how he would react to some of my relatives' questions and opinions—he would certainly stop listening to them after the first two minutes.

Every temple that my family and I visited, my mother prayed for me to find a nice Indian guy while I begged God to not listen to her.

Time went by in a blur.

And the day of execution was here.

Since the whole family has breakfast together, Ria and I had decided to lay it all out then. Ria was planning to go to a nearby park for our call. She was all ready to head out and Abhi had already called me for breakfast once.

"You ready, Akira?" Ria asked.

I had a pillow pressed to my stomach to stop the nonstop churning. I'd already rehearsed my words a thousand times, and the occasional shivers had still not passed.

"Yes?" I said.

"You can do it, Akira. Sooner or later, this was bound to happen. And Sam and I will be with you all along," Ria said.

She was right. If not today, then I'd have to have this conversation the next time I came home. If I delayed this conversation right now, I'd have to go through six more months of lying till I was back in summer.

No.

I can't deal with lying.

Each lie had been brutal.

Better to say the truth, and later blame the family for not being open-minded enough. *If this is what helps you admit the truth today.*

At least I wouldn't feel guilty for being in the wrong.

"Akira, come down. The tea is getting cold," Aakar shouted from the dining room.

Ria rolled her eyes and got her bag and phone ready.

"Let's go, Akira." She held my hand and dragged me to the door with her.

"What if they don't accept us?"

Ria smiled softly and squeezed my hand. "They're not going to. We're just going to see who does, and we'll take it from there."

I nodded.

Before I lost courage, I called Sam.

He picked up the phone on the first ring.

"You ready, sweetheart?" were his first words.

"I'm so scared, Sam. But yes, I'm ready," I said and looked at Ria. She gave me an encouraging smile.

Sam blew out a nervous breath. "I love you, Akira. And no matter what happens, I am here. Right beside you. You're so brave. Fuck, you have no idea how much I admire you."

His words.

This is the reason I asked him to be there.

Just the knowledge that he'd be right there with me was enough.

"I love you too, Sam. Let's do this," I declared with as much confidence as I could gather.

I added Ria on the conference call, put my phone in the pocket, and we headed out.

I went to the dining room while she headed out to the park.

"There you are," said Abhi, the moment I stepped into the dining room.

Everyone was here.

I went and took a seat beside Aakar, at the end of the table. He always made me feel protected, and if things got too much, I hoped he'd protect me. Or at least support me.

The moment I was seated, Aakar frowned at me. "You okay?"

Before I could say anything, Mom came to the table and placed a cup of tea in front of me. I didn't think I could stomach anything right now, even tea. Looking at everyone seated at the table, laughing and talking, had my heart pumping to an erratic beat. My stomach was roiling, and my underarms were sweating.

Aakar placed a firm hand on my knee under the table, stopping my rigorously bouncing leg that had started unconsciously.

"What's going on, Akira?" he asked softly, concern etched in his eyes.

"Everything okay?" Dad asked, just as Aakar was done. Sitting on the other end of the table, he looked at me from above the newspaper in his hands. Concern and confusion lined his forehead.

My ears were burning up.

Oh God, I can't. My heart. I was sure Aakar could hear it pounding. I pressed my hand on my chest, trying to hold it still.

"Akira?" Dad asked again, putting down his newspaper and making me his sole focus.

"Yeah? Uh... Yeah, I'm fine," I blurted.

Oh God, I can't. How do I begin? All my rehearsals and practice. Nothing. I remembered absolutely nothing. Sweat rolled down at the back of my neck.

Could Sam guess how terrified I was? What would Ria and he be thinking? Would they be talking? Guessing if I would back out?

I pressed my hand on the phone in my pocket.

Sam was with me.

Aakar's sharp gaze was on me as my dad tried to figure out what was going on with me.

Abhi had also stopped eating his breakfast on his seat opposite mine and was now sharing a look with Aakar.

"Akira," Dad softly said my name.

I met his eyes, and with a gentle gaze, he asked, "What's wrong, *beta*?"

And the seal broke.

"I love someone," I blurted.

Everything. Stopped.

The entire table went silent.

Fourteen gazes fixed on me.

I kept my eyes on the wooden table. I physically couldn't raise my eyes beyond that.

A strong hand rested on my shoulder.

"Akira," Aakar said.

I raised my eyes and looked at Abhi, my younger brother, who had the ability to brighten everything. His smiling face reflected at me calmed me a little.

I then met Aakar's eyes. He squeezed my shoulders in silent support and looked at Dad, encouraging me to do the same.

I followed his gaze and met my dad's eyes. Mom was already standing behind Dad, her hand on his shoulder.

Everyone had a gentle smile on their face. That was only there because they didn't know who I was in love with. My parents would have been fine with an Indian Hindu guy. Their accepting eyes screamed their expectations at me.

Before anyone could say anything, I finished the sentence. "His name is Sam."

That should give them a hint.

My dad asked, "As in short for Sameer?" Of course, there would be an Indian name that could be shortened to Sam. Dad's eyes clearly conveyed that the answer he was expecting was a big, fat yes.

I met my dad's eyes and said, "As in short for Samuel."

Sharp gasps filled the room.

"What?"

"Impossible."

"Akira, No."

The hand on my shoulder tightened, and I looked at Aakar. I didn't look at anyone else as murmured rejections filled the room. He didn't look anywhere else as his gaze stared back.

"Akira!" Mom called my name with a panicked voice, "Akira, tell me that's not true."

I didn't meet her eyes. I couldn't.

I kept looking at Aakar for strength and said, "It is. I love Sam, and I would really like it if you guys would give me a chance to explain how amazing he is."

"Is he an Indian boy?" my father asked, wanting to hear it out loud.

Still looking at Aakar, his accepting gaze giving me the strength to say the words. "He's American."

Mom's sob filled the room.

My aunts rushed to her side. I could feel the disappointed glares thrown at me. Tears rolled down my cheeks and I kept looking at Aakar.

"Is that why we sent you to America?" Dad's voice thundered in the room.

A sob broke through my lips.

I felt another hand clutching mine. Abhi.

"Dad," Abhi began.

"Do not come between your sister and me!" He glared at Abhi.

I was so thankful he tried to fight for me. I squeezed his hand in thanks. He showed me his support and acceptance by squeezing it back.

"Akira, start talking. And look at me while I'm talking to you," Dad said.

"He is really a great guy, Pappa. At least give him a chance." I tried to meet his eyes.

"I thought we had sent you there to study. We were so proud to tell everyone that you were studying in America. At Columbia University. But no, your focus wasn't in studying at all, was it?" His words pierced my heart. Why did I feel as if I'd betrayed my family?

I wiped my tears and said, "It's not like that, Pappa. I am doing well in my studies. I just fell in love along the way."

My dad scoffed, then looked at my crying mom and told me, "You don't just fall in love, Akira. There's always a choice. You made yours. Without even thinking what it would do to your family."

"I did think about the family. That's why I am asking you all to support me. To give us a chance," I begged.

"What's your plan, Akira? You want to marry this stranger?" Mom asked, her lips wobbling, tears clinging to her eyes.

"I want to, yes. One day. With your blessings." I looked at my mom, pleading with my eyes.

"This is unacceptable, Akira. You are not marrying an American. We do not lack in good Indian boys. I would have been okay if you had brought even a non-Gujarati boy. But American? Are you out of your mind?" Dad railed on.

"But, Pappa, if you would just—" I tried again.

"No. Absolutely not. I forbid you from having any relations with this guy. You are not seeing him again. In fact, you are not going back."

My stomach dropped. Air left my lungs, and a gasp tore through my lips. My grip on Abhi's hand tightened as I tried to keep my wits.

Shock paralyzed me.

"You can't do that, Dad." Aakar spoke for the first time.

"I can and I will," Dad said in his most stern voice.

"She has to study. Get her degree," Aakar argued back with the sternness that matched Dad's. His hand squeezed my shoulder.

"If Akira actually cared about her studies and getting a degree, we wouldn't have had to see this day," Dad shouted, disappointment leaking through every word he spoke. His refusal to even hearing me out gutted me.

"Pappa, please! At least give us a chance. Sam and I love each other, he respects me and our culture, he's a topper in our course, he's so perfect, Pappa. If only you'd give us a chance," I begged. My voice was hoarse with all the tears lodged in my throat.

The anger and disappointment in my parents' stare broke me more than my dad's next words. "We're done with the discussion, Akira. You're not going back. You'll finish your master's here."

He stormed out of the room as though he hadn't just crushed my heart. My mom gave me her tears and followed my dad. Everyone else left. The room emptied.

And I just sat there holding one brother's hand and crying in the other's shoulder.

∼

Sam

Hopelessness was a bitch.

I heard.

Every word that hit Akira.

Her sobs.

Her pleading.

The anger thrown at her.

The rejection.

I heard it all.

Ria tried to soften the language by giving me the gist of the conversation.

I refused to take that.

I asked her to translate what was being said.

And I wish I hadn't.

Every time Akira's voice broke, my heart stopped. For every time she pleaded, I wanted to scream. Her silent sniffles when her father shouted at her had my throat closing up. Her repeated begging to give us a chance, just to see her fighting so fucking hard for *me*, for us, had tears rolling down my eyes.

Hearing me sniffle, Ria had said, "Sam, we knew this was going to happen."

"No, we didn't," I'd said, my phone clenched in my hand.

The only reason I hadn't thrown it at the wall was because I needed Akira and this was my lifeline to her.

Fuck, if I had known this would happen, I would've never let her go. Or I would have gone with her. But dammit, this was all fucked up.

You're not going back.

Her dad's last words.

It was at that point when I had asked Ria to just cut the call and go back to Akira. I was glad she had her brothers, but Akira needed someone who knew us both.

But before she cut the call, I had asked Ria to convey a message to Akira. "Tell her I heard what her dad said. And that I'll support her in whatever she decides to do. Tell her, Ria, that if she chose her family, I'll support her. And if she still chooses me, I'll do whatever it takes to help her figure shit out."

Now, sitting in my cold empty apartment in the middle of the night, the silence haunted me.

Akira might not come back.

We just might be over.

I might never get to touch her again.

Hold her again.

Never watch her smile in my bed again.

Hot tears burned my eyes, and a scream that had built up all through the phone call tore through my chest.

I fucking smashed my phone.

And ran out the door.

Out on the silent New York street. I fucking ran.

Akira fought with her family just so she could love me.

Me.

I ran faster.

She risked everything to just be with me.

Me.

And I ran faster.

No one should have to fight the world just to love someone of their choice.

Akira's parents wouldn't have batted an eye had she fallen for an Indian guy. *Any* Indian guy.

How was that fair?

She fucking *begged* for us.

I picked up the speed even though my feet protested.

Unshed tears clouded my vision.

I wasn't there to hold Akira when she poured her heart out.

I. Wasn't. There.

A few tears rolled down my cheeks. I swiped them away. What would she be doing right now? Did she need me?

Should I give her some space to decide what she wanted next?

Did she even have any choice right now?

Did I lose the only person I'd truly wanted for myself?

She's the one.

"Fuck," I yelled in the still night.

I had no idea how long I ran, but I came home to find Luke on the phone. The moment he noticed me walk in, his eyes widened, and a few mouthed *fucks* came out of his mouth. He continued to look at me as he kept talking on the phone while I surfed through the top shelves of our kitchen cabinet.

Vodka.

"He's here. I'll get him to call you back in a bit... Yeah... Take care, Akira," he said and cut the call.

Akira.

"Was that Akira?" I asked him.

She wouldn't call him for no reason. I might have not heard her call. Luke stared at me while I patted all my pockets for my phone.

"You smashed your phone," Luke stated.

Oh. Yeah. I forgot.

"Give me your phone. I know Akira called for me." I put

the bottle on the table and walked over to Luke in the open living room. He was looking at me weird and his silence grated me.

I extended my hand for his phone, but instead of handing me the phone, Luke had the gall to say, "Sam, you need to calm down, man."

An angry laugh came out of my mouth.

"Give me your phone, Luke. I don't have time for this," I demanded. Akira needed me, and Luke was wasting precious minutes. He didn't know how difficult it was to get even ten minutes of uninterrupted time to talk.

Luke glared at me. "You have been out, God knows where, in the middle of the night, without a fucking sweater or jacket on, and it is fucking twenty degrees outside."

I glared back. "I am fucking fine. Now, give me the phone."

The fucker walked past me.

"Luke!"

He turned on the pot of coffee, got the cups out and said in a tone that was meant to calm me. "Akira told me what happened. She didn't have much time, so I just know the gist of it. Care to explain more?"

I scoffed. "Not right now." He was wasting my time when I could be talking to Akira.

"Will you look at yourself? This is not you. You've got tear tracks on your cheeks and fucking snot running down your face. Akira would just love to see you right now. A big help you would be to her." He tossed me the tissue box in disgust.

When I went to the washroom to get cleaned up, the sight that greeted me in the mirror made me angry all over again.

I *hate* her parents.

I hate her culture and values that bind her so much.

I hate it.

I took a near-scalding shower. It also brought back some of the sense that I'd lost in hurt and anger.

I looked at the mirror once I was cleaned up. The red eyes and swollen cheeks were still there.

Fuck it. I grabbed a sweater and went back to the living room, where Luke handed me the cup of coffee and sat at the dining table.

I sat across him and took a sip. Spiked coffee. Perfect.

I took a few more sips. The vodka-infused coffee and the warm cup made me realize how cold I was.

"Thanks for this," I mumbled and finished the first cup.

Once I had the second cup in hand, I told Luke everything. The phone call. Ria's translations. Akira's sobs and pleading. Hearing her dad shout at her. My message to Akira via Ria.

Except for the occasional swearing, Luke listened as I vented.

"Fuck, man. That's fucked up. I'm never going for an Indian girl," Luke said.

"Not helpful." I glared at his nonsense talk and continued, "What did Akira say?"

He got serious. "She told me to let you know that she is fine. And to call her during her nighttime. She needed to talk to her family right now."

It was her noon right now. So about ten hours from now.

Fuck.

"Give me your phone," I said, and put my hand palm up on the table between us.

"But...she told you to call her at night," Luke argued.

"I don't care," I said, and gave him the glare that had him handing me his phone with a grumbling, "Your funeral."

I walked into my bedroom with the phone and dialed her number.

After about six rings, I finally heard a soft, "Hey."

A lump lodged in my throat at the sound of her voice.

"Akira... Fuck..." was all I could say before I felt my voice breaking.

Her sharp inhale was enough to calm me.

"Are you okay?" I asked.

"Yeah," she answered.

"I know you didn't want me to call you before night, but fuck, I needed to talk to you. If only for a minute," I explained.

"It's okay," she said, with a soft voice.

"Are you with someone right now?"

"Yes."

"Is that why you're using one-word responses?" I asked, my lips turning into a smile.

"Yeah," she said. A sad laugh tore through me. Even at a time like this, Akira could make me laugh.

"I'll let you get to it, then. I love you, sweetheart. And you were very brave today. I am so fucking in awe of you. Call me anytime you need me. Any fucking time. You hear me?"

I heard a sniffle and a "Yeah" from Akira.

And just to make her smile, I added, "And you love me too?"

She chuckled, and I could imagine her rolling her eyes when she said, "Yes."

"We'll figure everything out. I'll wait for you, Akira. For as long as I have to. So, don't worry. Okay?" I couldn't stop talking to her. I knew she was giving me the time to cope. I had to cut the call.

"Yeah," she said, relief clear in her tone.

"I'll leave you to it, then. Talk to you soon."

"Bye," she said and cut the call.

Akira seemed fine. But I was losing hope.

I rubbed the spot where my heart ached, trying to soothe the pain as I replayed our conversation in my mind.

She never told me that she would be coming back.

CHAPTER 22

"To us, family means putting your arms around each other and being there."
  - Barbara Bush

Akira

"Is that how you talk to my future brother-in-law? Where's the love?" asked Abhi, finally breaking the silence that had descended in my room in the last half hour.

I glared at him, but he made me smile.

"What the hell, Akira?" Aakar glared at me.

"Aakar," Ria said, but shut up at the glare that he threw her way.

"You knew and didn't consider telling me?" Aakar asked, voice rising with every word.

"Bhai, please, I asked her to keep it between us. It's not her fault," I said.

"So, you think I'm not trustworthy enough?" Aakar challenged, his eyes daring me to deny his accusation. And I wouldn't. He had been my rock out there.

"We, bhai. I'm trustworthy too," Abhi interjected.

"Not now, Abhi," Aakar scolded our little brother.

"You guys are trustworthy. And I'm sorry for not sharing with you earlier. But I didn't want to put you in a position where Mom and Dad could blame you for knowing everything before them."

"We would have been better prepared to support you, Akira," Aakar said.

"Exactly my point. You would've had the time to prepare yourselves to support me. The rest of the family didn't have that. And they would have used that fact when you showed me your support. But now, despite knowing everything at the same time as them, you both supported me. And held me up. And that would send a better message. Wouldn't it?"

"She's right, you know?" Ria said.

"Fuck!" Aakar whisper-yelled.

Abhi was sitting beside me on my bed. Ria was on her bed beside mine, a nightstand between our beds. And Aakar was walking back and forth along the length of the room.

We all gave Aakar the time he needed to process everything.

I was watching him walk when Abhi bumped his shoulder to mine and whispered in my ear, "So, what does *jiju* look like?" Jiju meant brother-in-law in Gujarati.

I loved my little brother. He wasn't that little anymore. He was twenty-one and a foot taller than me. But he could always make me laugh. And he was the first person in my family to actually ask something important about my Sam.

I smiled and unlocked my phone. I scrolled through my pictures and showed a photo of Sam, where he was smiling at the camera in the middle of sketching. We were in the studio that day and had just started working again after the midterms. He was a little too happy because the busy days and heavy workload had kicked in.

Abhi took the phone in his hand, stared at the picture and scrolled to the next. His eyes brightened at the picture, and a teasing grin surfaced on his devil face. I snatched the phone away.

"You weren't supposed to scroll, dumbass," I growled.

It was a photo that I had clicked right after the one I showed Abhi. In this photo, instead of smiling, Sam was blowing me a kiss.

"I now know why," Abhi teased, waggling his eyebrows.

I rolled my eyes at him but couldn't stop the question, "So? What do you think?"

Abhi smiled and said, "Well, he's no Chris Evans. But I see why you love him. He'll do."

A laugh escaped me, and I took my brother's arm in both hands and laid my head on his shoulder. "Thank you, Abhi."

"It's cool." He shrugged.

At that, Aakar glanced back at both of us and raised his eyebrows. "The situation not serious enough for you two?"

"I was just seeing—" Abhi began, but Aakar shut him up with a glare.

"Go make some instant noodles for the four of us. I doubt there's going to be any big lunch today," Aakar ordered.

"What are *you* going to do?" Abhi asked.

Aakar glared at him with a clenched jaw. "I'm going to go and check what the others are feeling. We already know about Mom and Dad. I'll find out where everyone else's mind is at. Call me when you get lunch here."

Abhi squeezed my hand and headed toward the door when Aakar shouted, "And for God's sake, do not spill or burn anything."

With that, both of them parted at my door and headed in different directions.

Once they were gone, I lay back on my bed.

"He really loves you, you know." Ria was talking about Sam. We hadn't had the time to talk about her conversations with Sam since she was back home.

"Was he okay?" I asked, afraid to hear the answer.

"You talked to him. He was more worried about you. He got emotional when you cried." Ria's words pierced my heart and squeezed it so hard I gasped.

Sam. God, I wanted him so much.

"Did he...did he say anything?" I couldn't get the words out. I hadn't asked him to be with me to hurt him. But I know hearing the conversation with my family did end up hurting him.

Ria stretched across from her bed and squeezed my hand. "He asked me to let you know that whatever you decide, he'll be with you. And that if you still choose him, he'll figure shit out with you."

I sniffled and stopped the tears that threatened to fall.

"I love him so much, Ria,"

"We'll figure it out, Akira. You'll see."

I nodded and got my phone out. I already had a message waiting from Sam.

> Sam: Just ran and got a new phone. Just msg me if you need me, baby. I love you.

> Me: Hey... U there?

> Sam: I'm here. U Ok?

I could imagine the frown on his face.

> Me: Yeah. I love you, Sam. So freaking much. I never thanked you for being there with me. So, thank you.

> Sam: Are we going to talk about what your father said? Was he joking? Was he serious?

He was definitely not joking. I must've sighed loudly because Ria asked me, "What's wrong?"

I looked at her and asked, "Do you think Dad would let me go back? Or was it just his anger talking?"

Like me, Ria stared at the ceiling. "I don't know, babe. But we have a week left. We'll convince him by then."

> Me: He was serious. But we have a week to convince him. I'll be back, Sam.

> Sam: How can I help?

> Me: Don't lose hope. I don't know what else you can do. It's all up to my family now.

> Sam: I hate this.

> Me: I know... :-(

> Sam: But I love you

> Me: I know... :-)

Abhi's arrival alerted me.

> Me: TTYL. Fam here.

Abhi brought four bowls of noodles. He put two on Ria's desk and passed the bowls to us. He called Aakar to inform him that lunch was ready and that we were waiting for him in the room.

We all ate our noodles in silence.

"Thanks, Abhi. For everything," I said.

Abhi stared at his noodles and shrugged, a defeated look on his face. "Of course, Akira. Mom and Dad are being unreasonable."

Before I could respond, Aakar walked in, followed by Dad's younger brother, Sunil *kaka*, his wife, Ekta *kaki*, and my grandparents. All of them stared at me. I looked at Aakar, waiting for some indication on what to expect. He simply grabbed his bowl of instant noodles, pulled Ria's chair at her desk, and started eating.

I looked at *kaki*. She moved from the doorway and grabbed me in a hug. I didn't hear anyone shuffling in because I was busy crying in my aunt's arms.

"Oh, Akira. *Beta,* everything will be all right," she murmured in my hair.

I pulled myself together and looked at my uncle and my grandparents.

"I have to say, you shocked us, Akira," *Kaka* said. He led my grandparents to Ria's bed across me and took a seat at the end of my bed.

I couldn't meet their eyes as I said, "I'm sorry for disappointing you all. I know Sam isn't who you would've chosen for me, but I really love him."

I wiped the stupid, errant tear that kept appearing now and then. It was my grandmother who spoke up. "Akira, you did not disappoint us. Like your uncle said, you shocked us. Not disappoint. Okay?"

Once I nodded, she continued. "Now, tell us about your friend."

Her kind and gentle smile made me smile. I pulled out my phone and showed her the picture that I had earlier shown Abhi. My grandmother pulled off her glasses, brought my phone close to her nose and looked down.

"He's so white, Akira," she said, her face awestruck.

"Show it to me too, Bhavana." My grandfather took the phone from her hand.

He did the same with his glasses. "Akira, he looks so much fairer than you, doesn't he, Bhavana?"

"Yes. Akira, are you sure about him? He will look better than you in the wedding pictures," my grandmother said with all the seriousness. Like that was the biggest obstacle for me right now.

"Yes, *Daadi*. He is also a very genuine guy. He respects me, loves our culture, and always supports me. And we aren't marrying anytime soon." I got up and stood beside my grandmother to look at the picture too. Sam's smile melted my heart. Always.

At my last comment, *kaka*'s eyebrows rose to his hairline. "Then why are you announcing your relationship to everyone?"

As I looked around, everyone seemed to have the same question written across their faces. How did they not get it? "Because someday, I *am* going to marry him. And I didn't want to continue having a relationship in secret. Wouldn't you all have felt betrayed if I had told you guys about Sam after three years of a relationship?"

"You're in a complicated situation, Akira," Ekta *kaki* said, sympathy shining in her eyes.

"I'm glad all of you are here to give us a chance and learn more about Sam." I couldn't expect any more than this from my family.

"He has honest eyes," Grandpa muttered from beside my grandmother as he peeked into the phone to look at Sam's picture again.

Aakar came up behind Grandma to look at Sam's photo. "He's good. You're not with him just because an American guy is making you feel special, right? And is he just a pretty face?"

I glared at Aakar. "He is a topper in our class. He is smart, passionate, and is best at what he does. And he loves me and respects me."

Kaka came up behind my grandfather to look at the picture. It was getting crowded around the phone. I moved back to my bed and sat beside Abhi, who was happily enjoying the drama. *Kaki* also went to look at the picture.

It was just Ria, Abhi, and me on my bed while the rest of them looked over Grandma at Sam's photo.

"What does he plan to do? Does he have a job?" *Kaka* asked, staring at the picture.

"His father has a construction company. He will be taking over his dad's firm once he graduates," I said.

"So, his family is rich?" *Kaki* asked.

"I guess. They have their own company. They live in a great house." *Shit.* I shouldn't have mentioned the house.

The gasps from my aunt and grandmother, and the glare from Aakar and my uncle was the proof of that.

"You've met his family?" my grandmother asked, hurt evident in her gentle voice.

Guilt gnawed in my gut. "He invited me to their home for Thanksgiving. It's an American traditional holiday. I couldn't refuse. It would've been disrespectful."

"Whatever, don't tell this to Mom and Dad. You'll make it worse." Aakar tried diffusing the topic. I knew why they felt hurt by that. I was open about our relationship with Sam's parents, but not my own family.

"I didn't tell you all sooner because I was so scared. I didn't even know if he was worth the risk. But as I got to know him, I became sure of my feelings for him. He makes me happy. And I needed to tell you all about this face to face," I explained.

"Oh, Akira, this is a lot to process. Is there anything else that we need to know?" *Kaki* asked.

Their willingness to even hear me out and talk about Sam meant the world to me. "Nothing important," I said.

My grandparents, *kaka,* and *kaki* seemed to have a silent conversation for a minute before Abhi interrupted. "Do you all have any questions for Akira?"

Everyone looked at me. Sweat gathered behind my neck. I was so afraid to lose the support they'd shown. *Kaka* shook his head and took a seat near Ria's desk. "Akira, we are here for you. And we are willing to listen to your and Sam's story. Would you like to tell us?"

The stupid tear that kept falling made an appearance. Again. I didn't stop it. I nodded to my uncle and everyone took a seat around me. After taking a few deep breaths to compose myself, I began.

I told them everything. The first time I met Sam. Our decision to be studio partners. The time we spent doing research and site visits together. The little things he did for me, like dropping me off every night, getting me coffee as an apology for being rude, helping me in my research papers. His effort and enthusiasm to learn my culture, and his unwavering support since the day we decided to date. For hours, I told my family about the love of my life. I gave my all to show them how happy Sam made me and how perfect we were for each other.

Hours passed. *Kaka* and *kaki* had gentle smiles on their face. My grandmother was clearly pleased. And finally, when my grandfather spoke, I couldn't have stopped the tearful laugh even if I'd tried.

"We'll try talking to your parents."

Finally, a ray of hope.

Seven days left to convince my parents to let me go back.

CHAPTER 23

"A true romantic will break the rules for the right reasons. He will not conform to the ideals bestowed upon him by society. Instead, he will fight for a climate of freedom that allows him to pursue and obtain his heart's true yearning. He will appear incorrect in his upright form, but such perception only through the eyes of those traveling under the hypnotic notion of social paradigms. Do not judge he who is breaking the rules, rather try to understand his motivations. If his intent is pure then his fight is not in vain."

- Nicole Bonomi

Akira

Three days passed.

We were in a stalemate.

Mom and Dad were as disappointed and angry as ever.

Navin *kaka*, Dad's older brother, and his wife, Radhika *kaki*, were not saying anything. They neither supported me nor were they very supportive of my dad's decisions. The rest of the family and the kids were supportive of my relationship with Sam.

Ever since the day I announced my relationship, family breakfasts had stopped altogether. We tried the first day after the announcement. But the moment Sunil *kaka* tried to talk about hearing me out, Dad walked out of the room.

For the past three days, everyone had their tea and breakfast in their own rooms. All of us siblings had breakfast in mine and Ria's room. Since Ria and Aakar had jobs, most of my time was spent with Abhi and chatting with Sam.

I hadn't informed Sam about the recent changes in the household. The only information that I'd provided him was that I was coming back.

Every time he asked if my mom and dad were okay with us, I told him to give them time and that everything would be fine.

There was no need to worry Sam. He would only end up feeling helpless. He can't come here and talk to my parents for me—that would just make everything worse. I had to talk to my parents with a calm mind and maybe talk to them privately.

Mom hadn't called me to help in the kitchen these past days. I missed it. Missed talking about a bunch of stupid gossip and eating freshly cooked home food.

Today, I just decided to march into the kitchen head-on. The moment I stepped in, all the heads turned my way. My mom, aunts, and Raju *kaka* looked at me without blinking. At all. I met my mom's eyes and quirked my eyebrow just to check if she hadn't gone into shock.

The moment I did that, Mom pursed her lips and looked away. Nothing. She had no words for me. Her eyes were silent in resignation. She seemed to have built gigantic walls around her.

It hurt.

I wanted my mom. I needed her to take me in her arms and tell me everything was going to be okay. I wanted her to stand by *me,* not Dad. And she would. If only she understood.

The silence was broken when Mom said, "Akira, I'll call you when food is ready." She didn't meet my eyes. Not once.

Without a word, I went back to my room. Ria was at work already, Sam would be asleep at this time in New York, Abhi was at college, the kids were at school. It was just me. I dropped on my bed and stared at the ceiling.

I didn't know if Mom and Dad shared similar reasons for their refusal to hear me out or even give Sam and me a chance.

I understood that my parents' reluctance came out of fear.

Fear for me. Fear of a new culture. Fear of the unknown.

My words hadn't been enough to convince them that it was okay to fall for someone from a different country. That it was okay to love someone who was different from you.

That day, lunch and dinner were sent up to my room. My siblings had dinner with me. We discussed the possibilities of convincing my parents to let me go back. No one had any helpful ideas.

Two more days passed, and the day before I needed to leave for New York arrived. My parents hadn't talked to me. After two days of deliberation with Sunil *kaka*, Ekta *kaki*, my siblings, and my grandparents, we'd reached the conclusion that it was time I confronted my parents directly.

At night, after everyone had retired to their rooms, Aakar, Abhi, and I headed toward my parents' bedroom. The boys were only coming to drop me off to my parents' bedroom, per my request. I was pretty sure I would've just bolted otherwise.

Abhi knocked at my parents' bedroom door. The moment we heard some shuffling from inside, Abhi and Aakar disappeared, leaving me all alone, my heart pounding. My father answered the door, staring at me with eyes full of turmoil.

I was afraid he could hear my pulse thumping. I swallowed before I said, "Can we talk, Pappa? Please?"

He looked at me. After thirty agonizing seconds of staring me down, he sighed and opened the door wider to let me in.

Just as I entered, Mom came out of the attached bathroom and jerked back in surprise. Or maybe shock. "Akira."

Dad took a seat at the headboard of his bed and folded his arms. "Akira has come to talk."

Just as I sat at the foot of the bed, Mom got a chair from the vanity and took a seat across the bed, right in between me and Dad. She didn't tell me where she stood, but if her seating position was to go by, it wasn't a bad start.

Once we were settled, the awkward silence descended. Mom looked at Dad and then me. She rolled her eyes and finally said, "What do you need to talk about, Akira?"

With a deep breath and frantic heartbeats, I said, "I need to go back."

"No," Dad said without a second's thought.

And I lost it. "What is the problem, Pappa? You wouldn't have had any problem if I had fallen for an Indian guy. What's wrong with Sam? Other than him being an American." My voice rose with every sentence. I couldn't tamp it down. The more I talked, the angrier I got.

With every word that I spoke, Dad sat straighter. His frown got deeper. At the end of my rant, he snapped. "Enough, Akira. He might be the best American guy out there, but you won't be marrying one."

Wow. I looked at Mom, begging with my eyes to explain it to me.

Mom shook her head. "What were you thinking, Akira? We have no idea who the boy is. What kind of family does he belong to? And that is just about the boy. As for you, did you not once think about our culture before you chose to pursue that boy? Or do you not care enough about our culture? Do you not care about us? Your family? You went to America to study. And we happily sent you. But we expected you to marry into an Indian family, even if they were in America. We wanted you to live like an Indian, pass on our traditions to your future generation. And now you are trying to abandon all our values and culture."

"But, Mom, I'm not abandoning our culture. I'm just sharing it with Sam. He loves Indian culture. He gets so excited seeing all our festivals, our movies, hearing about stories of India," I explained. "And as for his family—" Before I could finish, Dad stopped me.

"Our culture is not just our festivals, Akira. Tell me, if you marry that guy, what religion are you going to follow— Hinduism or Christianity? Does he even believe in God?" Dad questioned.

Mom interjected, "And what about kids? If you have kids, would they pray to Jesus or Krishna? What language would you teach them? And how many Indian values would you pass on to your kids? The ones that only you feel are right?"

The more they spoke, the more questions they started having.

"Think about it, Akira. Once you are done with a long office day in America, you would still go home to an American? And continue talking in English? When will you talk in Gujarati? What will your children speak? How would they talk to us, your family, Akira? Are you willing to give up all of this for an American boy?" Mom had tears running down her cheeks.

Tears ran down my cheeks too. I had nothing to say. I never thought my language could be an issue. Our different native language has never been a problem. I was decent in English and have managed well for myself so far. I never missed talking in Gujarati. Or maybe because I was so used to talking in Gujarati and Hindi with my Indian roommates, I never felt like I needed to talk in Gujarati more.

I couldn't meet my parents' eyes. I understood where they were coming from. In fact, they were successful in making me feel guilty for falling in love with Sam.

They had put so much thought into it. They had gone

through every consequence and negative impacts of me marrying Sam.

"Mom, please don't cry." I held her hand in both of mine.

I looked at my parents' worried faces. "All your concerns are valid. But Sam makes me happy. We are different people, but our core beliefs are the same. We believe in understanding each other's cultures. He doesn't want me to give up my culture or pick one culture. Our differences do not separate us. They have brought us closer. It has made us look at each other beyond our differences."

I looked at my father, my rock, the one who was the first person to support me when I wanted to go to the US for my studies. "I love him, Pappa. I wouldn't fall for someone who wouldn't be right for our family or who would disrespect our values and traditions. You have to understand."

When their gazes softened, I continued, "I need to go back. I can't leave my studies. And it's not like Sam and I want to get married right away. But we would like to see where our relationship goes. I am telling you all about Sam now because I didn't want to keep lying to you all and date him behind your backs. Please, Pappa. Please understand."

Dad sighed and looked at Mom. She just shrugged and put her forehead in her hands in defeat.

I had nothing more to say in my defense. Like Mom, I hung my head and waited for Dad to say something.

After about two minutes of dead silence, except for Mom's occasional sniffles, Dad said, "Akira, I understand that you love that boy. He might be great. But he is not for you."

My stomach dropped. Nothing was enough for Dad. Tears filled my eyes, and a sharp ache pierced my heart.

He continued, "Love and understanding are not enough in a lifelong marriage. Marriage needs a lot of work. And I don't trust their marriage culture. I looked into it the other day.

Internet says that the divorce rate in America is forty-three percent. Do you know the divorce rate in India?"

Oh, God. I never expected him to bring this up. I don't know why I thought he wouldn't talk about divorce rates. Most Indians were always boggled by foreign culture of divorce. It was shocking to know that people just divorced when they were no longer happy in their marriage.

The fact that they could divorce and even find other people to date and marry again was even more shocking. We have stereotyped Western culture as the do-what-you-please culture, and my dad was not hesitant to take advantage of that.

I might've zoned off at the shock of the direction my dad had taken our conversation because Dad repeated his question, "Do you, Akira?"

I simply shook my head, knowing where the conversation was heading and having no means to stop it.

With the utmost confidence, Dad said, "Four percent. Do you understand, now? I don't trust an American boy, Akira. I don't care how much he loves you right now or how happy he makes you. Because in marriage, there always comes a time when you are not as in love with each other or you might not be as happy with each other. Is he going to stick with you? What if you never love each other later the way you do now? Is he going to still stay with you or find his happiness elsewhere?"

My stomach was churning violently at this point. With every question Dad asked, I lost hope. Hope that my parents would understand. Hope that they would send me back happily. Hope that they would accept my relationship with Sam. Because I believed in Sam. I believed in our relationship. I had to. Right?

I hated to admit it, but Dad was successful in planting a seed of doubt in my mind. His questions, along with the distance from Sam, was enough to make me doubt Sam's intentions. His love for me. What if we stopped making each other happy?

No.

No.

Just no.

Stop being so negative, my mind screamed at me.

Sam loves me. He is waiting for me. And I promised him. I promised him I was coming back. Even if to confirm that I make Sam happy. *And also, to see if he makes you as happy as you think he does,* my mind muttered.

"What about my studies, Pappa? Aren't you worried about it at all?" I asked.

Dad frowned. He wasn't trying to be cruel. And that was the hardest part. He was just afraid of the unknown and basing his assumptions on stereotypes. "Of course, I am worried, *beta*. But we will find a university here to finish your studies."

"But..but I want to go back, Pappa," I sobbed. I needed Sam. I needed him to hold me up. To tell me that everything would be fine.

Mom got up from her chair and pulled me in a hug. "I am sorry, *beta*. We are doing this for you. You'll see. You will thank us in the future."

"Please, Mummy. Please, I need to go back. I promised..." I begged into Mom's arms as I squeezed her. My tears left wet splotches on her clothes where she hugged me. Her gentle hands ran through my hair, and I cried harder.

Gut-wrenching sobs that my mom's hug muffled.

"I'm sorry, beta." Dad joined and ran his hand along my back.

My eyes burned with hot tears and the guttural sobs made my chest hurt.

"Everything will be all right, Akira. We'll be fine. You'll see." Mom's constant murmuring didn't help.

One moment I was crying.

And the next, I was furious.

I tore away from the hug and flung myself off the bed.

Walking across their room, I wiped my tears and rubbed at the pounding headache because of the crying.

I sniffled and said with a hoarse whisper, "I am... I need to... I need to be out of here."

I stormed out of their room.

They refused to let me go.

How could they do that?

What would I do now?

I needed to talk to Sam.

I had to tell him.

The moment I entered my room, strong arms engulfed me.

"Akira, what happened? What did they say?" Aakar asked, his voice surrounding me.

He led me to my bed and sat beside me, holding my hands. I looked around and found Abhi and Ria sitting on Ria's bed, Abhi's eyes brimming with unshed tears and holding Ria's hand.

I looked at Aakar and said, "I...I can't. They refused to let me go back." I told them everything. All their questions. Their doubts. Their mistrust.

Aakar got up and walked back and forth in my room, and Abhi took his spot beside me. The three of us watched Aakar, as if he'd have a solution to this mess. He stopped midway and looked at us. "What? I don't know what to do."

Abhi squeezed my hand as Ria asked me, "Have you talked to Sam about this?"

God. How do I even explain this mess to Sam?

I shook my head. "I was hoping to return. I thought I'd be able to convince Mom and Dad. I didn't want to worry Sam over our family drama."

"God, Akira. What're you going to tell him? Or are you?

Fuck, what are we gonna do, Aakar?" Every concern I had, Abhi voiced it.

Aakar's frown deepened, and he growled, "Let me think. Shit." Aakar kept walking back and forth, running hands in his hair.

He looked at me and said, "Akira, it's late. Your flight is tomorrow night. Are you all packed?"

"Did you not hear me earlier?"

Aakar was worrying me.

"I heard. But we still have twenty-four hours. And we'll do something. You are going back. So, pack your bags. And be ready," Aakar said and stormed out of my room.

Silence.

Abhi, Ria, and I sat back in silence, looking at each other, as we tried to understand what just happened.

～

NOTHING HAPPENED.

For twenty-two hours, I waited for Aakar. I didn't inform Sam about my arguments with my parents. I opened my messages and read his last message.

Sam: Can't wait to hold you, baby. I'll be there to pick you up at the airport.

Me: Miss you, Sam. Can't wait to see you. :-*

And because of the stupid hope that my big brother had given me, I had replied to Sam with that message. Mom and Dad had come to my room around midnight. I had hidden my bags in the closet.

"We're sorry, Akira," Dad had said.

"We'll figure it out," my mom said and kissed my forehead.

I had been surprised when Mom and Dad had come to my room and told me that. I thought Aakar would have spent the day convincing them and allowing me to go. For the last half hour, I had been mulling over this and what Aakar planned to do—if he would be able to do anything at all.

It was half-past midnight now and if I wanted to catch my flight, I had to leave in an hour. I lay down on my bed, thinking about it, and too afraid to deal with what could happen in the next hour if Aakar failed.

A hurried whisper of my name jolted me awake.

Abhi.

"Oh shit. What time is it, Abhi? Did I miss the flight?" I grabbed his hand to check his watch.

Panic filled my insides.

"Akira," Abhi whispered loudly, grabbed my shoulders, and made me focus on him.

"What?" I whispered back.

"We are taking you to the airport. We have already put your bags at the back of the car. Everyone's waiting for you." I lost track of what was coming out of Abhi's mouth.

"What? Am I hearing you correctly?" Dread filled my stomach as I waited for his answer.

When he nodded, I jerked away. "Are you out of your mind? I am not running away!"

Abhi glared at me. "You are. Aakar said so. And Sunil *kaka* said so. Stop wasting your time. We don't want Mom and Dad to wake up."

No.

I couldn't.

It would break my parents' hearts. Any possibility of them accepting my relationship with Sam would be destroyed.

"This will ruin everything, Abhi. This is what Aakar came up with?" I asked, angry that I wasted an entire day for this brilliant idea. I could have tried talking to my parents again.

They might have listened.

"Akira, first of all, your flight is bloody expensive. Second, Mom and Dad are not ready. You need to give them time. I am scared too. Aakar said he'll handle Mom and Dad. And last, your classes start in two days."

My heart was pounding out of my chest.

How did things come to this? Never in my life did I imagine that I'd have to run away from my own home. Abhi looked at me expectantly as I walked around my room, trying to calm my racing heart.

His phone vibrated in his hand. He picked it up and said in the phone, "Yeah."

He looked at me and whispered back, "I am trying, okay? She is thinking too much.

Yeah, okay," he said and cut the call.

"Akira, we need to leave. There is no way Mom and Dad are going to let you go in the next two days. Do you really want to skip your semester? I know Sam would wait for you. Your studies won't. So, pick now."

God, why did Abhi have to make sense? Did he even make sense?

Fuck it.

I needed to go.

Sam would have understood and waited for me. But no, I couldn't give up my degree. I couldn't give up my studies for this.

"Okay. Fine. Let's do this." The moment the words were out, Abhi took me in his arms.

He hugged me till it hurt.

"You are so brave, Akira. Don't stop fighting, okay? I hope Sam is worth it." Abhi's words broke my heart.

I loved my family so much. They were my strength.

And I truly hoped Sam would be a part of it too.

"He really is, Abhi. You'll see."

We wiped our tears and sneaked out of the house. Two blocks down the street, I saw everyone, but my parents and Ria's parents, gathered around the car, waiting.

Everyone was huddled near the car, wearing sweaters in the cold January. Right as Abhi and I neared, Ria looked at me and ran over to hug me.

"What am I doing, Ria?" I murmured in her arms.

"We'll handle it here, Akira. It's all going to be fine," she said.

Everyone got settled in the car. I sat with my grandparents. Grandma held my hand the entire way as she kept saying, "I know my son, *beta*. He is just worried and terrified for you. I'll talk to him."

"They'll forgive me for running away, right?" I asked. I had no intention of disappointing my parents. But I had to make a choice.

"They'll forgive you, Akira. We'll make them," my grandfather said.

The rest of the journey was spent in near silence. A consolation here and there. My family was willing to sacrifice so much for me. Mom and Dad would be furious with them. Even feel betrayed by them. They might even blame me for half the family choosing my side.

"I am so sorry you guys had to betray them." I met Aakar's eyes in the rearview mirror as he drove.

Aakar shook his head and said, "You have nothing to be sorry about, Akira. Mom and Dad shouldn't have stopped you. I understand they are angry, but they don't get to take away your choice. I'll deal with it."

It took us an hour to reach the airport. Every second, I was worried Dad might wake up and figure everything out. So, the moment we reached the airport, everyone knew that we didn't have any time to waste in goodbyes.

Aakar and Abhi were quick to get the bags. I hugged Ekta *kaki*, thanking her for all she chose to do for me—betraying my mom and Radhika *kaki*. I hugged Sunil *kaka* for doing the same.

Hugging them made me want my mom and dad. I wanted them to see me off.

If only.

Once I was done hugging my grandparents, I hugged Ria.

Right at the entrance of the airport, Abhi hugged me tightly. "Don't forget us, Akira. If you want to share anything about Sam, I'm here. And we want to talk to Sam. Give us a call with him, okay?"

I nodded and let my tears fall.

It was only a month ago when I was tackled to the ground at this very entrance. I was at the same spot where Mom and Dad had welcomed me into the warmest hug.

And I was leaving them with a betrayal.

It broke me. Was my relationship more important than them?

Before I could focus more on that, Aakar pulled me into his arms. "Don't think about it too much. You deserve to take a chance. If I had fallen for a girl that they wouldn't approve of, I would fight for her too. I'll handle Mom and Dad. And soon, you'll be talking to them from America. You'll see."

I never expected my big brother to be such a rock. He had always been there for Abhi and me, but to go against our parents for my happiness? I couldn't comprehend how amazing my brother was.

"Thank you, bhai. If you ever need my help running away, I'll come running back from the States to help you. Or you could just run to the States and live with me." I tried to lighten the mood, but even as I finished my sentence, I couldn't stop the tears.

He hugged me tightly. Two arms came around us.

"Me too," Abhi said.

Another set of arms surrounded us.

"Me too," Ria said.

"Let's go now." This time, it was Aakar breaking off our hug and sending me off.

"Akira, take care." Aakar held my cheeks and kissed my forehead.

I grabbed the trolley of my luggage and headed inside the airport.

Before entering, I turned around and looked at my family, tears in their eyes but acceptance and encouragement too.

And that is what made me take the step into the airport and one step closer to Sam.

CHAPTER 24

"The simple lack of her is more to me than others' presence."
    - Edward Thomas

Sam

Akira's plane had landed more than an hour ago. I was standing at the airport lobby. It was late at night, and I hoped the traffic on the way home would be kind.

It felt like a century since I last saw Akira. The past week had been one of the most difficult weeks of my life. I'd been in a constant state of panic. Every missed call, every short message, every conversation with Akira had unsettled me more.

Something seemed off. She kept saying everything was fine and her parents would let her go in the messages she sent me, but she refused to pick up my calls. I had no idea what to think, what to do, or what to say anymore. I just needed to see Akira.

I missed her. I missed our conversations. Akira's bright, joyful laugh that lit up my insides, her funny takes on American shit, and most of all, just her.

People streamed out of the airport, some in groups while some roaming around alone. Laughter and squeals burst from people at seeing their loved ones after a long time. Excited chatter filled the air. Besides the excitement, nervousness was apparent on the faces of hundreds of tourists.

I hated all of it. The conflicting emotions in every corner of the space unnerved me. People were laughing, crying, some were waiting for their loved one with hopeful eyes, and so many others were standing in the line for the cabs.

Where was Akira?

Every second of the wait had my heart beating faster. The atmosphere in the airport added to the pit of my tense stomach.

What if she couldn't come?

What if her father didn't allow her to get on the plane?

She did inform me when she boarded the flight though.

No, Akira was coming.

Sweat beaded at the back of my neck. She should be out any time now. Some groups of Indian families had already passed by me. Some more Indians followed. I tried looking around the groups, hoping to find Akira.

And that's when I saw her.

In a big black sweater and blue jeans, her inky black hair in a top knot. She pushed a baggage cart full of three giant suitcases topped with a mini carry bag. She was a thing of beauty.

Finally.

The tight knot in my chest loosened a little.

I took a few steps toward her when her eyes met mine.

Our world stopped.

She froze for a split second, let go of the cart, and ran toward me.

I ran toward her faster and caught her in my arms.

God, I held my entire world in my arms. A gasp left my chest as her arms came around me.

"Akira, sweetheart," I mumbled against her face, which was tucked into my neck.

A shudder racked her body. I felt it in my bones.

She clutched me tighter, and her silent sobs shattered my heart.

It. Broke. Me.

Every wet slide of her tears along my neck killed me further.

What had she been through?

What did her family do to her?

I clutched her tighter.

She dug deeper into my neck, her shoulders shaking.

"Akira, baby." I buried my face in her hair and placed kisses along her neck, hoping to soothe her.

"God, I missed you," she mumbled.

I needed her so much. I needed to do more than just hold her.

"Let's go home," I said, running my fingers in her hair.

Her smell. Her softness. Her arms around me.

My body finally started settling after a month of upheaval.

She nodded and gave me a heartbreaking, sad smile. After thoroughly rubbing her face in my T-shirt to wipe all the tears, she came out of my neck.

She didn't remove her arms from around me, and I didn't let her.

We walked to her abandoned cart and headed to the parking lot.

During the entire journey, Akira was silent. It had snowed a few days ago, and piles of dirty snow lined the roads. A month ago, the car would've been filled with her chatter and nonstop questions. Today, I could only feel her presence because of her tight grip on my hand. I rubbed my thumb along her fingers. She squeezed mine in return.

"How was your flight?" I asked, a stupid attempt to hear her voice.

"Good," she answered.

"Good," I mumbled back.

Why wasn't she talking? I so badly wanted to hear her voice. See her smile. But Akira was all silence. For the next hour of the drive, she slept with her head on my shoulder, clutching my hand. I was glad I borrowed the car from Dad when I left their place last week. I didn't want to pick up Akira and make her ride an hour and a half in a train.

Once we were home and I had parked the car, I finally took a good look at her while she slept. Her cheeks were swollen, her nose was red. Her lips were a little puffy. Her body was bowed with exhaustion.

I hated seeing her like this. So tired. So defeated.

My brave, beautiful girl.

I couldn't stop myself from touching her lips. Her hair.

The moment I placed a kiss on Akira's forehead, she opened her eyes.

Her gasp stole my breath away.

"Akira," I whispered, placing my forehead against hers.

Tears filled her eyes. She grabbed my shirt with both her hands and tugged me into her lips. She kissed me, over and over again.

I pulled her on my lap and kissed her more, reacquainting myself with her lips. Her cheeks. The throbbing pulse of her neck. The intoxicating smell at the juncture of her neck and shoulder that drove me wild. Akira didn't let go of my clothes, and her desperate kisses turned me wild.

"Akira, sweetheart." I held her cheeks. "We need to get inside."

She held my face with so much love, tears glistened in her eyes. My eyes filled up as I held her in my lap and pushed some of her hair behind her ears.

"Let's go," she said, and kissed me quickly, wiping the unshed tears.

Once we got inside, Akira went to take a quick shower while I got her bags settled. Luke was out with his family on a trip, so we had the apartment to ourselves. The moment Akira was out in just my T-shirt, I dragged her to my bedroom and in my bed.

And just held her.

The need to feel her in my arms choked me. I felt desperate to bury myself inside her. To show her how much I missed her. How desperate and helpless I felt without her. Her soft body fit perfectly in my arms. Akira burrowed herself in my arms, her hands roaming beneath my shirt. I couldn't stop my hands from running down her back, her hair, under her T-shirt.

Akira was finally in my arms. In. My. Arms.

I clutched her tighter. God, I needed to feel her.

Akira was happy to oblige. She held me even tighter and kept kissing me where she could. Our legs tangled under the comforter, her cold feet making me shiver.

After a long time passed where we breathed each other in, Akira, without meeting my eyes, playing with the button of my shirt, said, "I had to run away from home in the middle of the night."

My stomach dropped.

A sharp, stabbing pain spread through my body like a wildfire.

Was she in danger?

Was her family coming right behind her to take her back?

My hand tightened around Akira, and I pulled her tighter into my body.

"Alone?" I asked the most important question. I hope she had Ria's help.

Akira looked at me. She shook her head and held my hand.

"Ria?" I asked.

She nodded and said, "And most of my family. Aakar and Abhi planned it all, and they all came to drop me off at the airport. My uncle and aunt, my grandparents...they all came. I can't believe they all did this for me."

"Oh, sweetheart. I am so fucking grateful for them. And

why did you keep telling me everything was fine when nothing was fine at all?" I had to know. Did she not think that I could be there for her? Or did she think that I was incapable of trusting her?

"I can see the thoughts swimming around your head, Sam. Quit it. The only reason I didn't tell you about the gravity of the situation was that I didn't want you to drop everything and come to India. And you would've jumped on the next flight if I'd told you that my parents had refused to let me go even the day before my flight. I thought I could convince them with the help of my siblings, but things didn't work out very well."

The strain of the past days was visible with Akira's sad eyes, stress lines on her forehead and heaviness in her tone.

She did make it here with the help of her cousins. I didn't need to add any more stress on her.

I dragged her back into my arms. "So now what? Is your father going to come to the States to take you back? Should we be worried or taking any precautions or run away from New York?" What if her family followed her here and took her back to India? My hand automatically clutched her tighter to me.

She scoffed and a small smile broke through. I didn't expect that. At my raised eyebrows, Akira rolled her eyes. "No one in my family has a visa. It would take them at the very least three months to get a visa and follow me."

Thank the visa gods.

"Oh, I love America. Finally getting useful in protecting us mere mortals from ruthless parents," I mumbled in Akira's neck. My body sagged in relief.

Akira giggled sadly.

With tears in her eyes, she looked into my eyes and said, "They'll be devastated. I disappointed them. Again."

I wish I had something useful to say.

I wish I could take away her pain.

I wish I could change her parents' minds.

"Let's sleep for now. Tomorrow morning, we'll deal with the rest of the world," I said, placing kisses along her shoulders and neck.

I breathed her in. Again.

Akira was here.

"I love you so much, Akira," I mumbled in her hair and tugged her back to my front.

Akira turned her head to look at me and, with a soft smile, said, "I love you too, Sam. So much it hurts."

"Show me the ring, baby," I'd forgotten about the ring in the midst of everything.

When Akira placed her right palm in my hand, a shudder racked through my body and an insane surge of possessiveness bubbled up. I held her hand and kissed her ring finger.

Soon, this ring would be on the left hand.

Before long, Akira was asleep in my arms, her head in the crook of my neck and legs sprawled on my thighs.

I wanted this every day.

I had to do something to bring around Akira's parents.

She had done enough.

What was so wrong in loving each other?

That we looked different?

Why were people so afraid of *different*?

Why were they so reluctant to accept change?

Even if I were to scream a hundred times for them to accept the differences of people, I knew it wouldn't make a difference. It's human nature.

It is incredibly difficult to make people accept the differences.

But so simple to welcome people just like us into our safe haven. No questions asked.

So why not start finding the similarities among ourselves? Why not show everyone how similar we are to each other?

Maybe then, our differences won't matter so much.

I had to show Akira's parents how similar I was to them.

Like them, I hurt.

Like them, I felt joy.

Like them, I loved Akira.

Like them, I wanted to protect her.

Like them, I just wanted to make her happy.

The only difference that mattered was I was a man in love, prepared to fight till the end.

CHAPTER 25

"...what good would it do to shutter your windows, never dream of rainbows or find hope in promises? Why choose to walk away rather than hold your ground and fight for love?"
  - Ellen Hopkins

Akira

The early morning bustle of the city roused me from my sleep. I'd forgotten how loud it could get, living in low-rise apartments. Sam held me close to his front, his grip tight, as if to never let me leave again. I didn't want to.

A hundred thoughts swirled in my mind.

When my mom had asked me if I would like coming home to a place where I am not completely myself, I had no words to explain my feelings then. When Sam had crushed me in his arms at the airport, I had finally realized.

Home wasn't a place where I needed to talk in my native language or pray to my Hindu gods. Home was where I was unashamedly myself, with a guy who loved me, respected me, even celebrated me. A place, with him, where I wasn't forced to do something that I didn't believe in, where my choices were respected, and my opinions valued. And that's why every fight with my family was worth it.

I wasn't just fighting for Sam. Or for us.

I was fighting for me.

To be who I am.

To love proudly.

To live freely.

Gentle kisses along my neck brought me back.

"Morning, sweetheart," Sam said, pulling me closer to him, if that was even possible. It was.

Our legs tangled under the blanket. Sam's hands slid under his t-shirt that I wore and caressed my skin. Shivers raced down my spine. I turned into his arms and ran my nose along his throat.

Sam's arms tightened around me, and he pulled me on top of him.

"I missed you so fucking much," he whispered in my ear. Heavy breath fanned across my neck.

His words melted my heart. His wandering hands burned me. I placed kisses across his neck, nipped his jaw, and rubbed my cheeks to his scruff.

"I missed you too, Sam. So much." I trailed kisses on his naked chest.

"I still can't believe you're here," Sam said, his cheeks turning red.

He dragged me up from where I kissed along his hip and buried his face in my chest. He dragged my T-shirt up until it was thrown somewhere across the room and ran his nose along my exposed breasts. All the while, his hardness rubbed along my core, making me involuntarily rub myself along him.

The need to feel him, skin on skin, had me tugging his clothes off and tossing them to the floor. The moment our skin touched, groans filled the air. The soft, cool blanket rubbed my back as Sam's hot mouth bombarded me with a hundred different sensations. I clutched his shoulders as I pulled my panties aside to rub myself harder against his cock.

A loud groan from Sam had me kissing him harder.

"Off... Wait... Fuck, Akira." Sam's incoherent words went right above my head as I continued with my kisses.

His hands were everywhere—splayed on my back, clutching my ass, grabbing my hair.

His head arched up in pleasure as I kissed his neck.

"Wait, Akira. Panties. Off. God, wait a second, baby." He gripped my ass with both hands and dragged me off his cock.

I moaned in protest while he removed my panties.

The moment I was completely naked, I went back to what I was doing.

"God, Akira. Missed this," Sam growled in my ear and dragged my hips over him in a wild rhythm.

"Harder, baby," he said and rolled us in the blanket without leaving my ass. He rutted along my wetness, and the rapidly growing heat had me arching up for more.

"Inside me, Sam. Need...need you." I grabbed his hair and dragged him to my shoulder.

He fisted my hair with one hand and bit my shoulder, his other hand busy fumbling in the side drawer for the condom.

"Sam..." I moaned, my back arching for more.

"Fuck, sweetheart. A second." Sam's harsh breath spurred me further.

The moment the condom was rolled, Sam clutched my hips and held his cock in one hand while he pushed inside. Slowly. He pushed a little inside and pulled out.

A little more in and out.

He teased me like that for a while, getting me wetter.

"In now, Sam," I yelled and pinched his slow ass.

He huffed a burst of laughter and pushed himself completely inside.

He shivered. I arched up.

"I love you, sweetheart," he said, his voice a rough whisper. "Do not leave me again like that." The rare vulnerability in Sam's voice tugged at my heart. I clutched him harder to bring him closer. Kissed him deeper. Held him tighter.

"Never, Sam," I said, and poured all my love in my kisses, unshed tears clouding my vision.

Sam buried his face in my neck and picked up the speed.

The overwhelming emotions of reuniting, the realization of what we almost lost and the shared vulnerability, turned our pleasure into pure bliss.

Wetness slid along my neck. I ran my hand in Sam's hair and clutched his neck to show him I was right there with him. He held me tighter and moved as deep as he could. Heat sizzled in my core, tingling my spine. So close. I was so fucking close.

"Akira, fuck!" Sam yelled in my neck and with a hard thrust, erupted. He rolled his hips three more times, lost in his orgasm, as I cradled his hips between my open legs.

After a minute of catching his breath, he said in my ear, "Your turn to come, baby." Sam got out of me and threw the condom in the garbage bin.

"I'm so close." I ground my hips against his soft cock.

He moaned and moved down to my hips, placing kisses everywhere as he went.

"Yes," I hissed and pulled his head to where I needed it the most.

The moment his lips closed around my clit, a loud moan escaped me.

"Right there. Keep doing that. Just that," I chanted, and Sam followed.

He licked and sucked until I screamed his name and held his head between my thighs, squeezing out the last of my orgasm.

He let me ride my high, his face between my clamped thighs, and gasped loudly once I let him loose.

"Damn, sweetheart. Five more seconds and I would've fainted right between your legs," he said. I couldn't stop the snicker and the roll of my eyes.

We kissed for a few minutes but the loud honking of the ambulance and fire trucks on the street broke the happy bubble we had surrounded ourselves in.

After a few minutes of silence in Sam's arms, I said, "I need to call my family."

"Yeah, I figured. We'll do it together." Sam kissed my forehead and got out of the bed. He went to the attached bathroom in his room and freshened up while I got my bearings to face the family.

Once Sam was out of the bathroom, he said, "I'll get breakfast ready while you freshen up. We'll call your family after that. And we also need to sign up for lectures for the add/drop period. Classes begin in two days."

I got my phone from my abandoned bag, put it on to charge, and went to clean up.

I came out in the living room wearing Sam's T-shirt and boxers to find the dining table filled with food—my favorite breakfast food.

Chai.

Well, favorite breakfast beverage.

Sam looked up from his chair and said, "Umm...I've been trying to make chai the way you like it. You can make a new one if I didn't get it right." He straightened his already straight glasses, his face red. He'd never looked more adorable.

Stupid tears gathered in my eyes.

"It's perfect," I whispered and sat on his lap.

His arms came around me as I took the cup and sipped my chai.

Oh no. Not the best.

He raised his eyebrows. "And?"

I hid my smile in the cup and said, "A plus for effort and romance."

"And for taste?"

"B minus." He groaned loudly, making me laugh.

He bit my shoulder. "One day, I'll be making it better than you."

I didn't stop the loud snort. "Doubt it, Sam. The skill of good chai making is achieved through regular practice and precision. It needs discipline and dedication."

With a stupid laugh, Sam said, "Eat the toast. And some scrambled eggs if you'd like. I don't know if you'll have any appetite after the call. Not that it's going to be bad. But let's not risk it."

"Yeah," I sighed. I went to the opposite chair with my chai and took some egg and toast on my plate.

Breakfast was done way before I was emotionally prepared for the call. I even cleared the table and washed the utensils to delay the inevitable.

Sam ran his hand in my hair as I wiped my hands after washing the dishes and handed me my phone.

We went back to his bedroom and sat at the edge of his bed.

I switched on the phone.

Sam held my hand and played with the ring on my finger as the phone turned on. A gentle smile graced his lips, and I quickly kissed the side of his head. His eyes turned to my lips, and he captured them in a loving caress. He made me feel so freaking cherished. How could I not stand up for our love?

He nudged me with his shoulder, and I looked down at my phone.

A few missed calls from Aakar and Abhi. Two from Ria. One from my uncle.

None from my parents.

My heart rate spiked, and my stomach dropped.

"It's okay. Call your brother," Sam said gently.

I nodded and called Aakar. It would be around 10 p.m. in India. The call rang twice before Aakar picked up. "Akira, you okay?" was the first thing he asked.

"Are Mom and Dad okay?" I asked. He knew I wasn't okay.

Aakar sighed. I heard Abhi and Ria's voices on the other side.

"We're dealing with it. They're upset," Aakar said.

"*Bhai*, they get upset when you refuse to see girls for an arranged marriage. They must be furious right now. Please tell me the truth."

After a beat, Aakar asked, "Is your boyfriend with you?"

Sam had been patiently listening to my end of the conversation. So, when I looked at him, he raised his eyebrows in concern.

"Yeah," I answered, and nodded at Sam with a smile, hoping to convey that everything was fine.

"Maybe put the phone on speaker. He needs to hear this too. And I'll also talk to him," Aakar said.

This wasn't good at all.

"Okay," I said and turned on the speaker of the phone.

"Sam," Aakar said.

Sam looked at me, and at my nod, he said, "Aakar. Hi. Before you say anything, I just wanted to thank you for being there for Akira and supporting her. It meant a lot, man."

At the silence on Aakar's end, Sam looked at me with an apology in his eyes. I just mouthed thank you and held his hand.

"It's okay. She's my sister. If she's happy with you, I am happy for her. Don't make me regret supporting her, Sam," Aakar said. Always the straight shooter, my brother.

"I love her, Aakar. I just want to make her happy and be with her." I could see the love shining in his eyes as he held my hand a little tighter.

Aakar cleared his throat. "That's good. Now that is all clear..."

Abhi interrupted at that point. "We heard that too. Hi, Sam."

I mouthed Abhi to Sam, and Sam greeted, "Hi, Abhi, thank you to you, too, for supporting Akira."

"Of course, *jiju*," Abhi said, making me laugh, Sam frown, and Aakar groan. Sam would've totally blushed if he'd known that Abhi had called him brother-in-law.

"Let's get to the point, shall we?" Aakar asked, and the mood sobered.

"Yes, please. How did Mom and Dad react?" I asked.

"Well, not very well, as expected. Before they could find out on their own and feel betrayed, all of us went to them as soon as your plane took off and told them that we'd dropped you off at the airport," Aakar explained.

God. I hated myself for abandoning my family. Arms came around me. Sam's lips pressed against my forehead, and I said in the phone, "I am so sorry, bhai. I wish you had just blamed me that I ran away. That way, they would have only hated me."

Aakar scoffed. "Akira, that would have been worse. Our parents need to know that there are people in our family who support you. What else is going to convince them to give you guys a chance?"

"But, what about you all? How did they react?"

"Dad slapped Aakar," Abhi blurted, and I failed to contain the gasp.

"Fuck," Sam muttered. He pushed his glasses on his head and rubbed his eyes.

"Abhi... Shut up, will you?" Aakar scolded.

"Bhai...I am so, so, so sorry," I said, tears streaming down my cheeks.

"Look what you did!" Aakar scolded Abhi.

I heard a muttered, "She'd want to know."

I would want to know.

"What happened next?" Sam asked, diffusing the argument that was about to break out.

Aakar said, "Well, Mom cried and told us that we don't care enough about you. Dad told all of us, including Uncle, Aunt, Grandma, and Grandpa, that we had no right to make those decisions. Ria's parents threatened to get her married if she was adamant on being defiant, and we haven't talked to them since."

"God, I don't know what to say except that I am so sorry," I said. I ran away, leaving them all to deal with my shit.

"Do you think I should come back and convince them more?" I asked. Sam's hand tightened around me.

"No," Sam said at the same time that Aakar, Abhi, Ria, and now my grandmother said no.

"*Daadi*, I'm so, so sorry," I cried. Sam kept trying to soothe me by running his hand along my back and occasionally kissing my shoulder or forehead. But it wasn't working.

Every bit of this story had my guilt skyrocketing.

"Akira, *beta*...don't worry. He is my son. Give him some time. They are just worried about you, is all. He will come around. Your mom, too. We will make them come around," Grandma said.

Her words brought me more tears but also a kindling of hope.

"What should I do, *daadi*?" I needed to do *something* when my family was fighting for me now.

"Nothing, *beta*. Give them some time. We will continue reminding your parents that we stand by you and that we talk to you. They will soon miss their only daughter. Keep calling them, though. Remind them that you haven't forgotten them even though you left." Her steadfast support and simple solutions seemed a little too easy. But I would do as she said.

"Yeah, I'll do that. If only Mom and Dad would see how

good this is for me." At this, Sam held me tighter, and his eyes showed me the sympathy and support that I needed.

"They will," Ria added. They seemed to have put the phone on speaker too.

"We'll keep in touch, Akira. Don't keep thinking about this all day now. Live your life," Grandma said.

"Yeah. Keep me posted. Do not sugarcoat anything. I can take it," I said, and after a few more farewells, we hung up.

Once the phone call was done, all I could do was lie back on the bed in Sam's arms.

He was right.

I had no appetite anymore.

∼

Sam

A week passed.

Classes began in full force.

Akira chose the classes with the least amount of research papers. She chose to focus on building and technology courses, while I chose the ones with professional practice emphasis since I planned to join my father's construction firm right after I graduated.

We both wanted to go with whatever was easier to handle. With the tense atmosphere in our personal lives, neither of us wanted to deal with particularly difficult subjects this semester. We did have a studio together, the only common class we took this semester. However, I shared two classes with Luke this semester.

Akira had also moved back to her place after two days of living with me. She had spent an entire day catching up with her roommates, relaying everything that happened and discussing on how to approach her parents.

After the first call with her brother when she'd returned, she steadfastly called her parents every day. Neither of her parents have picked up the call. Every unanswered call stole some of the light from her eyes.

Akira laughed a little less.

Her smart-ass comments turned rare.

Her eyes stopped smiling.

I fucking hated it.

It had been great talking to her family. It was clear that they loved her. All of them. Some of them in ways that made Akira sad.

It was 11:00 a.m. and I was waiting for the class to begin when Luke dropped on the seat beside me. I was glad he wasn't at our place last weekend when Akira returned. He'd been off with his family to a volunteer program in Africa. Luke's family has always been involved in different charities and programs. I've joined them occasionally but not as much as I'd like.

"Hey, man. How's everything going? You know, after...?" Luke asked.

I nodded my head in greeting. "Good. Akira's finally back. I talked to some of her family."

Luke smiled in relief. "Oh, good. Glad her family allowed her to come back."

I stiffened at that.

"What'd I say?" Luke asked, worried at the tension seeping off me.

I shook my head, trying to shake off the anger brewing right under my skin. "Akira had to sneak off. Some of her family helped her get to the airport. No consent from her parents. They're not even picking up her calls right now."

Luke grimaced. "Fuck."

"Sums it up," I muttered.

"So, what are you guys gonna do?"

I shrugged.

Before I could expand on where we were, the professor came into the class and started the lecture.

"Later," I told him, and got into two hours of concentrating on something other than the fucked-up situation we were stuck in.

Luke and I walked to the adjacent building in the university for another class. He was up my ass and insistent on bouncing off ideas on how to deal with Akira's parents.

"What if you promise to move to India?" Idea number thirty-five from Luke.

At my glare, another idea bounced off his head and unashamedly through his mouth, "Bribe them with a world tour trip."

My lack of response to that was enough to get him frustrated.

"Ugh.." Luke said. "You might as well just call them and talk to them."

Hmm. I had been thinking about the same thing for a week now. But Akira had done the same thing. If her words had no impact on them, mine weren't going to do shit.

"You know, I have been thinking about it," I said.

"You wouldn't!" Luke's flabbergasted face almost made me laugh.

I surfed through my contact list on the phone and called the best person that could help me out.

After four rings, "Hello, Sam."

"Ria. Hi."

CHAPTER 26

"In the game of life;
   Sometimes we win,
   Sometimes we lose,
   Either ways, we should always keep playing."
   - Lailah Gifty Akita

Sam

Day 1 of Project - *Get Parents On Board*

I clutched the phone tighter in my clammy hands. Akira was at her place, so I could do this without her knowing. Sitting on the edge of my bed, I said a small prayer for luck and opened the contact details I got from Ria for Akira's mom.

I had asked Ria for Akira's dad's phone number. But she had shut me down quickly and told me to take a sensible risk and not jump off a cliff. Akira had once informed me that her parents understood English and they could talk a little bit too.

I opened the window of my apartment to let some of the cool winter air in.

I blew out a loud breath and before I could change my mind, pressed the call button.

After a few heart-throbbing rings, I heard, "Hello?"

Wiping my hands on my sweatpants, I said, "Uh... Hi, is this Akira's mother?"

A loud gasp echoed on the line.

"Yes. You are?" Akira's mother's voice trembled. With rage or fear, I didn't know.

"I'm Sam," I said.

And the call ended. Did she just end the call or did the call drop? I dialed again.

After two rings, the phone connected again.

"Do not call on this number again," Akira's mom said tartly.

"Ma'am, if you could just hear me out..." That was all I could say before the call ended.

This was going to take some work.

Day 5 of Project - *Get Parents On Board*

Akira's mother was one stubborn woman. For the past four days, I'd called her several times a day. She hadn't picked up any of my calls. If she thought I was going to stop, she was up for daily missed calls for a long fucking time.

I was on my way to the studio from my previous class. Akira was already in the studio and was waiting for me. I surfed through the phone as I walked and scrolled through all the unanswered calls to Akira's mother.

How could she not care?

The burst of anger had me calling her again. I kept walking to the studio.

I could just keep spamming her phone for the rest of my life as a punishment for hurting Akira.

A villainous laugh escaped me.

I called the number and waited for Akira's mother to end the call. While the phone rang, I nodded in greeting at some of my classmates that passed.

Except.

I saw the phone get picked up.

Fuck.

I quickly took a detour to the open smoking area and put the phone to my ear instead of giving the phone the stink eye. "Hello?" I asked.

"What do you want, Sam?" Akira's mother asked.

She had me blindsided, and I had absolutely nothing. I didn't have the speech prepared like last time. I wasn't amped up to call her out. God.

A deep breath. In and out. In and out.

"Ma'am, if you could only allow me to prove my love for Akira and explain why we could be so good together, I would really appreciate it," I said, talking quickly before she decided to drop the call on me.

Silence on the other side.

I checked the phone if the call had dropped.

No. She was still on the line.

I added, "If not for me, then for Akira, ma'am. Please."

A teary gasp came from her, and Akira's mother's voice trembled as she asked, "How is she?"

She was talking to me. Yes. I pumped my fist in the air. I could even break out in a dance in the middle of the campus.

I remembered Akira's face from last night and gave her the truth. "She is not doing the best. She misses you. She is always sad. She cries."

Akira's mother started sobbing. Her cries satisfied me far more than hurt me. She deserved to know how their actions hurt Akira. Their decision to not even consider giving us a chance and not allowing her to leave India had forced Akira to run away from her own home.

With a tearful sob, Akira's mother said, "Look what you did. Why would you ruin her life like that?"

My mind was still stuck at working through the *Look what you did.*

"Me...?" It was all I could ask.

"You distracted her. Because of you, she is not talking to her family. You should be ashamed of yourself." Boy, once she started, she didn't stop.

Each accusation chipped away at my deepest fear. Yes, I feared that Akira was just lost in the excitement of a relationship with an American. Yes, I feared Akira would resent me in the future if she lost her relationship with her family.

And I was ashamed of myself.

Not for falling in love with Akira.

But for doubting Akira, even after she already chose me.

"I love Akira," I said with a conviction that defied my fears.

With a sad huff, Akira's mother said, "If you loved her, you wouldn't come between her and her family." *I am not the one standing between Akira and her family*, I wanted to scream.

And then she conveniently ended the call.

All the guilt and all my hidden fears surfaced. Did Akira do the right thing choosing me? Was our relationship worth so much anguish within a family?

My phone vibrated in my hand, indicating an incoming call. *Akira calling...*

I picked up the call and heard Akira's melodious yet irritated voice. "Where are you? I need to discuss this design with you before the faculty arrives."

A lump of doubt and guilt had settled in my throat, making it difficult for the words to get out.

"Yeah. I'm on my way. Be there in five," I said, and ended the call.

I needed a minute to get my bearings. Akira's mother's words looped in my mind. I bumped into two people on my way to the studio.

The moment I entered the studio though, Akira's gaze

swung to me. A bright smile spread across her face as our eyes met. Love and real happiness shone through her eyes, and I fell in love all over again. Akira's mother's words came back to me.

Akira loved me. I loved her. *I* wasn't the one keeping her away from her family. Tomorrow, I'll try again, and explain that to Akira's mother. I didn't care if she thought I was right for her or not. But soon, she would know there was no one who loved Akira more than I did. That's for sure.

I walked to the seat beside Akira and ran the back of my fingers along her cheek. She nuzzled into my hand for a second and straightened up. She looked around the class and mock-glared at me.

"Everything okay?" Akira asked, concern dotting the line between her eyebrows.

I gave her a placating smile and said, "It's perfect. Now, where were you at the design development?"

Day 12 of Project - *Get Parents On Board*

After a week of constantly calling Akira's mom, I was getting frustrated. Even today, I'd called her twice already. But nothing.

Akira talked a lot with her family through WhatsApp. Maybe if I tried there.

I opened the app and clicked into her mother's profile to send her a message.

> Me: If you truly care about Akira, please pick up the call

I was willing to resort to stupid emotional blackmail shit if that would help.

After about half an hour of waiting, I got a call from Akira's mother.

I quickly picked up the call and said in a rush, "Please, ma'am, do not end the call. You need to hear me out."

"Is Akira okay?" she asked in a tired tone.

"Physically, yes. Emotionally, not so much," I explained.

"Say what you need to, Sam. I'm listening."

Relief spread through my limbs and I sat down on my bed from where I was walking back and forth across my room.

"Oh, thank God, I can't tell you how grateful I am," I said.

Akira's mother interrupted me in the middle of my gratitude. "Sam, I can't talk on the phone. Your accent is very difficult to understand. Can we talk in WhatsApp messages?"

Oh. Of course. Even though she could talk in English, I can't blame her for not catching up on the different accent.

"Yes, of course, ma'am. I'll message you."

Conveying my feelings for Akira in a text message seemed to trivialize the situation somehow. At least I wouldn't make a fool of myself since it gave me a chance to think before I send a message.

On the other hand, it also gives Akira's mom a chance to think about all the ways to reject me.

"Call me aunty, Sam," she said, bringing me out of my panic and relief-induced thoughts.

Wow. I got promoted from ma'am to Aunty. Akira would be so happy to know that. Except, I needed to be patient for now.

"Thank you, Aunty. I'll message you," I said, trying to talk slow and enunciate my words as clear as possible.

"Okay. Take care of Akira."

"Aunty, please call Akira," I said. I would have elaborately begged if my accent wasn't a barrier. But that's what I aimed to do through messages.

The moment the call ended, I drafted the text.

Me: Thank you so much for agreeing to hear me out. I wish I could have been there with Akira when she told you about our relationship. I never wanted her to face this alone. However, I will never let Akira go through that all alone ever again. I understand that our race, culture, and religion are all different. But, Aunty, I am just a human with different skin color, fewer festivals, and belief in even fewer gods. That doesn't mean I don't value and respect Akira's festivals, her culture and her belief in her Hindu gods. Just like Akira, I get sad when the people I love hurt. I want to succeed in life and make my family proud. I want to love someone and build a family with her, and I, too, want someone to love me unconditionally. Akira is that someone, Aunty. And you would never find a person who loves Akira more than I do. I only want to make her happy for the rest of our lives. I know you wish the same for Akira. How are we all that different from each other? Nothing would make Akira happier than her parents' blessings. She deserves all the love and happiness in the world.

I read the message a few times to make sure I got everything right.

And SEND.

DAY 20 of Project - *Get Parents On Board*

Still nothing. The messaging app indicated that the message was read. Akira's mother had been online multiple times a day. Oh yeah, I was watching.

Creepy? No.

Concerned? Very much so.

I did not stop messaging though.

Every day, I sent something. *Akira misses you, I will always care about Akira's values, she's doing so well in school,* and once in a while, just a photo. It hadn't been difficult to click a picture of Akira in a lost mood. Ever since she was back, she had been a little lost. A little sad, even at the happiest moments. A little guilty in every waking moment.

She tried to not show that outright. But guilt was a strong emotion. Most days, Akira spent the night at my place. It was easier for both of us. I didn't have to walk her to her apartment as I used to, when all we wanted to do was sleep during a hectic school load. Because of our separate classes, I only got to attend two lectures a week with Akira.

Thank God for that, because I got some time without Akira where I could harass and badger her mom without Akira knowing. They will call her sooner or later. Sooner if I could help.

> Akira's mom: You both are very different, Sam

Fucking finally.

> Me: We are more similar than we are different. Hopefully, you and Akira's father will give us a chance to show that to you.

> Akira's mom: How do I trust you with Akira?

> Me: The same way you would trust any other guy. Your daughter is a very smart woman, Aunty. If not me, I hope you trust her choice enough. You raised her well.

And I waited after that.
And waited.
Some more.

> Akira's mom: I'll talk to her father.

"Hell, yeah!" I didn't even realize I had jumped out of the bed. Finally. Relief blinded me for a minute there, and I took a seat back on my bed.

> Me: Thank you so much, Aunty. I won't let you down.

> Akira's mom: Please don't say anything to Akira for now. Let me talk to her father first.

> Me: Okay. I understand. Please don't mind if I keep pestering you for the status report. :-)

> Akira's mom: I didn't think you would stop. You are not too bad, Sam. Take care of Akira.

You are not too bad. No compliment has ever made me happier.

> Me: Loving Akira is my most important job. Take care.

∼

Akira

Day 30 of Project - *Get Parents On Board*

The blaring beats of "Believer" by Imagine Dragons jolted me from my sleep. A loud groan from beside me had me craning my neck in that direction. But before I could fully comprehend the surroundings, Sam groaned again and put his pillow over his head.

One of his hands was buried beneath his head and his other hand swatted at my side, waking me from the sleep.

"What the hell, Sam?" I barked. The pounding beats of the song and Sam's incessant nudging had my mind facing decibels above my tolerance level.

"It's your fucking phone. Shut it, would ya?" Sam's muffled voice from beneath his pillow was difficult to decipher.

But yes. It *was* my phone that was blaring in the middle of the night. Then why was there light out?

Keeping my eyes closed, I moved my hand all over the nightstand for the phone.

The moment I grabbed the phone and peeked at the screen from between my fingers, my eyes flew open.

The name on the screen had me scrambling out of bed.

"Sam! Sam...Sam..." I patted Sam's back and said, "Wake up, Sam! My dad's calling."

Sam did the same thing as me.

He flew out of bed.

Well, he tried to, but his legs got tangled in the covers and he fell on the floor.

"What? Your dad?" he asked.

"Yeah. Fuck. This is the second call. We slept through the first call. Oh God, Sam, the phone won't stop ringing." I held the phone as far from my body as possible, as if my dad would jump out of the phone.

Sam ran by my side and looked down at the phone screen. Perspiration dotted his forehead and upper lips.

"You're terrified, too, aren't you? Oh God, what do I do?" The walls were closing in on me. I needed some air. Looking around frantically, I opened the window in Sam's room and sat on the ledge.

"I'm not scared. I just get hot when I sleep," Sam lied. Because he did get hot when he slept, but not that hot.

Sam stood by me near the window and placed his one hand on my knee and the other held my shoulder in a firm grip.

A steely determination shone through his eyes as he said, "Pick up the phone, Akira. I'm with you this time. And put the phone on speaker."

His confidence had me sliding the answer button on the

phone screen before I could properly think. I put the phone on speaker and, at Sam's nod, said, "Hel...hello?"

"Akira?" My mom's voice trembled over the phone, and I gasped.

I bit my lip to stop my lips from wobbling, but tears slid down my cheeks. Sam squeezed my knee and shoulder lightly. Silent support in the storm of my life.

"Mummy? I am so sorry for running away," I hiccupped as the sobs broke free.

Mom cried on the other end. "Akira, beta, don't cry. We are sorry too. For forcing you to run."

"We?" Mom had said *we are sorry*. Did she mean...?

"Oh yes, your father is here too, *beta*. Here, talk to him." Mom switched to talking in Gujarati. Before I could protest, I heard the shuffling on the other end.

I looked up to Sam, trying to gauge his reaction.

He wiped my tears and, with a soft smile that melted my fears and my heart, kissed my nose. For a second, I forgot what was happening. My father's voice brought it all right back.

"Akira?" Dad asked, uncertainty and, if I'm not mistaken, a hint of guilt laced his tone.

"Pappa," I couldn't say more than that.

Before Dad could say anything, I continued. "I'm sorry, Pappa."

Sam's hold on my knee tightened.

Dad talked in Gujarati. I automatically switched to my native language.

"Akira, I understand, *beta*. You did what you had to. Your *daadi* and your brothers haven't been silent since you left."

"Please don't blame them, Pappa. They didn't do anything wrong." I didn't want my family to suffer because of my decisions.

Dad grunted on the other side. "Neither did you, Akira. I've had enough time to think about everything."

"And?" I asked. Nerves skated across my spine. Sweat gathered in my hands and under my knees. And I was pretty sure Sam could hear my heart beating from where he stood.

Dad talked in Gujarati. Sam had no idea about what was being discussed. I could see he was trying to figure out the gravity of the situation by reading the reactions on my face and the tension in our voices.

With a sigh, Dad said, "I admit that if you had fallen for an Indian boy, I wouldn't have reacted the same way. I am worried, Akira. I want you to have the best life possible, and I don't know if this American boy can provide that for you. And we don't want to lose you."

I looked at Sam, trying to contain my emotions.

I know Sam knew we were talking about him right now, because my dad said "American." I gave Sam a placating smile, but it didn't relax his tense face.

I continued in Gujarati. "Pappa, it would be the same case for any guy that even you choose for me. How would you know that he would provide me the best life possible?"

Dad scoffed. "At least I would be capable of destroying their family if they didn't."

I heard Mom gasp on the other hand followed by "Pravin!" the same time I gasped and said, "Pappa!"

"I'm right and you both know it. But in case of this American boy, he would be able to destroy your life, and I would be helpless. If you ever got into a bad situation with him, we wouldn't be able to be there for you in the next hour. It could take us months to reach you and be there for you. And what if he hurt you, Akira?"

The entire time my dad explained his point, Sam struggled to understand anything. Desperation to understand my dad poured off him in waves. I placed my hand over his on my knee and squeezed his hand. A sad smile crossed his face and his shoulders dropped.

Once Sam had pulled himself together, I said on the phone, "I understand, Pappa. But you must trust me in this. I know Sam. I have spent months getting to know him. He loves me so much, Pappa. He cares for me, he walks me home if it's dark, he brings me food if I forget to eat during the busy hours. Every little thing, Pappa. He notices every little thing. Please take a chance on him. You'll see how good he is when you meet him. You'll love him too."

After a long silence and some sniffles from Mom on the other end of the phone, Dad said, "All right."

I squealed before Dad could continue. "Oh my God, Pappa. Thank you. Thank you. You are going to love him."

Dad interrupted me. "Listen to me, Akira. Let me talk before you go crazy. Before I approve of him, I need to meet him. Our entire family needs to meet him."

Nerves churned my belly. *Meet him.*

Dad continued, "You both will come to India during the summer break. Is that clear? I will see for myself if that boy is good enough."

Summer break was when we went for an internship. That's like four months away. I needed to ask Sam if he would be willing to come.

I asked Dad, "Umm...we have an internship during that time. Can we maybe come to India in December?"

I cringed, waiting for Dad's answer. Sam frowned in confusion. I kept using English words like an internship, December, India. I was sure he could piece together some of the conversation.

"Do not test my patience, Akira," Dad said, his tone laced in a warning.

I quickly put the phone on mute and, without a second thought, asked Sam, "My dad and the rest of the family would like to meet you before approving our relationship. Would you uhh...be able to visit India with me on summer break?"

God, now he had to meet my parents. Embarrassment dotted my cheeks. I felt like a little kid that needed permission from her parents to go out.

Sam smiled at me and said, "If that's what it takes to get you, I am good with that."

Relief surged through me. I put the phone off the mute and said, "Okay, Pappa. I'll tell Sam to come to India. We'll book the tickets soon."

Dad grunted, "Okay. Good. And you tell that boy to stop pestering your mother with the nonstop messages."

My heart stopped. I looked at the confusion and worry dotted on Sam's innocent face. The reaction on my face had Sam tensing up. He raised his eyebrows in question. I just looked at him. I didn't know how to respond.

"Yes, Pappa. I am so happy you agreed. It means so much to me. Thank you," I said. My mind was still stuck on Sam messaging my mom. He got my parents talking to me. He had them apologize to me.

But when?

"We hate not talking to you, Akira. You better start calling us every day now. Are we clear?" Dad said, his tone gentle and emotional.

Tears blurred my eyes, and my nose flared with bubbling emotions.

"Yes, Pappa. I missed talking to you all. I am so, so happy. I love you guys."

Mom sobbed. "We love you too, *beta*. Call me every day. And tell Sam thank you. He forced me to open my eyes. He is not so bad."

And now I was sobbing.

"Now stop crying, you two. We need to end the call before I start crying too," Dad joked, making us laugh.

"Yeah. Okay. We'll talk soon," I said.

"Bye, Akira," they said, and ended the call.

With a deep sigh, I pressed my forehead to Sam's chest. He moved forward and took me in his arms.

"Are you going to tell me now?" Sam asked, his body still tense.

"They agreed to meet you and give us a chance," I said. I'll explain the word-by-word conversation later.

A big smile spread across his face. His eyes shone with tears. He wiped my wet cheeks with his thumbs. "Really?"

When I nodded in his palms, he pulled my face to him and kissed me.

I pulled away from the kiss and looked at him. "All thanks to you."

Realization dawned on his face, and color dotted his cheeks. "Um... Your parents told you, huh?"

I couldn't stop the smile at Sam's blush. I held his face in my hands and asked, "Why are you so amazing?"

He laughed, his face turning redder.

"Aww, you're blushing," I said, squeezing Sam's cheeks.

"And you are back, sweetheart. That's all I need," Sam said and caught my waist.

He pressed his forehead to mine and, with adoring eyes, whispered, "I missed you."

Love surrounded us, a physical force that was finally free to exist between us. It didn't have to worry about judgment from others and permission from the family. It could just thrive and grow now. All the barriers that stopped me from surrendering to this love broke free.

It pushed me to Sam, and I went into his arms. I opened myself to show him the love I had for him. Freely. Completely.

I surrendered myself to him, and it was the most surreal moment of my life. Sam's hands trembled on my waist. And when we finally kissed, our loved finally started living.

PART III

CHAPTER 27

"Have you ever been in love? Horrible isn't it? It makes you so vulnerable. It opens your chest and it opens up your heart and it means that someone can get inside you and mess you up."
- *Neil Gaiman*

Three months later

Akira

"We need to organize another tutorial for Sam before we leave for India," I said to my roommates, gathered around on my bed.

Megha, Vidya, Shruti, and I sat facing each other on my bed, chai in hand and a plate full of rusk, a type of tea biscuit, in the center. It was Saturday morning and none of us had any lectures.

Megha dipped the rusk in the piping hot chai for a few seconds, bit into it, and moaned, "Hmmm. These are so good." The moment she looked up from her chai and met my eyes, she said, "And of course, Shruti can do the explanations on the tricks to impress Indian parents."

Shruti already had her journal out and was busy taking notes.

Megha added, "I think Sam knows a lot of it after watching you interact with your family over the past few months. But yes, there are some things that we need to tell him that would gain him a few brownie points."

"Yeah. And we leave in ten days. How about we arrange this session over the next weekend. Since everyone's semester ends this coming Friday, we can rest in on Saturday and have a session on Sunday?" I asked.

After everyone agreed and we decided to gather in the living room at ten a.m., I got to work on my final assignments and preparing for the exams. I was a little relieved since I hadn't chosen any subjects with research papers for submissions. I just had to sit in my bed and study for regular old exams. I was already done with putting together the design drawings and presentations for our final studio submission.

> Sam: Status?

> Me: Your "Meeting the Indian parents" Tutorial session is next Sunday, at 10 a.m.

> Sam: Perfect. I'm almost done packing for the trip. You?

We still had ten days left. I didn't even know that we were supposed to start packing yet. I had not even finished buying gifts for my family.

> Me: Haven't even started. ;-) I still have a few things left to buy for my family. Can we go on Saturday?

> Sam: AKIRA!!! How will you be done with everything? When will you pack? Start today.

> Me: Yeah, I will. Mostly. :-* Now let me study. I have a test in two days.

> Sam: Yeah. Keep me posted. And you mind if I bring Luke around for the session?

> Me: Of course not. It was fun watching the two of you learn about our culture. And he'll learn a few things too.

> Sam: Perfect. I'll come prepared.

> Me: I know. :-*

Just like the last time, we put the whiteboard and markers against a chair. This was purely for dramatic purposes, as it made Shruti feel like a teacher.

And like true students, Sam and Luke arrived. One with a notebook and pens stuffed in his bag, the other with a hangover and coffee. Luke dropped on the sofa in our living room with a loud groan in the same spot where he sat the last time.

I went and tugged Sam's bag to bring him closer to me. His eyes twinkled at me, and he pulled me into him.

"Hey, sweetheart," Sam whispered near my lips.

With a soft peck on his lips, I said, "Hi... You excited for the trip?"

He scoffed and said, "More nervous than excited. Today should help."

Behind us, Shruti took her spot at the whiteboard, Megha brought out a tray full of snacks, and Vidya chatted with Luke. Seemed like everyone was set to begin.

I leaned closer into Sam and kissed his jaw and his neck. "Everything is going to be fine. You'll see. Let's settle in."

Sam quickly kissed me and sat beside Luke. The rest of us pulled out chairs from the dining table and settled around.

Shruti began with writing in bold letters MEETING THE

PARENTS, and then turned to us. "Sam, today's session is solely focused on you. Luke, since you are joining Sam and Akira on the trip to India, it might help you too. Although, you don't need to worry. You aren't asking for their daughter's hand. So, you can expect to be treated like a king. We Indians love impressing the foreign people."

By the end of this introduction, Sam's frown had deepened, and Luke's smile had widened. Before Shruti could continue, Sam raised his hand asking for permission to speak. He looked too cute with his learning mode on. Glasses on point, notebook open in his lap, pen clenched in his grip and ready to fly over the pages, a severe frown on his face. I so wanted to kiss off that frown and ruffle a few pages.

At Shruti's nod, Sam said, "Nothing important, just don't call it a *trip* to India. It is anything but a trip. Execution. Trial. Battle. A trip, it is not."

I snorted. Luke laughed as he patted Sam's back.

At that, Vidya chimed in. "If Akira's parents are willing to meet you and listen to you, it sure as hell is a trip."

Everyone laughed at that, including Sam.

"Touché," Sam said.

Shruti clapped her hands and started, "Let's begin. Sam, this is the first rule and the most important rule to follow. Never ever kiss Akira in front of her family." With each word that Shruti spoke, Sam's mouth tightened. "You can touch or hold her hands. Usually a hug is fine. But since it's your first time meeting the parents, let's limit the hugging too. No PDA of any sort."

"Not even a peck?" Sam asked, looking at me for help.

He had never looked cuter with his disappointed eyes and his adorable pout.

Before I could get lost in him, Megha piped in, "Not even a peck."

Sam nodded, but a rebellious look crossed his face. "Okay,

fine. We'll just have to sneak some in." And in his notebook, he wrote down in big capital letters "SNEAK KISSES."

I could so kiss him right now. Just to rile him up, I added, "Do you need to practice the no-kissing rule?"

He growled, "I'll show you no kissing," and jumped up from his seat. He had me in his arms and was kissing me before I could even process his words. I heard a few gasps and hoots around me. Before I could kiss him back properly, he pulled away. I couldn't help but chase his mouth, but with an evil smirk, he went back to his seat on the sofa. At my stunned expression, the cruel man just winked at me.

Shruti cleared her throat at us, and once our attention was on her, she continued, "Rule number two, Sam. Do not protest or raise your voice. Try to nod along at most of their conversations. You aren't much of a talker, so hopefully, this rule shouldn't be an issue."

Sam raised his hand to ask a question. Again.

At Shruti's nod, he asked, "Am I not going to fight for our relationship? How do you expect me to not fight for Akira?"

Poor guy. I stretched over from the chair and grabbed Sam's hand and said, "You didn't need to argue to convince my parents to give us a chance. You're good, Sam."

The relief in his smile was all the more endearing.

He nodded and said, "Okay, then. What's next?"

Shruti then proceeded to explain the ritual of welcoming someone after their long travel at the entrance of the house. Steps on how to join hands and close your eyes if and when Akira's mom puts a *tika,* meaning red dot, on the forehead, saying namaste or sometimes touching the feet of elders, and practicing sitting in Indian style and eating with hands.

By the end of four hours, Luke had already given up and was enjoying the show. Sam was determined to get everything right.

"You don't need to practice namaste. Even I don't say

namaste to my parents or grandparents." I tried to convince Sam to not worry about getting every little thing right.

"If all these little things could add even a little favor on our side, then I'm doing it. Now, let me focus, and you go pack. We leave in two days," Sam said. It made me equal parts happy and sad to see Sam working so hard to win over my family.

Happy because he loved me enough to do this for me.

Sad because I hadn't had to work hard to convince his family. But if our roles had been reversed, I would like to believe I would fight as hard as Sam was fighting for us.

But fortunately, Sam's parents were among the sweetest people I've met. Just the other day, we'd gone to his parents' place for dinner. I had the most fun hearing all about Sam's childhood and his young perfectionist stories. During our goodbye, Sam's mother had hugged me and said, "Take care of him, honey. Don't break his heart."

I had only been able to nod and say, "I promise."

And right now, Sam was engrossed in every word Shruti said, hoping to impress my family. He jotted down all the comments from Megha and Vidya, and even made them repeat if he missed something. I couldn't help but grab his face and kiss his cheek. He was just too cute with serious lines between his eyes.

He pulled back and said, "Go pack, Akira. We'll be done by the time you finish." He tried to sound strict, but he failed to wipe the smile off his face.

I rolled my eyes at having to pack and went to my room.

LUKE, Sam, and I were in the queue to the security check-in at the JFK International airport. Sam was his usual composed self with his pristine headphones around his neck, regulation-sized carry-on luggage, and a new neck pillow hanging from his bag.

He clutched his iPad and phone in his hand for the security check—no fumbling on his part. Luke and I, on the other hand, were more normal and a bit of a mess.

"Sam, could you hold my jacket, man?" Without looking at Sam, Luke extended his jacket toward Sam, as he tried to pull out his iPad and Kindle stuck in between the chargers. A few muttered curses left him, but I had no time to warn him about the little kids around us.

The stupid line kept moving and I had to keep dragging my half-open bag to get everything out. I needed to get my laptop out without spilling the things I'd jammed around it. Especially my spare undergarments.

"That's what happens when you pack at the last minute," Sam said primly and stepped around Luke and me to go first. Unfortunately, he didn't see the two fingers pointed at his back.

After an hour of the security check-in process, we headed toward the boarding gate. When we passed a liquor store, I commented, "Guys, drink all the alcohol you want right now or in flight, because you aren't getting any in my state."

At Luke's shocked gasp, Sam turned to him and asked, "Oh, did I forget to mention that? I'm sorry. Akira lives in a dry state. No alcohol, man."

Oh man, Sam can be cruel sometimes. I punched his shoulder. Luke punched it harder.

"Have your fun, man. We'll see who's having fun in India," Luke said.

Even though Luke's words sent a pang of fear through my body, I forced myself to think positive. We've gotten this far. We'd be fine. Everything would work out in our favor.

I jabbed my elbow into Luke's ribs and said, "Everything's going to work out."

A hint of guilt entered his eyes, and Luke wrapped an arm around my shoulders. "I know. Sam's unbeatable."

"You two"—Sam turned from where he'd walked ahead of

us—"let's get going. And no one is drinking during the flight. We need to create a good first impression, Luke."

Luke and I followed as Luke mumbled, "*You* have to create a good first impression."

Considering our two flights were going to take a total of twenty hours to reach India, we had way too much time for arguments. God save us all.

$\sim$

Sam

After twenty hours of a long journey, we finally fucking landed. The sky was washed with hints of orange and pink with the sun rising over the horizon. Two hours of immigration and baggage claim later, the airport was washed with bright morning light.

Everywhere I looked, there were people. So many people. The vast majority of them were Indians. It was very clear that Luke and I stood out. If not for my observation, the blatant stares at us were a pretty clear indication.

I could feel Luke's excitement as opposed to my anxiety. The overhead announcements switched from English to other languages that we didn't understand. It was the first time I couldn't understand announcements, which in itself was a little disturbing and left me feeling out of control.

After the final security check, we headed to the exit. My watch still showed American time, so I asked Luke if he had calibrated his watch to Indian Standard Time. He checked his watch and frowned. "It's nine a.m."

"Then why is the sun so bright right now?"

Both of us looked at Akira with a questioning glare.

She rolled her eyes at us and said, "It's the middle of May. Official summer season. It's going to be burning hot. Why do you think I insisted you wear long sleeves?"

"Fuck," Luke whispered.

Akira skipped along to the exit without a care in the world, her eyes searching among the people lined outside the airport to receive their family. I realized the moment Akira found her family. She was about ready to make a mad dash to them before I hurried and grabbed her arm.

"Do not run off without me, Akira." I grabbed her shirt.

At the same time, I felt Luke's firm hold on my arm. "Do not run off without me, Sam."

"Oh, I'm so sorry. But let's hurry, Sam. I can see everyone," Akira said, bouncing on her toes. Her excitement made me nervous.

"Sweetheart, Luke and I have the cart here. So, you need to slow down a little. And you're making me nervous."

Akira clutched my wrist where I was holding the cart. "Sam, I'll be with you all along. I promise. You don't have to worry about a thing. Almost all my family members are very excited to meet you. And you and Luke are our guests. They will treat you nicely."

She then looked at Luke and told us with a smile on her face, "And if it makes you guys feel better, they are more nervous to meet you than you are of them. Imagine going near pigeons. It's just like that. So please try and relax a little."

"Pigeons are afraid of nothing, the little fuckers," Luke murmured behind me.

Before we were about to step out the door, Akira warned us, "Brace yourselves."

For a second, I didn't get it. Neither did Luke, with the way he frowned. But *fuck*. The moment I stepped out the door, a blast of hot air almost threw me back into the cool airport. Holy fucking shit. This wasn't hot. It was scorching. Flaming. It felt like my skin was being roasted. I turned at Luke to see if I was exaggerating. Nope. The look of horror on Luke's face conveyed that I might be underplaying it a bit.

Beside me, Akira inhaled in delight, then squinted at me. With all that sun raining down on us, I was surprised she could open more than half of her eyes.

"Welcome to India in summer, baby," she giggled and turned to Luke. Luke had already put his shades on and was guzzling his water.

Sweat gathered at the back of my neck, and my shirt had started to cling to my back. The faster we finished the reunion, the quicker we might get to leave the heat.

Akira turned and started running to where her family was gathered. A guy ran toward her and lifted Akira in his arms in a hug. Luke and I walked toward the large group, with Luke pushing me to walk faster. I jabbed my elbow in his stomach while trying to keep a polite smile on my face.

As soon as I reached Akira, I recognized Abhi from the video call we've had a few times in the past few months. Akira's younger brother. The moment he let go of her, he pulled me in a hug too.

"Sam, good to finally meet you," he said after letting go of me. The resemblance between the siblings was evident in their eyes. They shone with barely restrained excitement and soul-deep joy. As I was introducing Abhi to Luke, Akira's older brother, Aakar, pulled her into a hug.

They seemed to be having some conversation that I couldn't decipher. Once introduced, Abhi and Luke started talking about the heat, where Luke complained and Abhi laughed. His laugh was so much like Akira's. A hand on my shoulder had me look over to Akira.

"Sam, Aakar. Aakar, Sam."

We had already seen each other in the video calls, but it was good to finally meet Akira's brother in person. He was the one I was most grateful for. This time, I pulled him in a hug. "Thank you once again, Aakar. For everything you did for Akira."

Aakar slapped me on the back in a brotherly pat, and we let go of the hug. "Anytime, man. Welcome to India." He smiled at me in reassurance. My anxiety over meeting the parents and the rest of the family might be too obvious on my face.

Akira came and stood close beside me so that our arms were touching. Aakar saw it but didn't comment. He just nodded with a smile and asked, "Akira, you ready to see Mom and Dad?"

Before Akira could answer, her mom had already marched to Akira, her father close behind.

"Akira, you crazy girl!" Akira's mom admonished and then pulled her into her arms, smothering her.

"I'm so sorry for running away, Mummy," Akira mumbled into her mom's arms. Another set of arms joined the mother and daughter. Akira looked up to her dad with tears in her eyes, and apologized, "Sorry, Pappa."

Her father huffed. "You will not repeat that stunt again. You hear me?"

Akira nodded and hugged her dad.

Finally. It had been weighing on Akira's heart that she hurt her parents by running away. The relief on her face had my heart calm a little.

If I watched the reunion any further, I might spill a tear or two. I turned to look at Abhi and Luke. They were looking at something on the phone and laughing at something. When I'd turned my head from the emotional reunion, I hadn't expected a comedy going on in the other direction.

They must've noticed my glare on them, because Abhi looked at me with a wide smile, and rolled his eyes. "This is the third reunion, including the time when we sent her off. I'm used to it."

Luke laughed and patted Abhi on the back. "I like you, man."

Aakar, who was standing beside me, nudged me with his elbow.

I turned to the three people staring at me with very different expressions on each of their faces.

Akira, with adoration and a little nervousness.

Akira's mom, with a little nervousness and curiosity.

Akira's dad, with no nervousness but a glint of warning in his eyes.

Sweat dotted my back and my forehead. I'd like to say the reason was the blistering heat, not the glare that Akira's dad was throwing at me. I went to stand across from the three of them. Akira quickly jumped to my side. Akira's father, not so much. I cleared my throat, joined my hands and said, "Namaste" to both parents.

Akira's mom smiled, looked at Akira, then me, and joined her hands in greeting. "Namaste."

Luke joined me and did the same.

Akira put her hand on my arm. "Sam, my mother, Shilpa. And my father, Pravin. Mom, Dad, meet Sam... Uhm, my boyfriend." Akira had gone all red, yet she continued. "And that's Luke, Sam's friend."

"Hello, Aunty. How are you?" I asked.

"You have a beautiful name, ma'am," Luke said. Did he just say she had a beautiful name? I looked from Luke to Akira's mom. Akira's dad did the same. And if I wasn't wrong, Akira's mom blushed.

"Oh, uh...thank you, Luke," Akira's mom said. Her face was still red.

Oh, this couldn't be good. I glared at Luke, and when I turned to Akira's dad, he was doing the same.

I decided to break the tension and offered my hand to Akira's dad. "Pleased to meet you, sir."

Akira's dad looked away from Luke to me, and shook my hand. "Same. Welcome to India, Sam."

We were interrupted when a loud female voice called Akira, "Oye, Akira."

All of us turned to a horde of people waiting to be greeted. Behind me, Luke muttered, "We're going to be here the whole day, aren't we?"

Aakar chuckled at that and put his arm around Luke's shoulder and said, "Let's make this quick, shall we?"

"Please," Luke begged.

Akira and I followed them while Akira's parents trailed behind us.

We stood in front of no less than ten people. Their stares ranged from cautious to elated. I recognized a few familiar faces from the video calls, and I smiled at them.

Akira started the introductions. "Everyone, meet Sam, and that's Luke. Sam and Luke, meet my family." Akira started introducing each person with names that I started to gloss over after the first two. I did try to keep in mind their relation to Akira.

She had two uncles, two aunts, grandparents, Ria and her kid brothers, and the two kids of her other uncle and aunt. If anyone asked me their names, I'd never be able to tell.

Everyone looked at me and just stared. Some smiled politely and some didn't even meet my eyes. I couldn't figure out if I was the nervous one or they were. Akira was right. I looked at Akira, and she gave me a kind smile that soothed my rapidly beating heart.

"Sam, hello," Akira's grandmother said.

I looked at Akira with a question in my eyes. With her nod of approval, just like Akira had taught me, I went forward and touched the feet of Akira's grandmother and grandfather, repeating, "Namaste, ma'am, sir,"

Excited gasps filled the air, and her grandmother giggled. She looked around to the other kids and said something to everyone that made them laugh.

At Luke's and my questioning glance, Akira translated, "She said, *"You see, kids. Such a sweet boy. When did you all last touch my feet? Learn something from him."* She loves you, Sam. Everything's going to be fine. You'll see."

Luke did the same, and people kept getting more excited. Unfortunately, I had no idea what everyone was saying, because the family had resorted to Gujarati, and we were left to wonder. Seeing that the adults were busy comparing their notes on their opinion of me while we melted into a puddle, Akira left my side and ran to Ria.

The women hugged for a long time, and Akira dragged Ria to where Luke and I stood.

Ria extended her hand and said, "We finally meet, Sam."

I would have hugged her if there weren't so many people staring at us. I shook her hand instead. "I cannot say how pleased I am to finally meet you. You are my hero, Ria."

Luke sidled up beside me. Ria pulled away from my hand and extended it to Luke. "I'm Ria. Welcome to India, Luke."

Luke shook her hand. "Thank you so much. Any way we can get out of this heat any quicker?"

Ria and Akira burst into laughter and called Aakar.

Looking at the sweat dotting out foreheads and the redness on Luke's cheek, Aakar announced, "Let's get going, everyone. We don't want our guests to get sick. It's getting hotter."

Everyone hummed in approval and started moving to different cars in the parking lot.

Aakar nudged me and said, "Our car's in that direction. Let's get the luggage."

Despite Luke's and my protests, Akira's brothers took the luggage cart from us and moved toward the car. Akira, Ria, Akira's brothers, Luke, and I got into one car. The rest went in the other cars.

The car interior was stifling. The moment my ass sat on the lava seat, I yelped.

Aakar cringed, while Abhi laughed.

"This is going to be so much fun." Abhi kept laughing.

Aakar glared at him and quickly turned on the car. Hot air blasted from the air conditioner.

"No more," Luke whined, as if he was being tortured.

My mind shrieked the same, but I tried to keep my mouth shut.

Akira patted Luke and kindly explained, "Give it a minute, Luke. Cool air will come out any minute." She pointed the air conditioner vents at us and held my hand.

Soon enough, the car started moving, and cool air wafted over us. Luke and I moaned in relief. I closed my eyes and relished the cool air hitting my sweat and making it that much cooler. Akira and her siblings giggled at me but fuck if I cared.

Aakar and Ria sat in the front. Akira, Luke, and I in the middle seat, and Abhi at the back. Akira sat in the middle so Luke and I could look outside. The entire way, she kept telling me the names of the roads we passed, what the area was famous for.

The architecture of the city was completely different than New York. There were no skyscrapers. Millions of people—and I literally meant millions—traveled on a two-wheeled vehicle like a Vespa. The cars drove nearly on top of each other.

I was afraid if Aakar took the car one inch to the left he was going to end up grazing the car right beside us. And the horns! We were clearly stuck in the traffic. If the cars could move forward, they would. But apparently, the people around seemed to be blind, because they did not stop honking their vehicles. It was nonstop.

I looked at Akira and asked, "Are they crazy? Why do they keep honking?"

Akira giggled and shrugged her shoulders. "It's just the way it is."

"Unbelievable," Luke said from the other side.

I know.

The roads were so interesting. They twisted and turned in multiple directions. The roads met at crossroads every now and then. Not even the crossroads had a regular geometry to it. The planning was very organic.

The same could go for the architecture of the buildings too. Every building was different. There seemed to be no uniform planning for the design. I couldn't take everything in quickly enough. I needed to roam around the streets to understand the architecture and the planning, or lack thereof.

Soon, we arrived at a gated housing complex. The streets were lined with huge houses. Since it was still early morning, and a weekend, the streets were quite peaceful. Few people walked along the street.

The car stopped at a huge house. Ria got down and opened the gate to the entry. We entered the vast parking space that could hold at least five cars. I got out of the car, and Luke came and stood beside me. Both of us were struck dumb with the sheer size of the house in front of us.

When Akira came and stood beside me, I hissed, "You're fucking filthy rich, aren't you?"

Akira laughed and shook her head. "You crazy? We're fifteen people, Sam. With the potential to grow. How else do you fit everyone in one house? We're upper middle class at best."

"Let's get in. The house is already cool," Ria shouted.

Luke and I ran like nobody's business. Akira's laugh trailed behind us.

CHAPTER 28

"Women love the last blow as well as the last word, and when they fight for love they are pitiless as a wounded buffalo."
   - H. Rider Haggard

Akira

Our car was the first to arrive. Instead of waiting for everyone in the living room, Ria decided to show us the sleeping arrangements.

"This is where you and Sam will sleep," Ria announced.

For a moment, Sam looked at me and smiled with relief and excitement. I expected his reaction to not being able to sleep with me a little different.

Luke slapped his hand on Sam's arm and pointed at himself. "You, as in me and you would be sleeping here, Sam. Ria was looking at me when she spoke."

"We can't even kiss in front of my family, and you thought they'd let us sleep together?" I asked with a laugh.

Sam frowned and put his bag on one of the twin beds. "I forgot for a second."

I laughed and hugged him. "Sam, I love you so much. I'm so

glad we came. Everything is going a lot better than I expected."
I looked at Ria to confirm, "What do you think?"

Ria sat on a chair at the study desk near her. "Yeah, I think
so too. The namaste and feet touching sure helped."

Luke dropped on one of the beds with a loud sigh. "Fuck, it
was a long flight."

At that, Ria pointed out, "Do not sleep right now. Breakfast
is in about an hour." She then looked at Sam. "You might want
to be prepared for some questions."

All color drained from Sam's already tired and pale face. I
clutched his hand tight and asked, "Sam, do you want me to tell
them that you guys want to rest?"

Luke and Ria looked at Sam.

"No." Sam sighed. "Let's get this done with."

"Let's all freshen up, and I'll come to call you guys when
breakfast is ready. Okay?" I asked.

When Sam and Luke nodded, Ria mentioned, "The towels
and other toiletries are in the washroom itself."

Before Ria and I stepped out of the room, Ria called out to
Luke. "No f-words or other cuss words. That'll get Sam rejected
before he gets a word out."

Sam's follow-up glare was enough to strengthen Ria's
warning. Luke cringed and made a show of zipping up his
lips.

With a laugh, Ria and I left the room, leaving the boys to
relax a little and freshen up. I hoped Sam was prepared. I was
pretty sure Dad was not going to delay the difficult conversation. I could only pray for everything to go well.

I HURRIED out of the shower and got to work.

If Sam was to be attacked, I had to take some precautionary
measures. I didn't have the time to build an entire bridge to

save Sam from the flood of questions, but I could at least give him a rope.

I had very little time before breakfast and needed to cover a lot of ground before I called Luke and Sam to join us.

First, I ran to my younger cousins. They were the two kids of my youngest uncle and aunt, and Ria's younger brother. He was eleven years younger than Ria. The kids were playing in the courtyard of our house.

I whisper-shouted at them to come closer to me, all the while flipping through some cash. Their eyes rounded and the money automatically dragged them closer to me.

I hid the money behind my back to get their attention. On cue, all of them looked at me with hungry, questioning eyes.

"You guys, you met my friends, right?"

"You mean your boyfriend?" Soham, Ria's younger brother, teased. And they all giggled.

I couldn't stop the smile even if I wanted to. I nodded. "Yes. My boyfriend. Now, listen carefully. During breakfast, if at any time, people start shouting or get angry at Sam, create a distraction. Cry. Fight. Drop the food. Anything."

The kids listened to me with rapt attention. When none of them even blinked in distraction, I continued, "If everything goes as smooth as possible, you'll get the money. Deal?"

While the two younger kids nodded, Soham, frowned and said, "Give us half as insurance."

He was such a businessman, just like his father.

I scoffed at him but handed over half the amount. I needed him, and he knew it.

Once I handed over the money, all three of them nodded and said, "Deal."

The moment I turned, I came face to face with Aakar and Abhi. Both of them had evil smirks on their stupid faces.

"Spoiling the kids already?" Abhi teased.

I rolled my eyes. "I was just coming to you guys."

N. M. PATEL

At their raised eyebrows, I continued, "Abhi, if the breakfast gets too tense, please, please, please try to lighten it up?"

Abhi smiled and put his arm around me. "You don't have to explain that to us. We're not kids."

At that, Aakar proved Abhi's point. "I'll try and handle the parents. It won't be needed as far as I can tell. Things have been getting back to normal in the past few months. But don't worry. We'll handle it."

I nodded and quickly hugged my brothers in thanks and ran off to the next person.

In the living room, I found my uncles reading a newspaper on their spots on the sofa and quickly sat between them. At their raised eyebrows, I joined my hands and begged, "Please, please, please don't ask too many questions to Sam. I think Dad is going to be enough on his own, don't you?"

My older uncle hummed and went back to his newspaper. "I'll try. I can't promise anything."

I sighed. That's as good as I could get from him.

I looked at my younger uncle with pleading eyes. He laughed and said, "Of course."

"Thank you, thank you, thank you," I whisper-shrieked, trying to not alert my dad.

"Where's Dad?" I asked.

My uncles just shrugged, their heads already back in their newspapers.

Moving on, I ran to the kitchen. The entire scene was nostalgic and something I'd missed out on in the last few days of my trip the last time. Radhika *kaki* sat on the counter near the stove, cooking and mixing the *bhaji*. Mom sat on the floor rolling the *puris* while Ekta *kaki* fried them in piping, hot oil. The combination of *bhaji*, a potato based dry *sabzi* and *puri*, a fried golden-brown flatbread, was a classic Indian breakfast. Well, at least the ladies were going all in to impress the guests.

"Akira, *beta*, help us arrange the table, will you? Raju *kaka* is busy making the tea," Mom asked.

I went near where everyone was busy preparing the food and plopped down beside Mom. "Mom, please go easy on Sam, no?"

Mom gasped. "Akira, how can you even say that? I would never be mean to a guest."

I raised my eyes at that. At that, Mom rolled her eyes and mumbled, "Fine. I won't say anything. Your dad will be enough." A sly smirk passed her face.

"Mummy," I whined. She was brutal. My aunts laughed.

I looked at my Radhika *kaki* and the container of spices in her hands. Before she could work her magic, I rushed, "*Kaki*, not too spicy. Sam and Luke are good with spices, but not *that* good."

She laughed. "No problem."

"Akira," Ekta *kaki* said, "I have to say. Sam is very good looking. And both the men are so fair. Right, Shilpa *didi*?" She looked at my mom who nodded. Her small smile was enough to soothe me a little.

"Where's Dad?" I asked on my way out of the kitchen.

Mom looked at me, laughter shining in her eyes. "Oh, did you want to ask him to be gentle too?"

Huh. So, she did notice. "What...? Where did you get that from?" I asked, trying to be convincingly confused.

All the ladies laughed, and with the rolling pin in her hand, my mom shooed me away. "He might be taking a bath. Wait for him in the living room. You father can't stay away from the newspaper."

I went back to the living room, where I found my uncles right where they were. But I also found my dad on the adjacent sofa with his head inside the newspaper.

I cleared my throat as I stood across from him. Dad flicked down the paper and looked at me from above the bent edge.

There was a certain awkwardness in the exchange. The last time we saw each other without the barrier of distance and video calling was when I had cried and begged in front of him to let me go back to the US.

We hadn't gotten the chance to say goodbye, and now, it was difficult to look him in the eye. Once we resolved the issues, I'd talked to my family through video calling almost every day. So, I knew everything was almost back to normal. Almost.

I needed that "almost" to go. I needed to be able to plop beside my dad without worry and demand he not go hard on Sam.

"I, uhh..." Why was it so difficult with Dad? We already hugged and made up at the airport.

"Yes?" Dad prodded.

"Uhh...are we okay?" I asked.

A small smile crossed his face. Dad put aside the newspaper and patted at the seat beside him. Each step toward the seat had my heart beating faster. My throat dried up, and I had to lock my feet from running back to my room.

It wasn't the fear that caused such reactions. It was guilt. Truthfully, I had no reason to feel guilty. But hurting your parents would always leave you feeling at least a tiny amount of guilt.

The moment I sat beside Dad, he placed his hand on my shoulder. My heart beat faster with anticipation.

"We are good, *beta*. You scared us, but I understand," he said.

A heavy sigh escaped me, spreading the rush of relief through my body.

"Thank you, Pappa. For understanding. For giving us a chance. I really hope you like him."

The smile on Dad's face disappeared. "We'll see."

Oh, God. He wasn't planning to play fair. I knew it. I held my dad's arms and begged, "Please be good to him? We just landed after a long flight. Please don't ask him difficult questions right away." I didn't know if I was asking, begging, or demanding. A snort came from behind one newspaper while the other newspaper shook with laughter. My uncles seemed to have found a neat little trick to spy on people's conversations.

"We're not your enemies, Akira," Dad said. He was barely controlling his laughter.

"So, you'll be good to Sam?" I asked. Dad wasn't showing any signs of cooperating except for the evil twinkle of laughter in his eyes. I had no idea what to gather. So, I added, "Please, Pappa. Promise me."

At that, he laughed out loud. "I promise no such thing, Akira. I will do what's best for my daughter."

Hmph.

As a last resort, I reminded him of the Hindu code of conduct. "*Atithi Devo Bhava*, remember?" *Guest is God.*

Now both of my uncles laughed out loud, their heads still concealed behind their newspapers. I threw evil eyes at the shaking pages.

"I'll remember, my Sanskrit teacher. However, I seem to recall, you didn't remember *Matru Devo Bhava* and *Pitru Devo Bhava* the last time you were here," Dad said. *Mother is God* and *Father is God.*

"I'll remember it from now on," I mumbled and fled from the scene. Three loud, obnoxious guffaws followed me until I reached the dining room where the breakfast was being set up.

～

Sam

Silence.

An utter, uncomfortable, awkward silence.

It had been fifteen minutes since all *seventeen of us* sat in the dining room for breakfast.

Fifteen. Long. Minutes.

Akira's grandfather sat at the head of the table on the furthest side from me, while Akira's grandmother sat on the opposite side. Luke, I, and Akira sat in that order, starting from her grandmother's side.

Akira's siblings sat across from us.

Beside Akira, her aunt Ekta and her kids, followed by Akira's elder aunt, Radhika, and her kid were seated at the other end of the table. Across them, Akira's father and her two uncles had taken their seats, probably to make it simpler to stare me down.

To mitigate the silence, the kids had resorted to occasional whispers and murmurs in each other's ears.

The churning in my stomach didn't help. An entire spread of food lined the long table. There was chai, potatoes, *puri,* pickled papaya, juice, toast, and coffee.

The chai had been even better than Akira's chai. The potatoes were delicious, and I had never had anything like the pickled papaya before. I wanted to ravish everything, but the silence from the people was too uncomfortable to savor the food. I had only had a bite or two of each food.

I looked at Akira, who silently sipped her chai. Her one hand stayed on my knee to show me that she was right there with me, and also maybe to stop my knee from bouncing.

I kept my head down. I knew I was surrounded by people who supported us. I looked at Akira's grandmother. Since she was already looking at me, she gave me a smile in assurance.

While it didn't help much, I looked around at the rest of the family. Abhi had an amused smile, as if he was metaphorically enjoying popcorn while he watched the show. He shared his amusement with Luke, who had the same expression.

Aakar sat right across from me, eating his food as if there

was nothing out of the ordinary on the table. It helped. Ria sat beside Aakar, right across from Luke, and she seemed to be enjoying the awkwardness too.

Akira's hand on my knee was firm and occasionally tightened in reassurance. I thought there would be fights and questions right off the bat. I was prepared for it. I wasn't prepared for this silence. It was so much worse.

I quickly moved my eyes over the other side of the table with all the parents. Only Uncle Sunil and Akira's grandfather met my eyes and gave me a small smile. The rest of them ate their food.

I didn't know if I should initiate any kind of conversation. Praise the food, maybe. Would it open the gate of questions and make the situation worse? I wanted Akira to eat first. It had been a long flight.

I mentally shrugged and decided to follow the vow of silence that everyone seemed to have taken up and started on the food. It was fucking delicious. And the perfect amount of spicy.

A loud *clack* sound broke the silence.

All of us looked at the source of the noise. Ria.

"Oh, it was just my hairpin. I was just testing," she said, her eyes playful. I was glad she talked in English.

"What?" Aakar asked. Confusion marred his forehead.

"I had to check if we could hear the pin drop," she giggled and burst out laughing.

Luke followed, and so did the rest of the siblings, including Akira. She then converted the joke in Gujarati for her grandparents, and they burst out laughing too.

In just a moment, the room was filled with laughter and lightness. I looked at Ria and nodded my head at her in thanks.

"So, Sam?" Uncle Sunil shook his head and looked at me.

"Yes, sir," I said. Finally. Someone to address me directly.

"How was the flight?" he asked. He was polite and his smile

assured me that it was just small talk to break the silence.

"It was good. Pretty long."

"Akira tells us that you both study together," he continued. I was so glad he had a list of questions. I wouldn't know how to carry on the small talk.

"Yes," I said, "we have some classes together." I tried to enunciate and speak slowly so that most people could understand.

Akira didn't translate, and the grandparents didn't ask for it. They might have guessed that the conversation was nothing but a get-to-know-each-other.

"Good. Good. So, what's your full name again?" he asked.

Fuck. I still remember Akira's comment on the irony of her future last name. I put my hand over Akira's that was still on my knee. I grazed my thumb over the ring on her finger. Her hand on my knee tightened, giving me the assurance I needed.

"It's Samuel Michael White, sir."

Aakar snorted. "So when you marry Akira, she would be Akira White?"

Why did he have to say that out loud? I felt color rising from my neck to the cheeks. I looked at him and nodded with a weak smile.

I heard several snorts and laughs where Akira's dad and uncles sat.

Luke laughed outright, as well as Akira. Akira translated for her grandparents and they too burst out laughing.

"Akira snorted the same way when she made the connection," I added, and that made her family laugh outright.

"*If* you marry Akira, that is," Akira's dad clarified. As if it wasn't obvious with the predicament that we were in. It still stung like a bitch. The mood in the room went from 0 to 5000 pretty fucking fast.

I had nothing to say. Well, I had several things to say. None too respectful. So, I sealed my mouth and clenched my jaw hard enough to stop the words. Akira would marry me. I'll make it happen.

"Pravin," Akira's mom chided.

"Pappa!" Akira said at the same time.

Akira's dad said something in Gujarati that sounded defensive, because guilt was clear in his eyes for ruining the laughter in the room.

"We'll talk about that later. Let the kids have food and rest a little," Akira's mom said in Gujarati, that Akira translated for us.

Akira's dad nodded and continued talking in Gujarati with the rest of the family.

Once he was done and left with his plate, Akira leaned down toward me and said, "He said that we'll have more discussion in the evening when everyone is back from work. So, we're good for now. And you were amazing, baby."

Not that I did much. Once her dad, uncles, and Aakar left the table to get ready for work, Luke, Abhi, and I dug into our plates filling it up again. I got some more chai, and Luke got some coffee.

"Akira," Akira's mom said, "once you and your friends are done with breakfast, let me know what you plan to do with the day. Do you want to stay home and rest today, or go for a walk outside?"

Akira looked at me and Luke and said, "It's too hot for a walk outside. We might go in the evening."

"You will have lunch at home?"

When all of us nodded, Akira's mom said, "I'll tell Raju *kaka* to get the mangoes out."

Akira shrieked, "Oh my God, Mummy. How did I forget the mangoes? You should have given it to me for breakfast too. Sam, you need to taste the mangoes."

Her excitement was addictive, and her smile always stole my breath away. I couldn't wipe my smile and joined in her excitement. "I can't wait for lunch, then."

I turned to her mom and her aunts. "Thank you so much for the breakfast, Aunty. The food was fantastic."

Luke joined in too. "Yes, I've never had Indian food this good in the US. I can't wait to try everything that you make."

I was relieved to see the slight blushes on the women's cheeks. At least I knew the way to the hearts of Akira's mom and aunts. Flattery was my best friend now.

"Now go rest, kids. We'll get lunch ready. Nothing too heavy today," her mom said, and everyone walked out of the dining room.

Luke, being the good friend he was, asked Abhi if they could relax somewhere. Ria was quick to suggest the courtyard, and the three of them got up. When they looked at us, Akira said, "We'll follow you in a minute."

Once it was just the two of us, I finally held Akira's hands. Looking around to find no one, I quickly dropped a kiss on her lips. Her loud gasp made me laugh.

"Sam!" She hit my arm but blushed nonetheless.

I entwined our fingers and asked, "You think everything went well?"

She tightened our grip and nodded. "Yeah. I'm glad there wasn't any heavy questioning. It's good we chose a weekday to come back. If it had been a weekend, my father would have started his interrogations right after breakfast."

It seems Akira wasn't too confident in me. I scoffed, "I am ready to face your family, sweetheart. Be it right now, or in ten days."

She almost put her head on my shoulder but stopped herself. "Don't be your sweet self. I need to resist touching you here."

I laughed and stood up with the plates. "Let's get this in the kitchen and join Luke and your siblings."

I quickly kissed her again, just because, and rushed to the kitchen to put away our plates.

CHAPTER 29

"I loved her against reason, against promise, against peace, against hope, against happiness, against all discouragement that could be."
 - Charles Dickens

Akira

I stretched myself over the *charpai,* a traditional handwoven bed, of our courtyard, after devouring five juicy Kesar mangoes. Our family always tied fabric over the courtyard to keep it cool and shaded in the summers.

The aroma of the Kesar mangoes—their sweetness, the flavor, everything about them—brought me joy. Especially the Indian mangoes. American mangoes were shit.

Our courtyard had two *charpai* beds, and the rest of the space was covered with thick carpets. Abhi, Luke, and Sam had occupied space on the thick carpets, right beside the air-cooler. Ria and I had taken up a *charpai* each.

A while ago, Mom had brought us a plate full of mango slices and I might have lost my chill for a minute there.

I felt a few stares boring into me as I let my stomach rest a little. I turned my head and, with all my effort, managed to open one eye toward Sam. His jaw hung open, and his hand held a big, juicy slice of mango that I could still eat, and his mouth had streaks of mango juices. I could lick it right off his lips. What would taste better—Sam's mouth or mangoes?

I looked down at the mango in Sam's hand. Definitely mango.

"Akira," Sam called me. "My eyes are up here, sweetheart."

I looked back up at him. "What?"

"You want one?" He offered me the slice in his hand.

I extended my hand from where I was resting, not moving my body. He stretched over from where he sat on the thick carpet and placed the slice in my palm. With a shake of his head, he said, "You just ate four whole mangoes."

And an extra slice. "Hmm...so?"

"So? You feel all right?"

Poor guy.

I smirked. "I can eat the highest number of mangoes in our family. Every summer, I get too much acne with the number of mangoes I eat, and yet, I can't stop."

"Why? Is India running out of mangoes or something?" Luke asked. Sam had the same question in his eyes.

Ria was sprawled on the carpet from where she answered, "Mangoes are only available in summers. And the good ones never last for more than three months."

I piped in. "And that's why you need to eat as many as you can."

"Looks like your mom is getting you ready for slaughter for the evening face-off with your father and uncles," Sam murmured.

I laughed but my stomach hurt. "Oww. Don't make me laugh. We'll handle it."

Luke was good with mangoes. He had not stopped eating them since we began. He didn't eat with as much gusto as Ria and me, but he hadn't stopped yet. I admired that. Sam seemed to have stopped right around the time when I might've snatched a slice from his hand for eating too fast. In my defense, he didn't have the passion for the mangoes like me.

A sense of calm had settled in my heart, knowing that Sam was sitting in my house. *In my house.* He was here, with me. And alive and eating mangoes. Who would've thought? I only wish my parents would quickly approve of us.

Sam had survived this far. We had to get the blessings from my parents. Intense murmurings woke me up from the mango-induced nap.

"What the hell? Show me." Luke wiped his hands with a cloth and extended his hand toward Sam.

Once he had the newspaper in his hands, severe frown lines marred Luke's forehead. I looked at Ria and Abhi and raised my eyebrows in question.

Ria shook her head and explained, "Sam read the headline on the decrease in farmers' suicide this year."

"And that's a bad thing?" I asked. Because I am, in fact, happy to hear that there's been a decrease in the suicide rate. It used to be severe not even a few years back.

Luke looked up at me with an intense expression that I'd never seen before. "If you guys think this is not severe, that's a problem. The article says, 'One hundred fifty fewer farmers commit suicide in 2018.'" Luke looked at Sam and continued, "And do you know the number of suicides in 2018? More than 2,500 farmers, Sam. Fuck."

Abhi and I stayed silent. What was there to say? We knew the country had problems. I guess the boys didn't realize that our country was still a developing nation. With a population of a billion people, there would always be people who suffered. These issues took time.

It was Ria who said, "There was a time when that number was above 15,000. In fact, one of my father's friends from our village committed suicide just five years back."

I remember. Every time we visited our village, Ria and I used to spend days playing with his daughter, Meera. She had the most infectious laughter and the biggest heart. Despite their poor economic conditions, she was always the first one to share her dolls with us.

I looked at Ria. "Remember Meera?"

Ria smiled sadly. Her eyes staring off, she said, "Yeah. I still remember riding on the truck with her and her dad. I wish her father hadn't done what he did."

I looked down at my sticky hands. "Yeah, me too. What's she doing these days? I haven't talked to her in a while."

Ria shrugged. "She was in her last year in Agriculture Science when her father passed. She finished early and came back home to Aunty and her little brother, and works as a government teacher in the village school. I have no idea what they did with their farm though."

The hundred slices of mangoes sat heavy in my stomach. God, I should probably call Meera sometime soon.

Luke seemed to be frozen solid, his head stuck in the newspaper, all while Ria talked. He looked like he had zoned out. Sam's attention was divided between Luke and me.

He slowly took a bottle of water from near my *charpai* and gently placed it near Luke. When I raised my eyes in question, he indicated he'll tell me later.

I nodded and said, "Meera, Ria, and I used to play a lot every time we visited our ancestral village. We used to have a farm there when my dad was younger. They sold it when they moved to the city. We just have a house there now. So, everyone in the village is like family to us. And Meera was so full of joy, you know. Always laughing. Always happy with what she got. Anything we got for her, like chocolates or clothes, she'd first share it with her little brother or her mother."

Sam squeezed my hand, the one that wasn't too sticky.

With a heavy throat, Ria said, "She isn't the same anymore, you know."

"I can't even imagine what she's gone through."

"Yeah," Ria said.

Silence fell around us. Abhi was silent the entire time.

God, I was such a bad host, making everyone sad the first day we arrived.

I looked at Abhi, waiting for him to meet my eyes. The moment he did, I widened my eyes and grimaced, telling him to change the mood.

"Luke, c'mon. Let's watch something. It's too hot outside, or else I would've taken you guys for a walk," Abhi said as he got up and stretched his arms.

Sam looked at me in gratitude and turned to Luke. "Yeah, man. I think it's a great idea. Luke?"

Luke let go of the paper with a heavy sigh. "Fine. let's watch something happy and Bollywood."

And that's what we did for the rest of the day. We watched a few Bollywood drama movies that would probably give Sam some ideas on how to tackle my parents' questions with emotional dialogues to win them over. And joked around at the improbable situations where the actors broke out into song and dance.

~

Sam

The day went by in a blur, and before I knew it, we were called in the dining room for dinner. The five of us had stayed in the family's TV room on the second floor for as long as we could. Luke and I were just happy to sit in the air-conditioned room.

Ria had chosen to work from home, and Abhi, like us, was enjoying the summer break. An hour or so ago, Akira and Ria

343

had gone down to the kitchen to help with the dinner preparations.

For the past hour, my feet hadn't stopped bouncing. I pinched near my knee to get them to stop for the duration of the dinner.

The moment Luke and I entered the dining room, all eyes turned to us. Or me, considering they didn't move even when Luke found a spot between Abhi and Ria. I gave a small smile to everyone and said, "Good evening."

A few nods here and there, but silence followed. I went and sat between Akira and Aakar. I squeezed Akira's hand in thanks for the thoughtful seating arrangement.

The dining table was laden with food items I'd never seen before. It had always been hit and miss for me when it came to any new Indian food item. A few plates were full of some weird yellow cut-up pieces of a cake-like thing. The top of each piece was covered with a sort of dark brown, burned surface.

"That's *haandwo*," Akira said with an amused smile on her face. Her lips pressed tight together as if controlling her laughter. She served me a gigantic piece of it with oil on the side. Before I could say anything, her mother came behind my chair and dropped a dollop of red chili powder in the oil. My throat closed up. My stomach started shutting down its system, violent in its protest.

Before I could come to terms with the dinner of the day, Akira brought in another container filled with tiny, rounded, green and yellow things. Fucking hell. What is up with the color of their food?

Akira shook with laughter as she put a few of those scary-looking pieces in my plate and said, "Another Indian delicacy. It's called *paatraa*."

Luke sat across from me, his face showing terror at having to try and eat this food in front of so many people. I was pretty sure my face reflected a terror far deeper than Luke's. Unlike him, I was here to impress and charm. With the amusement and laughter coming my way, I was doing a stellar job.

I held my fork and poked at the yellow blob of terror. Luke had taken a seat back, his eyes screaming *You brought me here, you go first, asshole.* Fair enough. I looked around. Everyone was eating it with their hand.

Akira's mom had gone into the kitchen since she had to keep bringing new, dangerous items to drop on the table. When she came out from the kitchen this time, she held a tray full of cups in her hands. She placed the entire tray in the center of the table and the cups got passed around.

Sweet Jesus. Finally, something that I recognized. Sweet, delicious chai. I blew on the piping hot tea and took a sip to calm some of my nerves.

"Aren't you going to eat, Sam?" Akira's mom asked.

"Uh...of course, Aunty," I said, sweat lined the back of my neck.

Before I was left to figure everything out, Akira touched my knee. When I looked at her, she smiled her sweet, amused smile and taught me how to break the piece of the soft, yellow, cake-like thing, dip it into the chili oil and eat it with my hand.

Huh. Not bad. Not bad at all. I looked at Luke and nodded for him to proceed. He smiled back and got to eating.

Akira did the same for the green and yellow stuff, and I tried it. Not my favorite. This was a little sweeter than what I liked in my food. But it wasn't bad. Occasionally, you're supposed to drink chai to push down the food. After five bites of the spongy yellow thing, I needed that chai.

A few giggles surrounded me every time Akira taught us something. When I looked up at the people around the table, I found most of them excited to see us trying their food. Heat spread across my cheeks at all the attention on me while I ate. I gave them all a small smile and looked at the ladies of the house. "The food is very good. Thank you."

"Akira helped us make the *haandwo*," Akira's younger aunt, Ekta, said, pride evident in her tone.

I couldn't stop the smile when I looked at Akira, who was now blushing. "Is that right?" I asked. Every ear in the room was tuned in to every word that came out of my mouth.

Akira smiled and nodded. "You like it?"

"It's delicious." I would've squeezed her hand or her knee under the table if every eye and ear wasn't tuned in to this small conversation between us.

The rest of the dinner was spent in occasional requests to pass the plates, more chai, and a few burps from people here and there.

Akira's dad cleared his throat once everyone was almost done. "Let's talk in the *chowk* after everyone's done."

My stomach swooped down for a second. At the same time that I nodded, Akira said, "Pappa, we've just arrived today. We're all tired."

"Forgive me if I want to have enough time for a conversation before you decide to run away with your friend," he said.

Fuck. That was a low blow. I squeezed Akira's thigh under the table in silent support. I clenched my jaw and stopped the words that threatened to spill in her defense. This wasn't the time to react. Her dad looked at me. I stared back, my eyes resolute. I was here, just for this. And I wasn't going to back down. Akira didn't need to fight this alone.

I gave Akira's dad a firm nod and finished my chai.

Akira grumbled under her breath and stabbed at the poor yellow food with one hand while she held my hand under the table with another.

All the adults of the house settled down in the courtyard, aka *chowk*, after the dinner was done. Akira and I sat on one of the beds or, as Akira called it, charpai, while the rest of the family got in sofas and chairs from the living room and the dining room. Ria, Abhi, and the younger uncle, Sunil, sat on the mattress on the floor where I was seated previously while eating mangoes.

I was bone tired. I was pretty sure Luke and Akira were too. Thankfully, we took a nap in the afternoon after a movie. But my body demanded an extended amount of rest. I told my body to hold off for a while.

Once everyone was seated and Akira's dad had taken up the center spot on the couch right across our bed, adrenaline kicked in. I sat a little straighter. Akira came a little closer. And when she looked at me, I found strength in her unwavering love. I hoped she found the same unflinching belief in us reflecting at her. Once she nodded at me, I looked up at her dad.

Akira's dad was about to speak when he was interrupted by Abhi. "So, Sam, how did you two meet?"

Uh. Okay. Was I supposed to answer that or let Akira's dad speak?

I looked at him. He nodded at Abhi's question and shrugged his shoulders for me to continue.

I nodded and looked at Akira. She had a big, dopey smile on her face as if she too had transported to that first meeting.

With a deep breath and a smile that I couldn't stop, I said, "Funny you should ask, Abhi. It was the first day of our university, and here I was, quietly sitting in my chair, when a girl in bright orange clothes dropped beside me. Almost everyone was dressed in dark colors, but not Akira." I chuckled, still remembering the passion with which she had talked about architecture. "We first talked to each other during the introduction session."

I smiled at Abhi. "To tell you the truth, I used to get a little irritated at how open and honest Akira was, how ready she was to discuss her work with others. I was not showing my work to anyone, worried someone would steal my idea. It slowly started to change when we became group partners in one of our classes and we had to work together. Akira was, and she still is, the brightest, most honest, and hardest working person I know. She is so brave to have left her country and is trying to make it in a whole new country all on her own. That is just remarkable."

Tears shone in Akira's eyes, and now that I looked around, in her mom's eyes too. When my eyes met Abhi's, he winked at me. I see what he did there. I nodded in thanks to him for setting up a positive outlook for the questioning. I loved Akira's brothers.

While I talked in English, Ria sat beside her grandparents, quietly translating our conversations.

Akira's dad cleared his throat. "Thank you, Sam. We are very proud of Akira. I love my daughter, and I don't trust you. To be frank, I could find a lot of better men for Akira than you."

"Pappa!" Akira started to protest but I held her hand.

"It's okay." I almost said sweetheart out loud. But Akira got it. Her smile was apologetic, but she nodded.

Akira's dad was not going to hold back. But he didn't say anything that I didn't know. I held her dad's stare and said, "I know, sir. Akira could have anyone she wanted. And I feel truly lucky that she chose me. I know you don't know me enough to trust me. I understand. But you trust Akira. You have trusted her enough to let her go to study halfway across the world. You trust her to survive and succeed. And I hope you trust Akira's choice of the person she loves. And with the more time I spend here, I hope we can get to know and understand each other better. I love Akira. I'd be a fool to not realize how lucky I am."

"Stop it. We're both lucky to have found each other," Akira said, her voice shaky with emotions. I looked around at the other family members. Almost all of them nodded in approval, even Akira's elder uncle, who had not been supportive of Akira when she'd run away from home.

Her dad ignored Akira and continued. "You say you love

her. But for how long? Love doesn't last forever. If you fall out of love with Akira, would you divorce her?"

Akira had told me about their conversation on the divorce issue before. And I understood. What I didn't understand was his concept of love.

"With all due respect, sir, I don't agree with your assessment on love."

"No?" Akira's dad frowned.

I shook my head. "I believe love has different forms. Forgive me, but I'm going to get a little poetic here. Right now, the love Akira and I share is beautiful, passionate, all-consuming. Like the brightest, newborn star. With time, it will cool down. It would transform into warmth, affection, comfort, habit, a part of one another. Like the sun, necessary to survive. I'm aware that our love wouldn't stay as bright and alive as we have now, but whatever form it takes, it would stay alive. Right along with us. So, to answer your question, sir, I wouldn't divorce Akira."

"God." Akira blew her nose in a tissue and wiped the stray tears. Aakar nodded in approval while Abhi said, "That's beautiful." Akira's family had big smiles on their faces, except for her father. He simply nodded.

Akira's mom shook her head as she wiped the stray tears below her eyes. "It makes me happy to know that Akira is loved, Sam. But you must understand. Our cultures and backgrounds are completely different. We are Hindu. You are a Christian. Our traditions and values are different. Even our languages are different." She turned her eyes to Akira, who sat rigidly beside me, and asked her, "Are you willing to give all that up for him?"

I felt Akira's hackles rise. She straightened in her spot and her fist near my leg tightened. I did not want her to be angry and defensive. Akira fighting with her family for a foreign guy would just be fodder for more doubts and rejection. I put my hand on her clenched fist and tightened my hold over her hand. Her intense glare softened a little when she met my eyes. Not wanting to spook her, I asked, "May I?" She nodded tightly.

I looked at her mom and said, "I'm not trying to answer for Akira here. I would just like to say something before Akira answers that question. If that's fine by you?"

Everyone's eyes were on us. Ria's murmured translations and the grandparents' questions filled the air. Akira's mom nodded at me to continue.

"Aunty, I'd never want Akira to give up anything for me. I'm no one to tell her what to do with her life. All I want is to be the one that Akira shares it with. Be it her traditions, customs, festivals, beliefs. I just want to be a part of her world and make her happy. Now we don't have as many festivals and traditions like you all, but I would love to share them with Akira, too. Please don't let our differences divide us. Please." I stared at her mom and met the eyes of every single person sitting in the room. I let them see all my vulnerabilities and weaknesses. My heartfelt desire to just make their daughter happy. I willed them to open their eyes to the simple truth of love.

I was no villain in their story.

A warm hand engulfed mine. I turned my head to Akira and found tears streaming down her face.

Without worrying about her family, I held her cheeks and wiped her tears. "Don't cry, sweetheart. I love you."

She sniffled and looked at her dad. "I love him, Pappa."

I squeezed Akira's knee in support and looked at her dad.

He sighed and nodded. "I know, *beta*. I see that." He looked at me and said, "I can see that you love our daughter, Sam. You are a good man. But it will take me some time to trust you."

Hope bubbled somewhere deep in my gut. I nodded and said, "I understand, sir."

He glanced around at the expectant looks on the people around us and grunted, "Call me uncle. Go see the city while you're here. We'll talk soon."

He then got up and walked out of the courtyard.

What. The. Hell.

I looked at Luke, who had taken a seat at the farthest corner of the courtyard, pretending to mind his own business. He shrugged his shoulders in confusion. A squeal burst near my ears. Akira's body flung around my neck and shook me in a tight grip. God.

"I'm so happy, Sam. We did it!" she said, her voice louder with every word.

I pulled her arms off from my neck before she strangled me and asked, "So your father walking out means an acceptance?"

She laughed and rolled her eyes. "You expected him to hug you and welcome you to the family?"

Well, kinda. My face clearly betrayed my thoughts because Akira snorted and bellowed with laughter. And it felt so fucking good to watch her laugh freely.

People started surrounding us.

Akira's older uncle came up to us and said, "Akira, you know you will never be able to afford a helper or a cook or a gardener, right? You'll have to do all of your chores on your own."

He was simply teasing, what with his wife hitting his arm and scolding him. She turned to us and said, "Don't listen to him, Akira. Sam, be good to our Akira."

I smiled at her and, with all seriousness, I promised, "Every day, Aunty."

But Akira wasn't done. "*Kaka*, I'll let you know. I do all my chores myself in the US, and I'm managing just fine."

Her uncle teased back. "What about when you have kids? You won't have time to manage work, kids, and house. It would have been simpler in India, you know?" He looked at me with a guilty expression and said, "I mean no offense, Sam. Have you both thought about settling here?"

My stomach dropped. Kids. Settling in India. This conversation was getting a little more adventurous than what I could handle. I was glad Akira's dad wasn't around and hadn't heard all this. He would've just *loved* the idea of us settling in India.

Akira was happy to defend my honor. "I'll have you know that Sam is not like the men in our family. He would be an equal participant in the kitchen department and the cleaning department. And I can assure you, he would be happy to share the responsibility of changing the diapers of our future babies too. Right, Sam?"

I had no idea how I was standing upright at this point. I remembered nodding.

This family. During dinner, they barely spoke to me. And now that Akira's father had approved of us, the conversation had reached to our future babies.

Soon after, Ria joined Akira and me as we stood talking to her mom, uncles, and aunts, and dragged us to where her grandparents were sitting. Both of us grabbed a chair and sat across them.

Akira talked to her grandparents in Gujarati, emotions pouring off them in waves. Tears rolled down Akira's face as she clutched her grandmother's hand and smiled as if a weight had lifted from her shoulders. Her grandparents looked at me as they talked to Akira and gave me an occasional pat on the knee.

Her grandmother looked at me and then said something to Akira. Akira looked at me and said, "Grandma is asking you to treat me with kindness and always keep me happy." Akira's red-rimmed eyes were lined with relief and joy.

I didn't want a translator between her grandparents and me. So, I put my one hand on each of their knees and with all my heart, promised them with a nod and a smile. A smile full of gratitude and joy. Their support had played an important part in convincing the rest of the family, and I'd never forget that.

Aakar and Abhi came up beside us, their mom right behind them.

Aakar had a bright smile on his face as he looked at the absolute joy on Akira's face. Happiness radiated from her and spread all around us. With a smile, he shook my hand and said, "Take care of her, Sam. You did good today."

Before I could thank him, Akira's dad came over at the balcony above the courtyard and shouted, "Kids!"

Everyone looked up.

"We're all going to the village during the weekend and will be staying there for two to three weeks depending on the weather and situation. Be ready."

All the kids screamed in delight while Akira's uncles went upstairs, probably to talk to Akira's dad. Aakar slapped me on the shoulder and said, "We'll talk later. I'll go see what this situation is that Dad's talking about."

I nodded, and before I could say anything, he was gone.

I looked around me, and my eyes met Akira's.

She'd never looked happier.

Maybe Akira's family needed to meet me before believing in us.

Maybe they needed to see us together, our love, to know that we were meant to be.

Maybe they just needed to look at us, looking at each other, to know our love was real.

Laughter and loud chatter echoed off the courtyard, but my mind was finally at peace.

CHAPTER 30

"Love does not begin and end the way we seem to think it does.
Love is a battle, love is a war; love is a growing up."
  - James A. Baldwin

Sam

Death flashed before my eyes.

I was pretty sure Akira was zooming us toward our end in full throttle. Air whipped at my face—that was covered with a handkerchief with only my eyes showing—as I clutched Akira's waist as tight as I possibly could. The name of Jesus was constant in my head from the moment I sat behind Akira on her death machine.

I was pretty sure if I let go of Akira, I'd fly off the vehicle into the farmland behind us and meet my end. But if I kept seated behind her on this vehicle hurtling on a dirt road at breakneck speed, we were sure to meet death on the other side.

"Tell my mother I loved her!" Luke screamed, his face covered like mine, from where he sat behind Abhi with the same tight grip on him as I had on Akira. They were on another two-wheeler vehicle three feet away from us on this narrow lane.

Akira chortled from where she drove her vehicle—called *Activa,* which looked like a big brother of a Vespa. "Do not laugh, Akira. Focus on the road," I yelled near her ear. She had covered her face and hair with a long scarf in a complex mechanism, had long gloves on her hands, and a helmet on her head.

She threw her head back and laughed. "Relax, Sam. I've been doing this for years. I know how to drive on such roads. You just enjoy the ride."

"Enjoy the fucking ride? My balls have climbed into my throat. How long till we're at our destination?" I didn't know if I should close my eyes or keep them open. Both scenarios were equally terrifying.

"Do you want me to go faster?" Akira was enjoying this way too much.

"No, please. Wasn't there any other way to go?"

She laughed. "There was. This way was just more fun. And I had to show you the normal way to commute here."

"You're fucking crazy!" I screamed and watched Luke, who was hunched behind Abhi, face scrunched in terror.

I flung myself off the Activa the moment Akira stopped. My footing was a little unsteady, but I lived. Thank fucking God. Luke joined me and, with a finger pointed at my face, said, "You. You owe me big-fucking-time."

I raised my hands to placate him. "I know. I know. The place might be worth the ride though."

Akira and Abhi joined us once they parked their vehicles. After ten minutes of waiting, Ria, Aakar, and Meera joined us. Meera was the same person that Akira and Ria had talked about in the courtyard. She seemed very different from what Akira had described then. We'd been in the village for about three days now, and I'd not seen her laugh. Not once.

We walked toward what looked like a temple. When I turned to check on Luke, he was just standing there, looking at Meera's slow, retreating form. I called out to him, and he almost jumped back. At my questioning look, he shook his head, plastered a smile on his face, and started walking with us.

Near the entrance of the temple, the street was lined with vendors selling soft drinks, chips, and chocolates. A small flower shop had its cart decorated with marigold garlands and piles of rose petals. A few tour guides lingered outside with brochures in their hands, talking to a few customers.

"Where are we again?" Luke asked.

"This is our village's Vav. Vav means stepwell," Akira said.

"Stepwells?" I'd never heard of something like that before.

Akira walked beside me, a bottle of water in her hand, and explained, "Stepwells are structures that actually originated in India. Historically, they were used to collect and store rainwater for the people in the community or a neighborhood. Some of them go very deep into the ground and they can be accessed through steps. And different stepwells have their steps designed differently, but the geometry of every stepwell is just extraordinary."

When we finally entered the top level of the stepwell, I understood.

A series of intricately carved colonnades ran across the length and the width of the structure, putting us in a grid of decorative columns.

Just ahead of me lay a series of steps along the width of the structure which led to the level below.

As we moved deeper, the place turned darker.

The shadows of the columns stretched across the steps. As I ran my hand along the columns, the cold and coarse stone contrasted with the weather outside. Moisture hung heavy in the air, and murmurs of people around us echoed in the space.

We moved down two more levels. The cool air was a balm

to the heavy heat of outside. Walls with carved windows and lintels ran along the length of the structure.

Luke had not stopped taking pictures. His eyes were lit with awe, and excitement poured through him.

Akira grazed her hand with mine. In the cool darkness of the well, her eyes lined with kohl, she looked exquisite. Her clothing style had changed a little since we'd arrived at the village. Her clothes were more traditional, she wore long earrings that reached her neck, and today, she even wore bangles on her wrists. Every time our hands touched, her cool bangles sent a shiver up my spine. She was so fucking sexy. Her traditional clothes—a long top and tight leggings—enhanced the curves that had been making me crazy for a few days now. I wanted to hold her against one of these walls and kiss her.

I needed us to be back home in the States and in our bedroom.

Another touch of her hand brought me out of my daze. She looked up at me with a shy smile and asked, "Want to sit down for a while?"

I clutched her hand in mine—I just had to—and sat one step below hers so our faces were closer. If I couldn't kiss her here, I was damn well gonna sit as close to her as possible. She didn't mind it. She didn't even leave my hand.

Neither Luke nor any of her family members disturbed us. Abhi and Aakar had taken a seat somewhere further up the steps on the other side, while Ria and Meera talked quietly in one of the niches. Luke roamed around the place documenting every corner. A few people wandered about, but no one paid us any attention.

"It's the afternoon and a weekday. Otherwise, this place would be packed."

I played with her fingers, letting myself enjoy the feel of her skin against mine after so long. "This is nice."

Akira laid her head on my shoulder and nodded. I asked,

"You think we're good with your family? I'm not sure when it comes to your dad."

She ran her fingers along my thumb. "It's going to take him some time. I'm just glad he didn't outright reject you. He'll come around and be all warm once he gets to know you."

"As far as nothing is stopping us from being together, I can deal with the rest."

We soaked up our freedom to sit so close to each other for a while before Luke stood over us. "We need to leave if we want to make it on time for evening tea."

"You guys go ahead. We'll be there in a bit," I said. I needed a few more minutes with Akira.

Luke nodded and got going with everyone else. Before leaving though, Abhi waggled his eyebrows, as if we were going to start making out in public. Akira shook her head and shooed him away.

We sighed in relief once they finally left.

It had been an overwhelming week since we'd arrived in India. It was the first moment where it was just the two of us. I'd missed the hell out of her despite being in each other's constant presence.

"How do you feel, sweetheart?" Fuck, I missed calling her that. I had to hold my tongue so often while in front of her family.

Akira closed her eyes and, with a beautiful smile, said, "I missed hearing that."

I quickly kissed her hand. Akira startled and opened her eyes. She shook her head and said, "I feel weightless, you know. I hadn't realized how much the worry of being rejected by my family had weighed me down. Or held me back from giving all of myself to you. I don't need to worry about loving you anymore. And it kinda feels weird. I'm allowed to love you as much as I want. And I don't know where that line ends."

If this was Akira holding back her love, how would it feel to have her unbridled love?

"There's no line, sweetheart. I fall a little more in love with you every day." I so wish I could kiss her right now. Just once.

Her eyes screamed *KISS ME*. Fuck.

"I know, Sam. God, I want us in our bed under a sheet," she whispered. She was going to kill me. I groaned.

"God, Akira. Don't say that."

"I love you so much. You have been nothing but amazing with my family. I can't thank you enough for being so supportive. It feels like a dream for everything to have worked out so well."

Unlike the last time, when she had to face her family alone, I was here with her to share the burden. "Together, Akira. We're in this together."

She nodded and, before I could blink, kissed me on my cheek.

She got up and straightened her top. "Let's go before Abhi comes back to drag me outside."

I held her hand as we climbed up the steps. "What now?"

She squeezed my hand and looked at me with her eyes so fucking full of love for me. "Now, we love. We rest and travel for the next two weeks. And then go home. And then we love some more. Every day."

"Every day," I promised.

◌

Akira

Life seemed unreal. Or maybe this was my new reality. I'd never imagined falling in love with a non-Indian guy, let alone stand up to my family and fight to simply love him and be with him.

Our days in India were coming to an end. Sam and I were

on the roof of my house in our village in the middle of the night. This was the only time when we could sneak out for some private time.

In the dark silence under the stars, we kissed with desperate hunger. Our bodies sang and begged to join. But neither of us wanted to be caught by any of my family members. Still, we didn't let go of each other.

For the past few days, this time had become sacred to us.

Most nights, we simply lay down together in silence, holding hands, or in each other's arms. Now that our main obstacle was over, loving Sam felt almost *too* easy. I didn't know how to do it without thinking about what others would think about it. It was going to take time.

I was excited to love Sam without worrying about the world. I knew our battles weren't over. We had a lot of hurdles ahead of us. Gossip by the relatives, loads of paperwork if or when we decided to marry or get engaged, racial jabs from people, irrelevant speculations on why we got together and so many more battles. But as long as we were together, I was ready.

Winning over my parents would've never been possible if Sam hadn't been such a rock since the beginning. Had he been unsure of us, I wouldn't have had any reason to fight in the first place. It was his steadfastness and solid support that gave me the assurance that I had him to fall back on. That he'd be there. For me. With me. And nothing short of that would've been worth risking my family. Only Sam.

"What are you thinking?" Sam asked. The gentle fingers running in my hair had put me deep into thoughts. I looked up at his face hovering near mine. His gentle smile and his sweet soul were mine to keep.

I returned his smile and touched his face. "I wish people didn't have to fight the world just to be able to love."

He held my hand on his cheeks and said, "Yeah."

"I can't wait to learn every little thing about you and fall in love with each of them," I said.

He bent down and kissed me square on the lips. Every single time, I wanted more. More him. More kiss. More love. I wouldn't say I was incomplete before I met Sam. I had my life, my studies, a plan to make it in a new country. And I was proud of all that I'd achieved. But having Sam with me certainly made my life a lot more exciting and beautiful.

"I can't wait to spend the rest of my life with you," he said as he nuzzled into my neck, placing a scorching hot kiss at my ear that had me tingling all over. I wish we were in the States.

I held him at my neck and said, "Hmm. I can't wait for you to start washing your ass instead of wiping—Ow!"

The jerk bit me on the neck! He laughed at my glare. "First, your timing for such words sucks. Second, you'll soon learn how to wipe, sweetheart. America will turn you into a wiper."

I snorted. "Yeah. Never gonna happen. I bet ya."

"You're on. What're the stakes?"

I thought about it, and when it clicked, I couldn't stop the evil smile. "Whoever loses would have to propose the other one for marriage."

"Fuck, Akira. That's awful and genius. I don't know if I want to win or lose."

"Me neither," I giggled.

"You're on," Sam said and rolled over me on the floor.

Under the clear sky on a cool, beautiful night, we kissed. And kissed some more till the first rays of dawn washed over us. Life could be so beautiful when we allowed love to thrive.

EPILOGUE

Almost a year later

Akira

Heart pumping. Absolute quiet. Colors in my hand.

The festival of Holi was upon us.

The early New York morning had woken me up before Sam, and I was ready. Our first Holi! Sam was asleep on his back, his mouth slightly open, his one hand resting underneath my pillow and his other hand on his chest.

And lucky for me, he was only wearing his tiny black boxers. His tousled hair sticking up everywhere was adorable. His worry lines about our assignments had disappeared.

All I wanted to do was cuddle up in his arms or wake him

up and make this morning a whole lot more tense and hot and sweaty.

But I couldn't.

I had a task to do. Color up Sam in pink, blue, yellow, and green.

Hell, yeah!

With the plate full of colors in my hand, I walked around the bed on Sam's side and sat at the edge near his face. A little bit of pink on his cheek. Gorgeous. A big blue nose. His nose wrinkled, and I ducked down. Nothing. Okay. Good. I got out and silently got back to work. I got green on my three fingers and ran them along his smooth neck. Yes.

I got a fist full of yellow for his chest. He was going to freak out. God, I can't wait.

The moment I was in touching distance again, Sam said, "Don't you dare, Akira."

I gulped and looked up at the mirth in his eyes, as if he was enjoying my Pablo Picasso moment. I fake-laughed and asked, "Uh...how long have you been awake?"

He wrapped his large hand around my small wrist. "Since you did something to my nose," Sam answered with a smirk.

Arrogant asshole. I smirked back and held open my hand so that all the yellow powdered color drifted down over his chest. Perfect.

"You fucking..." He dragged me over his colorful chest, making me shriek with laughter.

"Stop... No... Oh my God!"

He held me with one arm and jerked around to reach for the plate full of colors, "Where were we now? Yes." He placed the plate in front of me, his chest to my back, his one arm holding me to him, and he grabbed a fist full of pink with his free hand.

"Not so much!" I shrieked.

He ran his entire fist full of color, from my neck to my

boobs. "Yesss," Sam growled in my neck and turned me on my back.

He climbed on top of me and sat on my thighs. His one hand kept a hold on both of my wrists and pinned them above my head. His hardness aligned with all my right spots, and I couldn't stop my back from arching for more.

Sam pulled up my tank top, got another fist full of the green color, and ran his hand along my other boob, causing shivers to run down my spine. I gasped. He thrust over my panties.

"Now blue... Yes. So fucking hot, Akira," Sam moaned and ran his blue hand around my navel. He released one of my hands and held my palm with his blue hand. I ran my now blue hand around his neck and pulled him in for a scorching hot kiss.

Sam removed his boxers in a mad rush and got me out of my clothes. Quickly, he put on the condom and moved on top of me. The moment I had my hands free, I filled them with some green and pink and ran them along his back and butt.

Fuck, just the act turned me on more than ever. Sam groaned and filled his hands with God knows which color and held my cheek with one hand and my thigh with another.

We were all tangled limbs and bright colors. We rolled and tumbled. The colors were all gone from the plate, yet we kept playing.

Sam moved inside me with a fervent passion, his heart beating with mine. Our breaths puffed, sweat sticking the color to our skin, and we didn't stop.

He grabbed, I moved. I clenched, he yelled. We lost ourselves in a rhythm of colors and sounds and pleasure.

Our pace picked up and Sam moaned louder. "Fuck, Akira. God, kiss me..."

With my mouth on him, and my legs clenched tight around his waist, I burst with a million colors dancing behind my eyes.

"Fuck!" Sam clutched my hair in one hand and arched into

me. His grip on my hip tightened, and he moaned his pleasure in my neck.

We stayed like that for a while before we tried to roll over.

"Happy Holi, baby," I said as he rolled onto his back.

Sam turned his head to me with a dazed look in his eyes. "I love these festivals of yours. No wonder India is so fucking populated."

I burst into laughter at that. "It's the festivals, huh?"

"Definitely," he said.

I chuckled and was about to grab some color that had piled on the bedsheet when Sam was on top of me again, holding my hands above me.

"What, again? I need to recover," I whined.

His eyes shone with laughter but also with something else. He let go of my hands but entwined our fingers. He looked at me like I was his entire world. "Remember we made a bet a year ago?"

Tears filled my eyes, yet I couldn't stop smiling.

He wiped the tear from the corner of my eye. "You barged into my quiet world and turned it fucking upside down. And my life has never been better. I can't imagine not having you in my life, Akira. My light. My joy. My breath of fresh air. Despite all the challenges we've faced, I've never been happier, and every day I'm more in love with you than the day before. I want to spend the rest of my life trying to make up for all the joy you bring in my life every day. Will you please marry me, sweetheart?"

Tears clouded my vision of Sam. I blinked quickly, as to not miss out on the love shining in his eyes. Love for me.

"Yes... Yes!" I said and pulled him in for a kiss. That became two, then four and then a hundred. We kissed through the tears. We kissed through the joy. We kissed and kissed.

I already had his promise ring on my right hand. I never took it off.

"But wait! It counts as a real engagement for me, but my family might not accept it," I said, suddenly worried.

Sam kissed me again, mostly to shut me up for ruining the moment. "I already asked your dad for permission. I explained to him our American ritual and the value of a guy proposing to his girl. We have his blessing, sweetheart. This is as real as it gets."

Tears now poured out of my eyes and converted all the powdered color on my cheek into a paste. I didn't care. I extended my left hand. Sam's eyes clouded with tears as he brought the ring to my left ring finger. A gorgeous, unique ring with a single diamond in the center and colorful stones all around it.

With a hoarse voice, he murmured, "My mom gave it to me. It belonged to my grandmother. She said my grandmother would be thrilled for you to have it."

"It's stunning," I whispered.

With the beautiful ring in his hand, Sam's eyes asked me *May I?*

Mine screamed *Please.*

And he pushed the ring on my finger.

He pulled me in his arms and kissed me.

Our tears merged on our cheeks.

Love thrived in our small, beautiful world.

I broke the kiss when I remembered something. "Sam, our families need to meet, now that we're engaged," I groaned.

He huffed a sigh and mumbled into my neck, "Can't we just elope?"

"Only if you can prove to the world that we're dead, or else my family would do the deed."

"Can't wait for more family dramas," Sam groaned miserably, making me laugh.

~

Sam

Akira laughed, my ring on her finger, her face streaked with pink and yellow. Life couldn't get any better. Looking back at everything that we went through and fought for, it was worth it for this moment.

This moment where she wore my ring. This moment where she agreed to marry me. This moment where she loved freely. This moment where she loved me.

I held her cheeks in my palms and touched my forehead to hers. With love. With reverence. With a promise. "Forever, Akira," I whispered.

She held my wrist. She kissed my palm. With love. With reverence. With a promise. "Forever, Sam," she whispered back.

THE END

ACKNOWLEDGMENTS

Afsha – This book wouldn't have happened without you. You never let me give up, read every one of my drafts, and kept me motivated. Every one of your suggestions, comments and ideas have made this book a better work. I know I can come to you any time of the day, and you'll be there cheering me on.

Kruti – You are the best friend a person could ask for. My first and the worst draft was a pleasant surprise for you, and that gave me the confidence to finish my book. Our conversations of my story that lasted for hours made me believe in my characters, and that means the world to me.

Pallavi – I cannot thank you enough for reading so many of my drafts—no matter how little the revisions were. Your comments, your fangirling over different scenes, has been invaluable to me. Your constant support means the world to me.

Juliette Cross – I am so grateful that you offered to read my book. Your suggestions and guidance gave it the final push that it needed. I can't ever thank you enough.

Sophie – Thank you so much for beta reading my book. I lived for your comments on little scenes, your suggestions that got me thinking, and the little things you noticed that nobody else did. You're irreplaceable.

Malia – I am so happy and grateful you adored Sam and Akira. Thank you so much for surfing through ideas on my book cover with me.

Bhavi Mehta – Thank you for designing the perfect cover for my first book.

Aakriti – I cannot thank you enough for reading my book so many times. For believing in me, my story and telling me that people would want to read it.

Jalpa – I am so incredibly happy and thankful that you have read my book.

Mehzabin – I cannot thank you enough for not only reading my book but also working so hard in thinking through the initial ideas for my cover.

Jaini – Thank you so much for reading and loving my book. And flying through it.

Joyce – Thank you so much for teaching me how to be organized, how to outline my books, how to create Pinterest board and a million other things before actually starting to write. The book would have never taken its shape without that invaluable guidance.

Corina – Thank you for commenting and giving me suggestions along the way. Every little question and comment of yours helped me make my writing better.

Kiezha – Thank you so much for your constant guidance and the wonderful editing you did. I'm very grateful, and so glad that I could work with you.

Thank you to all the wonderful bookstagrammers who have constantly motivated me, have shown their excitement to read my book, and made me believe in the power of what this wonderful community can do for each other. I am so thankful to know you, talk to you and be in this community with you. And I am so humbled to share this story with you. Thank you so much for reading my book.

Adhish – The love of my life and my best friend in the world, thank you for believing in me. Thank you for constantly telling me that you are proud of me. Thank you for tolerating me when I was at my worst and was snappy. Thank you for being everything that I could imagine in a book boyfriend.

And a big thank you to my family who gave me the chance to go to the US that opened my world to millions of opportunities. All the love to you.

ABOUT THE AUTHOR

Born and brought up in India, N.M. Patel came to the US for her master's degree in Columbia University. After reading hundreds of romance novels, she longed to see more of her culture being represented in the stories. So, she decided to write a romance that reflected her Indian roots, her culture, the values and struggles of many Indians around the world when it comes to the matters of love. In her spare time, she reads romance books, socializes with her friends on her bookstagram account (liber_lady) and watches movies and documentaries with her husband.

instagram.com/liber_lady

Printed in Great Britain
by Amazon

26237344R00212